A QUESTION OF CHOICE

PRUDENCE ANDREW

A Question
of Choice

G. P. Putnam's Sons
New York

© 1962 BY PRUDENCE ANDREW

FIRST AMERICAN EDITION

Library of Congress Catalog
Card Number: 62-18245

NOTE

The author makes no apology for certain very minor liberties that she has, for her literary convenience, taken with history; such as by calling Queen Elisabeth's sons by their mother's name of Woodville instead of by their father's name of Gray; and by telescoping the events leading to the marriage of the King's sister.

1

BROTHER JOSEPH pushed the tip of his tongue between his teeth and wrinkled his short-sighted eyes. In front of him on the oak table lay stretched an oblong of parchment covered in fine Gothic script. It was very fine script indeed, as fine as the most expensive London scribe could produce. It was Brother Joseph's own work. But on this sharp March morning of the year 1468, the eve of the feast of his namesake, Brother Joseph was not concerned with the script. He bent his rickety back and peered at the initial letter. It was an 'O', for Brother Joseph was making a psalter and he had reached the psalm *Omnes gentes plaudite*. But this was not like the other 'O's. Instead of being a modest one-sixth of an inch in height it was a good inch and a half and as fat as a barrel. Instead of being drawn in black ink with a goose quill it was painted a beautiful red so that it glowed on the pale parchment like an altar light.

Brother Joseph grunted with pleasure. Round and round this great fat 'O' honeysuckle was twined, and from every twist of the honeysuckle a tiny angel peeped out, so minutely painted that for the eyes Brother Joseph had used a single hair pulled out of his own chest. Brother Joseph had been working on this particular illumination for twelve days. All his working hours had been devoted to it. Indeed, one might say that almost the whole of his life had been spent in the same way. For fifty years, whenever he was neither sleeping nor eating nor singing the services nor attending Chapter, he had been bent over his daubed table, a different-colour paint under each of his finger-nails and black ink ingrained in his middle finger. The book cupboards in the cloister were stuffed with exquisite examples of Brother Joseph's skill. Bound with calf, hasped with silver, decorated

7

with exquisite designs and covered with fifteen Gothic letters to the inch, Brother Joseph's works of art—psalters, missals, breviaries, epistles and Works of the Fathers—lay snugly behind oak doors.

No one ever read them.

Abbot Dominic greatly admired Brother Joseph's work. 'Very pretty, very pretty,' he would say. 'I have never seen aitches so delightful. I really must send this one to London to be bound, I doubt if a Gloucester binder could do justice to it.'

So the manuscript would travel all the way to London and in due course would be carried home again bound in blue or brown calf-skin, to be stowed away in one of the book cupboards. Very occasionally, perhaps when his eyes were troubling him more than usual, Brother Joseph would ask Sacristan to unlock the cupboards so that he might look at his life's work. Thus between Nones and Vespers he might review his whole life in the monastery from the day when as a newly professed monk he had ruled with trembling hand his first sheet of parchment to the day two years ago when he had written 'finis' at the end of his fifteenth psalter.

Brother Joseph bent low and studied the angelic faces. He knew they would very seldom see the light of day, certainly never leave the abbey. In his twenty years as abbot, Abbot Dominic had only twice allowed Brother Joseph's work to leave the abbey. A missal bound in white kid had been presented to King Edward IV on the occasion of his coronation seven years earlier. A pentateuch executed entirely in black and silver had been graciously accepted by the great Earl of Warwick after he and forty-nine retainers had once stayed the night. But Brother Joseph did not mind if few saw his works. He laboured at his texts not that they might be admired, not even that they might be read, but simply because he believed that by exercising his skill he was glorifying God.

So now he sat hunched happily over his sixteenth psalter, over the symmetrical script that no one would ever read and the great fat 'O' that only the Abbot would ever admire. He grunted and frowned. From his experience of 18,000 identical days he knew, without looking at the clock in the cloister yard, that in a few minutes the bell would start ringing for

8

Vespers. By the end of Vespers the light would have gone and his old eyes could no longer distinguish the colours by candle-light. Abbot Dominic allowed him two candles, but even two candles could not put the colours back into the paint-pots.

'I have just time for one halo,' thought Brother Joseph. The thought of the halo was like a hot brick, warming his stomach. He nibbled the ends of his cold fingers, scratched the bristles on his pate and selected his finest brush. He sucked the brush to a nice point, then dipped it gently in the pot of gold. Carefully he wiped the brush on the edge of the pot. He held his breath. He always held his breath when he put on the gold. As he bent closer, gouty knobs stood out on the back of his shorn neck. He lowered his face until the angels' faces came into focus. He marked with his eye the topmost angel on the left and slowly carried the golden brush towards him. But the brush never reached the angel. Suddenly a grey veil dropped between Brother Joseph and the page. The angelic faces were blotted out. The honeysuckle disappeared. All that was left was a blur of crimson, a block of black and a terror-stricken old man.

He blinked. He shook his head and blinked again, but the angels did not reappear. He laid down his brush and raised his streaming eyes to the light. At that moment a bell started ringing. But this was not the bell for Vespers. It was not the service bell. It was not the sanctuary bell nor the funeral bell. This was the bell that Brother Joseph had heard only once in the last ten years—on the day the kitchens caught fire.

This was the alarm bell.

Brother Joseph's own terror was swallowed up in a greater. He jerked to his feet, knocking over the stool and upsetting a pot of red paint. He groped his way to the door and fumbled for the latch and never saw the crimson stream that poured over his beautiful 'O' and dripped on to the stone floor.

The Prior of Woodchester Abbey in Gloucestershire sat in his room as far away from the fireplace as possible and worried.

It was in his nature to worry. Abbot Dominic often chided him that he would still be worrying in heaven. Just now he was worrying because, although he was not ill, he was sitting in a room with a fire. He had ordered the fire because his steward had told him that he could not present his accounts properly unless his feet were warm. But still Prior felt guilty. Deep in his conscience he was convinced that monks had no right to be comfortable. He hitched his stool a pace nearer the door and shivered as the draught rushed up his legs. He was a man of middle age and middle height, a man of excellent intentions but mediocre capabilities. He worried about many things, primarily about monastic affairs, without having the wit to see how they could be remedied. Since he had entered the abbey as a young man his career had been uneventful and he had reached his high office more by a series of unexpected deaths than by any striking abilities. He was conscientious, pious and inclined to dissatisfaction. A vague but perpetual anxiety had worn two grooves between his scanty eyebrows. At the age of forty-two he was already as bald as an egg.

Prior's steward tapped his teeth with his pen. 'There's your quarter's rents, then,' he said crisply. One after another he gave a push to the canvas bags in front of him. 'And there's your profits,' and he shot a smaller bag over the polished table so vigorously that it fell off the end and landed at Prior's feet. Prior bent and picked it up and weighed it in his hand.

'How do you always manage to make a profit, Steward?' he asked. 'I am sure my rents are the only ones that are all got in, never mind showing a profit. Sacristan is always complaining his steward cannot get his proper payments. Only yesterday he told me it was fortunate it was Lent because he doubted if he could find the money for more than two altar candles.'

'He'll have to look sharp before Easter, then,' sniffed Prior's steward. 'That Pascal candle will set him back a bit if I know the price of best beeswax.' He tapped one by one the canvas bags in front of him. 'All Sacristan wants is a new steward,' he said, and spat into the fire. 'The rents are there, you just got to screw it out of them.'

Prior stirred. 'But in the case of real hardship . . .'

His steward snorted. 'They're not doing too bad. It's not as if there's been a plague or a flood or a drought, not in years, not hereabouts. The crops is giving a fourfold yield and there's no scab or murrain—not this year—and judging by what I seen in Stroud market there's plenty of coin about. They can pay all right, you take my word for it, Prior. You just got to screw it out of them.'

Prior rose and selecting a large key from the bunch at his waist unlocked one of the great oak chests that lined one wall of his room. This chest housed Prior's fund, the rents and dues allocated to his office, which his steward collected for him and from which he paid for his servants, his horses, his personal expenses, building repairs and the monks' pocket money. This chest was three-quarters full, for Prior could not bring himself to live in the grand style affected by the Prior of Winchcombe, who had eight horses in his stables and employed only two servants fewer than the Abbot himself.

Prior's steward laid the bags of coin in the chest and Prior shut and locked the lid. Next he opened another chest in which he kept the profits of Prior's fund. This chest was almost empty, not because Prior's steward was inefficient or the lands allocated to Prior unfruitful, but simply because Prior was for ever handing over his own profits to make up the deficits in other officials' accounts. With a little thud, Prior's profits for the Lent quarter dropped into the bottom of the chest. Prior lowered the lid and turned the key in the lock. As he straightened his back he came face to face with the window. His room was high up on the east side of the abbey above the Chapter House; from it he looked out over the narrow Nailsworth Valley and over the Bath highway that twisted like a muddy ribbon in and out of the crowded arable fields.

Shifting his gaze upwards to the beech woods and sheep-walks of Amberley, he said: 'My father farmed a hundred acres, some of the best arable round Tewkesbury. When I was a boy he had four plough oxen. On one of my birthdays he harvested a sixfold yield of barley. He gave my mother a green dress, I remember, with something silver from Gloucester round the

11

neck, and he gave me a medal of St Anne.' He sighed and turned away from the window.

'Once a farmer always a farmer,' said his steward cheerfully. 'Maybe you missed your vocation, Prior.'

Prior lifted troubled grey eyes. 'Strange, is it not? This abbey owns twenty thousand acres between Nailsworth and Painswick, yet we farm barely an acre of it.'

'More money in letting than in farming,' said his steward promptly, stacking his account books in a neat pile. 'All you got to do is ride round and take in the money: no labour, no sweat, no worry. If things is managed proper—*if*, mark you—the landlord's in clover these days.'

'I suppose you are right, Steward,' sighed Prior. But he rubbed his finger and thumb together in the age-old gesture of a peasant feeling his soil. He smoothed his bald head, fingered the grooves between his eyebrows and suddenly burst out, 'By the fruits of their labour you shall know them.'

From under his fringe Steward shot him a startled look. 'You don't want to go back to all that, do you, Prior? Monks digging in the fields and milking the ewes and lugging dung and boiling their own puddings? Why, it's not been like that for hundreds of years. You wouldn't have a monk empty his own slops, would you?'

Prior did not answer, simply stared across the room at the flaming logs and shifted his cold toes in his sandals.

'Besides,' went on Steward, 'there's no profit in it, no profit in it at all.'

He made gestures of departure.

'No, no,' said Prior, 'you must eat before you go.'

Steward subsided. Prior rang a bell and when his servant appeared gave orders for refreshment.

'You can't run an abbey like this without you got money,' his steward persisted. 'Where'd you get your tapestries and your bells and your fancy plumbing and your new Chapter House?'

'The monks of Evesham, in the twelfth century, they built their own monastery,' said Prior.

'Did they now? And a fair mess they made of it, I'll wager.

You're not saying there's a monk here could do mason's work, surely? Have your monks build you a tower and I'll wager it'd tumble down inside a year.'

The door opened and two servants placed on the table a jug of ale, a pewter mug, a plate of salt beef, a loaf of wheaten bread and a wedge of cheese. Steward took out his knife and impaled a slice of beef.

Prior sat down on his draughty stool. 'I cannot understand it,' he said. 'This abbey is, after Evesham and Tewkesbury, one of the richest in Gloucestershire. Our income should be almost as large as Winchcombe's. Yet there is not one official besides myself who can show a profit in his accounts.' His voice sank. 'Even the Abbot is in debt.'

Steward belched. 'Well, what can you expect with that Abbot's Chaplain managing his affairs? He couldn't manage a fishery, let alone an Abbot's income.'

'But he has borrowed money!' cried Prior. 'The Abbot has borrowed at fifty per cent interest in order to build the new Chapter House. Surely out of our great resources we ought to be able to build without borrowing.'

Steward studied his beef. 'Of course, what you really want is what they got at Winchcombe,' he ventured. He peeped under his fringe to see how Prior was taking it. 'At Winchcombe they got one bursar for the whole lot. They've not got none of these separate funds. Everything's paid into Bursar's office and he doles out to the officials what each is due for. It's bound to be better when there's one chap checking the lot. See at a glance when he's overstepping the mark, can't he?'

Prior said nothing. He was not going to praise Winchcombe.

Steward polished off the last of the beef and poured himself a mug of ale. 'Your good health, Prior,' he said, and drank it down. He began picking his teeth with the point of his knife. 'There's a mort of reasons why accounts don't show profits,' he said. 'There's being stupid and there's being soft and there's being slack and'—he paused to tear off a hunk of bread—'there's being dishonest. Ever thought of that, Prior? A little bit here, a little bit there. Some monks got deep pockets.'

'And some stewards, I dare say,' retorted Prior.

Steward smiled. He hacked off four square inches of cheese. 'Don't you worry, Prior,' he said. 'I don't know why you fret so. You're all right. Your abbot's a decent sort and you've got a far cosier berth in here than you'd get outside. This monastery has stood for goodness knows how long and it'll go on standing, mark my words. You monks are as snug here as the mites in this cheese,' and he waggled the cheese on the end of his knife. 'I reckon you don't know when you're well off.'

Prior gazed at the white mites wriggling on the black table. 'Mites are parasites,' he said sadly.

His words were drowned in the sudden clamour of the alarm bell.

'God's truth!' gasped Steward, leaping to his feet. 'What's that, Prior? That's never——'

But Prior was gone.

'I am afraid there is not enough for the Pascal candle, Sacristan,' said Brother Paul on his knees in front of Sacristan's chest; 'not unless your steward can get the tithes from Cranham Church, but you know how hostile the Cranham parishioners are. They have never forgiven the abbey for appropriating their church and putting in a vicar. Last time your steward tried they threw him in the pond. I wonder if we could get the Rooksmoor mill-rent in advance. There are the Easter candles and the Easter tomb and the Easter vestments need some more gold thread round the bottom. . . .'

But Sacristan was not listening. He was reading a letter. He had taken off his sandals and thrust his fat feet close to the blaze. Everything about him was fat: his face, his lips, his chest, his rump, his fingers, his toes. The fringe of his tonsure gleamed red in the firelight. There were red hairs in his ears, over his eyes, in his nose, on the backs of his hands, on each of his big toes. He looked a caricature of a monk, a mountain of monastic fat so gross and so comic that the other monks often wondered why

14

Abbot Dominic had appointed him to his important office. It seemed strange to them that this monastic joke should be responsible not only for the fabric of their abbey church, for its vestments and its plate, its bells and paintings and books and statues and candles and holy relics, but that he should also be responsible for the holy oil, the holy water, the holy wafers and consecrated wine of the Sacraments. Prior thought him incompetent because he could not balance his books. His assistant Brother Paul thought him secretive and disliked his smell. The novices giggled when they saw him waddle across the cloister yard. His steward often wondered what he did with his rents, they disappeared so quickly.

Yet for all his scrimping and grumbling Woodchester Abbey had never yet gone without its Pascal candle nor its Christmas tableau, as the Abbot very well knew. No dying monk had been deprived of holy oil. No beam had yet been ravaged by beetle, at least not to the point of falling down. When Abbot Dominic asked for money to have one of Brother Joseph's psalters bound, somehow Sacristan always managed to find it— even if he had to borrow it from Prior.

'There are your fishery rents from Dudbridge,' babbled Brother Paul; 'perhaps if your steward saw them again ... and the brasses in the north transept badly need a clean. I shall speak——'

Sacristan snapped his fingers, once, twice, and Brother Paul scuttled out of the room. Sacristan was a man of few words. He returned to his letter.

To the Sacristan of Woodchester Abbey, in the shire of Gloucester, England, he read. *Brother, I greet you in Christ. I have noted your letter received the month of January five days after the Feast of the Holy Innocents. For the sum of fifty pounds, which I understand you have saved during some time for this purpose, I am able to supply a relic of the greatest value and importance. I share your distaste that such a great abbey as Woodchester should have beside its altar no better relic than the girdle of the blessed Honoria. I have made enquiries through my agents and for the said sum of fifty pounds silver, which includes the cost of transporting the relic to Woodchester, I can offer one, item one, of the relics named below.*

One of the coals on which Saint Lawrence was grilled.

The shaft of the arrow that pierced the heart of Saint Sebastian of glorious memory.

One of the Archangel Michael's wing feathers.

The toe-nails of Saint Peter the Apostle.

Each of these relics has worked many authenticated miracles and will be accompanied by a list of the same, vouched for by myself. The possession of one of them cannot fail to bring glory and renown to the Abbey of Woodchester.

If, Brother, you deliver the sum of fifty pounds to my agent in London, Signor Coppellini of Fleet Street, with a letter stating which of these magnificent relics you require, I undertake to have it delivered into your own hands in due time.

I am yours in Christ,

Andreo Belloni, Cardinal

Dated the third day of February, 1468. Rome

Sacristan laid down this letter and drew towards him the ink-pot, the pen, the sand-box and the parchment sheets. He dipped his pen in the ink and wrote rapidly, heedless of splutters and blots.

My lord Cardinal Andreo Belloni, greetings. I have this day, the twentieth day of March, 1468, received your gracious letter, for which pray receive my humble thanks. I am sending this letter to you and I am sending another letter to your agent Signor Coppellini in London together with fifty pounds silver. I pray you to purchase on my behalf . . .

Here Sacristan paused and laid down his pen. He read the Cardinal's letter again. He sank his massive head on his hands and pondered deeply, his golden ring gouging the flesh over his right eyebrow and his eyes disappearing into the rolling fat of his cheeks. The light faded and the fire grew low. Sacristan growled and shook his head in perplexity. At length he rose and lumbered across the room to where a wooden crucifix hung by a nail on the wall. Here Sacristan flopped on his knees and piled his hands one over the other. His puffy lips moved in prayer as he asked God to guide him. Soon he rose and returned to his letter.

. . . the toe-nails of Saint Peter the Apostle, he added, so eagerly that the pen made a hole in the parchment.

In the space of an hour the letter was finished, signed, sanded, rolled and sealed, and Sacristan had made arrangements not only for its despatch to Rome but also for the transport to London by six of his own armed servants of a letter and of a certain sealed, bound and padlocked chest which might, had he only seen inside it, have explained to Prior just exactly why Sacristan found it so difficult to balance his accounts.

When he was at last alone Sacristan leaned against his window-frame and gazed northwards in the direction of Winchcombe. He began to chuckle. He choked and wheezed and spluttered with delight. 'That has cooked Winchcombe's goose,' he crowed. 'Just wait until they hear about St Peter's toe-nails! We will be hearing a little less about St Kenelm's corpse come May.'

Then, because he was a man who for all his grotesquerie loved God and wished to serve Him, he went down on his knees in preparation for Vespers and remained in contemplation for so long that when at last the alarm bell shocked him into attention he found that both his feet had gone to sleep.

Brother Peter stirred and opened his eyes. Through the hay that all but smothered him he gazed up at the ribbed roof and at the stars of light that showed where Rector had forgotten to replace his tiles. He sighed and brought his lips down to the girl's ear.

'Alice, the time is running out,' he whispered.

Alice's eyes opened. They were a brilliant blue, as blue as periwinkles. 'Be un time?' she asked.

17

He gathered her into his arms and pressed his mouth on hers, but through the roaring fire of his passion he heard the icy voice of his conscience saying, 'Time enough to damn yourself.'

'I cannot help myself,' he answered it. 'I am engulfed, smothered, consumed.'

'You are damning yourself,' said his conscience coldly. 'Of your own free will you have broken your vow of chastity and have lain with a woman for pleasure.'

'For love!' his heart cried angrily. 'I love her.'

'A monk has no business with such love,' said his conscience. 'Only with the love of God. You are sinking into mortal sin, brother. The deeper the pit the higher the sides. Beware of sinking so deep you cannot climb out.'

Alice folded her white arms behind his neck. Her hands fluttered, half in protest, half in delight, over his shaved crown. 'Un bain't proper,' she whispered. 'Rector said——'

Brother Peter pressed his face between her breasts. 'It is only a little sin, for you. If you die in my arms—oh, my love, my love —you will not go to hell, I promise you.' He crushed and covered her and the small voice of his conscience was almost drowned by the triumphant cry of his heart, 'I never knew it was like this!'

The stars in the roof grew dimmer. 'Sweetheart, I must go soon,' he told her. 'Infirmarian will be asking for me and soon it will be time for Vespers.' He gazed at her sweet body, her innocent eyes, her two plaits lying like golden ropes on her shoulders. 'You love me? Tell me you love me.'

'Iss, 'ee be my sweetheart,' she answered. 'I doan't mind if 'ee be monk.'

He gazed at her lying beneath him, protected by her terrible and blind innocence. He could not help himself.

'I will come to you here at the same time tomorrow,' he told her. He hesitated, then added, 'God willing,' and crossed himself.

There were sudden footsteps outside the barn. Alice clutched him in terror. Frantically he pulled more hay over their bodies and they lay, breast to breast and mouth to mouth, their hearts hammering and their breath suspended while the steps passed by. He felt the girl's belly shudder. 'Do not be afraid, my love,' he murmured.

She stirred against him. 'I bain't afeared of t'strap, but I be desperd afeared along of 'ee. My da' 'ool wallop 'ee mortal bad if un catches 'ee. Un cass-n't abide t'abbey.'

She did not understand. It was his body she was afraid for, not his soul. She had no conception of how it felt to be moving, slowly and surely, step by step, down into the flames of hell. Brother Peter crushed her against him as if he had his conscience between their two bodies and was grinding it into little pieces with his passion. He closed his eyes and cried in his ecstasy, 'God forgive me!'

He had no very great hope.

When the alarm bell started it burst upon his ears like the trumpet of doom. He jerked up in terror and began fumbling for his clothes.

'What be matter? For why be thakky bell ringing?'

'I must go, I must go,' he cried, frantically struggling into his shirt. To his feverish mind it seemed as if his sins had been discovered and the terrible bell was broadcasting his transgressions to the world.

'Fornicator!' shrieked the bell. 'Adulterer!'

'Adulterer!' whispered Brother Peter.

'Adulterator?' said Alice. 'But 'ee bain't no adulterator. 'Ee bain't married.'

Brother Peter was wrestling with his cassock. At last he got it straight, threw it over his head and pulled the girdle tight. 'I am married to the Church,' he said simply.

She did not hear him for the clamouring of the bell. She clutched his hands as they fumbled with his sandals. 'Doan't leave I,' she pleaded. 'Doan't leave I.'

'Adulterer, adulterer,' clanged the bell.

Goaded by his fears, Brother Peter leaped down from the hay and pulled up the latch.

'Peter, 'ee cass-n't leave I!'

But Brother Peter did not turn his head. He disappeared into the outside world and closed the door with a thud behind him, leaving Alice kneeling in the hay clutching her naked breasts.

He never missed his minute-glass that had fallen out of his pocket into the hay.

In the lane he caught up with a knot of villagers all hastening towards the abbey.

'What is it?' he demanded.

'Thakky be alarm bell,' they told him. 'Ne'er bin rang afore nobbut once and thakky's going back a mort.'

'What be amiss, then?' someone asked. 'Be un fire, do 'ee thenk?'

' 'Ool un need t'buckets?'

'Tower falled maybe.'

'If un rings thakky way tower 'ool tumble for sure.'

'Bain't us hefting buckets, then?'

'Leave un heft thairn own buckets,' growled a grandfer. 'They monks be weedy batch! Make un wappered and whelmed! Make un moil!'

They bustled forward, eager for calamity. Brother Peter hitched up his skirts and ran faster than any of them.

'No, no, James Coles,' said Novice Master patiently. 'That is not good enough. You must learn the psalms perfectly or how can you sing them correctly in the services?'

James Coles bowed his head in shame and blushed. Novice Master returned him the book. 'Learn it again and I will hear you later.' He passed on to Andrew Alsopp and took the book from his hand. 'Now, Andrew Alsopp,' he said. 'Let me hear if you have psalm thirty-eight by heart.'

Andrew Alsopp rose. 'O Lord, rebuke me not in Thy wrath,' he began, for he was an industrious novice with a sound memory, one of the greatest blessings a monk can possess.

Novice Master allowed his attention to wander. He viewed his novices seated in a demure line before him on the stone bench.

20

A fair batch, he considered them: none brilliant, none stupid, all reasonably devout, all willing if not altogether eager to enter the Abbey of Woodchester and take the three monastic vows of poverty, chastity and obedience and to spend the rest of their lives in singing the divine offices, in praying for themselves and for the benefactors of the abbey and for the sins of the world, and in doing such work as the Abbot should appoint them to do. Their families had wanted them to spend their lives in this way and had supplied them with their dowries and their necessities, and so they had come and it was Novice Master's task to make them into good monks.

'There is no soundness in my flesh because of Thine anger,' droned Andrew Alsopp.

Novice Master shifted his weight to ease his ulcerous leg. He had three ulcers: one on the shin, one on the calf and one on the thigh. The one on the shin was so deep he could see the bone. He had had them four years and none of Infirmarian's remedies had done them any good.

'My wounds stink and are corrupt because of my foolishness,' chanted Andrew Alsopp.

Novice Master scratched his thigh through the stuff of his cassock. If medicines were ineffective that left only a miracle, but Novice Master did not think God was likely to favour him in this way because, for all his thin cheeks and domed forehead, Novice Master was not a good monk.

'When my foot slippeth they magnify themselves against me,' said Andrew Alsopp.

Novice Master winced, as if the words were salt in his sores. He had a sudden vision of an ugly mould and himself being squeezed into it by devils with two-pronged tails. It was not the monastic mould, it was not even the Catholic mould. The terrifying thing was that, although he closed his eyes to it, deep in his innermost heart Novice Master knew that it was the mould of heresy.

'Make haste to help me, O Lord my salvation,' concluded Andrew Alsopp triumphantly, and the other novices regarded him with awe.

They were eight novices: all young, all malleable, all clay in his hands.

'Place your books beneath you,' said Novice Master.

Eight books were symmetrically placed beneath the bench; sixteen feet were symmetrically arranged with their numbed toes on the line of the paving; sixteen hands were symmetrically tucked into their opposite sleeves.

'We will now consider the virtue of obedience.'

Eight pairs of eyes were meekly cast down. There had been a time, nearly two hundred years ago, when there had never been fewer than twenty novices sitting on this same bench; when in fact the novices sitting in the end places had been in danger of being pushed on to the floor. In those days every place in the choir had been filled and often the novices had been forced to sit on wooden stools. Now, in the year 1468, every novice had his own place in the back rows of the choir and at many services barely half the seats were occupied.

'They have no stamina, these young men of today,' thought Novice Master, eyeing the meek row from under his jutting temples. 'They are afraid of the cold and the discipline. They are too self-indulgent to renounce the lusts of the body.'

Thus he laboured to erect a barrier of platitudes against the heretical prompting that if young men of the day no longer became monks it was more likely to be because convent life no longer had anything to offer them.

'One of your first duties as a monk,' said Novice Master, 'is obedience. Obedience not only of the body but also of the mind. You must labour at all times to conform. Never question, even in your innermost thoughts, the instructions of your superiors. Allow no shadow of conjecture to darken your devotions. Let faith and faith alone order your lives in this convent. There is no danger so insidious in a monk as the danger of private opinion. Root it out without mercy. Be on your guard against every flicker of independence. You are here to conform to the Rule, to obey your superiors in all things and to express your devotion to God and the Church in the customary and accepted way.'

Eight cropped heads bowed submissively. Ah, if only he could do the same! If only he could practise as he preached!

'Let us now meditate,' he said, 'on this virtue of obedience and pray that we may be blessed with it.'

And none prayed more fervently than he.

He was still praying when the alarm bell almost split his ear-drums. The eight novices leapt to their feet and broke into excited chatter.

'Discipline!' roared Novice Master above the hubbub. 'Novices, remember your discipline. No novice may move from his place without permission. No novice may speak without leave.'

One by one they stopped their chatter and sat down, but not all the discipline in the Church could stop them peering through the cloister window at the tumult in the cloister yard beyond.

'Remain seated!' ordered Novice Master and he strode out into the cloister yard to find out what was wrong.

When the awful ringing burst upon him Guest Master neither jumped nor spilt his ink nor rushed from his room. Calmly he carried his documents and his accounts to his brass-studded chest. Calmly he laid them inside and turned the key on them. Carefully he examined his table and the floor under his table to make sure no scrap of parchment had been left behind. Only then did he pull tight his girdle, smooth his cassock with his tiny hands and carry his neat five foot one inch out of the Guest House to discover what calamity had warranted the ringing of what he could only suppose to be the alarm.

Guest Master was very busy cooking his accounts and, alarm or no alarm, he had no intention of being found out.

Brother Mark was in trouble again. Poor Brother Mark was always in trouble. He was a huge, plain, lubberly country lad;

23

stupid, said Novice Master; obstinate, said Sacristan; clumsy, said Cellarer; mistaken in his vocation, said Prior. Indeed, had it not been for Abbot Dominic, Brother Mark would never have become a monk at all. After the first six months Novice Master had reported that this farmer's boy would never make a monk of any kind, that he was too stupid to learn the services, too unskilled to be of use to the officials, too obstinate to do as he was told. 'He will never be a credit to the abbey,' Novice Master had told the Abbot. 'He cannot even sing in tune. Send him back to his pigs, Abbot, that is about all he is fit for.'

But Abbot Dominic had accepted him and no one had ever known why. 'I like him,' was all he had said. 'If he wants to be a monk then a monk he shall be.'

And there was no doubt that was what he wanted. With pathetic concentration he tried to remember what he had been told. Time and time again he tried to get through the service without a mistake but he had never yet succeeded. He was in a fair way to becoming the butt of the convent, poor Brother Mark. And the cream of the joke was that he never knew it. After every reprimand he bobbed up like a cork in a tank. He was, in spite of falling into hot water nearly every day of the week, extremely happy.

Just now the water was very hot indeed.

'Brother Mark,' Cellarer was saying sternly. 'Soon after Nones I sent you down here to check the grain sacks. Why have you not done so?'

Brother Mark grinned foolishly and stooped to fondle a little tabby cat that was caressing his bare ankles.

'Come, now,' said Cellarer impatiently. 'You can count, I presume? Have you nothing better to do than play with that wretched cat?'

Brother Mark straightened his back.

'A good monk,' said Cellarer, wagging his forefinger, 'a good monk has no business making pets out of animals. A good monk has his mind always on higher things. All his affection, all his attachment, all his love, must be directed to God and Holy Church.'

Surreptitiously Brother Mark rubbed the cat's flank with his ankle-bone.

'I very much fear, Brother Mark, that you do not direct your devotions wholeheartedly to the divine purpose. If I am not mistaken your pocket is at this moment full of monastic corn.'

Brother Mark thrust his hand into his pocket and extracted it with golden grain trickling between his massive fingers. ' 'Tis for t'birds,' he explained.

Cellarer blew through his nose. 'Cats! Birds! It would be better to devote such intelligence as you possess, brother, to learning your breviary.'

With a sniff and a shake of the head Cellarer turned away. 'I shall be expecting you before Vespers,' he warned him. 'With the correct number of grain sacks. Correct, Brother Mark!'

He disappeared up the steps, leaving Brother Mark in the gloom of the cellar with the little cat nibbling his toe-nails and grain trickling through his fingers.

Brother Mark poured the grain back into his pocket. 'Bide there, mommet,' he told the cat. 'I mun do straightways what un says and mind t'sacks.'

In the corner of the cellar he found a stick of wood. From the sheath in his girdle he took out his knife. 'One.' He made the first notch at the top of the stick. 'Two.' He made the second notch. 'Three.' But he never made the third notch. For standing behind the third sack of grain he saw his lord Jesus Christ, smiling at him as He had smiled so many times since he had become a monk. With his eyes on his lord, Brother Mark propped the tally against a sack and slipped his knife into its sheath. He sank on his knees and clasped his hands together. 'Lordy, lordy,' he said. His lord raised His right hand and blessed him. The faint light from the grating enclosed the three of them: Brother Mark, his lord Jesus and the little tabby cat who was curled up fast asleep between Brother Mark's calves.

Of all the ninety men in the Abbey of Woodchester, of the thirty monks and sixty servants, Brother Mark was the only one who did not hear the alarm bell.

2

I N THE cloister yard all hell was let loose. The grass was
being churned into mud by a panic-stricken mob of monks,
servants and villagers. They ran aimlessly about, clutching,
clamouring, praying and weeping, babbling of their sins, while
above them the ancient tower rocked to the clashing of the
alarm bell. What had started as a rush had become a panic.
Monks and laymen tore about like men lashed by devils, like
souls threatened by the Last Judgement. The terrible bell sounded
in their ears like Satan's joy at the warring of the world, at the
shattering of peace. Into their confused and frightened minds
surged terrifying pictures of civil wars, rampant heretics, disputed successions, a threatened Church, a Last Flood.

'O God, deliver me from my enemies,' muttered Brother
Joseph as he groped along the east cloister, convinced that it was
enemy figures that seethed in a mist before him.

'I will root out my passion,' vowed Brother Peter, as he
burst through the kitchen yard into the south cloister.

'Thank heaven I got the men off with the money before the
alarm,' thought Sacristan, tottering on his sleepy feet.

'They have run mad,' thought Guest Master, seeing a
woman on her knees in the mud beating her breast and shrieking,
'Lordy, save I.'

Infected by the horror about him Novice Master clung to a
pillar and, his novices forgotten, whispered over and over again,
'Make haste to help me, O Lord my salvation.'

Meanwhile Prior was fighting his way towards the south
transept. At the corner of the north cloister he collided with an
onrush of novices whose discipline had failed to stand this
arduous test.

'It is the end of the world!' shouted a young monk, flinging himself face downwards in the mud.

'The end of the world!' clashed the bell.

Someone came running with torches, whose eerie light made gargoyles of the terrified faces. To and fro they surged, trampling and screaming like lunatics, like men driven crazy by fear.

The bell stopped.

Instantly they froze like statues. Their clamour was cut off, as if every soul had been stifled where he stood. Even the boy with his leg broken in two places, even the woman with her hair burned, even the baby torn from the breast, all held their peace.

Instinctively every face turned to the north-east, to the great tower silhouetted against the darkening sky and pricked by two lights in the belfry windows. Overhead even the rooks were silent, circling the church as if they too waited to hear the worst.

The door of the tower creaked open and on the steps, torch in one hand and crucifix in the other, stood Abbot's Chaplain. The crowd gasped. He was as beautiful as the Archangel Michael, was Abbot's Chaplain. He stood there in his white cope and his black cassock, his skin gleaming in the torchlight, his wonderful eyes shining like stars, flames illuminating his magnificent features. When he had stood silent long enough he spoke. His voice was like a rippling stream or a thrush's song or any other miracle of nature.

'Brothers and good people,' he cried, gazing straight over Prior's head. 'I have ill tidings. I grieve to tell you that our beloved abbot, our much-revered and august Abbot Dominic'— he paused dramatically—'has succumbed to a seizure. In fact, brothers and good people, he has fallen in a fit.'

He closed his handsome mouth and the hubbub rose again But among the villagers the panic was over. It was only the Abbot's fit after all, not the destruction of the world or the threatening of the Church or pestilence or fire or flood or any other of nature's punishments. So they crossed themselves and murmured regrets and took their leave, a little shamefaced, anxious to get outside the walls as soon as possible. The boy's leg was strapped to a broom-handle, the baby was retrieved and put back to the breast, and the villagers trailed away to their neglected duties.

After some shuffling and muttering the three-score servants followed their example. They straightened their coats and pulled up their stockings and drifted away: cooks to the kitchens, bakers to the bake-house, grooms to the stables, gardeners to the cemetery, masons to the foundations of the new Chapter House, Prior's steward to the prising of more rents. This was monks' business, they argued. This was their grief. The abbey still had to eat and be clothed and sleep and work even if the Abbot was dying.

The last groom crept sheepishly from the cloisters. One by one the monks sank on their knees exactly where they stood.

'Incline unto our aid, O God,' intoned Prior.

'O Lord, make haste to help us,' enjoined the monks, bowing their shaved heads.

They were shocked, almost numbed, by this calamity. Only a handful remembered any other abbot but Abbot Dominic. For twenty years he had been their father in Christ. His word had been their law. Almost every day they saw him in the morning Chapter, heard his instructions and listened to his sermon. At least once in the week, and on major feast days in addition, they received the blessed Sacraments from Abbot Dominic's stubby hands, one with the forefinger missing and one wearing a ruby set in gold. '*Omnipitens semiterne Deus*,' they chanted, praying that he would recover and that life would plod on as before. They did not want change. They knew their abbot and they liked him and they did not want him to die. They felt—and it was a ghost of what they had felt when they had heard the alarm bell—they felt their security threatened. 'Dislodge a stone of that tower and it will tumble down,' a wit had once said. Yet what, after all, could happen to them? If their abbot died they would have to elect a new abbot. There was nothing new in that. Abbots were mortal and died and had to be replaced. But they were not happy these thirty, no, these twenty-nine monks, kneeling in the muddy cloister yard. Their abbot was dying and they could not help fearing that a part of their abbey was dying too.

Prior opened his eyes and rose to his feet. Before he spoke to the monks he sent up a silent prayer. 'Lord, give me strength to bear the burden placed upon me.' Then he said, 'Brothers, we will proceed to Vespers.' While the monks marshalled themselves in two lines in the east cloister Prior asked Abbot's Chaplain where the Abbot was.

'I have had his servants convey him to the infirmary,' Abbot's Chaplain replied.

At this news Infirmarian bustled away with Brother Peter, who was his assistant, in tow. 'Pray God we shall be able to nurse him back to health,' said Infirmarian.

'Pray God,' repeated Brother Peter. But he was thinking, 'Now I shall not be able to meet Alice in Rector's barn tomorrow.'

In the cloister the double line of monks was almost complete. At their head Cantor held aloft the single Lent taper. He started the first psalm. 'The Lord said unto my Lord, sit Thou at my right hand,' he sang. Behind him Guest Master stroked his chin and pondered that it was indeed unfortunate that Abbot Dominic should fall ill and it would be even worse if he died. For now there would be real guests in the Guest House: physicians, couriers, bishops' men, guests who ate and drank and had hungry horses and were more than numbers and figures in his account books.

The procession began to move. As each pair of monks reached the south door they bent and took off their sandals and placed them neatly against the wall in Lent fashion. Some of their feet were so numb with the March cold that they could not feel the additional cold of the pavement. 'Thine shall be dominion in the day of Thy power,' sang the monks, as two by two they disappeared into the transept. A second before the door closed there was a puffing in the cloister and Brother Mark tumbled into the church.

'Be summat up?' he asked.

Without pausing in their chant the monks unhooked their white choir copes from their pegs and put them on. They tucked

29

their hands in their sleeves, glad of the warmth on their chilly fingers. They went once round the nave with their eyes fixed on the bobbing taper ahead, then into their places in the choir, half to the left, half to the right, novices in the back rows, officials in the front. There were many empty places, places that had not been filled for a hundred years or more and that Prior feared never would be filled, such was the waning of enthusiasm for the monastic life.

'He shall drink of the brook in the way, therefore shall He lift up His head,' they sang.

All faces were correctly turned inwards but all eyes strained their sockets to glimpse the Abbot's chair, standing forlorn and empty on its dais near the altar steps. Brother Joseph began to cry: for his abbot, for his sight, for all the unhappiness that had struck him out of the blue. The psalm ended and with scarcely a pause for breath Cantor burst into the *Confitebor tibi* and the monks threw out their chests and raised their voices in the familiar hymn of praise.

Even Brother Mark sang, rejoicing that here was a piece that he knew by heart. 'I will praise Thee, O Lord, with my whole heart,' they sang, and despite their sorrow they sang loudly and joyfully, for it was one of their duties to praise God with cheerful voices, whatever the trials and tribulations of their lives. And, as they sang, verse by verse and phrase by phrase, comfort came trickling back into their little world. *This* would never sicken and die, *this* would never be threatened with destruction. Abbots might come and go but this would go on for ever: the age-old liturgy, the Gregorian chant, the candles and images, the Sacraments in the tabernacle awaiting morning Mass, the vestments in the vestry, the holy water in the stoup, the prayers and offerings. This service and all the other services of the monastic day were built into the very fabric of the Church and of course the Church would last, impregnable on St Peter's rock, for ever.

Honest or dishonest, weak or strong, selfish or unselfish, there was not a single monk, not even Novice Master, who did not believe that God was present in their abbey church, as He was in every church. 'Everything will be all right,' thought

Prior, as, with a creaking of misericords, the entire community sat down for the next psalm. He fingered the grooves between his eyebrows.

They sang their fifty-seven psalms, rising to their feet for the fifty-seventh and for the *Magnificat* that followed it. Then they sank on their knees and Cantor, who was Priest for the Week, sang the collect for the day and the Pater Noster in which they all joined. Six Hail Marys, a prayer for the Abbot and a sprinkle of holy water and Vespers was over. The monks filed out of their stalls, proceeded once again round the dark nave, doffed their copes and buckled on their sandals and departed to supper and a warm-up in the warming house. They all felt a great deal better.

The top notes of the *Magnificat* filtered through to the infirmary.

'That is Abbot's Chaplain singing the descant,' said Infirmarian. 'What a pity the Abbot cannot hear it.'

They were in the small ward, he and Brother Peter and two servants and the Abbot. It was a tiny room with a bed, two stools, a crucifix, a cupboard and a window in the east wall that looked straight out to the other side of the valley. In daylight this window gave one the impression of being on a cliff, the monastery was perched so high and the ground fell away so sharply. But now the window was a coal-black oblong and no one had eyes except for the man in the bed.

He seemed short and stocky, because although he filled the bed from side to side his toes did not reach the bottom. He lay on his back with his hands crossed over the sheet. He breathed heavily and his chest creaked like a rusty hinge. His eyes were tight shut but his eyelids did not seem to fit his eyes. Under his head there was a pillow that had bent back one of his ears. His face was swollen purple and blue like a colossal bruise.

'Is he going?' whispered Brother Peter.

Infirmarian felt the sick man's pulse. 'I do not know. I have known men fall like trees and lie like logs and yet live for weeks and months.'

A third servant entered with a hot brick wrapped in wool. Infirmarian tested it with his hand. 'Put it at his feet,' he ordered. When the bedclothes were turned back he pricked each of the Abbot's feet with a pin and, when the feet did not so much as quiver, he shook his head. 'His legs are dead. If the deadness mounts to his heart he will die.'

'What can we do for him?'

'We can pray for him.'

'But can we not administer medicines? Any potions? Surely it is not right to rely on prayers alone?'

'Of course I shall administer drugs,' answered Infirmarian crossly. 'Do not try and teach me my business, Brother Peter. I will try foxglove poultice on the dead limbs. I have often found it efficacious.'

The hours passed. The sick man's breath rasped his throat like a saw on stone. Candles were placed at his head, illuminating his ghastly features. The ruby on his right hand shone without winking. Brother Peter made a rhubarb brew and blew it with a straw drop by drop down the Abbot's swollen throat. He rolled pellets of crushed beetle in his fingers and squeezed them through gaps in the Abbot's teeth. From the waist down the Abbot was plastered with foxglove poultice and then wound in bandages. For every third turn of the bandage Infirmarian said a Hail Mary.

In the church the monks, warm from the fire and from their supper of chicken broth and oatbread, sang the office of Compline and lit two candles at each of the three altars, in supplication for the Abbot's recovery. They intoned a last *Benedicat* and went their ways to bed, the officials to their own rooms and the ordinary monks to their icy dormitory. Sacristan made the last rounds of the church, shooting the bolts and turning the keys. The torches were extinguished in the cloister yard. The monks said their private prayers, then took off their cassocks and sandals and swung themselves into bed, buttocks first, in the prescribed manner. The servants tucked themselves away in holes and corners like so many maggots. Down in the village the smoke dwindled as fires were banked for the night. The only sounds were the hoot of an owl and the sobbing of a child in a nightmare. Quiet descended on the abbey.

But not sleep.

Prior was composing a letter. He sat at his polished table with his shoulders sagging under the weight of his responsibilities. The same hand that had struck down his abbot was forcing him into a prominence for which he was not fitted. He had neither the character nor the ability to administer the Abbot's estates, preside at Chapter, inflict discipline, direct the building operations and, should the Abbot die, superintend the intricacies of an abbatical election, to say nothing of continuing his prior's duties. In other abbeys it was often a settled thing that on the death of the Abbot the Prior should be hailed unanimously as the new superior. But if the Prior of Woodchester was certain of anything it was that these monks would never elect him and that if they did he would decline the honour.

He sighed and pulled the candle towards him. He scratched his naked head with the tip of his pen and began:

To my lord king Edward, ruler of England, Wales and Calais, greetings. I take up my pen on this day of grace the twentieth of March in the year 1468 to inform your Majesty that his loyal subject Abbot Dominic, Abbot of Woodchester in the shire of Gloucester, baron of the realm, has this day been struck down by a seizure and lies grievously sick in the abbey infirmary. In the event of the abbot's demise I will send word to your Majesty forthwith. I remain your loyal servant in Christ, Simon, Prior of Woodchester.

'Yet what interest will the King take?' he thought as he watched the wax sizzle in the flame. The King was young, strong, not long married, secure on his throne at last now that the old Lancastrian king Henry was shut up in the Tower. To fill his days he had his court, his queen, his lords, his statues and books

33

and pictures. Why should he worry about an old abbot dying in a far-away corner of England? It was many years since the kings of England had bothered over abbatical elections. A *congé d'élire* to permit the election to proceed, confirmation of the candidate selected—what more had the King to do than this? Abbots were no longer of any political importance. In the House of Lords they outnumbered the bishops by three to one, yet for more than a century no king had ever listened to their advice. Why should the King care that another abbot lay dying?

Prior let the wax drop on to the parchment, then stamped it with his prior's seal. Perhaps King Edward might feel a prick of regret, might at least order candles, perhaps even a Mass. For Abbot Dominic had been loyal. He had taken his oath of homage to the York dynasty without a murmur. Seven years before he had bowed to the revolution that had swept the Lancastrian Henry off his throne. 'An abbot has no call to meddle in politics,' he had said, submitting gracefully to the *fait accompli*. At the expense of a month's income he had entertained Edward in 1463. He had even given hospitality to the great Warwick, the King's mentor and kinsman, who had truly earned his nickname of Kingmaker by lifting his young cousin on to the English throne; and Warwick's entertainment had cost the abbey even more than the King's.

The King's letter sealed and despatched, Prior wrote to the Bishop and then to a distinguished physician who lived in Gloucester, requiring his immediate attendance. Before the last letter was finished there came a tapping at his door and Abbot's Chaplain entered. He crossed the room and sat down beside the ashes and began inspecting his beautiful nails.

'Yes?' said Prior coldly, careful not to lay down his pen.

Abbot's Chaplain smiled, showing admirable teeth. He noted the furrows in Prior's forehead and his inky middle finger. 'I have come to assure you, Prior,' he said in a comforting voice, 'that while he is unable to attend to it you need have no fear for the administration of the Abbot's estates. I am fully conversant with his affairs. As you know I have acted as his steward and treasurer for eleven years.' His tone was sweet and reasonable

34

but Prior recognized a warning when he heard one. He laid down his pen. A decision so soon! Could he not be allowed even one night's peace? Now that the Abbot was laid low it was his duty to see the Abbot's rents collected and to supervise his household, but he did not have the strength to suppress the glorious relief that now flooded him at the prospect of shedding this load. He straightened his sagging back.

'I am grateful to you,' he said. 'You will of course bring the quarterly accounts to me for my inspection.'

Abbot's Chaplain rose. 'Of course,' he said.

At the door he turned and added: 'Perhaps you would care to be relieved of the administration of the building fund? I am well aware of the Abbot's preferences and I have copies of all plans and estimates in the Abbot's lodgings. With this multiplication of your spiritual duties it is scarcely to be expected that you should any longer personally supervise the raising of the new Chapter House.' He remained poised in the doorway with his hand laid gracefully on the latch.

Prior hesitated. He longed to stand firm but he could not help thinking of the daily sermon he must preach and the extra Masses he must perform.

'So be it,' he said at last. 'I will inform the master mason that he must take his instructions from you.'

Abbot's Chaplain bowed but he did not close the door. 'I will send servants for the money,' he said gently, eyeing the chest that lay nearest to the door.

Prior looked startled. 'You wish to remove the chest?'

'If I am to instruct the masons,' replied Abbot's Chaplain smoothly, 'then it is reasonable that I should also pay them their wages. I shall have no authority over them if I do not hold the purse-strings. Besides,' he added, with a wave of his white hand, 'half the building fund comes from the Abbot's own income. Can it be wrong for Abbot's Chaplain to have the handling of it?'

'Very well,' sighed Prior. 'You may send for the chest. But I shall require accounts. You must account to me for every penny you spend.'

'Of course,' said Abbot's Chaplain, and closed the door.

Prior returned to his letter. He felt guilty and unhappy. He thought of his decision twenty years ago to seek the seclusion and security of monastic life. If only he had realized then what responsibilities that life might bring him!

Guest Master sat at his table with his tiny feet crossed neatly at the ankles and his ten finger-tips placed accurately together. He thought he saw his way clear. Only let him persuade Prior that all visits connected with the Abbot's illness were Abbot's visits, then Prior was bound to sanction their expenses being paid out of Abbot's income. Only let him do that and with any luck he need scarcely fork out of his own fund at all. After all, he had precedent to support him. When King Edward had paid his visit five years before, Guest Master had contrived that only the horses and their grooms should become a charge on his own fund; and he had fobbed them off with dead meat and mouldy oats.

Guest Master viewed his plan with satisfaction. If he contrived things cleverly his son Francis would have the money for his shop by midsummer. Only let the quarter's rents be raked in and the sum would be made up. At the image of his son, Guest Master blushed a rosy pink. Even the thought of a battle with Abbot's Chaplain could not spoil his pleasure.

In the dormitory all was dark, but all was not still. As soon as he thought the others were asleep Brother Joseph crawled out of bed, pulled on his night-boots and crept to the door. Inch by inch he levered it open until he could slip through. Blindly he groped his way through the kitchen yard to the infirmary. He knocked timidly at the door and a servant opened. 'I wish to speak to Infirmarian,' he said to the pale blur that was the servant's face. Too flabbergasted to object, the servant allowed Brother Joseph to push past him. Brother Joseph felt his way to the main ward where many times he had been bled and where Infirmarian was at this moment squeezing foxglove ointment into Novice Master's ulcers.

As Brother Joseph advanced into the centre of the room Infirmarian looked up in astonishment at this trembling, weeping old man clad in nothing but his shirt and drawers and his felt night-boots. 'Why, Brother Joseph!' he exclaimed. 'What are you doing out of bed? Have you come to enquire after the Abbot?'

Brother Joseph stretched his skinny arms towards the light and cried, in such an agony of sorrow that both men started to their feet, 'I cannot see you!'

Infirmarian guided him to a bench. Between sobs Brother Joseph explained how his sight had suddenly deserted him so that now he could see light and dark and black and white and fire and the outline of shapes but he could no longer see to write his texts or paint his illuminations. 'What shall I do? What shall I do?' he kept pleading. 'If I cannot write my manuscripts, what shall I do?' When the purpose of a man's life is suddenly snatched away he may be forgiven for becoming querulous.

Infirmarian examined Brother Joseph's red and streaming eyes. 'We will try the foxglove ointment,' he said. 'I have often found it efficacious in the treatment of eye ailments.' With a spatula he spread the ointment thickly on to a bandage which he then pressed on to Brother Joseph's eyes and tied tightly in a knot at the back of his head. 'Come to me every day after High Mass so that I may make another application. When the time is right I will take it all off. But you must try not to cry, Brother Joseph. I cannot have your tears diluting the ointment.'

At last the old man was calmed and, full of hope, was sent back to the dormitory with a servant. He had forgotten to ask after the Abbot.

There was a tap at the door and a servant entered followed by Abbot's Chaplain. Greetings were exchanged. Novice Master took his leave. 'I have come,' said Abbot's Chaplain, clasping his elegant hands under his chin, 'to enquire after my beloved superior. What is the Abbot's condition? Have his senses returned?'

'You shall see him,' said Infirmarian, and led the way into the small ward.

As soon as Abbot's Chaplain beheld his abbot stretched out like a log—his breath whistling in his throat, his bloated lips spattered with foam, his features fused into a leaden mass—something twitched the corner of his mouth. He lowered his eyelids until his black lashes rested on his cheeks. 'Can he recover?' he asked softly. 'Will there be a new election?'

Infirmarian folded his lips together. 'Do not bury him before he is dead,' he said severely.

Abbot's Chaplain went on his knees at the bedside and prayed aloud in his musical voice for the Abbot's recovery. Then he asked, 'I do not suppose he has spoken?'

Infirmarian shook his head.

'Perhaps,' said Abbot's Chaplain, 'it might be as well if a servant sat by the Abbot's head. It is possible, is it not, that he might let fall a murmur? . . .' Here he moved his jaw, a surprising gesture in one so graceful. 'Perhaps he might indicate . . . God might give him strength to indicate whom he wishes to be his successor.'

'Are you hoping for that honour yourself?' asked Infirmarian, fastening his fingers on to the sick man's wrist.

'God forbid!' said Abbot's Chaplain.

Eventually he left the infirmary and retired to his own room in the Abbot's lodgings. He thought for a long while. At length he too decided to write a letter describing the Abbot's serious condition. He called for writing materials and wrote in his elegant script:

To Richard, Earl of Warwick, premier earl of the realm, at Middleham in Yorkshire. My lord, I greet you in Christ. . . .

In the bed nearest to the door—naturally, since it was in the full draught from the stairway—Brother Mark lay dreaming. Into his dreams a strange sound kept obtruding. He grunted. It came again, delicate and yet insistent. At last his eyes came open. There it was again, right outside the door. Scratch, scratch. Scratch, scratch. Brother Mark scrambled out of bed and opened the door. There was nothing to see, nothing to hear. Everything was pitch black and as quiet as the tomb. He shut the door and stumbled back into his bed and shoved his huge feet down into its icy bottom. His toes touched something soft and warm. The thing moved. It was the little cat. Twice Brother Mark steeled his heart, lugged her out and dropped her on the floor. Twice she sprang up and wormed her way down to his toes. At last he gave up trying to shift her and fell happily asleep with his feet resting on something as warm as a hot brick and far, far softer.

Two hundred feet below the abbey walls, in the dark and sleepy village, there was one house where a light still burned. It was the house of Alice's father, John Leys, one of the abbey's most articulate tenants. He was well-to-do for a peasant, was John Leys. He had high hopes that his eldest son, or perhaps his eldest son's eldest son when, God willing, he grew up and got one, would call himself a yeoman and build a house with stone tiles and marry his daughter to a gentleman.

John Leys had a stone chimney and an oak press for his wife's best dress and stone paving on his ground floor. He had two windows in his roof and a bed with a feather mattress and two pewter plates. His house was made of laths and plaster and had a tidy thatch. From the abbey he rented sixty acres of pasture and arable, the rent being collected by Novice Master's steward and going into Novice Master's fund. He grazed seventy sheep on the Selsely sheepwalks. He had a thrifty wife, four growing sons and a dutiful daughter and not a hare-lip among them. He was ambitious, quick-tempered and honest. He was by way of being leader in the village, much looked up to and much listened to. John Leys did not care for the abbey nor for its thirty monks. To him the abbey loomed like a feudal castle, blocking the way to better things. To him the Abbot was only a *rentier* who would not sell him his land. To him the monks were simply bald men in skirts who gobbled up his rents and did not make good the dilapidations.

'I tell 'ee, Rector, un bain't right,' he shouted, pounding the table with his fist. 'I 'oon't brook it. T'abbey did ought to sell I my land. I hae offered fair price, God knows. I be mortal sick of spewing up t'rent and nought done toward draining or fencing. I hae aksed thakky Novice Master time on time—or his'n steward, 'tis all one—and allus un says, "The Abbot will not allow it." Thakky be what un says. "T'Abbot will not sell." '

'Perhaps he never asks the Abbot,' suggested Rector.

John Leys growled and shook his red head.

'You must remember, John, that the monks have to live, too. If they sell their land the money is soon spent and then where is their income to come from?'

'They monks ought to mind summat else every once-while, besides theyselves. But thakky be monks all over, squatting on thairn backsides——'

'On their knees, John, on their knees.'

'. . . blathering and walloping they bells. T'monks doan't farm thairn own land, just bides still and gobbles up t'rents. Un bain't no good to we. . . .'

'They pray.'

'Ar, but un doan't pray for we! Un do pray desperd bad for theyselves and for they as gived money for t'abbey. 'Ee scratch I and I 'ool scratch 'ee, thakky be t'size of it.' Rector took a pull at his ale. 'What good be they?' thundered John Leys, rushing on before Rector had time to swallow. 'Who minds they? Who visits they, let alone un be after a bed for t'night? I tell 'ee, Rector, un ought to sell I my land. I tell 'ee——'

Rector raised his hand. 'Calm yourself, John. Do not waste your breath. You cannot make the abbey do what it does not wish. Nor can you stop it doing what it does wish.'

John Leys grunted and drained his mug. 'I cass-n't twig 'ee, Rector. 'Ee got no cause to love they, no more nor I. Abbot 'ool snatch yourn church off of 'ee if 'ee doan't watch un. Abbot 'ool wheedle Sir Thomas Arundel and Sir Thomas 'ool tilt 'ee out and pop in a weedy vicar.'

'Perhaps Sir Thomas Arundel will not agree,' said Rector.

John Leys snorted. 'U'll give in quick if Abbot promises un to pray for his'n soul for nought.'

'But the Abbot is ill, they tell me. Perhaps when he recovers he will have had a change of heart. After all, he is not a bad man. He only wants to raise more money for the new Chapter House.'

'Thakky Chapter House! Thakky bain't no good for we. Village 'oon't e'er get inside un.'

John Leys poured more ale for himself but Rector covered his mug with his hand. 'Of course,' he said thoughtfully, 'the Abbot might die.'

'Ar, most like, but what good 'ool that do for we? Un's all tarred likewise, un's all suckabloods. . . .'

Rector rose. 'Do not allow your temper to get the better of you, John. The Abbot is powerful and your lease is nearly up. You do not want to be turned off your land.'

He turned to the door and John Leys unbolted it. Together they sniffed the frosty air.

' 'Nation good for drying,' said John Leys.

'Aye,' said Rector. 'I have a mind to turn the hay in my barn tomorrow.'

3

THE King stretched out his hand. 'Beautiful, beautiful,' he murmured. On to his handsome face crept a look the court did not often see, a look of awe, almost of reverence. 'Worcester, that is a lovely thing. Look, Chancellor, look, Gunthorpe, is it not lovely?' He picked up the statue and held it aloft in the light of the candles. 'Beautiful,' he crooned, rubbing his cheek against its flank. It was a bronze cherub, a plump little fellow with minute wings, naked except for a pair of gauzy leggings. In his left hand he held a lyre. There were feathered wings on his chubby heels. 'See the colours?' cried the King. 'Green and gold and brown. Who would have thought that bronze could hold so many colours?'

'It is the best Italian workmanship,' said Worcester, his cold face warmed into something like life. 'It was made by Donatello. I bought it from his workshop in Florence.'

Chancellor leaned forward and inserted his little finger into a dimple. 'Exquisite,' he whispered. 'The metal breathes, does it not, Gunthorpe?'

The Queen's chaplain gazed into the jaunty infant face. 'I have never seen finer work,' he said gravely.

The three scholars nodded their heads, momentarily united by the beautiful thing between the King's hands.

'Is it not—you will pardon me, my lord . . .' It was the Bishop of London, a man so old that he no longer bothered to be careful what he said. 'Is it not—how shall I express myself—is it not pagan?'

The young King, the most handsome man in England, a golden giant with eyes like the Mediterranean Sea, regarded the statue. 'Pagan? How do you mean, London? How pagan?'

London pointed a tremulous finger. 'He is naked,' he explained. 'He delights to be naked. Could he not in decency have pulled his draperies higher? He is a shameless thing, my lord. He'—the ancient voice squeaked in indignation—'he *flaunts.*'

'You do not understand, London,' said the King kindly. 'Things have changed since you were a boy. These Italians understand the beauty of the human body.'

London turned pale. 'My lord! There is no beauty in the human body. It is a snare enticing men into sin. The more men see of the human body the worse it is for their souls.'

The King laughed and placed the cherub on the table. Over the cocked head and the smiling mouth he eyed his queen feeding dainties to her falcon and thought that if her body was bad for his soul he was willing to be damned in hell for it. She had all the charms that experience could give. Her breasts were high and round, her waist narrow, her belly plump and her buttocks generous. Her hair was twisted into a golden structure a foot high and pierced twice with blue ostrich feathers. Her skin was white and her teeth good. She did not look her age. The King studied her. He did not regret marrying her, although by doing so he had raised a storm indeed. Elisabeth Woodville. Elisabeth Woodville whose father had been a bailiff. Elisabeth Woodville, a woman of mature years with two grown sons. Elisabeth Woodville, widow of a Lancastrian knight killed by Edward's forces at St Albans, whose mother was rumoured to dabble in witchcraft, who had an ambitious Woodville father, five aspiring Woodville sisters and seven needy Woodville brothers.

'Come, my love,' called the King. 'Come and see the pretty cherub.'

She dropped her titbits and came towards him and there came with her her son Richard Woodville and her son Thomas Woodville, her sister Catherine the new Duchess of Buckingham and her eldest brother, Lord Scales. Her father, the new Earl Rivers, lately appointed treasurer of England, was playing chess against the wall but he looked round as she passed.

The King pinched her breast and laughed with pleasure. Indeed he had much to please him. For the first time in seven

43

years Edward Mortimer, descended in the female line from the second surviving son of Edward Plantagenet, felt safe on the throne of England.

Seven years before, after years of bloody civil war, his cousin Richard Neville, the great Earl of Warwick, had pulled from its high position the rotten Lancastrian government with its babbling king, and had put a Yorkist government in its place. Seven years before, Warwick and the great tribe of the Nevilles had placed the crown on Edward's young head and presented him to the people as the true king, the only king whose government was capable of restoring peace and justice to England. And the people of England had been so thankful to see on the throne a sane man with a strong-minded government that they had thrown their caps in the air and shouted, 'God save the King.'

Then had followed some uneasy years, but now that mad King Henry VI—descended in the male line from the third surviving son of Edward Plantagenet—was safely shut up in the Tower and his wife the Bitch of Anjou and her whelp son were trailing round the continent with a queue of beggarly Lancastrians at their heels—now indeed Edward IV felt secure.

'Is it not a pretty cherub?' he said, squeezing his wife's waist. 'Does it speak to you of the lust of the flesh, eh?' He began to bite her neck and she pouted prettily.

'Donatello cast this bronze by a new method,' Worcester explained. 'There is much investigation into such matters in Italy at this time.'

'And into other matters,' said Gunthorpe. 'They tell me there are scholars working on Greek manuscripts——'

'Greek!' breathed the King. He straightened his back and his blue eyes roamed the four walls of the hall. 'How old the world is!' he murmured. 'And how big! There are so many things to know.'

'Do you believe in the pursuit of knowledge, my lord?' asked Gunthorpe.

The King pondered. 'Yes,' he said. 'It is good to learn.'

'To learn what, my lord?'

'Why anything, Gunthorpe, anything.'

44

London blew bubbles, so indignantly did his wrath burst through his lips. 'My lord! How can you say such terrible things? It is man's duty to learn only such things as can make him more pious or more orthodox or more useful to the Church. Learning is for confounding heretics not for reading heathen texts! Knowledge is dangerous. Leave it alone. You do not know where it will lead you.'

'Nonsense, London,' cried Chancellor. 'You are out of the fashion, I assure you. Man loves what is new: new skills, new arts, new languages, new lands. Why, the Portuguese have just discovered some new islands. Would you have us pretend they are not there?'

London threw up his hands in horror and shuffled away. The King fondled the cherub's thigh. 'My cousin Warwick would not approve of this,' he remarked. 'He would say it was immodest and tie a handkerchief round it.'

In a spurt of devilment he whipped a napkin out of Chancellor's hands and tied it apron-fashion round the cherub's loins. 'There!' he shouted, his blue eyes snapping with fun. 'Now Warwick cannot complain. Out of sight, out of mind, eh, London? But you churchmen are pure-minded fellows, I am told. Why should the organ upset you when you have forsworn the use of it?'

'Warwick has not forsworn the use of it,' said Chancellor.

The King laughed. 'Forty years of age and only two daughters to show for it. The use of it cannot give him much pleasure.'

The court looked uneasy. In four years of marriage the Queen had produced only two daughters. The sudden hush was shattered by the Queen's scream of laughter. 'Two daughters in twenty years! The tree may be strong but the seed is weak. Perhaps he should have tried planting it in more fertile soil.'

The Woodvilles began to laugh. Against the wall Earl Rivers flung back his head and roared: 'I am surprised there is anything weak about the great Lord Warwick. To hear him talk one would think him the buttress of all England.'

'He carries England on his shoulders like Atlas,' sneered Richard Woodville. 'He says so often enough.'

'He keeps royal state,' giggled Thomas Woodville, prostrating himself in the rushes.

Lord Scales began prancing across the hall in devilish imitation of Warwick's stately walk. He leaped astride a bench and
cried: 'What? Would you have us fight on foot? I tell you no
Neville ever fights except on horseback.' He waved an imaginary
sword over his head.

Earl Rivers snatched up a scarf and wound it round his head.
'It is unseemly for a noble to remain uncovered,' he intoned,
twisting the ends of the scarf into a likeness of Warwick's famous
hat. He shot a glance at the King's smiling face, then he leapt up
on a stool and began bowing to right and left in a parody of
graciousness. The Fool took the hint. He dropped on all fours
and, crawling through the rushes to the Earl's feet, knocked his
forehead on the ground and smacked his lips in kisses. 'A
Warwick! A Warwick!' he piped, mocking the war-cry of three
northern shires.

'A Warwick! A Warwick!' they screamed, unleashing
behind the shelter of a joke the hounds of their jealousy. One by
one the Woodvilles crawled to the Earl's feet and saluted him,
and after them crawled the courtiers and the servants and the
retainers, every one of them owing their fortune to the man they
were now ridiculing, the man who had placed their royal master
on his throne. 'A Warwick!' they shouted, with man's primitive
instinct to tear down the mighty and humble the proud.

Intent on their sport, the Woodvilles did not observe the
King's radiance cloud nor the sparkle die out in his blue eyes.
Not even the Queen observed the frown of guilt that marred his
young forehead. 'Enough!' he muttered. Chancellor heard him
and touched his sleeve. Below the hubbub he murmured in the
King's ear: 'I am most anxious to confer with your Majesty.
Will your Majesty accompany me into another room?'

The King hesitated. His queen and her sister had got their
father in an armed chair and were plying him with imaginary
dishes, shuffling to and fro on their knees with shrieks of amuse-
ment. The hall was filled with mocking cries. Spite, envy and
hatred had found legitimate expression in a charade. Chancellor

touched the King's sleeve. 'It will be quiet in the ante-chamber,' he said. He did not want to cross swords with the Woodvilles.

'Very well,' said the King.

The little procession of King, Chancellor, Worcester, London and half a dozen attendants passed through the tapestry hangings and came into the ante-chamber. Chancellor and London sank stiffly on to oak chairs. Worcester ran his nail over some embroidery. The King dawdled over the fireplace and kicked a log with his foot. Chancellor received a parchment from his clerk and consulted it. 'News has just reached me, my lord, that His Holiness the Pope has awarded a cardinal's hat to the Archbishop of Canterbury. A great honour for the English Church, is it not?'

London screwed up his mouth. 'George Neville will not be pleased. Ever since he has been Archbishop of York he has been hoping for a cardinal's hat.'

'York!' exclaimed Chancellor. 'How could York expect a cardinalate? Every Vatican clerk tells tales of his whoring. They say he will not let his priest leave his side, not even when he is taking his nightly pleasures, lest he should be struck down and die unabsolved in an act of mortal sin.'

London replied: 'I did not say George Neville should have a cardinal's hat, Chancellor. I simply said he will be angry when he hears that Canterbury has got one.'

The King raised troubled eyes from the fire. 'Warwick will not like it,' he said. 'He will call it a slight on his brother. He will blame me.'

There was an uncomfortable silence.

'How can he blame you, my lord?' said Worcester at length. 'It is the Pope's decision.'

'He will blame me,' the King repeated. 'He will say I could have bribed the Pope to bestow a cardinal's hat on whomever I wished.'

'And would your Majesty have wished one on George Neville?' asked London slyly. 'Would you have asked His Holiness to honour a harem?'

The King did not reply.

'The Nevilles are powerful enough without further honours,'

said Chancellor, thinking a little smugly how only the previous year the King had taken the chancellorship away from George Neville and given it to himself. He consulted another document. 'My lord Warwick has just arrived at Middleham from France. I am informed that in presents he received from the King of France'—here Chancellor consulted a list—'two greyhounds with silver collars, a butt of wine, a white hunting-horse and a dagger with an emerald in the handle.'

The King shifted uneasily. He had good cause to know of his cousin Warwick's preference for France and things French. It was because of this preference that, four years earlier, Edward had married his Elisabeth Woodville in secret, not daring for four months to break to Warwick the news that he was no longer free to marry the French princess. Six foot four inches tall, twenty-six years of age, handsome, secure, popular— Edward IV of England felt his belly stir even now at the memory of Warwick's speechless wrath. Four years before, Edward had made Warwick look a fool, and now it seemed as if he was bound to do so again.

'You will have to tell him,' said Worcester, turning over Brother Joseph's missal. 'You must not keep him in the dark too long. It is better if my lord Warwick hears of the treaty with Burgundy from your own lips. Do not give him the excuse to say that you feared to tell him.'

The King threw back his golden head. 'I am not afraid,' he said proudly. 'If I and my counsellors have decided to conclude a treaty of friendship and alliance with Burgundy——'

'Warwick is your counsellor too,' put in London. 'Yet I do not recall you taking his advice.'

The King whirled round. 'I have done nothing but take Warwick's advice,' he said furiously. 'For years I have taken his advice. He has lived my life for me, breathed my breath, thought my thoughts. I cannot take his advice for ever.'

'Yet he won you your throne, my lord,' pursued London. 'In common gratitude——'

'Gratitude!' shouted the King. 'I have given him gratitude. Must I be grateful for ever?'

48

There was no sound but the spitting of the logs. The candles burned steadily.

'I will tell him,' said the King suddenly. 'I promise you I will tell him at Easter. He will understand that a treaty with Burgundy is best.' Out of sight Chancellor raised doubtful eyebrows. 'Chancellor, see that my cousin Warwick is invited to Ludlow for Easter.' Chancellor bowed. The King flung himself on to a stool and bit into an apple. 'What news from the Tower?' he demanded cheerfully, for his moods were a young man's moods, black and gold chasing over his nature like colours over a stream.

Chancellor smiled. 'Excellent, my lord, excellent. King Henry—or should I perhaps say Henry of Lancaster since of course he is no longer a king—he is very frail and babbles of saints and martyrs and thinks he is a little boy.'

'Does he talk of me?'

'He talks of nothing, my lord. He knows neither his name nor his station. He does not know the year or the place or the names of his warders.'

'He does not speak of his wife and son?'

'He does not even know they exist.'

The King sighed and flung out his legs. 'I wish I had his family in with him,' he muttered. 'That bitch wife of his is capable of any devilry. She would stab her mad husband, I do believe, if she could get at him, and the deed would put her whelp on the throne.'

Worcester laid down Brother Joseph's missal and brought his cold face near to the King's fresh cheek. 'Do not fear her, my lord. I had news of her on the continent. She and her whelp son were found begging—begging, my lord!—in the French king's train. What harm can she do to you while she has to beg for her bread?'

The King flung his apple core over his head and roared with laughter so heartily that he fell off his stool. 'Margaret of Anjou a-begging!' he crowed. 'The Bitch of Anjou with a begging-bowl!' He rocked to and fro on the ground. 'I must tell Warwick,' he gasped. 'He said it would almost be worth going to hell to see Margaret of Anjou burning there.'

At this point the tapestries twitched and the Queen slipped into the room. Seeing her husband prone on the floor she knelt down beside him and pressed his golden head to her breasts. 'Come, my dear lord,' she murmured, 'the tailor is ready with your new suit of clothes.' Over her naked shoulder she stared insolently at Chancellor and Worcester. She made no attempt to arrest the King's groping hands. London threw up his hands and hobbled away. Worcester studied the couple on the hearth as he might have studied a pair of marble statues.

'Come, Worcester,' whispered Chancellor. 'Leave the King to his pleasures.' They withdrew and took the attendants with them.

'The suit, my lord,' murmured the Queen.

The King scrabbled at her bosom and little pearls flew into the fire.

'My lord! They are waiting.'

But she did not move her arms, not until the King burst from her embrace and crushed her in his own enormous arms and proved to his own satisfaction that he had no more cause than the bronze cherub to feel ashamed, and to her satisfaction that, while her weapon lasted, it was a very strong weapon indeed. But she was startled, none the less, to hear him mutter, 'I will wager Warwick never did *this*.'

It was late when they rejoined the court. They had supped privately and in the hall the food had been cleared away and the heavy trestles stacked against the walls. The hall was filled with chatter and laughter, the yelps of dogs, the scraping of viols, the clicking of dice. For this was a young court. Most of the grey-beards had been killed off in the civil wars, leaving their young sprigs to inherit. There was Buckingham still a minor and Gloucester and Clarence not yet twenty and Devonshire only lately come of age. There was a king in the prime of his golden youth and a queen who if she could not be called young certainly could not be called anything else.

Through a host of rainbow dresses and coloured stockings the King made his way to his new clothes laid out on the dais. He kicked off his shoes and untied his flaps and let his servant peel off his plum-coloured hose. The servant undid the twelve silver toggles and pulled off his jacket and the King stepped forth in his shirt and drawers, as beautiful a king as had ever sat on the English throne. The court crowded round, clamouring, admiring, feeling the King's calves and pinching his biceps. The Woodvilles raised high voices in praise of the royal beauty. Earl Rivers in particular launched into ecstasies of admiration over the straightness of the King's legs and the massiveness of his muscles bulging under the linen shirt. And well he might. For four years before he had been nobody, an adherent of the losing side, a man of common birth with an enormous and needy family. But almost overnight his daughter had rocketed into eminence and power, and in her wake the Woodvilles—father, brothers, sisters, cousins—had come trailing like comets, intent on outshining the constellation of the Nevilles.

'Oh, exquisite!' cried Earl Rivers, clasping his hands. 'What line! What symmetry!'

The King tied the last string and looked with satisfaction down his long and shapely legs, now clothed in butter-yellow and embroidered in gold from ankle to knee.

'The jacket, my lord.'

The jacket was put on, a harmonious composition of apricot velvet slashed with green silk and studded with seed pearls.

'The hat, my lord.'

The King pulled over his golden curls a circle of beaver fur and adjusted it so that the tail covered the back of his neck.

'The shoes, my lord.'

The King eyed them where they lay side by side on the dais. They were of purple kid, narrow and tapering into long points. 'A measure!' he said, snapping his fingers. The tailor whipped a tape out of his pocket. The King looked slowly round his court and his eyes travelled inch by inch down the rainbow stockings to the ground. They shuffled. The dandies among them edged their feet under their ladies' skirts, but there was no escape.

'Ladies, retire to the wall.'

They had no choice but to obey. They whispered together and plucked their lips.

'Come!' said the King. 'Make a line here.'

A servant ran forward with a lump of chalk and, kicking away the rushes, marked a white line on the gritty floor. One by one the courtiers advanced: lords, nobles, gentlemen; Woodvilles, Herberts, Hastings, Dacres, Berners, Buckingham, Worcester —only the churchmen were excused.

'Heels in a line!' ordered the King without a flicker of a smile.

Thirty pairs of shoes heeled the line: blue, silver, scarlet, gold, violet, green, white, marigold. All were narrow. All had points, some so long that the tips were fastened to the knees with silver chains.

'Undo the chains!' said the King sternly. Someone tittered nervously. 'Tailor, see the points are stretched straight.'

The tailor darted from end to end of the line, pulling straight the point of every shoe. Straight as dies they lay stretched, sixty shoe-points side by side, while above them their owners trembled with apprehension. Solemnly the King marched to the top of the line, preceded by a page with a crimson cushion, and followed by Gunthorpe with a slate. The page placed the cushion at Rivers' midnight-blue feet and the King went down on his knees with his tape and measured the toes of his treasurer's shoes.

'Five inches and three-quarters,' he announced.

Gunthorpe's scratcher squeaked. The King rose, the page shifted the cushion to Richard Woodville's ruby feet, the King sank on his knees and applied his measure.

'Six inches and five-eighths.'

And so on down the long line, from Worcester's five-inch brocades with satin rosettes down to little Buckingham's golden slippers with the toes wired in the Turkish fashion. At last the thirtieth pair of shoes was measured and Gunthorpe's slate was full. The longest points belonged to Richard Woodville. Six inches and five-eighths. For the thirtieth time the King rose from his knees. In his brilliant yellow hose he advanced to the dais. He lifted his tape. He measured the toes of his new shoes. The tailor peered under his arm and shouted: 'Seven inches! They are seven inches!'

The tension snapped like a bow-string. A sigh like a rushing wind rose from the court. Seven inches! Longer than the longest by three-eighths of an inch. The King began to laugh. Richard Woodville giggled, Chancellor smiled, even old London twitched the corners of his dry mouth. Seven inches! The lords and ladies roared with delight and slapped one another's backs. Servants leant against the walls and wept with laughing. The Queen shrieked at the King's joke. Her son Thomas shouted, 'How long are my lord Warwick's toes?' And a wit answered, 'Long enough to kick your arse with.' Fluid with relief, the court melted and flowed. The musicians struck up a tune, the Fool juggled his coloured balls, the Queen threw her arms round her husband's neck and bit his ear.

The clamour was at its height when a messenger was admitted and approached the King where he sat twiddling his new shoes with his queen's arm round his waist.

'From Woodchester Abbey, my lord,' he said, presenting his letter.

Chancellor took the letter and broke the seal.

'My lord, the Abbot of Woodchester is dying,' he announced. 'The Prior has written to acquaint your Majesty with the fact that very soon there may be an abbatical election required at Woodchester.'

The King did not turn his head. 'Woodchester?' he said. The Queen whispered something in his ear and his hand dropped to her knee.

'That is Abbot Dominic,' said London. 'A good fellow, a good fellow. I have spoken with him many times at Westminster.' And he sighed to think how near his own death approached.

'You recall him, my lord?' asked Chancellor. 'You stayed at the abbey in the second year of your succession. The abbot presented you with a missal bound in white leather, the work of one of the monks.'

But the King was not listening. An abbot was dying, what was that to him? He did not care who was abbot. There was not a single abbot among his counsellors. To this extravagant and lusty young king an abbot dead meant only a *congé d'élire* for the election of a new one and a period, before the *congé d'élire* was granted, during which all the dead abbot's income was raked into the royal coffers.

'Woodchester?' said Worcester, observing with distaste how the King's hands busied themselves. 'That is near Winchcombe, is it not? A large abbey, Chancellor?'

Chancellor turned an enquiring look on London. 'A large abbey, London?' he asked.

London turned to his chaplain and raised his eyebrows.

'About thirty monks, your Grace,' said his chaplain. 'An income in all of about one thousand pounds a year.'

'Any scandals?' said Chancellor.

'I think not, I think not,' said London. 'I believe it to be an admirable establishment. Human without being worldly, pious without being uncomfortable. You will not find any saints in Woodchester.'

'Nor sinners either, I trust,' said Gunthorpe with a smile.

Chancellor cleared his throat and said loudly: 'Has your Majesty any instruction to give about an election at Woodchester? When the Abbot dies have you any objection to the election proceeding according to rule?'

The King freed his lips and spoke over his shoulder. 'Let them elect their prior,' he said. 'That is what they usually do, is it not? Only not too soon, Chancellor. Let me have the Abbot's income for a few months. It will buy me a statue like Worcester's.'

He spoke as if Abbot Dominic were already dead.

Before he retired for the night the King heard prayers in his private chapel and confessed his sins to the Bishop of London, for although he mocked London's old-fashioned notions he did not altogether disregard them. Advanced he might be, setting high store by learning and art and beauty and all the delights of life that the Church frowned on, but in his inmost heart he still wondered if he were not sinning with his wife when she inflamed in him a passion he had never experienced with any other woman.

She lay waiting for him in the huge bed, canopied in rose and silver, with three feather mattresses beneath her, linen sheets and fur rugs above her, a silk pillow under her head. She had let down her yellow hair and combed it over the covers in a becoming way. A candle burned at each corner of the bed. A fire crackled in the hearth and flickered over the ebony crucifix. It could have been a young girl lying there waiting for her husband, except that no young girl would have worn on her handsome face such a compound expression of determination and lust.

In the shadowy hall the King prowled up and down in an attempt to tire his limbs. He had already had a bout of fisticuffs with one of the grooms and an exercise with the short sword with John Woodville. He was restless, vaguely dissatisfied, pricked by guilt. In front of Worcester's cherub he stopped short and twitched the napkin from its chubby loins. He said aloud, 'I will not be tied to any man's apron-strings.' Yet when before seeking his bedchamber he ran his fingers down the razor edge of his sword, he could not help remembering how patiently Warwick had taught him the art of the short sword, at Ludlow when he was a boy.

The King's servant removed his new clothes and tiptoed out of the room. Before seeking his bed the King stood staring into the fire, seeing in the flames the grave face of his cousin Warwick. It was a face he had known from the cradle. It was a face that had shown comfort to his father York in the bloody years of his boyhood, that had turned on himself looks of encouragement and hope in the terrible days after York's death, when the Lancastrian arrows had scraped their very heels. It was the face of his cousin Richard Neville, the eldest son of his mother's brother; of the man who had fought and toiled to put him on the throne of England; of the man who now demanded it as his due that he should stand at the right hand of the King and order his doing.

'Can he not give a little?' groaned the King, laying his forehead on the warm mantle. 'Can he not learn to share? Must the Nevilles rule the world?'

'My lord!' It was the Queen calling to him from her nest of feathers.

With one bound the King leapt into the bed and seized her. But he was astonished to feel not flesh but linen. The Queen was wearing her shift. 'What is it?' he stammered, blushing like a boy. 'What have I done?'

The Queen smiled and crossed her arms over her breasts. 'I have a favour to ask of you, my lord. Only grant me my request and I will take off my shift.'

The King's hands went to rip the stuff from her shoulders but, such was her power, he hesitated when she whispered: 'You would not take me unwilling, my lord? A man will never get a son who rapes his own wife.'

His hands trembled. 'What is your request?' he asked.

The Queen's eyelids drooped. 'The Abbot of Woodchester. When he dies I ask you to present my cousin Nigel Woodville as their next abbot. He is looking for a good place and I believe Woodchester would suit him very well. Only present him to the monks, my lord. They will elect him gladly when they know it is your wish.'

The King laughed. 'Is that all? I shall be glad for your cousin to have the place. I wish all requests could be so easily granted. I will tell Chancellor in the morning. And you had best write to your cousin and tell him of his good fortune so that he can learn to put on a pi face and order a hair shirt!'

With a wrench of the wrists the shift was ripped from neck to hem and the King set about collecting his reward.

It never entered his head to enquire after Nigel Woodville's qualifications.

4

RICHARD NEVILLE, Earl of Warwick, Newburgh and Aumarle, Earl of Salisbury, Premier Earl of England, Knight of the Illustrious Order of the Garter, Baron of Elmley and Hanslape, Lord of Glamorgan and Morgannoc, High Chamberlain of England, Keeper of the Seas, Captain of Calais, High Steward of the Duchy of Lancaster, Constable of Dover, Warden of the Cinque Ports, Master of Mews and Falcons, Warden of the East and West Marches—owner of one hundred and twenty-six manors, fourteen castles, two towns, eleven town houses and one forest—sat with his friends and relations at the high table at Middleham and picked a chicken bone.

Outside the wind howled and snow beat against the shutters. Inside four great fires blazed, fifty pounds of candles burned, the rushes smelled sweet and the huge hall was filled with the air of decorous goodwill that is found only in well-ordered households.

On Warwick's left hand sat his wife, Ann Beaumont, with her two daughters Isabella and Ann and their ladies. On his right sat his brother George Neville, Archbishop of York; his brother John Neville, Earl of Northumberland; the Earl of Oxford; the Earl of Kent; Lord Mountjoy, until lately treasurer of England; and finally Warwick's dear confidant and friend, Lord Wenlock.

Warwick nibbled his drumstick and surveyed his world, snugly packed as an onion, layer upon layer. Below the salt the long trestles stretched away into the shadows by the door. At the first table sat his household: his chancellor, his treasurer, his comptroller, his master of horse, his chief steward and his almoner. At the second table sat his courtiers, knights and squires and gentleman of the shire, all sedately dressed in brown and black and olive-green, and their ladies, none of whose dresses rose less than four inches above their nipples. At the third table sat his sergeants-at-arms and those of his retainers who were not on duty; every man with an extra knife at his belt and his bow propped against the wall and the badge of the White Bear above his left breast. They spoke low among themselves because when he was present the Lord Warwick did not care for clamour. They drank sparingly because when he was in the hall they did not dare to be seen drunk. And they left the serving-maids alone, because when the Lord Warwick was in residence he would allow no wenching within doors. At the fourth table sat the upper servants: stewards, clerks, chaplains, surgeons, head grooms and falconers. At the fifth table, in the draught of the door, sat the lower servants: the huntsmen, messengers, barbers, tailors and armourers. And round and about like ants in a hill scurried the army of servers, cooks, butlers and pot-boys. And down on their bellies in the rushes crawled the dogs and the sweepers and the slop-boys scrabbling for titbits among the boots and slippers.

Warwick surveyed his household, two hundred souls eating his meat and drinking his ale and carrying away afterwards as much meat as they could spear on the points of their knives; and he knew that, however diverse the company, however wide the gulf between highest and lowest, a common purpose united them all. They revered him. His dark eyes roamed the rafters and in his mind he surveyed the ten times two hundred souls whose allegiance was also his, whose fathers had been his men and whose grandfathers had been his father's men; men who had fought the Lancastrians under his banner and whose loyalty was owing firstly to the Nevilles and only secondly to the King; men who scorned the Woodvilles as fiercely as he did and who felt in their own hearts every slight offered to himself.

'It is an insult, a damnable insult,' growled George Neville in his ear. 'Why should Canterbury get the cardinal's hat? I will wager the King did it to spite me. First he takes the Chancellorship away from me and gives it to that pi-faced Bath and Wells and now he snatches the very hat off my head. And do not tell me the King had nothing to do with it. He has done nothing but insult us ever since he married that Woodville whore.' Warwick settled his famous hat more firmly on his ears but before he could reply George Neville grunted: 'The King could have wheedled the Pope's agent if he had wished. But it is all of a piece, brother, all of a piece. We put him on the throne and what thanks do we get for it? Ungrateful young pup. Takes the treasury away from Mountjoy here and gives it to that Rivers who goes to bed in his boots and adds up figures in his sleep. Marries the heiress of Exeter to his brother-in-law instead of to our nephew. Spits in the eye of the French ambassadors——'

'Come, George,' said Warwick with a smile. 'You exaggerate, I think.'

'A metaphor,' said George Neville, waving his fat hands. 'You cannot deny he insulted them, Richard, and they your own guests. Kept them waiting in the ante-room five hours, and when you presented them said he had a game of tennis waiting and did not even let them speak.'

Warwick sighed but did not deny it. 'His Majesty is young,' he murmured. 'He has not the experience of his father.'

George Neville sniffed. 'He needs a sharp lesson. Someone had better teach him he cannot do just as he likes, not in England in this day and this age. If he lacks experience he should listen to the advice of tried counsellors, not to the yappings of a pack of Woodville jackals.'

Warwick threw down his drumstick and wiped his fingers on his napkin.

'King's barons have a right to be consulted,' grumbled George Neville, worrying his grievances like bones. 'Now take this question of the French alliance. . . .'

At the mention of France John Neville craned round his portly brother and said: 'And what news of France, Richard? Did the French king receive you kindly? When are we to view the presents he gave you?'

Warwick fingered his black French beard. 'They are on the road from Newcastle, John. We shall try the hounds before they are many days older.'

'And the French king? What did Louis say about the treaty?'

Once again Warwick smiled, seeing the little bird of French friendship hovering above his outstretched hand. 'He was civil, very civil indeed.' he replied, fishing a rib out of the sauce with finger and thumb. 'He expressed great regard for our king and agreed that it was most desirous that there should be peace between our two countries.' He swallowed his meat and drank his wine and by the time he spoke again the hall was hushed, for with only the evidence of their eyes the court had realized—as indeed it always did—that Warwick was saying something of importance. Warwick never spoke secretly, for he had nothing to hide and nothing to be ashamed of. He was too proud for secrets. 'We must ensure peace with France,' he declared, insisting on what he had many times insisted on in the King's presence. 'It is not many years since the terrible war with France ended. There are still many in France who favour an invasion of our country. Some even cast their eyes on Calais. We must conciliate France. We must grasp the hand of friendship that King Louis extends. To refuse it is to offer him a mortal insult and cast our country back into the pit of war.'

He was on his feet, his hand raised, his dark face flushed.

'A Warwick! A Warwick! Peace with France!' shouted a sergeant-at-arms.

'A Warwick! A Warwick!' they cried, eyes shining, limbs braced, forgetting their ancestors skewered by French arrows and their kinsmen blasted by French cannon, seeing only the lord and master whose word was their law. 'A Warwick! A Warwick!' they shouted banging their mugs on the table.

Warwick sat down and called for more wine. Immediately his chamberlain rose and cried, 'Wine for my lord Warwick.'

Against the wall the steward cried, 'Wine for my lord Warwick.'

Down the passage to the pantry echoed the same cry, 'Wine for my lord Warwick.' And presently the jug appeared, beaded with ice and borne aloft by a servant in brown stockings. The servant presented the jug to the steward, the steward presented it to the chamberlain and the chamberlain presented it to the highest in rank, next to Warwick, at the high table. This was John Neville, who rose to his feet, and, edging behind his brother George, filled his brother Richard's cup from over his right shoulder. He returned the jug to the chamberlain who in turn returned it to the steward who in his turn returned it to the servant who then proceeded to fill the cups of all the lords and ladies at the high table. This ceremony completed, fresh dishes were carried in: a stuffed swan, a herring pie, half a pig and half a sheep stitched together; and eating and drinking began again.

'And how does the King of France propose to cement this friendship, my lord?' asked Oxford, with his mouth full. 'Promises are easy and cost nothing. Oaths are broken every day.'

'King Louis has a nephew, the Duc d'Orléans,' replied Warwick, knife in hand. 'And King Edward has a sister, Margaret. Both are of marriageable age. King Louis is willing for the friendship of France and England to be consummated in the union of these two.'

George Neville gave a low whistle. 'So the lion and the cock shall bed down together! The rose and the lily shall mingle their roots in the same soil! Burgundy will throw a fit when he hears of this.'

Warwick frowned. 'Burgundy is no friend of England,' he declared. 'To smile on Burgundy is to offend the French for ever.'

'And when will this marriage take place, brother?' asked John Neville, slicing into the thigh of the swan.

'I have promised to escort the Lady Margaret on a visit to Paris at midsummer.'

Further down the table Kent cleared his throat. 'And what does his Majesty say?'

Warwick dipped his spoon into his blancmange, cutting in two the 'W' picked out in almonds. 'His Majesty will understand that it is in amity with France that the hopes of England lie.' He paused to swallow, then added, 'He will understand that when I explain it to him.'

'And when will that be, my lord?'

'I shall speak to him at Easter, when the court meets at Ludlow.'

'Mind you get him alone,' sniffed George Neville. 'You will

not get a word in edgeways if those Woodvilles know anything about it.'

Gravely Warwick adjusted his long sleeves. 'I held the King in my arms when he was an infant,' he said quietly. 'His mother was the sister of my father. I taught him how to balance in the saddle in full armour. I showed him how to tilt in the meadows of Herefordshire. I fought beside his father York at the battle of St Albans. After our defeat at Ludlow I took Edward behind me on my horse all the way from Southampton to Barnstaple and there I bribed a boatman to carry us to Calais. I rallied his forces, and with the help of my family I defeated his enemies and placed him on the throne of England. I am his senior earl. He owes his place to me. It is his duty to listen to me.'

'He has not always done so,' grunted George Neville. 'He has married a nobody. He has robbed me of my Great Seal and now of my cardinal's hat. He has surrounded himself with men who hate us. Beware he does not untie the apron-strings.'

For the first time Warwick's composure wavered. He glanced at his brother with troubled eyes. 'But I do not wish to tie him to me,' he muttered. 'All I want is my rightful place. The King has no right not to listen to me. He has no right to act without our approval.'

Right. Right. In his mouth the word was heavy, weighting his tongue with its importance. In the ordered world that Warwick inhabited it was right that called the tune and set the measure. It was the yardstick by which everything was measured. In Warwick's world a man had his rights and to rob him of them was to fly in the face of God who had given them.

'I have a right to be heard,' he muttered. 'The King must listen to me. He is young, inexperienced. He needs my counsel. How can he hear sense when the Woodvilles deafen him with their importunings?'

He rested his beard on his fists, a proud and disquieted man, and brooded over his wrongs.

He was interrupted by the entry of a messenger who handed a letter to his chancellor. The chancellor approached. 'From Woodchester, my lord. From the Abbot's chaplain.'

Warwick broke the seal and read the letter in which Abbot's Chaplain, who was a second cousin of Warwick's second steward, informed him of the Abbot's illness and probable death. He tossed the letter to his brother George. 'Excellent beds at Woodchester,' he said. 'Good hunting, too. I shot three fine stags in the Abbot's park. Let us hope the new abbot employs as good a huntsman.'

'They will elect their prior?' asked John Neville.

Warwick yawned and stretched. 'Their prior, their almoner, their sacristan, it is all the same. One abbot is like another. The convent moulds them all.

He flicked Abbot's Chaplain's letter with his nail and called to his brother John: 'And how is the crazy Henry of Lancaster? Does he show any signs of dying?'

But he never heard the answer for at that instant the main doors burst open and a courier rushed in, in a blast of freezing air, mud to the groins, icicles hanging from his eyebrows, a letter clutched in his numb hand. 'From Adam Thorpe,' he croaked, going down on his frozen knees. 'From Westminster.'

'Oho, so we have spies at court, eh?' chuckled George Neville.

Warwick did not reply. He tore open the letter and while he read it two hundred souls stopped their chatter, two hundred pairs of eyes were fixed on his face. Even the dogs looked up from their bones.

'What is it, brother?' asked John Neville, alarmed at Warwick's ashen cheeks.

'Tell us what it says,' said George, wondering what honour the Nevilles were to lose next.

Warwick stood erect, a black pillar in his black hat with twisted ends and his black tunic falling nearly to his feet and his black beard. 'The King has agreed that his sister Margaret shall marry the Duke of Burgundy,' he said heavily, the coldness of his voice belying the fire of anger that raged inside him. 'The Bastard of Burgundy is at Westminster now and a treaty of alliance has been signed.'

No one dared speak. If the King himself had stepped on to the dais and slapped Warwick on both cheeks these people could not have been more aghast. Warwick lifted his trembling hands, and, shaken by anger and disappointment, apprehension and outrage, cried, 'He did not even ask me!'

'It is the Queen,' growled George Neville. 'She will not be content until she has wheedled the King into doing every single thing she knows we disapprove of.'

'An alliance with Burgundy!' groaned John Neville. 'And it was the King himself who sent you to France!'

'This will send Louis to the Lancastrians,' whispered Kent. 'The Bitch of Anjou will not be begging in his train for long, not when he hears this bit of news.'

'There is another apron-string snapped, brother,' said George Neville. 'Those Woodvilles are breaking them one by one.'

Warwick leaned heavily on the table, while below him his followers began to whisper and gesticulate. His shoulders sagged. The courier spoke again: 'Master Thorpe said to tell you the Queen has persuaded his Majesty to present a new abbot to Woodchester when the old abbot dies. It is her cousin, he said. Name of Nigel Woodville. He told me to tell you particular.'

Warwick's jaw dropped. The King presenting a new abbot! Such a thing had not happened within living memory. Not since Henry IV's reign had any king concerned himself with abbatical elections. Abbots were no longer of any importance. Politically they were insignificant, spiritually they were ignored. No one bothered about abbots any longer. Abbeys lay in the backwaters of English life, like quaint islands whose inhabitants had lost touch with real life, doing nothing but sing services no one heard but themselves and saying prayers for people no longer living.

'Master Thorpe said to tell you the Queen wants to provide for her cousin and she reckoned Woodchester Abbey might do because it's got a lot of land.'

So it was a whim of the Queen's! And why should the King refuse her? He had only to tell the monks to elect Nigel Woodville and they would do so at once, for monks were noted for their obedience. There was only one snag that might arise and that was a rival candidate. There had not been a disputed abbatical election for fifty years, but suppose there were to be one now, at

Woodchester? Suppose there should appear in opposition to Nigel Woodville a notable rival, a rival of excellent qualifications, with the backing of a wealthy and influential patron? What then? Then the election would have to go to the vote; monks could be persuaded, cajoled, wheedled, threatened, even bribed.

Warwick worried his beard. For four years he had suffered in silence the accumulative pinpricks of the King's growing independence. He had bowed to the new queen, although he had not brought himself to grace her coronation. He had stood god-father to her first daughter. He had remained silent when the King insulted the French ambassadors. He had sat at the same council table as Earl Rivers and Lord Scales and drunk wine from the same cup. In silence he had witnessed his kinsman Mountjoy dismissed from the treasury, his brother George deprived of the Great Seal. He had stood silent with his back to the wall while the King romped with the Woodvilles or made love to the Queen in public. He had simulated interest in dog-eared manuscripts and shameless statues. On his trips to France he had bought frippery and embroideries and noted, for the King's interest, the length of the points of the French king's shoes. He had negotiated loans for the King. He had forgiven him for not inviting a Neville to his last two councils. He had given him advice, he had besought him to listen to older and wiser heads. But he had been ignored and insulted. He had been sickened by the Woodvilles' vulgarity; he had fallen over their shoes; he had been horrified by their lusts and ambitions. Yearly he had watched the King change from a grateful and amenable boy to a thankless and headstrong youth. He trembled for the fate of England if her policies fell into the hands of the Woodville mob.

'Master Thorpe said to tell you the Queen and her brother made a mock of you in the court and Earl Rivers poked fun at your hat.'

Silently but inexorably the last minute straw dropped on to Warwick's shoulders. He sat down suddenly. He called to Lord Wenlock, whom he trusted and loved more than any man on earth. 'Wenlock, you are acquainted with my aunt, the Prioress?'

'Certainly, my lord.'

'I wish you to take her a message. I wish you to ascertain if, amongst her ecclesiastical acquaintance, she knows any man suited in character and abilities to be the next Abbot of Wood-chester.'

He did not once consider the man who had written to tell him of the Abbot's illness. If Abbot's Chaplain fostered a secret ambition to be abbot, let him kill and bury it at once for it would never grow to maturity.

When the candles were burned almost to their sockets the Earl of Warwick retired for the night. He got to his feet and as one man the hall rose and bowed. He did not move from his place but stared at the silver salt-cellar so minutely he might have been counting its rigging. No one so much as shuffled. Even the dogs were still. At length Warwick raised his eyes and spoke to his chancellor. 'Write to the King,' he said sadly, 'that the Earl regrets the state of the roads does not permit him to accept his invitation to attend the Easter court at Ludlow.'

It was the first time in his life he had refused a royal summons.

He bowed to his court, took his wife's hand and led her to their private chamber in the south turret. His friends and retainers watched him go, a grave, upright, serious man, but only his wife Ann Beaumont saw him beat his forehead on the mantle and heard him cry: 'Give me my place! Give me back my place!'

5

EASTER was over. A glorious April reigned over England, burning out of men's mouths the salty taste of winter. In the fresh pastures lambs kicked up their heels. In the woods piglets tectered after their colossal sows. Every cow had her calf, every nanny-goat her kid, every mother her baby. It was a time of joy so inexpressible that boys and girls resorted to cuffing one another and rolling in the new bracken. The winter was over. Christ was risen from the dead. Soon He would ascend to heaven to sit on the right hand of His Father, promising eternal bliss to those who did not die in mortal sin. The way to heaven stretched plain for all who chose to take it. Man was saved and spring was come and the weather was glorious. The melancholy of winter peeled away as cleanly as willow bark, as sweetly as a dirty fleece under the shears, leaving men light-headed with happiness.

The delights of Gloucestershire shone very bright in Nigel Woodville's eyes as he and his party trotted southwards along the Chipping Campden highway and journeyed farther and farther away from Stratford where until now Nigel had been employed as chaplain and clerk to Lord Hastings. Nigel smiled cheerfully and tweaked the orange plume of his hat. He relished the thought of being an abbot, of ruling a household of thirty monks and sixty servants, of owning twenty horses and a lodging with seven bedchambers, of having his own chamberlain and steward and chaplain, of being bowed to and revered and obeyed instead of being at the beck and call of an ignorant lord who scarcely knew one end of a book from the other and whose idea of entertainment was to set the dogs on his Fool. Ever since he had taken orders ten years before—he was now thirty years old —Nigel Woodville had been waiting for such a chance as this.

When he had received the Queen's, his cousin's, letter he had, it is true, felt a momentary disappointment that he was not to become a bishop. But he reminded himself, for Nigel Woodville was a sensible man, that none of the bishops was sickly and only old London was likely to die soon and the King would never give London to a man of thirty, not even if he was a Woodville. Better an abbot now than a bishop twenty years hence, he argued, and how could he be sure the Queen would not soon forget him? She was notorious for her whims.

At midday they stopped for refreshment at an inn and while they were still sitting there they heard a clatter of hooves on the cobbles and in rushed Thomas Woodville, the Queen's son and Nigel's kinsman, followed by six retainers with badges of the Rising Sun over their left breasts.

'Praise heaven I have caught you!' gasped Thomas, flinging himself on to a bench and seizing the nearest mug. 'I have a message for you from the King.' He drained his mug and pulled Nigel by the sleeve away into a secret corner among the onions and hams. He rolled his eyes, relishing his news. 'There is another candidate!' he announced. 'He is on the road to Woodchester now. The King has just had news of him and sent me after you with instructions. When the Abbot dies, if this new candidate persists, there will be a disputed election and the decision will have to be by the votes of the monks. The King is adamant that you must win. All his influence and wealth will be at your command. He has sent me to be your agent and supporter.' Here Thomas thumped his chest and shook his curls.

Nigel stared, flabbergasted. He was a Woodville, it is true, and therefore had claims on the King's generosity. Further, he was a man after the King's heart, being young, ambitious, interested in the new learning, a connoisseur of Italian painting and Flemish embroideries. But that the King should do this for him! Send his step-son to support him in what promised to be an expensive abbatical election when he had hundreds of presentations in his gift of which any half-dozen would have served the same purpose of providing for an obscure cousin of his wife's.

'I am pledged to give you all the help in my power,' said

Thomas, importantly. 'If you need money you have only to say so. "Spare no expense," the King said. "We must see to it that Nigel Woodville becomes the next Abbot of Woodchester." '

A thought struck Nigel. 'Who is this other candidate?' he asked.

'Henry Osborne.'

'And his calling?'

'He is a canon of Salisbury Cathedral. He is fifty years old. His uncle was brother-in-law to the late Earl of Salisbury's chaplain.'

Light was beginning to dawn.

'And his sponsor?'

'The Earl of Warwick,' said Thomas Woodville, and spat at an onion.

Warwick! So that was why the King was so anxious for Nigel to win the election. What Woodville did not know of Warwick's jealousy, of his obsession to keep the King if not in swaddling-clothes at least in leading-reins? There was not a Woodville in England who had not divined the King's determination to live his own life, think his own thoughts, choose his own court and his own friends, even his own advisers.

Thoughtfully Nigel Woodville plucked the orange plume from his hat and put it in his pocket. He inspected his dark-blue gown and his leather boots. He fished his ivory crucifix out of his bag and hung it round his neck. He tweaked his men into tidiness. He surveyed Thomas Woodville's ringlets, his stuffed doublet and twenty-two-inch sleeves, and wished heartily that the King's representative had been more soberly dressed.

'Let us go,' he said at last. 'The King need have no fear that I will not win. When the monks of Woodchester hear of my plans for their abbey they will beg me on their knees to be their abbot.'

They mounted and rode away southwards, half blinded by the April sun.

Twenty-five miles away to the south, Henry Osborne too was nearing Woodchester Abbey. He patted his wallet where lay the letter written to him by the Prioress, the great Warwick's aunt. He had brought it with him because he still could hardly believe his good fortune. He was not distinguished. He was not venerable. He had no reputation for piety or learning. It was true that he was discreet and temperate and dependable, but there must have been dozens of other clerics known to Warwick or his aunt, all as capable and as orthodox as he. Why should he be singled out as Warwick's candidate in the Woodchester election? He never questioned Warwick's right to interfere in the election. There was not the remotest connection of the great Warwick who did not know how grieved the Earl was at the King's ingratitude, how his noble heart bled to see the King surrounded by minions and fawners, and how he longed to steady the reins of government with his own capable hands.

The lowliest Neville knew the immense debt that Edward IV owed to Warwick and his brothers, and felt in his own heart Warwick's sorrow that the King should forget his debt so easily. Henry Osborne understood perfectly well why Warwick was putting forward a rival candidate. What he did not understand was that it was his own complete ordinariness that had prompted the Prioress to choose him on her nephew's behalf.

Henry Osborne was a man who had no brilliant ideas, who was never going to set the world on fire or take the monks by the ears; a man, in short, after Warwick's own heart; a man who knew his own place and the place of all other men in society. To Warwick it was the Henry Osbornes of this world who were the firm ground under his feet. They were dependable, loyal, unimaginative. They played with no dangerous toys like Greek translations or voyages of exploration or indecent statuary. They were stay-at-homes. To them the future was the past all over again. To them the world was flat and the sun went round the earth and God had created mankind in layers.

'Woodchester Abbey,' said a servant, and Henry Osborne set his eyes for the first time on the convent that he hoped to make his home. With the April sun behind his head he gazed up at the abbey walls behind which, if only to please Warwick, he hoped to die. Ahead of him the Bath highway stretched straight and white in the sunlight all the way to Stroud. Up from his right hand sloped the green steeps of Amberley, half clothed in beech woods, their feet in arable, their heads dark against the periwinkle sky. On his left hand ran the little Avon brook, brimful with brown water; above it nestled the thatched roofs of Woodchester village and the tiled roof of the parish church; far above that stretched the rolling sheepwalks of Selsely; and in between the two, like a huge rock embedded in the hillside, loomed the grey mass of Woodchester Abbey. From the highway all that could be seen of it were the lofty walls, studded here and there with windows, and the glorious spire soaring two hundred feet into the blue sky, its bronze Cross shining like a beacon in the sun.

'Looks prosperous,' said Lord Wenlock in his ear. 'Good walls.'

Henry Osborne said, 'They have stood there for over three hundred years.' Their permanence warmed him. He seemed to see their roots growing down through the hill towards the centre of the earth. While so much was in flux it was good to consider a way of life that had continued day in and day out for as long as, and far longer than, those walls had been standing, and which would continue for thousands of years to come.

'On this rock I will build My Church,' said Henry Osborne, for although he could not be called a pious man already he was preparing to be very pious indeed. He knew his appearance favoured him, for he was many people's idea of a monk, with his neat tonsure and dark robes, his plump cheeks and roly-poly figure and stumpy fingers. Indeed, he had another advantage, one that the Prioress did not know about. He had something of the look of Abbot Dominic.

'Come,' said Lord Wenlock, touching Henry's black sleeve. 'My lord Warwick is anxious for you to arrive before Nigel Woodville. First impressions are most important, he said, particularly with monks.'

They swung their horses to the left, splashed through the brook and began the long toil up to the abbey's south gate. And high above them in the clear air a hawk watched the two parties converge on the abbey, one at the south gate and one at the north gate, so that the distracted Prior did not know whom to greet first.

The hawk was not the only one to spot the parties converging. Guest Master stood in the bell-tower and watched the two cavalcades climb the hill and swore a very unholy oath. He had lost his battle with Prior over the entertainments. Prior had brought out the ancient Rule of the Order and had shown him—delighted that for once there could be no argument—where in Rule 42 it stated that the Abbot's fund was responsible for entertaining all Abbot's visitors *except* religious visitors and their parties. In the background Abbot's Chaplain had smiled his beautiful smile and gone back to directing the master mason, and now Guest Master was left with the prospect of spending on these unwelcome guests all of the official fund that he had illicitly secreted for his son Francis.

'Thirty-five horses,' moaned Guest Master, counting. 'And thirty mouths. The servants will eat their heads off in my Guest House and the gentry will be given the best of everything in the Abbot's lodgings and it will all be charged to me.' He pictured the little shop in Stroud that he had set his heart on for Francis. It had a green shutter that was pushed up at night and a wooden staircase leading into the attic and a nice workroom at the back where Francis could make his saddles. Francis' apprenticeship ended at Michaelmas and his father had set his heart on giving him a shop for a present. The monks of Woodchester would have been surprised to see Guest Master beating his neat fists on the stone wall of the bell-tower, his usually composed features distorted by fury. Before he returned to the Guest House to receive the visitors' servants and the visitors' horses he had to dabble his hands in the fishpond to get rid of the blood.

At the south gate Abbot's Chaplain was receiving Henry Osborne while at the north gate Prior was receiving Nigel

Woodville. Reconciled to being passed over, Abbot's Chaplain had staked everything on getting Warwick's candidate elected. By so doing he had burned his boats, for a new abbot could appoint his own chaplain and through his partisan policy Abbot's Chaplain was making it certain that, should Nigel be elected, he would lose his high position. But Abbot's Chaplain carried much weight, especially with the younger monks who had not yet had time to get to know him nor to see through the façade of beauty to the hollowness within. Like his patron Warwick, Abbot's Chaplain rated very highly the virtue of gratitude, and never once through the lengthy and close-fought campaign did it occur to him that Henry Osborne might not want him for a chaplain.

Abbot's Chaplain bowed to Lord Wenlock but to Henry Osborne he went on his knees, knowing that within the hour every monk and every servant in the abbey would know he had done so. He kissed Henry's hand, remarked how effectively the Abbot's ring would fit Henry's fourth finger and led him and Lord Wenlock to the Abbot's lodgings, leaving the horses and retainers to a speechless Guest Master.

Now to reach the Abbot's lodgings from the south gate they had to traverse the length of the abbey, crossing the kitchen yard, passing the stables and bake-houses and smithy, walking along the west cloisters underneath the officials' rooms and skirting the west end of the abbey church. Between the cloister and the west door was a narrow arch and a narrow passage, and in the middle of this passage Abbot's Chaplain, Henry Osborne and Lord Wenlock came face to face with the King's retainers who had accompanied Nigel Woodville and who were on their way to the Guest House. All stopped. Abbot's Chaplain waved his elegant hand at the fifteen Rising Sun badges, which immediately bunched together.

'Let my lords pass,' said Abbot's Chaplain sternly, making his marvellous eyes flash. The King's retainers huddled like cattle, heads lowered and jaws working. Abbot's Chaplain seized his wooden Cross and waved it dramatically in front of his shapely nose. 'In the name of the lord Jesus Christ,' he intoned, 'I command you to move.'

Confronted with the Cross the bunch wavered and broke up. Seven retainers flattened themselves against the right-hand wall, eight against the left. Through the lane thus formed the three men passed, running the gauntlet of baleful stares and silent oaths. As soon as he had presented his back to them Henry Osborne was struck on the left ear by a stone. He spun round, blood trickling down the side of his neck, but all he saw was fifteen hessian backs retreating down the passage.

In silence they entered the Abbot's lodgings and ascended the stone stairs to the hall on the upper floor where, ensconced in front of a roaring fire, they found Nigel Woodville and Thomas Woodville and, at a suitable distance from the flames, Prior. The candidates eyed each other and introductions were made, while their hands made mechanical gestures of politeness; Henry with the blood still wet on his neck and Nigel frozen almost to dumbness by Prior's chilly demeanour.

But if Prior showed unresponsiveness it was simply a weapon, his only weapon, against despair. That there should be two candidates! That he should be pitchforked into the turmoil of a disputed election when all he wanted, all he had ever wanted, was peace and quiet. He had instructions from the King that Nigel must be elected. He had instructions from Warwick that Henry must be elected. He had been dropped head first into that hell that had been his nightmare from a child, the hell of decisive action, where decisions clawed at him and gnawed his stomach and bound him with spiked chains. Ahead of him in the nethermost pit he glimpsed a decision so momentous, so appalling, that he pulled down a shutter in his mind to blot it out.

He watched the group gathered between him and the fire, watched them eat and drink and nod their heads and chatter or remain silent according to their natures. He wondered which of these two candidates could do the most for Woodchester Abbey. He even wondered, and he was the only man in the abbey to do so, what kind of abbot Woodchester needed and what kind of abbey Woodchester needed to be. Inexorably the old speculations and uncertainties crept back into his mind. The books would not balance; the monks were unpopular with the village; Abbot's Chaplain was overbearing; the number of novices was falling off; too much time was taken by administration; none of them bent their backs to honest toil; there was not performed one task that could not be better done by professionals.

And yet . . . the grooves between Prior's eyebrows deepened. His bald head gleamed in the firelight like an egg. And yet . . . where else but in a monastery like this were the services said with such daily regularity: the seven Holy Hours, Low Mass, High Mass, prayers for the living and the dead, psalms, anthems, Ave Marias and Pater Nosters without number, the Epistles, the Martyrology, sermons, the Works of the Fathers?

Out of their devotions monks built both a wall to keep back the powers of darkness and a path to lead into heaven. From the early days of the Church no one had ever denied that the highest form of life was the life of religious contemplation. What did it matter that meat was eaten four days a week and a quarter of the choir stalls were empty, so long as the wall of prayers was kept in good repair?

Prior shifted his bare toes. What was it the wit had said? 'Meddle with the fabric and the whole edifice will come crashing to the ground.' In his very bones he felt the moment of decision drawing nearer. Like a ship approaching harbour, it was sounding its signals and each signal was louder than the last.

In front of the hearth Nigel Woodville suddenly flung out his arms and said, 'But the finances would be far more efficient with a central administration.'

And Henry Osborne rolled his thumbs and replied, 'I see no need for change, no need for change at all.'

In the infirmary the dying abbot still lay like a log, while two hundred paces away they spoke as if he were already dead, gathered round his own hearth like vultures round a kill. Since the feast of St Joseph the deadness had mounted from his feet to his waist but still he hung on to life, as if he wanted to spare his prior the agonies of choice. On his right hand the ruby shone

75

unwinking in the candlelight. His breath wheezed in his throat, too feeble to disturb the contours of his barrel chest. He lay motionless with his eyes glued shut, his hands folded over the sheet; the only change in his appearance the bristle of hairs on his tonsure and the dark growth on his jaw. His face lay on the pillow like a leaden mould. Already his feet were turning black and there was a smell of decay about the room as if death crouched in a corner.

Brother Peter held the bowl in one hand and Infirmarian's minute-glass in the other. Infirmarian slipped the knife into the vein and out welled the dark blood, abbot's blood, blood that three hundred years earlier would have contained healing properties. Brother Peter turned the glass again and again, five times in all. The blood rose in the basin. When the sand had run through for the last time Brother Peter said, 'Enough.' Infirmarian clamped his thumb on the vein and Brother Peter tied round the Abbot's arm an apricot bleeding-band decorated with silver thread. A servant took the basin and emptied the blood out of the window.

'Will you not try sheep's parsley?' whispered Brother Peter. 'I know where it can be found, in Amberley wood.'

For twenty-two days he had been able neither to see nor communicate with Alice. Her lovely face came between him and his devotions, even between him and the Cross. For twenty-two days he had scarcely eaten or slept, torn between his passion and his conscience as a criminal was torn between horses.

Infirmarian looked at his haggard cheeks and wild eyes and relented. 'Go tomorrow,' he said. 'Go as soon as it is light and enjoy a little of God's fresh air. You have been watching too long and too late. Find the herb and I will administer it after High Mass. I will ask Prior to excuse you your morning devotions.'

He turned to his medicine-chest and so missed the ecstasy that leapt into Brother Peter's face. He fumbled and grumbled as he returned his minute-glass to the cupboard and said for the twenty-second time, 'I cannot think what has become of your minute-glass, the one with St Peter carved on the bottom.'

After Compline the candidates came to gaze at the dying abbot, to try and stimulate him into indicating a preference for one or other of them. Each in turn thrust his face close to that leaden mask and shouted: 'It is I! Abbot Dominic! Do you not desire me as the next Abbot of Woodchester?' But shout how they liked not a flicker disturbed that deadly repose.

'Give him a pinch,' whispered Thomas Woodville, but Nigel shook his head.

'He will never rouse now,' he said, privately hoping that he never would, for what if he named Henry Osborne as his successor or Prior or that colossal monk with red hair seen trimming the Pascal candle?

'Has the Abbot never indicated whom he wishes to succeed him?' asked Henry Osborne, thanking his stars that this prior was so obviously unfitted for the Abbot's shoes.

'Never,' replied Prior, remembering how on his knees he had besought his abbot never to express a preference for *him*.

They remained in the infirmary for an hour. Both candidates managed to weep noticeable tears which they were careful to leave undried until they had reached the Abbot's lodgings. But not a word of regret was spoken. How could they feel regret when this man's death was to make the fortune of one of them?

Sacristan finished trimming the Pascal candle and put his knife back in his belt. He was as pleased with events as he could be while yet grieving for the sickness of his abbot. It was true that St Peter's toe-nails had not yet arrived—he could not begin to expect them until the end of the month—but his sacristan's fund was now on a much firmer financial basis. Finding himself short of cash for the Easter necessities, he had cast about for a way of raising some money and had been fortunate in selling the freehold of six acres at Inchbrook, whose rents were part of his official fund. The buyer was Robert Cordwell, a peasant living in the village, and he had paid cash on the nail after selling a dozen sheep in Stroud market. With this windfall Sacristan had bought his Easter candles and the materials for the Easter sepulchre and his wine and oil. And if his conscience pricked him because he had sold land without his superior's permission he soothed the place with the reflection that it was all done with the loftiest intent, namely the acquisition of the most important and meritorious relic Italy had to offer, a relic that the Abbot of Winchcombe would surely give his big ears to possess.

6

I T WAS morning. Matins, Lauds and Prime had been sung.
Low Mass had been celebrated. The whole abbey was in a
state of suspension waiting for High Mass and the first official
appearance of the two candidates. Already the monks were
looking to the future, for it was of great moment to them who
was to be their next abbot, seeing that his word was their
law, that he must be bowed to and revered, obeyed and never
interrupted, that he appointed all officials, received novices and
inflicted penances, that he represented the abbey in the law
courts, had a seat in the House of Lords and was the ultimate
authority for sales, purchases and loans. An abbot could make or
mar a monastery, just as he could make of his monks' lives a
heaven or a hell. It was natural the monks should crane round
corners and stare up at the Abbot's windows and speculate about
the natures of Nigel Woodville and Henry Osborne.

There was one monk who could not easily satisfy his curiosity
and that was Brother Joseph. 'What are they like?' he kept asking
Infirmarian when the bandages on his eyes were changed. Infirmarian smeared another layer of foxglove poultice on eyes that were
two solid scabs of dried ointment, and tied on a clean bandage.

'Nigel Woodville is quick and dark and wiry,' he told him,
'and Henry Osborne is plump and fair-skinned and smiling, after
the manner of our beloved abbot.' Infirmarian did not care for what
he had heard of Nigel Woodville. His seed carefully planted, he
took Brother Joseph by the hand and led him into another room.

'What is it? What is it?' cried Brother Joseph, feeling warmth
strike him in the face.

'It is for the good of your eyes,' said Infirmarian gently. 'Do
not be frightened. I will assist you.'

Brother Joseph shrank back.

'Be brave. It is not so terrible.'

With shaking hands Brother Joseph undid his girdle and allowed Infirmarian to pull over his head his wooden crucifix and his black woollen cassock. He fumbled with the strings of his linen shirt and that too was drawn over his head. Next Infirmarian removed his sandals and peeled off his linen drawers. Brother Joseph crossed his hands in front of his crutch and bent his head as if to hide his naked chest.

'Come,' said Infirmarian. 'It will do your eyes good.'

Brother Joseph's old fingers crawled round the wooden rim. 'Must I?' he pleaded.

'Yes.'

'Will it make my eyes see?'

'It may.'

'You will stay with me?'

'Yes.'

Brother Joseph raised a skinny leg and rested his foot on the rim, curling his toes as he felt the heat strike his sole. Slowly, with many backslidings and false starts, he inched his leg into the fiery water, toe, heel, ankle, shin, knee. He gasped and clung and thrashed his arms. A servant came running and together they manœuvred the second leg into the steaming water and lowered Brother Joseph on to his sharp buttocks, so that all that could be seen of him was a shaved head, a stringy neck and a band of white bandage looming through the steam. Brother Joseph stopped gasping. He waggled his hands cautiously under the water. He made islands of his knees. He smiled. At seventy years of age he was having the first hot bath of his life. Even blindness had its tiny compensations.

'I have heard that Henry Osborne is a great believer in the efficacy of hot baths,' said Infirmarian, reconciling himself to a hundred and fifty Hail Marys for his untruth.

From the edge of Amberley wood, sheep's parsley in hand, Brother Peter vainly searched the fields below him for any signs of Alice's geese or Alice's goats or Alice herself. He had combed the wood from end to end and not found her. 'Let us hope she is within doors,' said his conscience, 'where you cannot seek her out. You are very anxious to damn yourself. What is it that excites you so? White skin, golden hair, rosebud nipples, breasts like apples and legs like birch trees—soon they will be crawling with worms and you will be roasting in hell for having succumbed to their delights. You have taken a vow of chastity from which you cannot be absolved. Is it impossible for you to stay safe within the abbey walls? Even if you cannot root out your passion is it impossible for you to sin with your love only in your dreams?'

'Impossible!' cried Brother Peter aloud, startling the drowsy rooks. 'I cannot live without her.'

He plunged down the hillside, crossed the stream by the wooden plank and made straight for Rector's barn. It was locked. Flabbergasted, he read the scrap of parchment nailed on the door: 'Closed by the order of Wilfred, Bishop of Worcester, for default of taxes.' So Rector had not paid his taxes. Relieved that at least Alice had not been pining for him in the hay, Brother Peter hurried up the steep street towards the Leys' house, so desperate for a glimpse of his love that he could scarcely put one foot in front of the other. The Leys' door was closed and barred. Shutters covered the windows. No smoke poured out of the chimney. They were all on the arable, a neighbour told him. They were hoeing in the spring corn and Master Leys was up Selsely way with his lambs and if it was a message from the abbey—but Brother Peter was gone, retching with despair. He dragged his feet up the track towards the south gate, panting like a man in a desert, aware only of grit between his toes and a monstrous weight on his chest.

And then—and then he saw his oasis, his sweet pool of water. The weight rolled off him and he heard it bounding away down the path behind him. A huge hand fastened on his bowels. For there was Alice, coming down from Selsely with a new-born lamb in her arms and the sun in her face, smiling such a welcome that he wondered the bells did not all burst out ringing.

'Where 'ee bin, then?' she asked him.

'I have been nursing the Abbot,' he said, going red and white and red again.

He put his arm round her and drew her into the copse of willows that fronted the abbey gate. In silence he took the lamb from her arms and placed it in a nest of last year's leaves. In silence he laid her among the young willow shoots and knelt down beside her. The morning sun shining through the young leaves made patterns on her skin. 'What if a body come?' she whispered. 'What if my da'——' But Brother Peter would not let her speak.

'My love, my love,' he said, over and over again. 'My love, my dearest love.' He covered her with kisses and into her sweet body he released all his pent-up passion so that afterwards he lay beside her almost contented, almost thoughtless.

When at last, just in time for High Mass, he returned to the infirmary he found that he had lost the sheep's parsley, so he told Infirmarian he had not been able to find it. When a man is already swamped in mortal sin, what does a venial offence signify to his hereafter? He cannot be more than damned.

The morning sun streamed through the east window of the infirmary, gilding the dying Abbot's ghastly features. All was still. Infirmarian was bathing Brother Joseph. Brother Peter was searching for his love. The two servants sat silently one on each side of the Abbot's head. At the side of the bed, his knees grinding into the stone floor, knelt Brother Mark. The little cat washed her face beside him. No one had stopped them. When Jesus Christ had appeared to Brother Mark in the buttery, where he was trying to count the wine pitchers, and had told him to come and comfort the Abbot, he had obeyed Him immediately. He had dropped his tally and his lump of chalk and had followed his nose to the Abbot's sick chamber, the little cat close at his heels like a minute and jaunty shadow. Now he knelt motionless, like an image in plaster. He had clasped one ham-fist over the other. His grimy heels stuck out beyond his cassock. Obediently, he comforted the Abbot. 'Jesus send 'ee a mort of comfort,' he prayed. 'Jesus love 'ee.'

The servants' eyes stood out on stalks. From another room came muffled splashes. The cat leapt lightly on to the bed and curled herself between the Abbot's ankles. Brother Mark lowered his fists on to the blankets. He sank back on his heels and laid his head on the Abbot's pillow. 'I 'ool give 'ee a mort of comfort,' he murmured in the Abbot's purple ear. 'Jesus told I to comfort 'ee.' He clasped one of his huge hands over the Abbot's hands and one of the Abbot's sticky eyelids flickered. Positively it flickered. The two servants shot like bolts out of their seats and hared from the room hollering that the Abbot was come to life.

Infirmarian dropped the scrubbing-brush in the water and rushed out to meet them. They gabbled incoherently, waving and pointing. Brother Joseph tried to crawl out of the tub but could not scale the slippery sides. The servants rushed into the kitchen yard yelling the news. 'The Abbot budged! The Abbot come to life!'

Like ants out of their holes they came pouring. As a village drops everything at the sound of the hue and cry, so the abbey dropped everything and came pelting to see the miracle. Came Sacristan from the vestry with a taper clutched in his fat fingers. Came Novice Master with a queue of novices. Came Guest Master from his accounts, Prior from his private prayers, Nigel with only one shoe on, Lord Wenlock unlaced, Henry Osborne sucking a drumstick, Thomas Woodville with only half his hair curled. Came Abbot's Chaplain with his pi eyes cast up to heaven. Only Brother Peter, deep in his love, missed the excitement. They jostled in the doorway and crammed the infirmary with sweating bodies. They swirled round Brother Joseph in his cooling bath. They pressed so close round the bed their heads met over the blankets and Brother Mark was all but smothered. They craned for a sign of life. If they could have moved their arms they would have crossed themselves.

But they were disappointed. The Abbot lay as before, dead to the world, his bruised flesh rigid as marble.

'I seen un bat his'n eye,' the servant insisted. 'Brother Mark held his'n hand and un batted his'n eye.'

'Did he speak?' Infirmarian asked Brother Mark. 'Did you ask him who he wanted for abbot? Did he make any last request?'

Brother Mark stared stupidly at the crowding faces. He put out his hand to protect the cat. 'Ar,' he said at last. 'Un uttered summat.'

They swayed over him. Abbot's Chaplain levered himself closer with his pointed elbows. 'What did he say?' he demanded.

Nigel shifted uneasily. Henry Osborne tried vainly to get his drumstick to his mouth.

'I doan't know,' said Brother Mark at last· 'I didna twig what un said.'

Cheated of its sensation, the crowed muttered and shifted and, as those on the outskirts drifted into the yard, began to melt away.

'I do not believe you heard anything,' said Abbot's Chaplain. 'You have fabricated a story to draw attention to yourself. I do not believe the Abbot moved at all. Beware of vanity, Brother Mark.'

He stalked out. One by one the others followed until there was left only Infirmarian, the two servants, Brother Mark and the little cat—and the stricken Abbot.

'You can tell *me*,' said Infirmarian gently. 'Did the Abbot really speak?'

But Brother Mark had learned to beware of men, however kindly. He rubbed his face with a colossal hand and muttered: 'I doan't know. Maybe I bin a-dreaming.'

Brother Peter and Infirmarian were not the only monks to tell lies that day. For Brother Mark knew perfectly well what the Abbot had said.

The Abbot had uttered a name.

It was not until Brother Peter came rushing in without the sheep's parsley that Infirmarian remembered Brother Joseph, squatting patiently in his stone-cold bath.

While the monks were assembling in the cloisters composing their minds for High Mass, down in the village Rector sat in his tiny room tacked on to the shady side of the parish church and counted his money. So much from the offerings. So much from the sale of three hens. So much from two buryings and a marriage. He sighed. He was still short by five shillings of the money to pay the Bishop's taxes, to say nothing of putting by for his old age or for when the Abbot persuaded Sir Thomas Arundel to let him appropriate the parish church and turn Rector out. The Bishop would never unlock the haybarn until the taxes were paid in full. Already Rector had had to buy hay for his cow, who was in calf, and if the old hay was not turned soon it might get damp. He counted the money again but it was still short by five shillings.

Ah well, if he was to have his hay back he would have to agree to John Leys' suggestion and arrange a marriage for his daughter Alice. 'I cass-n't hope for gentry,' Leys had said, 'but her be bonny wench and I 'ool pay thirty sheep for dowry. I be arter a body a cut above t'village, Rector. I be arter a body with his'n own horse and a spot of cash and a tidy bed to lay she in. I be arter a body as 'ool be credit to I. 'Tis time her be wed. Thee cast about, Rector. I 'ool give 'ee ten shillings. Ahead of time, if 'ee want.'

Rector sighed again and swept his coins into his purse. Advance it would have to be, if he was to recover his own hay. He would collect the ten shillings from Leys, then he would hitch a lift to Gloucester, pay his taxes to the Bishop's agent and retrieve the key of his barn. And on his way back through Stroud he would call on George Fulham the wool dealer who had a seat on the town council and who was looking for a good wife for his son Edwin. But he would have to be very quiet about it because if the Bishop heard he would be very angry and might lock up the hay again, for the clergy were forbidden to arrange marriages, at least for payment.

Rector tied his purse on his belt and went out to find John Leys. He did not bother to lock his room because there was nothing there worth stealing.

In the east cloisters the procession was formed. Because it was a special occasion Prior had given permission for the girdle of the blessed Honoria to be taken from its niche beside the altar and carried in the procession. All was ready. At the head the Cross was already aloft, its bronze arms blazing in a shaft of sunlight. Behind the Cross, in vestments so stiff and so long he could almost have dispensed with his legs, stood Guest Master who was Priest for the Week. But now he was no longer Guest Master who fiddled his accounts and had fathered in his youth an illegitimate son. He was no longer a man, no longer a monk, with his dishonesties and jealousies and ambitions. He was a priest. He had the power to work a miracle, to turn wine and bread into the blood and flesh of Jesus Christ and put the flesh into men's mouths. Standing patiently at the head of the procession, half smothered in his peacock colours, his purple cap slipping towards one ear, dazzled by the Cross, chary of the tapers, worried about his finances, Guest Master held in his tiny hands the power to baptize, to absolve from sin and to give men a taste of God. He was God's instrument; and whatever his own sins he could shoot the bolts of hell against any repentant sinner.

Behind him in his festal cope stood Prior, as unhappy as if his lean feet were indeed crammed into Abbot Dominic's stumpy shoes. On his left stood Henry Osborne in his black robes, on his right Nigel Woodville in his dark blue, and between them poor Prior felt like grist between millstones. Behind them Abbot's Chaplain reared his invisible wings and behind him Lord Wenlock and Thomas Woodville stood stiffly with two paces between them, backs half turned to accentuate their hatred. On their heels the officials waited, two by two according to their seniority, all except Novice Master who brought up the rear with his clutch of novices and Sacristan who insisted on keeping an eye on the relic.

Behind the officials, the monks stiffened like figures out of an ark, their black robes and white copes falling in wooden folds, wooden hands in wooden sleeves, wooden necks bent, only their eyes alive, darting about under their wooden eyelids like silver fish. In their midst, carried by poles on the shoulders of four monks, was the litter bearing the relic. It was covered with

86

liver-coloured brocade and bordered with gold tassels, and its ivory canopy was embroidered with crimson roses and fringed with yellow silk. Under the canopy, reposing on a crimson velvet cushion, was a mother-of-pearl box with a glass lid, and under the glass lay what was—as yet—the abbey's most precious possession, the girdle of the blessed Honoria, the early Christian martyr who had had her eyes picked out by ravens for refusing to give up her faith. Unfortunately, unlike St Kenelm's corpse at Winchcombe, this relic had never, so far as was known, worked a miracle. But there was always hope. That was the great benefit of the Christian faith. There was always hope. Except of course for those who died in mortal sin.

The procession terminated in a queue of servants, sixty in all, and in a crowd of thirty retainers. There was a good deal of jostling among the King's retainers who were intent on shoving their Rising Sun badges to the front. Two retainers' noses were bloodied, for neither Thomas Woodville nor Lord Wenlock had got Warwick's uncanny power for keeping rough men in check. A Woodville rib was cracked and one of Warwick's men was jabbed with a knife through the centre of his White Bear badge. But the wound was no more serious than Henry Osborne's had been and since the blood had not been shed within the church little notice was taken of it.

But violence was simmering, knocking like steam at the lid.

All was ready. Prior gave the signal and Cantor took a breath to sound the first note of the psalm. But there was an interruption. A high voice quavered: 'Where are they? Where are the candidates?' Unnoticed, Brother Joseph had felt his way along the inner wall to the head of the procession. Inspirited by his hot bath, emboldened by his disability, he was beginning to perceive some of the tiny advantages of extreme old age. Like the Bishop of London he was learning that antiquity earns privileges. 'Where are they?' he cried, extending his meagre arms, his fingers groping.

Both candidates started forward but, although he was farther away, Henry Osborne reached Brother Joseph first because Abbot's Chaplain hooked his elegant hand into Nigel's belt and held him back. In an abbey, age usually means influence, so Henry flung himself on his knees and guided Brother Joseph's hands towards his face. Brother Joseph's bandaged eyes looked down and his hands crawled over him. Even now, after weeks of inactivity, traces of old paint lingered under his nails and the contours of his finger-tips were still stained with black ink. The old fingers inched over Warwick's candidate, over the sturdy neck and bland features and over the monk's tonsure, the shaved circle that measured four inches from the crown of the head and was the invariable insignia of those in monastic orders—unless, like Prior, one was already totally bald. The fingers seemed satisfied.

'I pray you to elect me as your abbot,' cried Henry, in a loud voice. 'I swear on this holy Cross'—here he rose and stretched over Prior's shoulder to touch the Cross—'that when I am abbot I will rule this abbey as Abbot Dominic has ruled it, making no innovation. His word shall be my law. What he has wished so I shall wish. That is his desire.'

It was the first public declaration of his policy.

Brother Joseph nodded as if pleased. Life as he had always known it, with the addition of hot baths. What more could an old monk ask for? Except—ah, except his sight, except his sight.

Thomas Woodville drew his dagger and jabbed Abbot's Chaplain's beautiful wrist. Nigel fell forward at Brother Joseph's feet. He seized his hands. 'And I swear,' he cried in his young clear voice, 'I swear that I will make this abbey rich and famous, a pearl among abbeys. I will make it more famous than Winchcombe. I will make the name of Woodchester sing in men's ears. I will make it a paragon, a model of piety and learning and magnificence. I, Nigel Woodville, swear it.'

A breath of uneasiness, like the precursor of a storm, passed over the ranks of religious. One of Brother Joseph's hands came to rest on Nigel Woodville's head, on the centre of the shaved crown. The fingers splayed, feeling for the edge of the hair. They stopped, the tips buried in the thick fringe. Something was wrong. Brother Joseph brought up his other hand and made a frantic investigation of Nigel's head, crown, fringe, ears, forehead and nape. Then he raised his bandaged eyes towards the roof of the cloisters and announced, in a voice that quivered with shock, what everyone had realized from the moment Nigel Woodville set foot in the abbey but which no one, not even Abbot's Chaplain, had dared lay tongue to. 'He is not a monk!' cried Brother Joseph. 'This is only a priest's tonsure. This man is not a monk.'

Nigel shouted: 'I intend to take vows. I have already written to the Bishop——'

His words were drowned in the hubbub. By voicing the obvious, Brother Joseph had made it seem so much the worse. Indeed, Nigel Woodville had great disadvantages to overcome.

At last order was restored. Brother Joseph was led back to his place. Cantor sounded the note, the first word of the psalm burst forth, the Cross flashed and the procession began to move, while John Leys paused at the south gate with a lamb under each arm to see what mumbo-jumbo the monks were up to now.

'*Jubilate Deo, omnis terra alleluja,*' sang the monks, their eyes on the bobbing bronze Cross. They proceeded up the north cloister past the novices' bench and the book cupboards and right into the passage where Henry Osborne had been hit by a stone; once round the Abbot's lodgings, skirting his herb garden, his stables and his dovecote; back into the west cloisters, under the officials' rooms; past the masons' lodge and the henhouse and the smithy into the kitchen yard; once round the kitchen yard, past the door of the infirmary and the Guest House; back into the south cloisters past the lavatories and the towel cupboards; past Brother Joseph's scriptorium with its red paint still caked on psalm forty-seven; back into the east cloisters and through the door of the south transept into the church.

'*Lauda, anima mea, Dominum: laudabo Dominum in vita mea,*' they sang, and each verse peeled off another preoccupation. For this was their life, the liturgy and the Mass and the prayers. This was what they were trained for. This was their core where lay the secret of life. To praise and to pray, these were their duties. To follow the ritual devised by St Bernard of Clairvaux a thousand years before. To be poor, to be chaste, to be obedient.

This was the life that all men recognized as holy and desirable, and would have embraced themselves had worldly ties not proved too strong. The monastic life had always been first best and these monks knew it. And if they could not have explained just what it was that was so good about it, that did not mean that its goodness did not exist.

They went once round the nave, empty as always except for the dead abbots lying over their own bones staring stonily at the vaulting, and for the devils on the rood screen putting their victims through highly coloured torments, and for the thirty-two plaster statues, twenty of our Lord and twelve of our Lady, and for Jesus Christ depicted fourteen times on the walls. The religious mounted the chancel steps into the choir, leaving the laymen in the nave to peer through the screen: abbey servants in the middle, Thomas Woodville and the King's Rising Suns on their left, Lord Wenlock and Warwick's White Bears on their right.

The two lines of religious divided, and filed into opposing choir stalls so that the candidates glared at each other. A cloud of incense engulfed them, so strong they would carry the smell of it in their noses through dinner. Guest Master approached the altar, his servers on either hand. Sacristan saw the blessed Honoria's girdle safely into its niche and closed the grille with a snap. Abbot's Chaplain chanted softly, saving his voice for the antiphon. Novice Master glared at James Coles who was picking his nose. Brother Peter's drawers rustled with last year's willow leaves.

High Mass proceeded. Abbots might come and go but the Mass went on for ever. It was the rock on which the Church was built. 'Take, eat, this is My body,' He had said. 'Take, drink, this is My blood.' These were truths no one denied except a few crackpot heretics who never escaped the furnaces of hell even if some managed to elude the Sheriff's bonfire.

When the time came, the monks approached the altar steps in order of their seniority and knelt at the rail from the left to the right. First came Prior, Cellarer, Sacristan, Infirmarian, Abbot's Chaplain, Cantor, Chamberlain and Refectorian. Novice Master waited as usual to communicate with his novices. Now

Prior and Cellarer were both thin men and neither filled his eighth of the altar rail, so as soon as Guest Master was turned to the altar Nigel Woodville darted from his stall and slipped into the space between them, clamping his hands on to the brass rail. Here he was at Prior's right elbow, as if he were Prior's favourite.

Seeing his opponent thus ensconced Henry Osborne marched out of his stall and tried to insinuate himself likewise, but by the time he had approached the altar rail the officials had grasped what was happening and had shifted flank to flank until the only spare space was a dozen inches at the extreme end between Refectorian and the south wall. Into this niche Henry crammed himself.

'*Ecce Agnus Dei, ecce qui tollit peccata mundi,*' said Guest Master, scowling at the disturbance.

But worse was to come. In the nave words buzzed about what had occurred. Immediately Lord Wenlock and three White Bears rushed up the chancel. Wenlock and one retainer jerked Nigel Woodville out of his privileged position and the other two wedged a scarlet Henry Osborne in his place. Angry cries broke out behind the chancel screen. The officials clung to the altar rail like drowning men. Into the fray rushed half a dozen of the King's Rising Suns, headed by Thomas Woodville in crimson stockings. Blows were exchanged. Dust rose from the sacred pavement. The monks shrank like snails into their shells, hiding their heads from a violence they thought they had abandoned for ever at the convent gate. Prior stood up and waved his arms but it was not his authority that stopped them, nor was it Guest Master's, for all his vestments and the blessed Sacrament between his hands. Nor was it either of the candidates. It was Sacristan who hoisted his enormous bulk on to his feet and, filling his colossal lungs with incense-laden air, roared, 'The next man to strike a blow is excommunicated!'

They heard him, believed him, and stopped. For not one of them wished to be expelled from the bosom of the Church and denied the consolations of his religion. They abandoned their candidates and slunk away into the nave, followed somewhat sheepishly by Lord Wenlock and Thomas Woodville.

'Come, Infirmarian,' said Sacristan. 'Let us give our places to those that obviously need grace so badly.' And he pushed Nigel and Henry side by side on to their knees at the rail. It went not unnoticed that he put Henry nearest to the Prior's right hand.

'*Corpus domini nostri*,' quavered Guest Master, placing the sacred wafer on Prior's tongue.

When the younger monks had received the Sacrament, Brother Mark remained where he was at the rail because he had caught sight of his dear lord Jesus Christ nodding to him from a spot a pace to the left of the altar Cross. He smiled at Him placidly until in the end he was rudely pulled away by Cellarer who did not encourage such demonstrations of piety.

Brother Peter, too, remained where he was because he had been made faint by a sudden vision of the hell that awaited him, for not only had he broken his vow of chastity and thus entered a state of mortal sin but he had dug for himself an even deeper pit by taking the Sacrament while unabsolved. 'Perhaps after all,' he thought, 'one can be more than damned. Even in hell there must be graduations of torment.' In his vision he saw the most agonizing ones being prepared for him. Yet even to escape these terrors he could never bring himself to confess his sin and repent and renounce his guilty love. If only he could rid himself of this passion that burned like a fire in his loins!

When at last he dragged himself away it was to give up his place to Novice Master, for whom was reserved the worst horror of all. He was last of all the religious to communicate. He opened his mouth to receive the wafer and the instant it touched his tongue he knew, without a shadow of doubt, that this was not the body of Jesus Christ. The foundations of the church shook. The altar rail trembled. He shut his eyes and swallowed, but he knew he was not swallowing God's flesh. In a flash of light he realized that the teaching of the Church was founded on a delusion. 'Take, eat, this is My flesh,' He had said, but He had added, 'Do this in remembrance of Me.'

With audible clicks the puzzle fell into place in Novice Master's brain. He realized it was not devils that had been prompting him but his own reason. Why should the one utterance be taken as gospel rather than the other? Did Jesus cut His vein and let His blood into a basin? Did He cut off bits of His own flesh with a knife? Why should the Church insist that the wine turned to blood and the bread to flesh? Anyone with taste could tell that the wine and the flesh did not change their properties. 'In memory' was what He had said. The Mass was an act of memory, of representation. Novice Master could not understand why he had not seen the truth before. But now he had seen the truth—or perhaps it was only what he thought to be the truth.

He walked calmly back to his place. In one minute all his doubts had been laid to rest. The months of self-torture, self-questioning and self-doubt were at an end. His reason had lain down with his faith and out of that union had sprung a new faith, a faith blessed by God. So Novice Master thought. He sat quietly intoning the last psalm and thanking God that He had shown him the truth about the Sacraments. He was unaware of the horror that pressed about him, that Brother Mark could see like a black cloud round his head. Out of this cloud he peered serenely at the other monks. They were the heretics now, not he.

It was as he knelt down for the last prayers that Novice Master felt the onset of a fourth ulcer, high up under the left buttock.

As Guest Master raised his right hand in a last blessing Abbot Dominic gave up the ghost. He gave up breathing and his soul left him and flew out of the window into the bright spring sunshine and started on its journey to heaven to join the saints and martyrs. His death was not known until Infirmarian returned from High Mass because the two servants set to watch him had fallen asleep with their heads on his pillow.

7

'**B**RAVA, brava, my lord!' shrieked the Queen, seeing her husband's lance strike Lord Hastings full in the chest and send him sprawling.

'Brava, brava!' shouted the ladies, jubilant with relief.

The hot April sun, surely the hottest April sun in living memory, poured down on the brilliant scene; on peacock colours and ivory flesh, on emerald grass and rainbow embroideries and on dazzling armour that an hour in the sun made too hot to touch. 'Brava, brava!' they screamed, wagging their towers of hair, craning perilously out of their seats so that the knights might admire their breasts.

The King turned his horse and trotted heavily towards the dais. With a hand swimming in sweat inside its mailed glove, he pushed up his visor, revealing a scarlet and sweating face and a fringe of wet hair plastered to his forehead. 'Did you see, my love?' he cried, for indeed he was, in his enjoyments, a very young man. 'Plumb in the middle. My cousin Warwick could not have done it better.'

A frown creased the Queen's forehead. Warwick! Always Warwick! Even now, when rumours were buzzing like poisoned darts, it was always Warwick. The King snapped down his visor and trotted to the enclosure where his squires, standing on step-ladders, removed his blue surcoat and his blue ostrich plume and doused his horse and his armour in cold water. Through the vertical grille of his helm the King peered at the lists and a momentary panic overcame him, imprisoned in his leaden armour, unable even to dismount without help, peering between steel bars. Suddenly he longed to be a boy again, to feel Warwick's hand on his wrist and hear Warwick's grave advice.

He contemplated the bloody and dangerous years of his boyhood, when, to both him and his father York, Warwick had been like a rock, a dark rock firmly bedded when everything else was shifting; the one sure support in a world of flux. But now the flux was over; there was firm ground under the throne. Why could Warwick not move with the times? Why must he still insist that the throne needed a prop and that the prop must be himself? Was the King to trust no men but Nevilles for the rest of his days? Was he never to build up a party dependent solely on himself?

The King would have sighed had the weight of his armour allowed it. Across the emerald meadow he watched a pulley hoisting Lord Dacre into the saddle. A fresh surcoat was thrown over his own head. A rosy plume was stuck in his helm. A trumpet sounded. Two squires raised the lance and tucked it into the King's right armpit. His open glove received the weight of the shaft. He jabbed with his spurs and the horse moved forward. Over the meadow Lord Dacre fixed his lance. 'Never swerve until you can see his eyes through the visor.' That was what Warwick had said, long ago in the meadows of Ludlow. There was a grinding of metal joints as both horses lumbered into a trot.

'My lord! My lord!'

It was Chancellor, running after the King like an old blackbird, waving a parchment roll. Agitated courtiers gave chase but Chancellor knew what he was about. 'From Woodchester, my lord,' he panted, clutching a spur and cutting two of his fingers. 'You gave orders . . .'

The King halted his horse and lowered his lance until the tip rested on the turf. 'Open it,' he commanded. Chancellor broke the seal and read aloud news of Abbot Dominic's death. For one glorious, carefree moment the King had it in his mind to throw in his hand, to give orders for Nigel Woodville and Thomas Woodville and the fifteen Rising Suns to be recalled, to let Henry Osborne be abbot and give Warwick his little triumph. What, after all, did Woodchester matter? An abbey among hundreds of abbeys, undistinguished, unimportant, humdrum. What did the King care who was abbot? There were places in plenty for Nigel Woodville.

The lance quivered, rose an inch and then fell. If only the King had raised it again, charged Lord Dacre and forgotten Woodchester Abbey, how many lives might have been saved, how many buildings left whole? But at that moment the Queen fluttered her scarf and blew kisses and patted her high stomach where his third child lay coiled. If he angered her she would deny him and if he forced his will on her that child would never be born a boy.

The King signalled with his left glove. The lance was taken from him, he was lugged from his horse and set free from his armour, then he walked with straddled legs into his pavilion to discuss affairs of state. In the flush of unseating Lord Hastings he might congratulate himself on the stability of his throne, but in fact matters were not entirely satisfactory.

The Burgundian alliance was ratified and his sister Margaret was at this moment trying on the olive-velvet gown that she was to wear at her wedding with the Duke Charles. On receiving news of the marriage Louis of France had sent neither regrets nor threats, but he had removed the Bitch of Anjou, mad Henry of Lancaster's wife, from his train of beggars and had installed her and her whelp son at his court in Paris with fifty servants and eight horses; and it was rumoured that he had promised her powerful aid if she made a bid to rescue her husband from the Tower and put him back on the English throne. So far had Warwick's alarms been justified.

'What can the Bitch do?' said the King scornfully, rubbing his thigh where a joint had pinched it. 'She has little support here. She cooked her goose when she ravaged the Midlands. And who wants a babbling lunatic on the throne? It is she who would be ruler.'

'There is her son,' said Chancellor. 'He is of age.'

'Somerset's love-child! Who believes him to be Henry's boy? Sterile for ten years and then out of the blue the seed blossoms. Who believes that tale?'

To divert his attention, Chancellor again raised the question of Woodchester. 'I wish Nigel Woodville to be elected as the new abbot,' the King announced. 'I will show Warwick he is no longer my tutor. Send ten more retainers to Woodchester. Set spies to discover anything discreditable about Henry Osborne. Instruct Thomas Woodville to unearth any possibilities of blackmail or bribery among the monks. Place coin at his disposal.'

Thus he harnessed a lion's strength to do a mouse's work—and all to prove his independence of the man who had won him his throne.

But King Edward IV of England was not so independent that he disregarded his own safety. The day he received news about the Bitch of Anjou, he ordered his chamberlain to provide for his personal protection a bodyguard of two hundred archers at the princely wage of eightpence a day. But to Warwick the bodyguard had been ordered the day the King received the news that Warwick declined the invitation to Ludlow.

Thus they laboured at their wall of misunderstanding and distrust.

On the first day of May, Warwick stood in the bows of the *English Rose*, two hundred tons of English teak creaking under his feet, two thousand square yards of English canvas bellying over his head, and watched the white cliffs of Dover rearing and dipping beyond the swell. The sailors, busy with the rigging, one eye open for Channel pirates, never lost their consciousness of the trim black figure and the black hat with twisted ends and the black French beard. All sailors loved Warwick, for as Keeper of the High Seas he had blasted the Channel clear for peaceful shipping.

'Fine run, my lord,' shouted Mountjoy in his ear. 'We shall be in Dover for supper.'

Warwick nodded. He was disquieted about the Calais garrison and not inclined to pleasantries. Their wages were overdue again and with Louis of France eyeing Calais and jingling his money-bags under their noses he would not be happy until the King had despatched their dues. If only the King had listened to him! If only the King had not allowed the Woodvilles to tilt him into this Burgundian alliance! In Calais Warwick had had news of the Bitch of Anjou, the woman he hated above all women. It was she who had sold Maine to the French, who had promised Louis Calais if he would help her lunatic husband back on to his throne. It was she who had incited the men of Pontefract into beheading Warwick's father Salisbury after the battle of Wakefield. It was she who had allowed her troops to murder and pillage and rape all the way up the Great North Road. And here she was ensconced in honour at the French court! And all because the King would not listen to trusty advisers!

An hour before sunset the *English Rose* sounded her signals outside Dover harbour, furled her sails and was rowed to her berth. With the same grave deliberation with which he did everything Warwick walked down the plank to the quay, and was escorted by a mob of enthusiastic Kentish men to Dover Castle where he was to spend the night. Warwick was very popular in Kent, being a diligent Warden of the Cinque Ports, a Constable of Dover and owning several estates in the shire.

At the castle bad news greeted him. There was a letter from his agent at the Papal Court stating that the agent had been unable to obtain from His Holiness the Pope the necessary dispensation that would allow Warwick's elder daughter Isabella to marry the King's young brother Clarence, whose cousin she was. This was an old scheme, laid when the King was newly crowned and Isabella and Clarence still children. A postscript added that it was common report in Rome that the English king had bribed the Pope not to grant the dispensation and that the Pope had bowed to his wishes in the hope that the English king would send more money for the crusade against the Turks.

Warwick jerked his head as if a glove had slapped his cheek. Sufficient money had been sent, he knew, to buy far closer marriages than this. It was not as if the young people were first cousins. There had been no murmur of opposition until now. And without a word! Warwick ground his teeth, picturing

Clarence taking his pick of the Woodville sisters. It was a sight that set his pride quivering.

On the London road next morning a messenger from Westminster presented a letter from Chancellor announcing that the King had decided to relieve Warwick of his post of Great Chamberlain and bestow it on the Queen's brother, Lord Scales. Then a cry went up among the apple and cherry orchards that boded ill for Woodchester Abbey. 'After all I have done for him!' So it turned out that, before even the second letter from Abbot's Chaplain reached Warwick at his London house, the decision was made, the die cast. On hearing of Abbot Dominic's death, Warwick suffered no indecision such as had haunted the King in the meadows of Westminster. The letter read, he dictated letters of his own to his clerk. To Lord Wenlock he wrote that Wenlock was to get Henry Osborne elected at all costs; and he despatched the letter in the care of six armed retainers, together with extra funds. Then for the first time in his life Warwick put his pride in his pocket and wrote the following letter to his lord the King.

To our sovereign lord Edward, King of England, Ireland, Wales and Calais. We send our humble and loyal greetings. It has grieved us greatly of recent times .that we have not enjoyed full accord in our policies. We beg that you will receive us in audience so that we may speak in private of these matters and assure you that we have in our heart only your good and the good of the realm.

It had the ring of a last appeal.

Prior drooped over his table, his egg-like head propped up by his hands, grooves as deep as scars between his eyebrows, his shoulders sagging under his cares. Everything worried him: the quarrelsome retainers, the whispers and conjectures, the way the candidates kept backing his monks into corners, the funeral arrangements, even the unnatural weather—day after day of unbroken sunshine, no rain, no wind, nothing but a burning sun and a blue sky. He was made no easier by having heard that morning from the Bishop who gave him his instructions as to how the election was to proceed. In twelve days' time the whole convent was to be assembled. Since there was a disputed election they were to elect by acclamation—for the Bishop had no liking for the vagaries of majority voting—six monks, that was one-fifth of their number. These six monks, plus Prior as the acting superior of the abbey, were on behalf of the community to elect —by unanimous vote—the new abbot. This final voting was to take place later, on a date to be specified by the King. It would be the duty of Prior and the six acclaimed monks to consider the inclinations of the religious and to elect as their abbot a man not only acceptable to God but also acceptable to the monks of Woodchester.

Prior groaned and clutched his naked head. Here was the snag! Acceptable to the monks and to God! How were they to know, he and the six unnamed monks, who was acceptable to God? And even if they did, what if the monks of Woodchester did not find him acceptable? Prior forced himself to consider the two candidates. Which did God favour? Henry Osborne? He had been a monk for thirty years. He was steeped in monastic tradition. He would step neatly into the shoes of the dead abbot whom he resembled and whom all had liked. He would change nothing. Under his rule life would sail on as it had always done. Under him tradition would rest untouched. The abbey would amble on peacefully in its traditional, cosy, quiet, pious, in-efficient way. And who was to say it was not the safe way?

But Nigel Woodville? Nigel Woodville was a different kettle of fish. Who was to say it was not God's intention that Woodchester Abbey should be turned inside out? Nigel would make Woodchester famous, he said, and Prior did not doubt he meant it. He would reorganize the finances, realize her vast potential wealth, leave nothing untouched that could be improved. He would make Woodchester as affluent and as well known as Winchcombe, so that pilgrims would queue at her gates and novices clamour to enter her cloisters, learned men to consult her library, the sick to touch her relics. She would become a second Evesham. So Nigel Woodville said. And the services would not be neglected. With increasing numbers there would never be any lack of monks to say the Holy Offices and maintain in good repair that wall of devotions that kept Satan at bay.

And yet . . . Prior curled one bare foot round his ankle-bone and groaned again. What did God wish? Oh, what did God wish? There was a sickness in the monastery, Prior could feel its taste in his mouth. All was not well. The spirit was missing, even from the liturgy. The air within walls was stale. And yet—might not a blast of change be more of a damage than a remedy? 'You cannot touch the fabric of the Church for fear the whole edifice will come tumbling down.' That was the joke, but might there not be a grain of truth in it?

Prior rubbed a bare calf with bare toes and suddenly there flashed into his mind a picture of himself as a little boy, watching monks cutting rushes in a meadow near Tewkesbury. The monks had tucked up their cassocks. Their thighs were brown. Prior and his father were making the return journey from market with salt and herrings and Prior had stood up on a salt-barrel to watch the monks longer. They straddled their legs thigh-deep in the water and cut the reeds with sickles. There was blood on their fingers. Before the road curved the bell began ringing for Vespers, and the monks hoisted their baskets on to their heads and began the trudge up to the monastery for their evening prayers.

It was a beautiful picture, one that had coloured the whole of Prior's life since he was eight years old. It was this picture, and his own timid nature, that had sent him into Woodchester Abbey. But he had been disappointed. In the abbey he had found protection for his timidity but he had lost the earth between his toes, and since he had donned the cassock he had never seen blood on his fingers. Prior ground his knuckles into his eyes. The time was rapidly coming when he would have to favour one candidate or the other. How could he choose? Which did God favour? Which did Woodchester need? Which—ah, this was the mountainous question, the pinnacle of doubt—which did the Church need?

Prior sank on his knees and prayed God to tell him how to decide. But God did not answer. He placed squarely on Prior's cringing shoulders the responsibility of choice.

The body of Abbot Dominic lay in its open coffin on the altar steps, awaiting burial. At each corner a two-foot candle burned, beside each candle a monk knelt, breathing prayers for the Abbot's soul and clicking the beads of his rosary. *'Pater Noster qui est in caelis'* . . . *'Ave Maria'* . . . *'Requiem aeternam dona eis, Domine'* . . . they prayed, wondering how long the Abbot's purgatory would be, and then how long their own, and picturing the glorious ranks of prophets and saints and martyrs that would welcome them when at last they reached heaven. Of one thing they were certain. Being monks they would reach paradise far more quickly than laymen, for they led much holier lives.

Brother Peter was not one of them.

As soon as Abbot Dominic's body was cold Nigel Woodville began his proper campaign. Not yet knowing the Bishop's choice of election procedure, he concentrated on the officials; not on Prior, for there was something about Prior's haggard face that warned him to step carefully, but on Novice Master and Sacristan and the other administrators of separate funds.

Novice Master puzzled him. It was as if the man were deaf or blind or otherwise cut off from human contact. When Nigel approached him in the north cloister and asked him if he did not consider it essential that the entry of novices be kept up, Novice Master stared as intently as if he were counting Nigel's ribs but did not answer. When Nigel enlarged on his schemes for making Woodchester an abbey that novices would fight to enter, Novice Master only scratched his left buttock and gazed calmly before him, oblivious for once of his novices who craned, eyes popping and ears twitching, on the bench behind him.

But Henry Osborne was more fortunate. He was so often fortunate, usually by virtue of doing very little. One morning after Low Mass he crossed the baked grass of the cloister yard and stood listening at the open window of the north cloister. He had no motive for listening. He had no real campaign. He had the enormous advantage over Nigel Woodville that change was anathema to monks. He had only to declare, loudly and often, that he wanted to alter nothing—and to see that Warwick's retainers matched the King's.

The novices were considering the Gospel for the second Sunday after Easter. 'This teaches us,' said Novice Master, 'that we must never be like Thomas. Happy is he who believes without any doubt. It is one of man's greatest happinesses to know that what he believes is true. To be certain. To be sure.'

Andrew Alsopp raised his hand, for Novice Master had taught his novices to ask questions about what they did not understand. Andrew Alsopp rose and asked, 'I have had a doubt, Novice Master, that I pray you to resolve for me.' Novice Master inclined his head. 'When the holy wafer has been consecrated,' said Andrew Alsopp, 'it is eaten at the altar rail by those who are communicating.' Novice Master bowed again. 'If there is any left it is put in the tabernacle and the door of the tabernacle is shut and locked.' Novice Master shifted his toes. 'Now suppose,' pursued Andrew Alsopp, 'the devil makes the priest forget to shut the tabernacle door, and a raven enters the church and he eats the holy wafer. Does he eat God's body? He has never been baptized. Does he swallow God's flesh, like a son of the Church?'

Silence. Long afterwards Henry Osborne remembered that silence. It seemed to fill the cloister and, by very pressure, to be squeezed out of the window. At last Novice Master answered: 'No. He does not eat God's body.'

A little devil prompted Andrew Alsopp to pursue his enquiries. 'But the wafer has been consecrated. When does it change back into ordinary bread? Is it when the raven takes it into his mouth? Or when he swallows it?'

The silence was so complete Henry Osborne could hear

Novice Master breathing. Into the silence, like stones into a lake, the weighty words dropped, shattering the calm surface and setting in motion God knows what undulations. 'The wafer has not become God's body,' said Novice Master. 'The wafer never becomes God's body.'

Henry Osborne tiptoed away. He was horrified. But he was also silent. It seemed to him that Novice Master was more likely to support Henry Osborne than Nigel Woodville. Also he had no intention of being involved in a scandal.

8

THE third day after his death, Abbot Dominic was buried. For three days he had lain in his open coffin on the altar steps, with candles to ward off devils and monks to pray for his soul's safe conduct to heaven. He had offered his deaf ears to three Nones, three Vespers, three Complines, two Low Masses, two High Masses, three Nocturns, three Lauds, two Terces and two Sexts. His body had been ritually cleansed. His stomach, chest, nostrils, palms and soles had been anointed with holy oil. He had been dressed in white robes and nailed up in his oak coffin together with a wafer of consecrated bread. An impression of his features had been taken in life, for it never does to forget how Death the Great Leveller lies in wait for all men. So now his effigy, fashioned out of wax, dressed in the Benedictine habit and painted in a more than lifelike manner, stretched its length over its own corpse and waited composedly for the procession to form.

They had shortened Prime by four psalms so as to gain extra time to rub ashes over their faces and fasten sackcloths on their shoulders. They were no longer grief-stricken but they were sobered by the contemplation of death, the mysterious state that the righteous had no reason to fear but that every reasonable man did fear, just as a child fears the dark however often he is told that if he is a good boy nothing will come and snatch him away in the night. Even the retainers were quiet, and elbowed their way into prominent positions in silence.

The bronze Cross was raised. The monks lit their tapers from the Pascal candle that had burned itself down to a cube. The plaster statues were lifted down from their niches and borne aloft. Once again the girdle of the blessed Honoria saw the light. Prior donned his amice, his alb, his cincture, his maniple, his stole and his mourning chasuble and took his place behind the relic. The dead man and his wax image were manœuvred on to a litter, then hoisted on to the shoulders of the eight largest servants. Nigel Woodville and Henry Osborne took their stations behind him and began to weep, although not so effectively as Abbot's Chaplain. Prior nodded his aching head and Cantor began his chant. *'De profundis clamavi ad te, Domine,'* he sang, and they burst into the funeral psalm with the relief of men who need not seek far for expression for their sorrow because their Church in its liturgy expresses it for them.

The long procession began to move. Abbot Dominic's bones had a long journey to go before they could be laid to rest in the stone tomb that awaited them. Round the nave they shuffled, tapers fuming, censers swinging, images bobbing like corks on water, tonsures shining like full moons. The eight servants shrugged their shoulders to get the poles into the hollows. The retainers went tiptoe to see what was happening in front. They journeyed twice round the nave, with a pause at every one of the fourteen stations, then out through the north transept into sunshine so brilliant it swallowed up the flames of the tapers and left only the smoke. The procession crawled round the Abbot's lodgings, and then three times round the cloister yard. The more psalms they sang the heavier their sins weighed on them; which is the purpose of penitential psalms. Now the bronze Cross emerged into the glare of the kitchen yard and the heat of the sun struck at their naked scalps. Three times they circled the kitchen yard, with hot wax dripping on to their fingers and sweat in their armpits, then they wended their way out through the south gate, to attract in their passing, as a flame attracts insects, almost the whole of the village which, in spite of indifference or hostility, had still given itself a holiday for the occasion. Even John Leys joined the procession, together with his wife and his four sons and his daughter. The procession went down the precipitous slope to the village, the four servants under the back poles bending their knees to keep the coffin level. The village trailed behind and tried to forget its peas and oats not germinated for lack of rain and its wheat scarcely a finger high and the clouds of dust raised even by these funeral feet. 'My moisture is like the drought in summer,' they all sang together; but John Leys was thinking that these abbey-lubbers did not really care about the weather. It was like a wall, this indifference to the weather.

It separated the lay from the religious far more effectively than renunciations of family or even sexual abstinence. *They* had no need to fuss about the weather nor about flood or forest fire or cattle disease or sheep-rot or drought. They were not farmers dependent for their living on good harvests and healthy stock. They had their living. Generations of benefactors had given them their living so that they could live cosily on their rents, praying behind their grey walls, unmoved by storm-clouds or red sunrises, by lambs lost or pigs overlaid or cows run dry. This was what John Leys thought and he was influential in the village.

It was also what the novices thought. At first Prior had been reluctant to let the novices out of the abbey because he was afraid the sights of spring might seduce them back into the world. But he need not have worried. The novices eyed such signs of agricultural distress as a brook run dry and bullocks butting each other off the longer grass, and they thanked God that it need no longer disturb *their* sleep.

At the bottom of the hill the procession halted, while the coffin was shifted on to the shoulders of another eight servants. The monks wiped their sweating heads with their sleeves. But they never stopped singing. The Cross flashed, the coffin lurched and they plodded on, past Leys' house and Rector's church and Rector's barn with its door unlocked at last and its remaining hay already quarter-turned; past the mill and the dipping-pens, past the dusty arable and the baked meadow and the wishbone houses with their dry thatch; ceaselessly chanting their psalms of sorrow. By the time they had traversed the village and come again to the south gate they had sung their penitential psalms five times over.

At the south gate the villagers stopped, for they hardly ever entered the abbey except on business. It was business, naturally, that prompted John Leys to slip in after Prior and ask him, under cover of the Introit, to say prayers for rain. He argued that if God was going to answer any prayers He was most likely to answer monks' prayers, since praying was their profession.

The procession wound its length round the nave for the last time, then departed into the chancel, leaving the laymen to goggle through the lattice-work of the screen. There the monks performed the proper rites over Abbot Dominic. They prayed that his sins should be forgiven him and that the blessed Angel Michael should bring him into the holy light. They celebrated Mass and cried on the Lord for mercy. They sprinkled his bier with holy water and each of them gave the kiss of peace to his wax image. As the Abbot was carried down into the nave and lowered into his stone tomb they sang, 'May the angels lead thee into Paradise.' They laid him with his feet to the east so that, when the last trumpet sounded on the Day of Doom, and his corpse pushed up the stone lid, he would be facing the holy city of Jerusalem. They placed the wax image on the lid of the tomb and pulled its cassock straight. '*Requiescat in pace*,' they chanted, satisfied that they had done all they could for him.

Before they went to the refectory for the funeral feast there was one more ceremony to perform—Nigel Woodville's admission to the Benedictine order. Already his noviciate had been waived. Already Prior had given him a copy of the Rule and had publicly, in morning Chapter, warned him that if he took monastic vows he must be humble, chaste, patient, abstemious, serious, diligent, devout and obedient to his superiors, above all to his abbot.

Prostrate on the floor with his mouth in the dust and his scalp still raw from its shaving, Nigel had smiled a little because he was determined to be abbot himself. Now, on the day of the dead Abbot's funeral, Nigel Woodville stripped himself of all his clothes while Prior, whom for this occasion the Bishop had granted suffragan powers, said, in a loud voice, 'May the Lord put off from thee the old man, with his deeds.'

Then, naked as a new-born child, Nigel knelt on the altar steps and cried: 'Take me, O Lord! Take me, O Lord! Take me, O Lord!' afterwards prostrating himself on the pavement in the shape of a cross. Still naked he rose and recited aloud his profession of faith and his vow to obey the Abbot whom 'the more judicious portion of the whole congregation may by God's will elect'.

On the Bishop's behalf, Prior then admitted Nigel Woodville to the Benedictine order, throwing over him a black cassock and a new white cope with the words, 'May the Lord put on thee a new man.'

But Nigel Woodville was not a new man. He was the same man: young, capable, ambitious, itching to set about Woodchester Abbey, to do good to it and make it popular and efficient.

They were all the same men. Monks no longer shed their humanity when they entered a monastery. A thousand years before, St Benedict had inspired a new race of monks who had cast their sins and obsessions as snakes cast their skins. These monks of old had literally become new men. They had been born again in Christ. But the monks of the fifteenth century did not kill off their old Adams. If they had, John Leys would not have disliked them so much.

9

NIGEL WOODVILLE resumed his campaign next morning. He approached Chamberlain, Refectorian and Cantor, who were all old men and who had got used to Abbot Dominic's ways and had no wish to get used to any other. For twenty years each had been digging his own rut—it might as well be a grave, Nigel thought impatiently—and the thought of being lugged out of it horrified and distressed them. To them a central financial administration simply meant robbing them of much of their employment. 'But what will we do,' they complained, 'if we have no rents to collect and no accounts to do?'

'You could say extra prayers,' Nigel told them. 'Shorten some soul's purgatory by reciting two extra rosaries each day. Perform private Masses for your dead relations. Or you will be able to study the devotional works that I shall obtain for the new library.'

But they only shook their heads. A private prayer night and morning, the seven Holy Hours, the two daily Masses—since their coming of age this had been the pattern of their devotions. They were too old to change it. 'Let things go on as they are,' they said, in whispers, for fear the retainers might hear them.

There were retainers everywhere now: in the cloister yard, in the cloisters, in the nave, skulking behind pillars and scratching their initials on the abbots' tombs. They were big fellows, for ever throwing dice and spitting and fornicating in the village and beating on the south gate after curfew and getting drunk in the ale-house. They sharpened their knives on the chancel steps. They scowled murderously at one another. They trailed after their own candidate, within walls and without. All of them had had their wages doubled. All of them were spoiling for a fight. They had brought with them into the abbey the loyalties and prejudices they had acquired in the world outside, so that they squabbled and bickered not so much over who was to be abbot as over who was to predominate, Neville or Woodville, White Bear or Rising Sun, Warwick or the King.

The monks went about their business in fear and trembling, terrified to voice their preferences lest they should be hustled, perhaps even beaten. Indeed it was a bad day for Woodchester when Warwick made it a disputed election.

Nigel approached Guest Master at an unfortunate moment. He picked his way over a dozen White Bears who were sunning themselves in the kitchen yard and climbed the stairs to Guest Master's room where he found Guest Master, who had heard his steps, turning the key in his oak chest and looking as dishevelled as a man can look when his head is shaved and his sole garment a woollen cassock with a girdle round the middle. There was a guilty flush on Guest Master's cheeks but Nigel did not know that it was not his natural colour.

'I am just setting off for Gloucester,' snapped Guest Master. 'I have particular business there.'

Nigel crossed to the window and eyed the retainers sprawled in the sun. He saw a giant Rising Sun jump up and kick a White Bear in the stomach. Instantly the yard was a mass of writhing, struggling bodies. Angry shouts bounded off the walls. 'I reckon they eat a great deal,' shouted Nigel, above the hubbub. 'If you had a central fund under a bursar you would not have to worry about what they cost you. You could draw what you needed from the central treasury instead of worrying about rents.'

For half a minute Guest Master considered this proposal. In theory it offered the same opportunity of embezzlement as he had now, but in fact a central bursary would mean a far closer eye on expenditure. 'The most efficient arrangement,' said Nigel, as the shouts dwindled, 'would be to have a lay bursar.'

That settled Guest Master. He could never pull the wool over a layman's eyes the way he had hoodwinked Prior. It was precisely for this reason, to squeeze the abbey like a teat into his son's mouth, that he had entered the abbey in the first place, two years after his son had been born to another man's wife. 'You must excuse me,' he said shortly. 'I have nothing to say to you.'

Nigel had no choice but to leave. He trailed dispiritedly down the stairs. But he was not without hope. Early in life he had learned that every man has his price, even a monk. All he had to do was to discover what the price was.

As soon as Nigel was safely out of sight Guest Master unlocked his chest, and transferred to his pocket a tiny package wrapped in a scrap of linen and tied with twine. With this he set off for Gloucester where he visited a certain Reuben Abraham who lived in Silver Street. On his way back he spent an hour in Stroud, admiring the green shutters of the shop he had bespoken for his son Francis.

Nigel had more sense than to approach Abbot's Chaplain. Infirmarian informed him, not unkindly, that he was too young to be an abbot. Cellarer stopped bullying Brother Mark just long enough to tell Nigel that no one was getting his vote who had been a monk only three days. Sacristan was more forthcoming. Not that he favoured Nigel. There was scarcely a monk in the abbey who looked on Nigel with any favour, except Brother Peter who should never have been a monk at all. But Sacristan greeted Nigel pleasantly because he was in a good humour. He had heard by direct messenger from London that St Peter's toe-nails were arriving at Bristol the following week. He had just completed his arrangements for having them met and conveyed with due honour to the abbey. He had already boasted about them in the district when he had handed to Robert Cordwell the freehold title of the lands he had sold him.

He mopped his colossal forehead with a handkerchief and pushed Nigel on to a chair. He wheezed and chuckled and waddled excitedly between the hearth and the window, waving his fat hands. 'Thirty-two authenticated miracles!' he exclaimed, grunting with pleasure like a cow rasping herself on a tree trunk. 'Thirty-two authenticated miracles and every toe-nail complete. It is the only complete set of Christian martyr's toe-nails in the world. Oh, they will come flocking to us when they hear about this. I am broadcasting the good news as far as Tewkesbury. This will take Winchcombe down a peg. St Kenelm's corpse cannot hold a candle to St Peter's toe-nails.' His fantastic face shone with enthusiasm. 'I will try them on Novice Master. He is a hard nut and he has four ulcers on his left leg. I will try them on Brother Joseph.'

'They should bring in a good income,' said Nigel Woodville.

'They will come flocking,' cried Sacristan, his piggy eyes glistening as he pictured them, on stretchers, on crutches, foaming at the mouth, possessed by devils, dumb, blind, with worms in their ears. He pictured them crawling in through the north door and bounding out through the west door, hundreds upon hundreds of them, all rejoicing and praising God and spreading the news of the wonderful relic at Woodchester Abbey. 'We will become another Canterbury!' he exclaimed, his cheeks quivering like two blancmanges. 'Twenty thousand pilgrims a year to peek at St Thomas Becket's brains in a glass box! How many more will travel to Woodchester to touch the toe-nails of St Peter!'

'You must have a shrine worthy of such an important relic,' said Nigel, who had caught a glimpse of light at the end of a long dark tunnel. 'You must have Purbeck marble at the least, and jewels, beautiful jewels, for the pilgrims to admire. And an enormous candle, a hundred pounds of best beeswax continually burning.'

But a cloud had dimmed Sacristan's shining face. 'Prior says we cannot afford such a shrine,' he muttered, thrusting out his bottom lip like a child. 'I cannot pay for it out of my fund. I have scarcely the money for the new supply of holy oil. My rents do not come in as they should.'

'Prior——'

'Prior tells me his fund cannot afford it either. He was angry I had not informed him about the toe-nails of St Peter.'

Two tears rolled down Sacristan's face, one on each side of his fleshy nose. Nigel got up and approached the crucifix. He raised his hand and touched it and said, 'If I swear on God's holy Cross that I will give you a shrine as splendid as Thomas Becket's will you vote for me in the abbatical election?'

Sacristan stared at this young man, this monk of three days, his scalp still raw from its ceremonial shaving; this candidate, this King's man, who it was rumoured would turn them all out of their offices if he was made abbot, and who sought to cure monastic maladies with a surgeon's knife. He said slowly, 'Purbeck marble?'

'Yes, or alabaster.'

'And jewels?'

'I will give you a casket set with jewels and lined with velvet to contain the sacred toe-nails. I will give you a book of parchment bound with kid-skin in which to write the pilgrims' names. And a golden bowl to receive their offerings.'

Sacristan licked his lips. This gesture was Nigel's undoing because he saw it as a sign of greed. 'It will be a marvellous addition to Woodchester's income,' he said with enthusiasm. 'Thomas Becket's tomb at Canterbury brings in two thousand pounds every year in pilgrims' fees. Think of that, Sacristan!' He jumped up and began pounding one fist against the other. 'We must have the shrine in the nave, by the chancel steps. The pilgrims can enter by the north transept—they must pay their pennies to come in—and go out by the west door.' His eyes brightened as he pictured the coins rattling in the golden bowl. 'We can maintain a stable in Gloucester and another in Ciren-cester,' he continued, his imagination blown up like a bladder, 'to carry the pilgrims on the last day of their journey. We can sell them candles to light at the shrine. Badges, too, to sew on their clothes to show that they have touched the toe-nails of St Peter. We can build lodgings outside the north gate.' He halted his frenzied striding and eyed Sacristan where he slumped, mouth hanging, his eyes so wide Nigel noticed for the first time what colour they were. 'I tell you, Sacristan, in five years' time the pilgrims' offerings will rival the Abbot's income. Your fund will be the richest of all the officials' funds.' In his ardour Nigel had forgotten all about his central treasury. 'You will no longer have to worry about getting in your rents. Pilgrims will flock here from all over the south to see our famous shrine and earn indulgences for their sins and buy mementoes——'

'And be cured,' whispered Sacristan, slouched so low it seemed his voice was trapped inside his enormous chest.

But Nigel did not understand. He was not undevout but his mind had not hardened in the monastic mould. At once he had too much imagination and too little. 'Cures?' he said, ignorant of the trembling of Sacristan's ponderous belly. 'Cures? Ah yes, we must arrange for some cures, eh, Sacristan? There must be some spectacular cures at the very beginning. There is nothing like news of a miracle for bringing them in. I am certain that for a moderate payment——'

He never finished. With a roar of rage Sacristan charged him, bursting from his place like an old boar from a thicket. A palm two inches thick slapped Nigel Woodville on the side of the head and knocked him against the wall. 'But the age of miracles is past!' Nigel protested. 'The Archbishop said so!' Sacristan stubbed his big toe against Nigel's ribs. 'But no one believes in all those miracles at Becket's tomb!' Nigel shouted, endeavouring to present his fleshier parts to Sacristan's blows. Poor Nigel Woodville! How could he know that it was a lunatic made sensible—before his own eyes, too, and in front of Becket's bloody scalp—that had made a monk out of Sacristan?

Sacristan did not waste any breath on argument. He beat Nigel until he stopped protesting that modern men no longer believed in miracles, then he rolled him out into the passage and left him there for Lord Wenlock, who happened to be visiting Cantor, to gloat over. Lord Wenlock was not normally inclined to gloat over the misfortunes of others but already the heat of the Woodchester election was warping his natural character, just as it was beginning to warp Henry Osborne's and Warwick's and the King's. Indeed, one had to be a very upright man to preserve one's integrity in a disputed abbatical election.

Eventually Nigel Woodville picked himself up and sneaked

back to the Abbot's lodgings. It seemed that he had cooked his goose. Sacristan fuming and the story of Nigel's beating in a hundred mouths within the hour! But still Nigel wrote his letter to the King begging him to despatch at once statuary and other necessaries for the toe-nails of St Peter. Nigel Woodville's power of recover was extraordinary. And had not the King said spare no expense?

When Novice Master heard that John Leys was waiting to speak to him in the parlour he emerged from his private pre-occupation just sufficiently to wonder what he wanted. Leys was one of the few tenants who did not owe him any rent. As soon as he presented his jutting temples in the doorway Leys told him what it was he wanted, for he was a man who believed in direct attack. ' 'Ool 'ee sell I my land?' he demanded. 'I be arter t'freehold. I be renting sixty acres off of 'ee, fourpence the acre arable and tenpence the acre pasture and eighteenpence t'meadow. I 'ool pay 'ee cash.'

Novice Master shook his head. Preoccupied he might be, but he was not so bemused that he forgot the abbey's watchword, 'Never sell.'

Woodchester Abbey, like all other abbeys, lived on its rents. If it sold its land what would it do with the money? How could it ensure a regular income? Was it to lend out its money at interest, like Lombards or Jews? Was it to enter trade? ' 'Ee sell I my land,' urged John Leys, screwing his coat in his cracked hands. 'Where be sense in I draining and making betterer when t'land bain't mine proper but on t'lease solely? I be arter freehold desperd bad so as my land cass-n't be snatched off of I.' Again Novice Master shook his head. Leys' anger soared. 'I 'ool hae thee know my lass be going to wed with councillor's son,' he shouted, stamping dust all over the parlour floor. 'I bain't nobuddy. 'Ee cass-n't jigger I. 'Ee sits on t'arse and gobbles t'rents. . . .' When Novice Master did nothing but hide his hands in his sleeves and shake his head John Leys lost all control.

'T'abbey hae sold freehold to thakky Robert Cordwell,' he bellowed. 'Thakky bellying pig wi' red hair, un sold land to Robert Cordwell and there be Cordwell crowing like t'cocks all o'er t'village.'

But Novice Master had stopped hearing him. He shook his head like a pendulum, and after a time John Leys stopped shouting at him and went away. As soon as he reached the village he began spreading the story not only that the monks had taken a sacred vow never to sell any more abbey land but also that both candidates had sworn, the moment they were elected, to appropriate the village church and turn Rector out. Leys was well thought of in the village and they believed what he said.

When Brother Peter heard through the parlour wall what John Leys shouted about his daughter, he turned to ice. In spite of the unseasonal heat, that made even the inner walls warm, he shivered and gasped like a man plunged in icy water. Alice to marry a councillor's son? 'Bravo!' cried his conscience. 'Now she will be snatched away from your lust. Now you can free your mind for the life-long penance that is necessary to wipe out your sin.'

Brother Peter did not listen to his conscience.

His first instinct was to rush to find Alice, to snatch what solace he could before the storm broke over him. His second and prevailing instinct was to seek out the two candidates. He found Henry Osborne with Lord Wenlock in the Abbot's garden, planning where he would plant cherry trees when he was abbot. He bowed and asked him if he would resolve a problem that had arisen in discussion with the novices. He asked if under any circumstances it was possible for a monk to be absolved from his vows, so that he could return to the world and marry and live a layman's life. Henry Osborne saw no strangeness in the request. He replied that there was no absolution possible for a monk once he had taken his final vows. He was married to the Church and he could not be divorced from the Church. Brother Peter thanked him and withdrew. Five minutes before the bell rang for Sext he approached Nigel Woodville where he stood watching Brother Joseph groping his way towards the south transept.

He repeated his question. Nigel Woodville exerted his intelligence. 'Has this monk been ordained a priest?' he asked. Brother Peter, after hastily explaining that it was a hypothetical monk, replied that the monk was not a priest. 'Then I believe absolution from his vows might be possible,' said Nigel. 'Just as His Holiness the Pope will under certain circumstances declare a marriage invalid, so he might be prevailed upon to declare absolved the marriage of a monk and the Church.'

Brother Peter trembled. 'What would be . . . how could he . . .' he stammered.

'It would mean an application in person to the Papal Court at Rome,' Nigel explained. 'It would also mean a considerable sum of money. His Holiness is of course at this time greatly in need of money for his crusade against the infidels. I believe he might be prevailed upon, provided the monk was not also a priest.'

'Oh, he isn't, he isn't,' cried Brother Peter, hurrying away into Sext less miserable than he had been for months.

Nigel Woodville looked after him thoughtfully.

Released from Sext, Brother Peter obtained permission to search for herbs—how damnably useful those herbs were, his conscience grumbled—and he searched, heart pounding and loins on fire, until he found his love alone with the pigs in Amberley wood. At first he could not speak to her. He made a hollow for them both among the beech husks and he kissed her between the lips, the breasts, the thighs, damning himself by his passion over and over again. When the sun came level with the Selsely beeches he managed to ask her if it was true that she was betrothed to the councillor's son. She blushed then and said, 'I mun do what my da' tells I.' He hid his face in her hair to hide his tears. She tried to comfort him. 'Sweetheart, what for be 'ee come a monk? I wish 'ee bain't monk.'

Eagerly he began to justify himself, to speak of his four older brothers, the entailed land, his aversion for trade, his cleverness with his books, his father's debts and the inducements of Infirmarian's steward. 'I was only sixteen. I had never had a woman. I did not know. . . .'

But she could never understand. She stroked his shaved head and said: 'My da' 'oodna mind 'ee so be 'ee bain't a monk. My da' cass-n't bide a monk.'

Much later Brother Peter put on his cassock and, having helped her to collect her straying pigs, kissed his love good-bye with such sadness and desperation that she was moved to tell him just why she was going to marry the councillor's son. 'I mun best be wed soon,' she said. 'I do be going to bear a baba.'

'I doan't know,' muttered Brother Mark. 'I reckon as how t'Abbot spoke summat but I didna follow what un be.' He wished Henry Osborne would stop asking what the dying Abbot had said.

'Think, Brother Mark,' said Henry Osborne, smiling and turning one thumb over the other. 'I am certain you can think of a name Abbot Dominic might have said if you put your mind to it.'

Brother Mark did not answer. He stretched awkwardly to his task of unhooking bunches of onions from the ceiling so that he might count the ones behind. It did not occur to him to bend down and count them from underneath. Brother Mark was very stupid.

'You know my name?' pursued Henry Osborne.

Brother Mark nodded. 'Henry Osborne, an aitch and an "O",' he said, not without pride in his learning.

'The Abbot mentioned my name, did he not? I am sure Abbot Dominic spoke my name when you held his hands.'

Brother Mark said nothing. He had found silence his only refuge. Nigel, Abbot's Chaplain, Lord Wenlock, Thomas Woodville, Cellarer, they had all been badgering him to tell what the Abbot had said. Henry Osborne stooped and fondled the little cat who by now was so attached to Brother Mark she had to be shut out of the church for fear she might do something unseemly during a service.

'If you will say that Abbot Dominic spoke my name and

wished me to be the next abbot I will give you a dog and make sure you are allowed to keep him.'

But Brother Mark said nothing. Nigel had been wrong. Here was one monk who had no price. He simply did what Jesus told him to do and Jesus had not yet ordered him to divulge what name the Abbot had muttered.

Of all the interested parties who had stroked the little cat and made to Brother Mark much the same suggestions, Henry Osborne was the only one who reflected how thin the cat's tail was.

'Now you must sit still, Brother Joseph,' said Infirmarian gently. 'I have to soak off all this foxglove poultice and it will take a long time.'

Brother Joseph sat patiently while a hundred and fifty applications of foxglove ointment were scraped off his eyelids. For fifty days he had been moving in darkness, buoyed up by the hope that when the poultice was removed the darkness would go with it. He had been very good. He had enjoyed his tiny privileges. He had relished his hot baths and his warm wine, and had even joked that he did not mind losing his sight if it meant such delicacies and immunities. But he did mind. He was like a man chained to a stake who stretches his ears for the click of the flint. Until the spark flies and the faggots kindle there is always hope.

Infirmarian scraped with his spatula. After every sixth scrape he wiped the spatula on the edge of the basin. Under their sealed lids Brother Joseph's eyes rolled wildly. They charged about like live things, stirring the heavy eyelids. 'We are nearly finished,' said Infirmarian cheerfully. He crossed himself, then laid steaming pads in Brother Joseph's sockets. The minutes passed. Infirmarian led Brother Joseph to the window and sat him down with his back to the light. Behind the old man's head hung an oblong of periwinkle sky, a strip of pasture, a fringe of elm. *In nomine Patris, et Filii, et Spiritus Sancti*,' said Infirmarian, and took off the pads.

Brother Joseph's eyelids sprang up. Which of them ever forgot the cry of triumph and thanksgiving that burst from Brother Joseph as he looked up at Infirmarian and saw a nose, a mouth, two eyes, a gleam of teeth, a wooden Cross? 'I can see! God be praised, I can see!'

He had only one purpose. He shook off Infirmarian's supporting hand and scurried as fast as his legs could go along the way that he knew blindfold, along the kitchen yard, past the vaults, between the refectory and the dormitory, into the east cloister and so into his own scriptorium where there awaited him the parchments and paints and inks, the gold leaf and the quills and the charcoal, and psalm forty-seven with its fat scarlet 'O'. After him came half a hundred retainers, thankful for any diversion, and a dozen abbey servants and a score of monks; for this was the hour of recreation and what happier recreation could there be than to see an old man made happy?

Brother Joseph rushed up to his table and scrabbled for a script. He was confused by the scarlet stain on psalm forty-seven and it was some minutes before he laid his shaking hands on another script. This happened to be the *Te Deum*, with a silver 'T' like a gallows-tree that Brother Joseph recognized. He faced the crowd that had jammed itself in the doorway, the window, the cloister outside, and he read aloud, holding the manuscript between a finger and thumb still ingrained with ink. '*Te Deum laudamus te Dominum confitemur.*'

Everyone began to smile and nod, even the retainers, even the Rising Suns who had least cause to love Brother Joseph. '*Sanctus, sanctus, sanctus, Dominus, deus Sabaoth,*' said Brother Joseph, and the monks all beamed at him; their disturbed little world made suddenly tranquil by the thought of old Joseph back at his usual occupation, tongue between his teeth, gouty neck bent, labouring at scripts that no one would ever read. '*Per singulos dies benedicimus te et laudamus nomen tuum in saeculum et in saeculum saeculi.*' Yes, yes, they all praised Him for ever and ever for restoring his sight to Brother Joseph. '*In te, Domine, speravi; non confundar in aeternum.*'

The ancient voice faltered and stopped. The page slipped

from his fingers and Brother Joseph sank on to his knees and laid his ancient forehead on the stones. He was indeed confounded. He had hoped; and his hopes had gone up in flames. He had been deluding himself. He could not really distinguish the script. All the letters ran into one another, like a snake. He had been reciting the psalm from memory.

They rushed to comfort him. They reminded him that he might still be able to paint the capitals even if he could not write the script. Brother Leo was not a bad hand at script, they told him. But Brother Joseph refused to be comforted. The purpose of his life was gone. All the hot baths in the world could not make up for what he had lost.

When those inside the scriptorium tried to get out they found the door blocked by a crowd that was being squeezed inwards by the pressure of bodies in the cloister.

'Back!' shouted the King's retainers, breasting the crush with their Rising Suns.

'We want to see!' shouted Warwick's retainers from the cloister, hurling their White Bears against the bulging wall of backs. Soon the cries of 'Back!' and 'Forward!' were mingled with gasps of terror from those caught between, whose breath was being wrung out of them. 'Push, push,' yelled the retainers, exerting their muscles so long unemployed. One by one the monks and their servants were cleared away, kicked underfoot or pinned to the walls by retainers who struggled to damage one another. Violence suddenly flared like bracken in the heat. Knives came out and battle was joined, trampling over the bodies of men too dazed or terrified even to pray for deliverance.

'A Warwick! A Warwick!'

The old cry brought Lord Wenlock from the Abbot's garden. With the flat of his sword he began whacking at any hessian he could reach. Sacristan crawled out from under a table and began at the top of his voice to pronounce God's curse on the contestants. Brother Mark tried to bite every lay leg that presented itself to him. Cantor arrived and had the presence of mind to start ringing the service bell, whereupon the monks stirred and began crawling through the thrashing legs to the sound. Thomas

Woodville curled up under one of the desks but Nigel and Henry both leapt into action, tugging coats and shouting directions, for they did not want it said that they countenanced violence.

The turmoil subsided. Boots kicked for the last time. Blows lost their aim. Knives were wiped and shoved away. A cook rushed to the scene a pot of steaming stew and like hounds on a scent the retainers followed it, their hatred momentarily swallowed up by the rumbling of their bellies.

They left tragedy behind. Cloister and scriptorium were littered with bodies. There was scarcely a man left unmarked except Sacristan who had been cushioned by his own fat. Of the abbey servants three had broken arms, one a cracked skull, six had bruised ribs, Prior's steward a crushed finger and a kitchen boy a knife-wound in the groin six inches long.

Of the monks four had broken ribs and one a fractured shinbone. Brother Mark had lost five of his front teeth, Brother Peter had a gash on his left temple, Guest Master's right ear was half severed, and Abbot's Chaplain's beauty was marred by a broken nose. Brother Joseph was nearly frightened to death. Two monks were unconscious, the rest beaten and terrified. What terrified them was not simply the violence but also its precipitancy. One moment, it seemed, their world was full of good humour and gentleness and the next moment it was a storm of knives and fists and boots against which they could not count on either prayers or curses prevailing.

Eventually order was restored. Infirmarian and Brother Peter were a long time stitching and strapping and poulticing, but there was a complement of bandaged and limping monks to croak their way through Nones. Not for fire, flood, plague, battle or other disaster might a service be missed. Not by so much as a chink might the wall of devotions be weakened.

The retainers' cuts were bound up. Eventually the monks' hurts healed. The servants recovered, all but the kitchen boy with the slashed groin. He died that same night and was buried outside the walls in the servants' cemetery.

It was the first death.

123

10

I T WAS the Eve of Ascension. There had not been a drop of rain for three months. For eight weeks there had been no cloud that was not as white and woolly as a lamb's coat. In the village Rector said prayers twice a day for rain. But without result. The villagers were growing more and more silent as their livelihoods shrivelled and wasted and pined in the fields. They grew surly with fear and cuffed their children and lay with their wives more often than usual, clutching the only comfort, after their religion, that was left to them.

Inside the abbey prayers for rain were said on Fridays and Sundays. In here it was a time of religious joy when in their services the monks shouted 'Alleluia' and pictured the Son of God soaring up into heaven in a golden cloud to take his place in a blast of trumpets at His Father's right hand. But the monks too had their worries. Their spiritual joy could not completely silence their human anxiety. The morrow was Ascension Day and the day following was the day ordained by the Bishop for the official nomination of the candidates and for their first election speeches and for Prior to explain the form of the election, whether it was to be by common declaration or by deputation, whether by unanimous or by majority vote.

But Prior was missing. A week earlier he had ordered three horses to be saddled and had set off northwards with only two servants, leaving his officials to keep the retainers in order if they could. This was a hopeless task. They overran the abbey like rats, lumping fellows with leather boots and badges over their left breasts, half Rising Suns and half White Bears. They recognized no authority except that of their own particular patron, that is Warwick and his mouthpiece Lord Wenlock or the King and his mouthpiece Thomas Woodville; and Woodville and Wenlock were more often than not away on discreditable errands, sniffing out unsavoury information about their rivals and their rivals' supporters.

A crucifix still had the power to check these retainers but the authority it wielded was daily weakening. What would happen if it lost its power to halt them? They could hardly all be excommunicated. At least four out of the seventy now swarming in and out of the buildings had been heard to boast—publicly too—that they did not care if they *were* excommunicated. Each patron had an archbishop in his pocket who would receive them back into the Church quickly enough. Soon the wretched monks could scarcely draw breath without dirty and unshaven faces leering over their shoulders. Threats bounded about like tennis balls. Each monk was continually warned that if he did not, when the time came, declare loudly and enthusiastically for this candidate or that, his liver would be cut out, his face carved into fancy patterns, his bones broken one by one or his feet roasted over a slow fire.

In despair Sacristan sent a messenger to the Bishop begging him to hasten the final election, but the reply came back that the Bishop could not act without the King's permission. And the King was in no hurry. While the vacancy lasted he was receiving most of the Abbot's income, and Nigel Woodville had sent word that he needed more time to ensure success. Thomas Woodville's spies had done wonders but it would need very damaging evidence indeed to spoil Henry's chances.

It was time for Vespers. The shadow of the abbey spire stretched eastwards down the parched hill until it touched Rector's churchyard. The monks had run the gauntlet of the retainers' knife-points and had arrived, scratched and breathless, in the sanctuary of their choir. Before the service began they sank on their knees while Cantor, who was Priest for the Week, prayed that this cup might be taken from them. They rose for the first psalm, grunting softly at their half-healed hurts. Abbot's Chaplain fingered his broken nose, Guest Master the bundle of bandages that was his right ear. Brother Peter's temple throbbed. Brother Mark ran his tongue over his torn gums. Cantor had ordered him not to sing now that his front teeth were missing. 'Come unto my help, O God,' they sang; twenty-eight bewildered voices. 'O Lord, make haste to help me.'

Sacristan comforted himself with the thought of St Peter's toe-nails. That morning he had despatched his steward and a party of servants to meet the toe-nails at Bristol docks and to escort them to Woodchester Abbey. 'The Lord upon thy right hand hath overthrown kings,' sang Henry Osborne, confident that however long the King delayed the election the great Warwick's candidate would still triumph. His ever-optimistic rival, Nigel Woodville, thought hopefully of the King's enormous influence and of his own excellent schemes and of what he hoped was Prior's inclination towards himself. '*Non nobis, Domine, non nobis*,' they sang, '*sed nomini tuo . . .*'

Without warning the west door burst open. All eyes swivelled towards it. Stiff monastic necks creaked an inch in the right direction. '. . . *da gloriam*,' they sang, far too disciplined even to falter.

Through the tracery of the chancel screen they glimpsed two shapes silhouetted against the blazing sunlight, but only Cellarer, standing behind the lectern, had a plain view through the chancel gateway. He saw Prior, his egg-shaped head black against the light. He saw a donkey, such as passed the south gate every day except Sunday, laden with wool for the Stroud market. And sitting on the donkey he saw a strange man, whose bony ankles dangled far below the donkey's belly. Prior jerked the rope and the donkey moved forward, stepping delicately over the pavement of the nave and nodding his gentle head.

'O praise the Lord all ye nations,' sang the monks, eyes popping out their sockets. Then without a pause they burst into the antiphon. 'Alleluia, alleluia, alleluia!' At the last triumphant shout Prior and the donkey and the stranger came to a halt at the chancel gate. Prior could not have timed it better. Before Cantor could open his mouth to chant the Little Chapter, Prior said clearly: 'I wish to present to you another candidate for the vacant chair of abbot. This is Brother Ambrose, sub-prior of Tewkesbury Abbey.'

A silence followed so profound that they could hear the thoughts buzzing like startled bees inside their shaved heads. The donkey breathed softly. Sacristan thought: 'How thin he is! Only rigorous fasting can make a man so thin.' Guest Master thought thankfully that a man like this would not have any servants. One donkey was not much to feed. For an instant Novice Master saw Ambrose's eyes like flaming torches that endeavoured in vain to hold back the night, then he relapsed back into his own preoccupations. Brother Peter speculated about Ambrose's views on absolution from monastic vows and concluded sadly that he would never countenance it. Brother Joseph strained his poor eyes for a glimpse of Ambrose's features but he did not need to see him to know that here was an unusual man.

Boldly Nigel Woodville turned his head through ninety degrees and studied Ambrose's lined forehead, the hollow cheeks, the brooding eyes. Here was every monk's idea of a saint. Here was an ideal powerful enough to commit the vacillating prior. It remained to be seen whether Ambrose could commit the rest of the monks also. Under his new cassock Nigel braced his muscles. He could do so much for Woodchester Abbey! He would never give up the struggle. Never!

Not a flicker disturbed Henry Osborne's placid features but his bowels stirred. For the first time since his arrival at Woodchester Abbey he felt his position seriously threatened. In the opposite stalls Abbot's Chaplain ground his beautiful teeth together in fury. Who would have thought Prior capable of such independence? Something must have happened to him since the day he so tamely handed over the building fund. It would now be even more imperative that a way be found to make Brother Mark divulge what name he had heard Abbot Dominic mutter—provided of course that it was Henry Osborne's name.

And Brother Mark? Brother Mark's mouth dropped open.

It was Jesus Christ he had seen riding up the nave on a donkey, his naked toes dangling a foot above the pavement. He realized now, of course, that it was not Jesus Christ, but from that moment he gave his allegiance, heart and soul, to Ambrose.

All was dark. The monks were in their beds. Ambrose at his own request had eaten his evening crust in private, and had lain down blanketless on three planks laid over trestles in the punishment cell. He had taken off his hair shirt for the night and Prior had contrived to hang it up outside the cell in the hope that the monks would see it. In the draught from the dormitory door Brother Mark lay quiet, his ears stretched for the familiar scratch at the door. At last it came, very faint. Scratch, scratch. Brother Mark opened and shut the door and scrambled back into bed to feel the customary fur cushion under his feet. But the little cat was restless that night. She whimpered a little and could not keep still. In the morning at the hour of Prime when Brother Mark threw back his cover in the dawn he was greatly distressed to find the bottom of his bed soaked in blood and the cat's tail missing. To escape Chamberlain's wrath he simply turned over his straw mattress and said nothing. The little cat recovered and followed him, tailless, as jauntily as before. Brother Mark never examined the severed edges. He never doubted but that she had caught her tail in a door or a trap and for days, even after Henry Osborne had badgered him again about what name Abbot Dominic had spoken, he searched everywhere for the cat's tail in the hope that Infirmarian might stitch it on again.

He did not say the name Abbot Dominic had murmured because his lord Jesus had not yet told him to.

'I fear not, Brother Peter,' said Prior next morning. 'I have no authority to sanction pilgrimages. You must wait until our abbot is elected and then you must petition him.'

'But I most urgently wish to make a journey of devotion to the Church of St Peter's in Rome,' said Brother Peter. 'I was born on the feast of St Peter's chains. I long to see them with my own eyes.'

'Wait and see St Peter's toe-nails,' said Prior unsympathetically.

He had become very firm since Ambrose's arrival. He looked almost happy. He had not only found a man whom he thought might cure the sickness in the abbey, he had actually persuaded him to stand for abbot and his superiors to allow it. Truly God had blessed Prior's endeavours.

'Then may I not visit our daughter house at Viterbo?' pleaded Brother Peter. Viterbo was only forty miles from Rome, and in Rome lived the Pope, the only man in the world who could grant him dispensation from his monastic vows.

'You are very anxious to leave the abbey, Brother Peter,' said Prior. He creased his face and it was an instant before Brother Peter realized that he was smiling. 'But I cannot give you permission to go. You must wait until the new abbot is elected.'

Nigel Woodville would let him go, Brother Peter thought. Nigel would not be afraid to let his monks breathe the outside air. Nigel's eyes were fixed on a horizon beyond the walls of the abbey. 'Pray God the election will be soon,' said Brother Peter aloud.

'Pray God,' echoed Prior.

Brother Peter left Prior's room to join the community at High Mass. But so great had grown his dread of swallowing God's body while in mortal sin that he kept the wafer under his tongue and after Mass rolled it into a ball and tossed it to the doves in the Abbot's garden. It did not matter if the doves ate it because to them, as to Novice Master, it was no more than bread. Brother Peter did this every day after Ambrose's arrival.

After High Mass Nigel sought out Brother Joseph, whom he suspected of being influential if only on account of his great age, and set himself with youthful guile to the lessening of Brother Joseph's prejudice against himself. He found Brother Joseph in his scriptorium, hunched over a page of Brother Leo's indifferent script, endeavouring to insert red roses into the interstices of a capital 'M'. At Nigel's approach he raised his crimson weeping eyes and waited for his face to come into focus. Nigel sat down beside him.

'I fear your plums are out of place,' he said cruelly.

Brother Joseph straightened his rickety neck. 'They are roses,' he said, pressing his shaky lips together. 'Brother Leo's capitals are inadequate. I have spoken to him a hundred times but he will not splay the legs of the "M"s.' He picked up his paint-brush and, at the second attempt, managed to dip it in the paint-pot.

'That is blue,' said Nigel.

'I intend blue,' replied Brother Joseph coldly. There was no doubt he disliked Nigel Woodville extremely; as was only natural in an old monk of seventy years who had adored his dead abbot and who asked for nothing more than that life should amble on as it had always done, without any innovation—except a remedy for ailing eyes. Brother Joseph bowed his head to within six inches of the parchment and dabbed uncertainly at the capital 'M'.

'Let me do it for you,' said Nigel. It was the final indignity. With a screech of rage Brother Joseph dropped his brush and fell upon Nigel with such suddenness that the bench overturned and they crashed to the floor. Feebly Brother Joseph pummelled Nigel where he lay underneath him, striking out at all the horrors that in fifty years as a monk he had learned to fear—novelty, cleverness, independence, initiative. 'You shall never be our abbot!' he croaked at the loathed candidate lying passively underneath him. 'You shall never have my vote. Never, never, never!'

'You do not yet know that you will have a vote,' said Nigel quietly, feeling Brother Joseph's knuckles no heavier than a fly's feet. 'But if you do, Brother Joseph, I want you to vote for me.' By this fantastic impudence Brother Joseph's fists were actually frozen in mid air. His jaw dropped. 'If you vote for me,' said Nigel, 'I will give you something that will cure your eyes. I shall go after Chapter tomorrow to Gloucester to order it.'

There was silence. The prejudices of a lifetime melted a fraction at the edges. 'How can you cure my eyes? I am too old for the cauterizing. Infirmarian said I would die under the iron.'

'I can cure you,' said Nigel. 'I can make your eyes strong again so that you can write your scripts and decorate your capitals. When I am abbot I shall build a fine library and I shall have shelves built to accommodate all your beautiful texts, so that everyone may admire them.'

Brother Joseph froze again. 'I do not labour for the admiration of men,' he retorted.

Poor Nigel Woodville! He felt his task was indeed a hard one. However carefully he trod he was for ever putting his foot in trouble. He eased himself out from under Brother Joseph's hams. 'Think about it,' he told him. 'I can make you see properly again. Only tell the monks that you would like me to be your abbot and I will give you back your ancient skill.' He went out and closed the door behind him, leaving Brother Joseph squatting on the stone floor, staring at temptation.

When Lord Wenlock and Thomas Woodville arrived back, severally, at Woodchester Abbey that night, each received news of the third candidate with gloom. Prior begged them to stay in the abbey and try to control their retainers, but each replied that he must be off again as soon as the election Chapter was over, for there was business to be done. This business was of course to nose into Ambrose's past, but neither of them had great hopes of unearthing anything damaging. Each had found plenty to discredit the other's candidate but neither was prepared to divulge it yet. Like archers facing a charge, they had to be sure of finding their target before letting fly their arrows.

While in Woodchester Abbey servants scrubbed the stone floor of the Chapter House and polished the reading-desk for the morrow's Chapter meeting; while the retainers honed their blades and fornicated in the village; while Prior's steward badgered for rents; while Sacristan ordered two watchdogs to guard—when they arrived—St Peter's toe-nails; while Prior, for the first time in his monastic life, felt that a decision of his had been blessed by God; while Brother Joseph could not eat for speculating how Nigel Woodville could—but of course he could never pay such a price—cure his eyes; while Brother Peter yearned over his love and Brother Mark searched for the cat's tail; while Abbot's Chaplain mooned over his broken nose and Henry Osborne racked his brains for compulsive things to say at the Chapter meeting; while Nigel Woodville covered six pieces of parchment with notes of his ambitious schemes; while Novice Master brooded and the novice Andrew Alsopp screwed up his courage to speak; while Ambrose prayed and Guest Master paid another visit to Reuben Abraham in Gloucester; while Mistress Leys eyed her daughter's belly; while Rector scraped aside the last of his hay; while the sun shone pitilessly and there was talk in the village of killing the beasts for salting while they still had some flesh on their bones; while John Leys and his friends pictured famine staring at them and prayers for rain went unanswered and in the village the accumulated resentments of generations began first to steam and then to simmer . . .

Then Edward Mortimer, King Edward IV of England, Ireland, Wales and Calais, sat in his private room in Ludlow Castle and waited for his cousin Warwick. He was receiving him alone, impressed by the proud Warwick's letter, eager as always for any excuse to stifle uneasiness. King Edward was always anxious for people to love him. While he waited he felt his heart thumping under his blue-silk doublet, and he prayed that Warwick would not ask of him what he was not prepared to concede. The tapestries twitched.

'My lord Warwick,' said a voice, and here was Warwick in the flesh: slight, dark, his beard trim, his eyes brimming with involuntary affection. Like iron to a magnet the King was drawn to this old friend, this counsellor, the master-mason of his fortunes. His queen was forgotten. He stretched out his arms. Blue silk enfolded black velvet. Cheek was laid to cheek in the kiss of peace. It was two years since they had last met.

They sat side by side on the couch, the golden king and the dark earl, bitterness and distrust swamped by a warm tide of love. If only this tide could flow for ever! If only it could submerge for ever Warwick's pride and the King's ingratitude. If only these two could be trapped like this for ever, like flies in amber, enclosed in happy memories, united by old loves and old hates. If only the last five years could be wiped off the slate.

They plunged happily into the past.

'We must try a bout with the short swords, Richard, like we did when I was a boy.'

'Have you remembered that flick of the wrist, Edward?'

'Your god-child can say the first of her Pater Noster.'

'How long it seems since I held her at her christening. I offered twenty candles for your father York's soul, Edward, on his name day. I have only to shut my eyes now to see his bloody body hacked by the Bitch of Anjou's men.'

'May she burn in hell for it!'

'And for my father Salisbury's murder also.'

'Amen.'

The King poured wine and they drank from the same cup, turning it so that their lips touched the same spot.

'My arse aches still to think of that ride to Barnstaple.'

'Do you recall the fisherman? He had a carbuncle on his nose, on the right side——'

'No, the left.'

They argued contentedly.

'And how we slipped through the Bitch's ships and made Calais under Somerset's nose!'

'Do you remember the old scars, Edward? See that and that and that.'

'They have faded little, Richard, in seven years.'

'Do you remember how your father York pretended to be reconciled with the Bitch in 'fifty-nine. You were only a lad then. . . .'

133

'I watched from the balcony. They went two by two like a Noah's Ark and my father squeezed the Bitch's finger so tight he broke a bone and she did not dare squawk. . . .'

They roared with laughter.

'Do you remember . . . do you remember . . . ?'

Heedlessly they floated on their tide of recollection, drawing nearer and nearer to the dangerous torrents of the present.

'Henry of Lancaster babbles like a baby, Richard. He cannot walk or talk. The physicians say he will never recover his wits. The Bitch can do nothing. Should she win back the throne—which she never will—she has only an idiot husband or a bastard son to put on it.'

For a space they happily abused Henry of Lancaster's queen, the woman each hated most in the world; then thoughts of one queen brought thoughts of another.

'The Queen is to be confined in September. It will be a son, Richard, you will see.'

Warwick bowed. His ear had caught the rushing of torrents. 'I trust the Queen is in good health,' he said politely.

Politeness fell like a blight on the conversation.

'I trust my cousin Northumberland is in good health.'

'You must convey my good wishes to my cousin Clarence and my cousin Gloucester.'

'Let us hope your lady wife and your daughters Isabella and Ann are well.'

The refused dispensation rose like a wall between them.

'I am grieved that my cousin the Archbishop of York was peeved he did not receive a cardinal's hat.'

'I pray your father-in-law Earl Rivers is not crushed by the colossal weight of his responsibilities.'

'Let us hope Lord Mountjoy has found employment more suited to his capabilities.'

'And how does Lord Scales manage my Chamberlain's duties?'

'As well, I dare say, as Lord Wenlock is managing the Woodchester abbatical elections.'

The torrents poured over Warwick. They felt very chill.

He shifted uneasily and muttered, 'I regret that we cannot agree who should be the next Abbot of Woodchester.'

The King leaped off the couch and began pacing the room, kicking up the rushes with his long-toed shoes. 'Nigel Woodville is the man for Woodchester,' he shouted, so loudly that a servant popped his head through the tapestries and as quickly withdrew it. 'The abbeys need men of new blood. They are sinking into a rut, Warwick. Some of them are so grossly mismanaged they will soon not be able to pay me my taxes.'

'Do not worry, my lord. With a Woodville as abbot you need never fear for your Woodchester taxes. A Woodville will pay the King's taxes even if he has to take them from the offertory bowl.'

The insult brought blood to the King's face. 'The abbeys need a fillip,' he cried furiously, trying to justify his succumbing to his queen's whim. 'Think what they used to be in the Plantagenets' day. No man of birth dared die without willing large bequests to an English abbey. The abbeys harboured saints and learned men. Their libraries and hospitals were famous. They were the finest farmers in the land. Young men begged on their knees to become novices. Their chronicles were unrivalled. Their texts——' In his vehemence he flung his arms wide, hitting his knuckles against a silver crucifix. 'And what are they now, Warwick? Backwaters! Has-beens!' He lashed himself into enthusiasm. 'They can be great again, if only they elect the right abbots.'

'And who are the right abbots?' cried Warwick, jumping to his feet. Then, before the King could reply, he said: 'You do not care what kind of man is abbot. If it was Henry Osborne who was full of ambitious schemes you would still oppose him. If Nigel Woodville were a deaf mute you would support his candidature, simply because the Queen had asked you and because I favoured the other side.'

It was evident that both the King and Warwick had been kept well informed of events at Woodchester.

They stared at each other, appalled. Their breathing was heavy. Malicious devils sat in their ears, urging them on.

'It was you who set your candidate up against mine, Warwick. You want the Church to rot in a rut, to languish among the memories of past glories.'

'Why must you be for ever changing things, my lord? For ever surging forward into dangerous innovations? What was good enough for our fathers must be good enough for us.'

'My father did not find the government of England good, so he sought to change it. So did your father, Salisbury. So did you. You changed the government of England, Warwick. Why should I not change the government of an English abbey?'

'But I did not seek to change it!' cried Warwick in anguish. 'The King, yes. Because the King was mad and his counsellors corrupt and inefficient. But the King is not the whole government. He must rule with trusted and weighty advisers, the barons of his realm. And you——'

'And I have not?' The King's eyes flashed. 'I take for my advisers whom I wish, my lord Warwick. The barons are as much backwaters as the abbeys. What baron has a flair for business? What baron can add up columns in his head? What baron can write decent Latin or see further than the end of his own hall? What baron can tell me the best market for my wool? You would have me offend Burgundy and lose my wool market. If that is baron's advice then I will dispense with it.'

'And plunge England into war with Louis of France!'

'I deem it an honour to go to war with a leper who keeps a live monk in a cage and harbours the Bitch of Anjou.'

Passion had seized hold of them and was riding them to calamity, trampling underfoot the affections and obligations of the past.

'It is your duty to consult your barons.'

'You mean it is my duty to consult the Nevilles.'

'We won you your throne.'

'I won it for myself; I and my father York. I do not remember my lord Warwick being signally successful at St Albans the second time or at Ludford.'

'Northampton——'

'Northampton was won because Lord Grey deserted the

136

Lancastrians and Towton was won because God blew snow into the enemies' faces and I managed very well at Mortimer's Cross without you and do not tell me how you recovered the northern forts because a month later they fell to the Bitch again and were not recaptured for another year.'

It scarcely seemed the King's own mouth that spat out the scalding words.

'I have yet to see the Woodvilles' capabilities. By what right do they govern England?'

'By the right of the King's choice. I tell you I will appoint what counsellors I choose.'

'You are bound by English custom to summon all the barons to Parliament.'

'Custom is not law.'

'If that is your opinion, my lord, then you are not worthy of your throne.'

They glared and panted, now pale as ashes, now red as fire, knowing in their hearts they could never be reconciled; for an impassable rift had opened between them so that one stood in the past and the other in the future.

'Withdraw Henry Osborne from Woodchester Abbey!'

'Never. Withdraw Nigel Woodville from Woodchester Abbey!'

'Never!'

At length they parted. They did not kiss in peace. The bed was never used that the King had ordered for them to sleep in together.

On the evening of Warwick's departure the King elevated all his remaining brothers-in-law to the peerage, so that there were now fifteen Woodvilles or Woodville connections in a House of Lords that could seat only fifty—and of those fifty twenty-five were abbots, none of whom was of any significance. The King also bestowed the Constableship on his father-in-law, Earl Rivers, doubled his bodyguard of archers and refused to pay the wages of the Calais garrison. He sent money and encouraging messages to Nigel Woodville and precipitated the despatch of a marble statue of St Peter. He also begged Nigel to inform him as soon as he considered the time was ripe for the final election.

Warwick returned immediately to Middleham, giving audience at Ludlow only to Lord Wenlock. He paid the Calais garrison out of his own pocket, making sure they realized where the coin came from. He declined to escort the King's sister Margaret to Burgundy to marry the Duke Charles. He wrote letters both to Henry Osborne and to Abbot's Chaplain begging them to call on him for any assistance they required.

When eventually the King and Warwick received news of the third candidate they were not as perturbed as their advisers expected. For, however they might protest, their real preoccupation was the failure of the other's candidate rather than the success of their own. The election of a stranger, whatever his character, was infinitely preferable to the election of a man whose patron one had once loved and now dared love no longer.

11

IT WAS the day of the preliminary election Chapter. Beyond the baked sheepwalks of Minchinhampton the sun came up as bright as a copper coin. This sun held no mercy. It baked the earth as solid as stone. It withered leaves, roots, blades, even bark. The air was deathly still. The birds were too languid to sing. Sheep drifted sluggishly over the parched grass. Udders shrivelled. Lambs and calves pined away. Only the pigs kept any semblance of vitality, but they grew lean and savage among last year's acorns. In that quivering heat the end of the world approached very near. Villagers who never confessed more than once a year began to bombard Rector with their sins. As the Avon brook dwindled, so within themselves a latent spring of pessimism welled up; seeping into their veins, their arteries, their brains, muscles, bones and sinews; so that they walked about like men weighed down with chains.

God was angry. God had sent a drought to punish them, just as he had sent a plague on the Egyptians. In the evening, when they were protected from the sun by Selsely Hill, they gathered together in the churchyard and, enlivened by the shadows, bewailed their lot and grumbled about the monks whose well was still three-quarters full and about the monks' stewards who were dunning them for their rents and about the retainers who had got three girls with child already. Unfailingly in their midst was John Leys, his energies scarcely impaired by misfortune, exhorting them to dig for water, to salt their cattle, to drive their sheep into the woods, to set guards on their well, to ration the water. Dry as husks these villagers were, but they were not dead yet; and it is the driest tinder that leaps most readily into flame.

Nor was the abbey unaffected. In the shade of the cloisters

the monks sweltered in their woollen cassocks. The retainers stripped off their shirts, scandalizing the religious by their display of so much human flesh. The stewards squeezed the tenants hard for any coin they still had about them. So few had any money left that the stewards were in many cases reduced to accepting new fleeces in lieu. Outside the south transept Sacristan's watchdogs panted on the end of their long chains, waiting for the toe-nails that still had not arrived. Cellarer counted the grain sacks and reckoned they had a comfortable six months' supply provided the retainers were gone soon. If the milk supply failed they could import cheeses from Ireland. The cellars were well stocked with beer, wine, onions, hams, dried peas, oatmeal, flour, salt, raisins and spices. The abbey would not starve, despite the drought—but the retainers must go the instant the final election was over. 'Pray God the King does not delay the election,' he told Sacristan. But Sacristan was too worried about St Peter's toe-nails to reply.

Long before the hour for Chapter the retainers were encamped in the east cloister. Those that could find no space in the cloister squatted in the cloister yard. Those that could find no space in the yard seized the masons' ladders and leaning them against the east wall clambered up and clustered like flies round the unglazed windows. Thomas Woodville and Lord Wenlock pitched stools on the threshold, united only in their determination that the door should not be shut in their faces.

Chapter Mass was celebrated. A procession was formed of the monks and the three candidates. Nigel and Henry assumed the conventional expressions of piety. Ambrose did not have any need to alter his expression, nor would he have dreamed of doing so. There was no room for a circuit of the abbey so they contented themselves with a tour of the nave. Then they passed out of the west door, under the round Norman arch and the fine semicircles of dog's-tooth decoration carved by the Norman masons, and edged their way to the Chapter House. In silence they filled their places. On the dais, on the right of the Abbot's empty chair, with his back to the blazing windows, sat Prior. On his right sat Ambrose. On the left of the Abbot's chair sat Nigel Woodville and on his left sat Henry Osborne. Facing them on the long stone bench sat the officials: Cellarer, Sacristan, Guest Master with his ear still a lump of bandages, Novice Master, Infirmarian, Cantor, Refectorian and Chamberlain, and on the extreme end Abbot's Chaplain. Behind them sat the body of the monks, many still bandaged and bruised, one with his leg in splints and a crutch beside him. Behind them, in a line to the left of the open doorway, sat the novices who were present only as observers.

The monks tucked their hands in their sleeves and glanced at each other without turning their heads, in a manner perfected only by monks. The novices, free of their master's supervision, whispered and fidgeted. Behind both Wenlock and Thomas Woodville a retainer was posted, to relay the proceedings to his comrades outside.

Prior rose. He moved to the reading-desk, his shadow darkening one by one the faces of the officials below him, and plodded through the routine matters of the day. When he had finished, a ripple of expectation disturbed the shaved crowns. This day was a landmark in their placid territory, a red-letter day in their monotonous calendar. This was a day on which the Church actually expected them to think for themselves. Prior took into his right hand the Bishop's instructions. He had no need to collect their attention. Every ear within hearing was stretched to its limit. A hundred men were hanging on his words. Quietly he read the Bishop's letter. If no candidate was universally acclaimed, here and now, by the fully professed monks of the abbey then those monks were, here and now, to appoint six of their number. These six, together with Prior, were to be the mouthpiece of the abbey and would, on a day to be decided by the King, elect one man as Abbot of Woodchester. This final decision was to be unanimous. As in a papal election, they would be shut up in the tower until they signalled that they had come to an undivided opinion.

It would be the duty of Prior and these six chosen delegates to consider the wishes both of the monks and of God. Private considerations must play no part in their decision. They must pray for guidance and ruminate devoutly on which of the three candidates before them was the right abbot for Woodchester. The acclamation of the six delegates would proceed at once. These six, plus Prior, would elect the new abbot at some future date as yet undecided by the King.

Prior paused. A sigh of relief rose from the stone benches. Only six of them would have to face the final question of choice.

'Monks of Woodchester!' called Prior, hope fluttering in his heart. 'Is there one man you wish to acclaim with one voice as your new abbot?'

But there was silence. They faced the retainers' scowls at the windows. Retainers' eyes bored into their backs. There was not one monk brave enough to shout Ambrose's name. Better leave it to the delegates.

Three times Prior called and three times the monks silently shifted their responsibilities. Disappointment deepened the creases between Prior's eyebrows. He mopped the sweat off his bald head, frustrated in his hope that Ambrose would be spontaneously acclaimed and the whole affair finished and done with.

'Before choosing the six delegates,' he announced, 'the convent will listen to the addresses of the candidates.' He sat down with a sigh and Nigel Woodville rose, clutching his parchment sheaves. As youngest candidate it was his misfortune to speak first.

Nigel eyed the ranks of religious, itching to know the six he was addressing, depressed by the knowledge that Prior was committed elsewhere and had the power to hold up a decision indefinitely. But Nigel was optimistic and young and determined that a good report of his endeavours should reach the ears of the King.

'Monks of Woodchester,' he began—and then he was away, rolling on the billows of his own excellent intelligence, instructing the monks exactly how their abbey could be made rich, efficient, famous, popular, a paragon among abbeys. 'I will make this abbey renowned throughout Christendom,' he cried, losing all his parchments in his enthusiasm. 'You complain that, for all her vast possessions, your abbey is in debt. You complain that scarcely any of the officials' funds show a profit. Pilgrims never knock at your gates. The number of novices decreases yearly. Soon, you say, there may be no novices at all and then who will maintain the Holy Offices? The villagers dislike your abbey. No men of learning visit it. Your late abbot was of no account in the King's council. Brothers, there is a sickness in this abbey and if you will elect me as your abbot I will cure it.'

He paused to retrieve his parchments and Abbot's Chaplain sniffed very loudly through his broken nose. Brother Peter's eyes shone and he forgot the throbbing of his temple, for in Nigel he recognized his best hope. Brother Mark heard but did not understand a word. Novice Master never even heard. The mention of pilgrims set Sacristan wondering if after all Nigel Woodville did intend to present a statue to grace St Peter's toe-nails. Silently Guest Master swore that nothing on earth would induce him to vote for a man who would make such a vigilant and efficient abbot. And Brother Joseph shuddered with loathing while at the same time wondering if perhaps Nigel Woodville was hoping to cure his eyes with the ashes of a coal-black cat.

Nigel proceeded to give them details of his cure. 'We must have a central administration,' he told them. 'These separate funds are wasteful and inefficient.' Guest Master closed his eyes. 'Our possessions must be properly valued. Rents must be increased and rigorously extracted. Income must be distinguished from capital. We must have a lay bursar to oversee the accounts. The Abbot's income must be open to convent inspection.' Abbot's Chaplain raised his elegant hands towards the roof. 'We must take back our old domain and farm it ourselves instead of relying only on our rents and leases. We must set the peasants an example of efficient farming. We must enclose large areas and raise sheep and find better methods of drainage and irrigation. By farming some of our own lands we shall treble our income in five years.'

On the threshold Thomas Woodville crossed one puce leg

143

over the other. 'Woodchester will become a place of pilgrimage. When I am abbot I will erect a shrine for our holy relics that will draw pilgrims from the far ends of England.'

'Then he does not intend to give the statue unless he is elected,' thought Sacristan.

'We can make this abbey into a famous centre of learning,' cried Nigel, oblivious of the stunned stares of the officials in the front row. 'I will make a great library instead of a new Chapter House.'

Here Abbot's Chaplain rose to his feet and slowly sat down again. 'If we take back all our quarries into our own hands we can raise the building for half the cost. I have the word of the Earl of Worcester that he will give us Greek and Latin manuscripts. With the pilgrims' offerings we can buy many beautiful and learned books that wise men will be glad to consult. We can buy printed books and lend them to poor scholars.'

Printed books! Brother Joseph could not believe his ears. Printed books! 'What an honour,' cried Nigel, beside himself with excitement, 'to be the first English abbey to install its own printing-press and print works of devotion, works of scholarship, works . . .'

Poor Nigel Woodville! Every word he uttered was a nail in his coffin. They stared at him glassily. Their brains reeled. Greek! Lay bursars! Printing-presses! Farming! What would their peace be worth if Nigel Woodville became abbot? Like dust in the corner they shrank from the new broom. They longed to lie quiet in their cosy obscurity, not be swept into a hustle and bustle such as they had fled from as young men. As Nigel expanded his views the monks, all except Brother Peter, grew stonier and stonier. Nervously Thomas Woodville twisted his yellow ringlets. Henry Osborne twiddled his thumbs. He smiled. He did not fear competition from this quarter. Ambrose studied his gaunt toes and felt God's spirit rising in him like sap.

'The King wishes you to elect me as your abbot,' concluded Nigel in triumph. 'If you elect me I will make Woodchester more famous than Winchcombe.'

He sat down. He was hailed by a deathly hush. He dabbed his mouth nervously, sensing his failure. In the cloister yard the King's retainer reported the gist of the speech, which was greeted by a mixture of cheers and jeers.

Prior waved a hand and Henry Osborne rose. In the windows retainers eased themselves into more comfortable positions. Lord Wenlock leaned forward with his hands between his knees. Henry turned slowly to the left and then slowly to the right so that the monks could study his profile, so reminiscent of Abbot Dominic's. He smoothed his skirts as Abbot's Chaplain had instructed him and cleared his throat with a recognizable imitation of Abbot Dominic's wheeze. And suddenly their dead abbot was amongst them again, smiling at them with his back to the morning sun, predictable, human, unimaginative, impressionable, conservative, kindly—and safe.

'Monks of Woodchester,' said Henry Osborne. 'Our Lord said it was foolish to put new wine into an old bottle for fear it would shatter the bottle. Brothers, I shall pour no new wine into this ancient abbey. I intend no sacrilegious innovations. I shall not damage the sacred fabric of the past.'

Abbot's Chaplain smiled with pleasure at his own fancy phrases. There was a slackening of monastic muscles. Henry Osborne raised his left hand, bending forward his first finger so that in silhouette it seemed to have been amputated at the big joint, as Abbot Dominic's had been. 'If you elect me as your abbot your hallowed life shall continue unchanged. I shall not touch the administration. I shall rob no official of his duties. I shall never become preoccupied with riches and fame. It is an unholy slur on your late beloved abbot for a youthful and inexperienced man to talk of reversing the policy of his elders and betters. What does Nigel Woodville know of convent life? What right has he to dictate the fortunes of this monastery? He has been a monk for only a few days. I have been a monk for thirty years. Elect me as your abbot and your abbey will be safe from interference for ever.' He made gestures of sitting but a murmur from Abbot's Chaplain jerked him up again. 'If you are anxious to attract more novices,' he declared, 'spread it abroad that the monks here are now allowed one month's holiday each year instead of two weeks and that the pocket-money is now five shillings a quarter instead of three shillings. Tell people that in future there are warm socks during bitter weather and that monks here no longer have to learn the whole psalmody by heart. I promise you that when I am abbot there will be no lack of novices.'

On the left of the doorway the novices whispered in excitement. Brother Peter began calculating the cost of the journey to Rome in terms of increased pocket-money. Guest Master gloated over how easily he could pull the wool over Henry Osborne's eyes. Abbot's Chaplain exulted in having the future abbot in his pocket. Brother Mark stared at Ambrose. He had the strangest feeling, as if his heart was tied to Ambrose's heart by a long string which was being steadily wound round a winch somewhere inside Ambrose's emaciated chest.

'It is no part of a monk's duty to farm or quarry or run a printing-press,' Henry Osborne declared. 'A monk's duty is to pray for miracles and sing the services and get to heaven as quickly as possible. If the abbey wishes to add to its income let it appropriate the incomes of the parish churches.'

Brother Joseph beamed. Here was a man after his own heart. But he wished all the same that the man he wanted as abbot could be more to him than a black blur surrounded by blinding light.

'A sound fellow, a sound fellow,' thought Sacristan, 'he will never throw doubt on the validity of miracles.'

'I have reason to believe,' concluded Henry Osborne, who was not by nature an untruthful man, 'that on his deathbed Abbot Dominic uttered my name. . . .'

Ambrose lifted his head and looked straight into Brother Mark's eyes. Brother Mark heaved himself to his feet. 'Un ne'er did thakky!' he roared. 'Un said sommat name but un bain't yourn neither!'

All heads twisted in one direction. Henry turned pale. Hope blossomed in Thomas Woodville's heart. Pandemonium broke out in the cloister yard. Prior clanged his bell and shouted:

'You should have spoken sooner, Brother Mark. On your holy oath you must tell us what name Abbot Dominic said.'

'Hold your noise!' roared the retainer at the door. 'Hush up there. He be going to let on who old Dominic wanted for t'Abbot.'

Brother Mark filled his lungs with air. 'Jesus!' he shouted. 'Un said Jesus. Thakky be what un said. Jesus.'

Jesus!

Now there was only one man who looked like Jesus and that was Ambrose. All eyes turned towards him. Slowly he rose and stretching out his arms in the attitude of the Cross cried: 'O Lord, have mercy upon us, miserable sinners. Break the chains of our sins. O monks, repent you of your sins. Pray for the sins of the world.'

The monks' jaws dropped. Ambrose's high voice floated out into the cloisters, hushing the uproar. It was as if he had struck a note to which even the rudest ear was tuned. Brother Mark fell on his knees. For the first time in days Novice Master focused his eyes on reality and felt the rawness of his four ulcers.

'*Dies ira, dies illa . . .*' cried Ambrose. 'On the Day of Doom the world shall be laid in ashes, every sin, every deed, every thought, shall be dragged from hiding. How then shall our lives appear, when even the holy shall be afraid? What must we do to prevent God casting us into the burning pit on that terrible day. Kneel down in prayer! Repent of your transgressions! Cast out lust, covetousness, pride, anger, gluttony, avarice, deceit, malice and worldly preoccupations. Cheat Satan of his nourishment. Let us furnish here a hearth whereupon may be kept for ever burning the fire sent down from heaven. Turn your backs on sauntering comfort. Be a shining example to this faithless and slippery age. Burn out the rottenness that crawls through the body of the Church. . . .'

One by one the monks fell on their knees. They were carried out of themselves. Cries burst from them. Guest Master's deceit, Brother Peter's lust, Abbot's Chaplain's vanity, Sacristan's temper, Prior's weakness, Brother Mark's incompetence, Brother Joseph's pride—all their sins swelled to terrifying size.

Hell gaped at their feet. The sun in their eyes was like a consuming flame.

'Repent!' cried Ambrose. 'Fix your eyes on Christ's passion. Suffer as he suffered. Mortify your flesh. Deny yourself comforts. Become the salt of the earth. Emulate the saints and martyrs. Cast aside your servants, your fleshpots, your creature comforts. Watch and pray that you may gain heaven all the sooner. Distribute your wealth in alms. Labour in the fields as St Benedict instructed. St Benedict said "To labour is to pray" and in Thessalonians it is written "If any would not work neither shall he eat." '

Hands fumbled in the sign of the Cross. Many retainers burst into tears. Lord Wenlock knocked his forehead on the stone floor. Even Thomas Woodville stopped twiddling his curls and groped for his rosary. Only Novice Master sat on undisturbed by the general hysteria. Monks prostrated themselves on the pavement. 'I have made the right choice,' thought Prior triumphantly. 'Surely they will acclaim him now.'

But they did not.

At last the ecstasies subsided. The monks wiped their faces and dusted their skirts. Ambrose lowered his arms and sat down. With a calm that belied his bitter disappointment Prior called on the monks to name their six delegates. For a long time there was silence. Then at last a bashful voice whispered a name, then other bashful voices whispered other names. Names were timidly advanced from the stone benches. In voices made hoarse by their recent lamentations, the monks of Woodchester croaked the first names that came into their heads, until six names were scrawled on the stone wall. Brother Joseph. Sacristan. Brother Peter. Brother Mark. Guest Master. Novice Master.

Why were they chosen? Why indeed? Who can explain the vagaries of choice of men unaccustomed to thinking for themselves, of men temporarily carried out of themselves by religious ecstasy? Some voted for the monk sitting next to them. Some voted for the oldest monk, some for the youngest. Some voted for Brother Peter because they had no conception of his admiration for Nigel Woodville and because he had stitched their cuts and bathed their bruises. The most recently professed monks voted for Novice Master. Some voted for Sacristan because they remembered him quelling the retainers at Mass. Several of the older monks voted for Guest Master in order to spite Abbot's Chaplain whose sworn enemy he was. Abbot's Chaplain's name was not so much as breathed, for since his nose had been broken in Brother Joseph's scriptorium his old authority had been halved. On that day his beauty had been robbed of its power to blind men to his sins.

The six chosen monks ranged themselves with Prior at the foot of the dais and all seven swore a holy oath that they would unanimously elect, on a day to be decided by the King, a new abbot for Woodchester. And the rest of the convent swore an oath that they would accept whatever abbot the seven decided on.

The Chapter concluded with a prayer; then the monks once again formed their procession and proceeded back to their choir, under the west porch and the dog's-tooth decoration, to sing Terce and Sext and celebrate High Mass.

Lord Wenlock rode off immediately for Monmouth, where Ambrose had been born, hoping to ferret out unpleasantnesses about this candidate who contained more authority in the tip of his skinny finger than Henry Osborne contained in his whole ample body. But although he left Woodchester before noon he and his party did not pass through Gloucester until six hours later. Thomas Woodville, aghast at an election speech that had no basis in reason and therefore could not be countered with reason, paid a visit to the infirmary to consult with Infirmarian about a devil that was gnawing his breastbone. Infirmarian and Brother Peter were both at Mass but Thomas Woodville waited for them a long time, alone in the small ward. Eventually he left without seeing them.

Straight after High Mass Nigel Woodville also rode towards Gloucester, for his intelligence told him that religious ecstasies were often temporary and that it might be possible despite his reception to bribe his way to victory, being well supplied with royal funds. He reached the city safely and ordered a cure for Brother Joseph's eyes from a shop in Northgate. At three o'clock he and his three servants directed their horses' feet back along the Stroud road.

News of the Chapter spread quickly to the village. With seventy retainers whoring and drinking in the neighbourhood information did not stop long inside the abbey walls. A mass of men gathered in the churchyard, for now that their skinny sheep were sheared and their wilting hay cut, there was little they could do in their parched fields. Their lips were cracking. Their throats were choking with the dust that covered everything: trees, houses, grass, stones, ponds—or what was left of the ponds. To these frightened men things were beginning to look larger than life. Famine stared them in the face. Drought was a calamity they could do nothing about. They could no more make it rain than they could cure a plague or quench a forest fire or hold back a flood. Only God could do that and it did not seem that God was pleased with Woodchester at this time.

'Can 'ee wonder at un?' shouted John Leys, clutching clumps of his red hair. 'Thikky bain't God's work they abbey-lubbers be a-doing. 'Ee heared what be afoot in t'abbey's innards. Them be going to turf we off of ourn land. Them's a-buying up t'leases and tilting we out. Whereby be us going to live then? Be us to moil for thakky monks at a penny a day?'

'Surely they cannot intend to farm *all* their land themselves,' said Rector mildly. 'And there is such a thing as tenants' rights. You could take it to the courts.'

'Oh ar! And what be un going to cost we? Where be cash to bribe t'jury? And what do happen when thakky monks send them retainers to wallop t'judge? I 'ool give 'ee courts! There bain't no brave justice for such as we.' There were growls of agreement. 'And now them do blather of swiping back t'quarries,' pursued John Leys, who was a man who struck hard on hot iron.

A thick-set man with yellow hair threw up his arms. 'Swiping t'quarries?' he exclaimed. 'But I hae rented t'quarry for ever, and my da' and my da's da'. They monks be going to snitch un off of I?' He spat. 'I 'ool see un in hell first.'

'Thakky be whereabouts un do belong,' snarled a man with black whiskers. 'Them guzzles salmon and sucker-pigs and screws t'rents out of we. . . .'

'Them 'ool be a-turning Rector out of t'church straight-ways,' put in John Leys.

They muttered and shook their fists at the grey walls that loomed over them.

'Them doan't do nought for we,' shouted a man with a hare-lip. 'Squatting on thairn arses . . .'

Rector raised his hand. 'They pray,' he reminded them. 'They say the holy services and are nearer to God than ordinary men. They are the Church's bulwark against Satan. I have always taught you that a monastery must be revered because it is the haven of orthodoxy. Our Catholic faith is nowhere safer than within those abbey walls.'

They shuffled their dusty feet. Their eyes dropped. It was true. They could not deny it. Monks lived holier lives than common people, that was something they had known from their cradles. They said prayers. . . .

'Them bin saying prayers for t'rain,' grumbled John Leys, 'and nought be come of un. Where be good of being holy when nought come out of un?'

The man with the hare-lip said, 'There 'ool be a-walloping if them retainers doan't keep thairn mitts off of my cabbages.'

'Reckon there bin a lamming up in t'abbey, there be half of un wappered and slashed and scathed.'

They burst into grievances. They shouted and wrangled, made violent by the heat and the dust and their dread of famine. At length Rector gave up trying to quiet them. He sought refuge in his haybarn and continued scraping aside the last of his old hay to make room for the new that was being carted up the next day. His rake struck something, a small object. It was

a minute-glass. Carved on the bottom was a tiny replica of
St Peter.

'I 'oon't tell 'ee!' screamed Alice. 'I 'oon't, I 'oon't!'

The belt descended again and again across her naked back.
John Leys had stripped her of her clothes to shame her and was
beating her to make her tell who had got her with child. 'I
'ool jigger un! I 'ool hackle un! I 'ool larrop his'n guts! 'Ee bist
spoiled goods. Councillor's lad 'oon't wed with 'ee now.' He
gave a last lash, then flung the belt into a corner and jerked
her face upwards on the mattress.

Her golden plaits were soiled with sweat. She crossed her
arms over her trembling belly. She was not surprised. She had
known she would be beaten sooner or later, when her mother's
sharp eyes spied her secret. John Leys seized her shoulders and
shook her as a dog shakes a rat. Her breasts jumped. 'Tell I who
t'man be! Tell I and he 'ool marry 'ee even if I mun bust un in
shatters.'

Alice gasped for breath. 'I 'oon't tell 'ee!' she blurted out.
'Un canna marry I. Un be married.'

In fury John Leys struck her on both cheeks. 'Slut! Whore!
Thikky bain't no rape, else thee 'ood hae hollered long since.
A lass of mine tumbling in t'hay——'

Alice gave a cry of terror. Her hands flew to her mouth as
the chance arrow struck the target. John Leys sank down on his
hams in front of her. 'In t'hay?' he said, with a dreadful softness.
'What hay?' Alice squeezed her lips together. 'What hay?'
When he saw she would not speak he fetched his belt from the
corner. He twisted the punched end round his fist and swung
the buckle to and fro, to and fro, like a pendulum before her
eyes. ' 'Ee split who un be and where 'ee bin with un or I 'ool
larrop 'ee into shreds and none 'ool cobble 'ee up neither.'

'I 'oon't split, I 'oon't! There bain't no good I telling. Un be
married. Un cass-n't marry I.'

John Leys flourished the buckle round his head. 'I can lam

un!' he bellowed. 'And bust his'n bones and burn his'n house.'
A devil seized hold of him. He slashed the buckle across her belly.

Alice shrieked. As the buckle was raised for another blow
she screamed: 'Rector's barn! In Rector's barn!'

Appalled at his own violence John Leys dropped the belt,
thankful that he could stop beating her without losing face.
'Bide 'ee there then,' he told her. 'And 'ee best pray for un, for
when I find un I 'ool lam t'flesh off of his'n bones.'

He went out and down the ladder. He went to see Rector
but before he went he sent up her mother to her with foxglove
ointment.

During the hour of conversation the novice Andrew Alsopp
begged audience of Prior. He had at last screwed himself up to
speak. As Prior listened to him the stones began to tremble under
his feet. The walls shook. The room spun round. He clung to the
table with whitened knuckles. 'On Friday,' he heard Andrew
Alsopp say, 'he told us that the wine was not really Christ's
blood but only to put us in mind of Him. And yesterday he
made James Coles read out of Luke where it says "Do this in
memory of Me" and he told us that the Church is deluded in
thinking the bread really turns into flesh. He said it was never
certain in the old days and it was not made holy doctrine not
until Paschasius in the ninth century. . . .'

Prior listened aghast and his spirit, buoyed up by Ambrose's
holiness, sank like a stone. Heresy! Heresy in an abbey! Not in
some inexperienced and hysterical young monk but in an
official, a priest, a Novice Master responsible for the moulding
of the novices' minds. If heresy could creep in among professed
monks what hope was there for the ignorant peasants? And this
was no minor heresy like questioning the virgin birth or doubting if monks should go hunting or refusing to pay tithes to an
immoral parson. This heresy struck at the roots of the Church,
at the rock bottom of the Catholic faith. Whoever doubted the
miracle of the Mass was no better than a Moslem or a Hindu.

At length Andrew Alsopp stopped speaking. Prior opened his eyes and told him in a trembling voice that he had done his duty and God would bless him for it. He might now return to his master and tell him Prior wished to speak to him in his room. Before he went Andrew Alsopp explained that he would have spoken sooner but he had been expecting Henry Osborne to report what he had heard, considering it only right that he should leave such a serious matter to a senior monk, but when nothing happened . . . Yes, yes, he had done his duty, Prior told him, and might go now. As soon as he was alone Prior sank on his knees and prayed God to lift this curse from Woodchester Abbey. He prayed that Novice Master might be cured of his delusions and scandal avoided. He prayed that the King might allow the final election soon so that the abbey could be freed of the retainers. He prayed that the six delegates might agree with him in electing Ambrose as abbot. Surely now, when they found heresy in their midst, they would see their need of a holy and ascetic man.

The door opened and Novice Master entered with the exalted aspect of an early Christian braving the lions' den. He dragged his left leg on which three of his ulcers had bitten down to the bone and released putrid matter. Shakily Prior rose from his knees. He pressed together his trembling hands. 'Novice Master,' he said at last. 'I have heard that terrible errors have crept into your teaching. I wish you to repeat after me the cardinal beliefs of the Church and swear to me on God's Holy Scriptures that you believe them to be the truth.' He placed a bible in Novice Master's hands. 'I believe . . .' he began.

But he got no further.

The door crashed open and in burst Sacristan; scarlet, sweating, speechless with rage and horror. His monstrous cheeks shook with fury. He gabbled incoherently, unable to decide which ghastly bit of news to impart first. At length he achieved speech, saving the worst calamity for the last.

The Abbot's ruby ring was missing!

Monks of Winchcombe had attacked Sacristan's servants on their way back from Bristol and had stolen St Peter's toe-nails!

12

Prior almost sank beneath his burdens. Had it not been a mortal sin he would have wished to drop dead. What had they done to deserve such punishment?

Even heresy was momentarily forgotten in the panic. Sacristan heaved himself on to his horse, tucked his skirts round his thighs and, despite the hour, galloped away northwards to Winchcombe; and after him rode a straggle of retainers, White Bears and Rising Suns, eager for an evening's sport. They never had their sport. They found the gates of Winchcombe closed and barred. Sacristan pounded the oak and bellowed that they were to give him back his relic but the only reply he got was the clashing of Winchcombe's bell. Sacristan shook his fists. 'Thieves! Thieves!' he roared. 'Now I know St Kenelm's corpse is a fake or why should you want to steal St Peter's toe-nails?'

Eventually he turned away, muttering most unholy curses, and they trailed back to Woodchester in the moonlight to find village and abbey both wide awake and agog with the scandal that Novice Master had been confined to his room under suspicion of unorthodoxy and that Prior had sent a message to the Bishop. Abbot's Chaplain had already set a rumour circulating that the Abbot's ruby ring, which ever since Abbot Dominic's death had been locked in an oak chest with three locks in the Abbot's lodgings, had been made off with by Nigel Woodville, who had unaccountably not returned from Gloucester.

At dawn Sacristan sent a messenger galloping to the Bishop asking for dispensation to take a party of armed men to break down Winchcombe's gates.

Immediately after Prime the barber arrived for the customary three-weekly tonsure-shaving. He scraped the monks' pates and carried back strange tales with him to Stroud, but he never shaved Brother Peter because Brother Peter deliberately avoided him. First he hid in the latrines then, when there was no religious in sight, he slipped out by the north gate and went in search of Alice. Before he found her in the woods, still smarting from her beating, he had once to hide in the brushwood to avoid being seen by Ambrose, who was toiling northwards alone on his donkey. He lay with her among last year's acorns and was so lost in his love that he arrived back in the abbey too late to go into Chapter. But such was the excitement in there no one missed him.

'I say it is Nigel Woodville who has done this thing,' cried Abbot's Chaplain in his choir voice. 'He has been staying for weeks in the Abbot's lodgings. It would have been easy for him to steal my keys in the night and extract the ring. And where is he? Why has he run away if not to sell the ring? I tell you he is a thief and a deceiver, not at all the man to be abbot.' He fingered his broken nose. 'Think what a serpent you have been hiding in your bosom! A man who would steal the Abbot's sacred ring! But what can be expected of a candidate who maintains such sacrilegious advisers?' and he pointed an accusing finger at Thomas Woodville where he was throwing dice in the doorway.

Thomas Woodville sprang to his feet. Abbot's Chaplain's sneers suddenly pricked him into prematurely letting fly one of his cherished arrows. 'And who are you,' he shouted, dancing with rage on his skinny legs, 'to cast stones? *You* are a deceiver, Abbot's Chaplain. You took priest's orders and you are not a whole man!'

Not a whole man! Even the novices knew what that meant. Every eye within range fastened itself on the unfortunate Abbot's Chaplain, on the skirts of his cassock. Not a whole man! It was a most serious charge.

'I am! I am!' Goaded by vanity Abbot's Chaplain tore at his girdle.

'I have proof,' shrieked Thomas Woodville. 'He is not a complete man. I can bring women from his village . . .'

Pandemonium broke out in the cloisters. Retainers bandied obscenities about. The monks shut their eyes but not so tightly that they did not see Abbot's Chaplain fling off his girdle, cassock, drawers and shirt and jump naked on to the dais in front of a distraught Prior and an embarrassed Henry Osborne. 'Now say I am not a whole man,' challenged Abbot's Chaplain, his chest flushed with anger. Appalling ruderies poured from Thomas Woodville. There were bellows of mirth from the retainers.

'Come on, then!' they encouraged him. 'Let we be seeing how whole 'ee be! There be plenty here . . .' The monks poked their fingers in their ears, horrified by such mud flying within sacred walls.

'I am a whole man,' intoned Abbot's Chaplain. 'In canon law I am a whole man.'

'What about common law?' shouted a wit.

Thomas Woodville did not pounce on Abbot's Chaplain's damaging declaration. It was enough that he had smeared him. There were plenty more shames to be exposed—at the right moment.

At last order was restored. Abbot's Chaplain dressed himself, gnashing his teeth in fury because Lord Wenlock had not divulged to him the reports of his own spies. How he could have struck back if only he had had the information!

Prior marshalled his monks and hustled them into the choir for Chapter Mass. The creases in his forehead were like knife-wounds. Where was Ambrose? Where was Nigel Woodville? Where was the Abbot's ring? What if they could not persuade Novice Master to retract? What would the Bishop say? When, oh when, would the King give permission for the election of the Abbot? In these last days Prior had almost come to thinking that any abbot would be better than none at all. The hours dragged. Servants made preparations for the Bishop's visit.

Prior hunched his shoulders over the accounts. He allowed himself to be persuaded by Guest Master that the guest fund could not finance the Bishop's visit. He had a stormy interview with Abbot's Chaplain. He informed him that Abbot's funds must finance the Bishop's visit but he won his point only after promising Abbot's Chaplain that no one would tell the Bishop about Thomas Woodville's serious accusation. When he was alone, Prior sank inch by inch down on to the stone floor. The King and Warwick between them had sent into the abbey violence, suspicion, slander, hatred—and now blackmail.

Straight after Chapter Mass Thomas Woodville rode off to Gloucester to Silver Street to which certain of his spies had directed his attention. Two hours after his departure an ox-cart drawn by a team of four lumbered to a halt at Avon brook. It contained a mysterious shape wrapped up in straw and sacking and fastened to the sides of the cart with hemp ropes. Accompanying the package, which measured seven feet by three feet by two feet, was a courier in the King's livery who was accompanied by eight royal servants. He carried in his panniers two other mysterious parcels sewn up in hessian. Four more oxen were borrowed to lug the cart up the precipitous slope to the abbey's north gate and into the Abbot's garden.

'For Nigel Woodville,' said the courier. Twenty servants eased the shape off the cart and laid it down in the shadow of the north transept. Prior saw the two small packages safely into Abbot's chest and hung the keys on his own girdle. The courier demanded in the King's name the Abbot's rents for that quarter. In vain Abbot's Chaplain and Prior pleaded the Bishop's visit and the cost of the retainers. During a vacancy these rents were the King's due and the King had no intention of giving them up. When the courier departed with his escort that afternoon his panniers were bulging with the last of the Abbot's stock of coin.

Still neither Ambrose nor Nigel Woodville returned. The baking hours crawled by. Between services Sacristan prowled in the Abbot's garden and eyed the shape. His sausage fingers itched to rip off the packing. After High Mass he led round the panting watchdogs and hitched their chains to the Abbot's fig tree which grew at the west end of the shape. They were grey dogs, lean as wolves. No one but Sacristan fed them. He put them on guard, patted the shape, and waddled off to try to persuade Novice Master to recant. In spite of the arrival of the shape he was very unhappy. What was the use of a statue without the relic it was supposed to honour?

None of the retainers had yet reached the point of daring to intimidate Sacristan; nor did the White Bears see the need to, because the whole abbey knew by now how Sacristan had beaten Nigel Woodville senseless. But the other five delegates —no, four—they could not get at Novice Master in his confinement, and in any event there were already rumours that he would not be eligible to vote, being under a canonical cloud—the other four delegates were meat and drink to these bored and prickly men.

It was while he waited in the church for the monks to come out of Chapter that Brother Peter was caught. Two White Bears, one with red hair and one bald, sidled through the door and closed it silently behind them. They tiptoed through the chancel gate and padded up to Brother Peter where he knelt at the altar rail with his forehead on the warm brass, beseeching God to help him. Hot breath tickled his ears. Clammy hands clamped his wrists. He tried to get up but two heavy boots ground his ankles into the pavement. 'Who be you favouring, brother?' whispered the bald one. 'Just you sing out who you be favouring so as us knows if you be for us or agin us.'

Brother Peter eyed the knife-hilts. One of them was scored by a row of notches. 'Prior has instructed us not to divulge our intentions,' he replied. The red-headed man tightened his grip.

'You'm a-telling!' he growled. 'Or us'll be minded to slit your belly.'

'That will do you no good,' replied Brother Peter coldly. But he thought to himself that a slit in the belly might be the greatest favour these men could do him. If he defied them . . .

'I have no intention of telling you which candidate I favour,' he said. The red-head drew his knife. The bald one jerked him to his feet and together they hustled him up the altar steps to the altar. They forced him on to his knees and rammed the palm of his hand on the brass grille that protected the girdle of the blessed Honoria.

The red-head pricked Brother Peter's neck. 'You make an oath that you'll vote for Henry Osborne or I'll shove this here knife in your ear-hole.'

Brother Peter's heart leaped. He closed his eyes and began to pray, begging God to forgive him his sins, trying to feel true contrition, hoping against all hope that if these men killed him by virtue of his martyrdom he might elude hell. 'I confess to Almighty God, to blessed Mary ever virgin, to blessed Michael the Archangel . . .'

The bald man leaned nearer. 'You be a-going to swear,' he muttered.

'May Almighty God have mercy . . .'

'I be a-telling you!' whispered the bald man, taking a screw on Brother Peter's sleeve.

'May the Almighty and merciful Lord grant pardon . . .'

'You be a-going to swear!' said the bald man, his cracked lips against Brother Peter's ear.

Brother Peter shook his head. 'No,' he said hopefully.

He braced his head for the knife but instead the bald man said, 'You'm best swear or I do be minded to tell Bishop I spied you lying with a wench in t'woods.'

Brother Peter groaned. So they had seen him. Either he swore an oath to vote for Nigel Woodville's enemy or he would be exposed to disgrace, punishment, imprisonment, enforced separation from his love. His thoughts raced. He splayed his sweating fingers over the grille and said clearly, 'I swear on these holy relics that when I gather with Prior and the other five monks for the election of our new abbot I will vote for Henry Osborne.' To his relief the two White Bears released their hold. They were not clever enough to spot the loopholes in his declaration. They sneaked away. Brother Peter wiped his face with his sleeve and followed them, reaching the cloister just as the monks came out of Chapter. He joined them unobserved.

All through Mass he fingered the bristles on his pate and brooded over his plan of action.

Guest Master was cornered after Vespers. He was unpopular with the retainers on account of his stinginess with the rations and his economies in matters of straw mattresses and warm water. Every day that the retainers stopped in the abbey meant one essential less for his son Francis' shop. The men sensed his antagonism without knowing the precise cause of it. A bunch of King's men grabbed him on his own steps and bustled him into his own hall. His four servants scuttled away, not caring enough for him to stop and defend him. The Rising Suns sat him down in his own chair. They sensed at once that he was a coward, for such perceptions were part of their stock-in-trade. Their problem was so to scare him that nothing the White Bears could do to him would make him fear them more. They knew that all their efforts might be nullified by Ambrose who had God knows what dramatic effects up his sleeve, but like their candidate they soldiered on in hope. You never knew. Like retainers the world over they were not without pride in earning their wages, and the King's retainers, thanks to the royal munificence, were paid very good wages indeed. Even if they had not received them for the last month.

Suddenly before their eyes Guest Master disintegrated like a sawdust doll pricked with a knife. He began to babble that he would promise them anything, would vote for anyone, if they would only leave him alone. He was a tiny man and by the time he had finished grovelling he was no bigger than a beetle. 'You vote for Nigel Woodville, then,' they told him. Yes, yes, he would do it, he swore it on his rosary. 'No fooling, mind. You stick out for Nigel Woodville and don't be shifted. At least they'll have to have another election if you won't be shifted.' Yes, yes, he swore it. In the end they could do nothing but leave him; suspecting that, religious or not, he would recant his vow and swear the opposite to the first batch of Warwick's men that accosted him. They were no nearer knowing his real mind.

And Guest Master, not so long after, did swear the opposite. He swore to a bunch of White Bears that he would try to get Henry Osborne elected. And this was a vow he was determined to keep.

The retainers caught Brother Mark after Compline. He had stripped off his cassock and his shirt and was on his knees in the cellar with a scourge in his hand trying to lash his back. The scourge was a rope with six knots in it. Brother Mark was no more efficient with it than he was with anything else. When they pounced on him he was flicking the rope over his left shoulder in an ineffective endeavour to mortify his flesh. The little cat watched him with her arms folded under her chest, her stump of tail twitching.

It was a party of a dozen that found him. They separated into two groups, Warwick's men and King's men. They made two semicircles round him under the dangling hams. The cat bolted behind the grain sacks. To begin with it was only a game. The taste of supper was still under their tongues. Brother Mark amused them by lumbering from one man to another trying to retrieve his scourge as it was chucked over his head.

'Up's a daisy!'

'Here un be!'

'Dinna get moithered, then.'

'Give un here!' shouted Brother Mark. 'If a chap bain't let have his'n rope . . .' He bumbled from hand to hand.

'O'er his'n head, now!'

'Quicky, un 'ool snatch un.'

A Rising Sun made to chuck the scourge and Brother Mark scrambled round to chase it. Thwack! went the rope on his naked back. 'Thakky addled un!' roared a White Bear. 'U'll get a bellyful of them if un doan't vote for Henry Osborne.' He grinned and threw the rope to a pal, who slashed with it at Brother Mark's ankles. Brother Mark skipped over it. There were roars of laughter. The rope slashed again. Brother Mark skipped. They whooped. Here was a good game.

But the time came when Brother Mark was not quick enough and the rope, wielded by a Rising Sun, ripped skin off one ankle. Instantly there were yells of protest from the White Bears, who did not care about monastic flesh but were spoiling for a quarrel.

'Dinna whiffle un!'

'You'm nobbut bullies.'

'You'm no betterer nor beasties.'

And then, fatally: 'You'll get nowhere thikky way. Thikky monk be going to vote for Woodville.'

'I bain't, I bain't!' roared Brother Mark. 'I be Ambrose's man. I bain't voting for t'others.'

In an instant every belt was off and they began to strike out indiscriminately: at Brother Mark, at one another, at the hams and onions and sacks. The gloom thickened with grain-dust. A Rising Sun lugged out the cat and twiddled her on the point of his knife and shouted, 'You'm choosing Woodville, monk, or 'twill be you up along here,' and he poked the squirming cat under Brother Mark's eyes.

Brother Mark's ham-fists smashed the man's face, knocking out two front teeth. With growls the Rising Suns advanced, but a noise checked them. It was the clash of the service bell —long after the last service of the day had been sung—and a stampede of feet in the cloisters above them. There was a rush for the steps; leather boots clattered away. Brother Mark lay down beside the dying cat and prayed for her. He was too stupid to be intimidated. Besides, when his lord Jesus Christ appeared underneath the grating and smiled and blessed him he was struck again by His resemblance to Ambrose. Eventually he picked up the dead cat and went up the cellar steps to see what all the commotion was about.

It was the second death.

Brother Joseph was caught in the cloisters, where he was sitting in the twilight of the south cloister, hearing but scarcely noticing the gurgle of water in the lavatories and the distant shouts of the retainers from the kitchen yard. He was enjoying the temporary lull. He heard the watchdogs clank their chains and a carp plop in the pond. Ah, if only it was always like this, as it had been in Abbot Dominic's day. Calm. Protected from the turbulence of common life. A cocoon of safety in which monks could get on with prayers and their worship and their monastic duties in peace.

A hot hand descended on Brother Joseph's pate and wrenched round his head, grinding his gouty vertebrae. 'Here un be!' shouted a Rising Sun. 'Who be 'ee favouring, Granfur? Now 'ee just say as how 'ee 'oon't vote fur thakky skinny Ambrose whatever un gits up to.'

Faces loomed at Brother Joseph, grinning faces covered in brown or black or red stubble. Mouths split like pods. Teeth stuck out like rotten posts. 'I cannot see!' he cried in panic as they closed round him.

'We 'ool soon put thakky to rights!' and the King's men whipped him up, stool and all, and rushed him into the kitchen yard for a bit of sport. They pushed and plucked him. They twirled him like a top. They shouted loud enough to split his eardrums that he must vote for Nigel Woodville or they would cut his lights out and let the dogs eat them. Then a wit remembered Brother Joseph's eyes and came running with a poker from the smithy. It was red hot and he whirled it like a devil, making a fiery pattern against the dark sky 'Thikky can cure yourn eyen,' he yelled. 'Thikky can!' they all shouted. And they made gestures of drawing the iron across their eyebrows in the time-honoured operation of cauterizing.

Brother Joseph found his voice.

'No, no!' he screamed. 'Infirmarian said I would die under it.' The fiery poker whirled and came nearer. 'No, no!'

They giggled at his distress. Even the White Bears joined in the fun. 'T'iron 'ool make 'ee see proper,' they told him. The poker darted to and fro like a snake's tongue. 'Catch hold of un, chaps. Un be like an eel.' Hands grabbed him. The poker advanced . . . .

And there was Prior in their midst, torches on either side of him, a bronze Cross held up in front of him. The Cross blazed. A hush fell. 'Release him,' commanded Prior. No one moved. 'Release him. In the name of God I order you to release him.' They stared at this bald man in skirts and at the Cross he carried that was the symbol of the Church's authority. They did not move. 'If you do not release him I will excommunicate every man of you. I will cast you out of Holy Church with bell, book and candle. If you die you will be cast into everlasting hell. You will be denied Mass. No priest will absolve you of your sins.'

Still no one moved. Forty retainers stood like statues. The Cross wavered in Prior's hands. If they should defy him—but they would not. If they defied the Church's most terrifying threat what hope was there for the abbey? For the world?

The Rising Sun flourished his cooling poker. 'Be damned to yourn threats!' he shouted. 'Be damned! Be damned!' shouted his friends. 'Be damned!' shouted the White Bears. The ground heaved under Prior's feet. The authority of fifteen centuries shivered in his hands. In an awful silence he spoke to his chaplain.

'Summon the brothers,' he ordered. 'We will go into the church. There I will excommunicate these men.' He turned, longing for them to call out, to release Brother Joseph, to relieve him of this ghastly duty. They neither moved nor spoke. They were defying the Holy Catholic Church and they did not care.

Prior turned his back on them and walked towards the west cloister. His chaplain scurried off to ring the service bell. In silence, his Cross aloft, Prior walked down the cloister and through the narrow doorway where once a long time ago Abbot's Chaplain had forced a bunch of King's men to make way. He came to the west door but finding it locked walked on to the door of the north transept, giving a wide berth to the mysterious package and the snarling dogs. A picture transfixed him. Ambrose. Ambrose in the light of a solitary torch that flared on the north wall. Ambrose on his donkey with a wooden box in the crook of his left arm.

'I have brought back the toe-nails of St Peter,' he said.

The service bell clashed. Sandals came pattering into the

choir. Servants came running at the unusual summons. Retainers crammed the nave to hear themselves excommunicated. In the kitchen yard Brother Joseph sobbed alone. On the last stroke of the bell the transept door creaked open and in walked Prior, Cross held high, and behind him Ambrose, his head bent and the wooden box between his hands. In a religious hush they edged their way into the choir and came face to face with Sacristan who was just turning from lighting extra candles. Sacristan's monstrous body quivered. His piggy eyes dropped to the wooden box. 'I have brought you the toe-nails of St Peter,' said Ambrose, and put the box into Sacristan's hands.

Behind the chancel screen there was uproar, but Sacristan did not heed it. He put the box down at his feet, knelt, and taking out his knife prised up the lid. Out of the wooden box he lifted a silver casket with four feet and a ring in the lid. He lifted the lid. He gazed. His fantastic face was lit by a light no candle can give. There they were, nestling in crimson velvet, the ten sacred relics bought out of his official fund, ten horny shapes from the ten toes of St Peter, the disciple of whom Christ said, 'Thou art a rock and on this rock I will build My Church.'

'Glory be to God,' breathed Sacristan, crossing himself. He heaved himself up and flopped on his knees before the man who had accomplished single-handed what he could not accomplish with a posse of men. He lifted Ambrose's hand and kissed it.

'I asked, and they gave it to me,' said Ambrose simply.

The monks fell on their knees. Cries of 'Alleluia' and 'Praise be to God' burst from them. Prior felt strength pouring like wine through his veins. Henry Osborne stopped twiddling his thumbs and saw a disquieting picture of his hard stall in Salisbury Cathedral. Abbot's Chaplain buried his broken nose in his hands and cursed so vilely he earned himself a penance of a hundred and fifty Hail Marys. Behind the chancel screen Thomas Woodville, just returned from Gloucester, gnawed his nails in fury and wondered for the thousandth time where his cousin Nigel had got to. Brother Mark forgot the dead cat in his bosom. Brother Peter wondered if the toe-nails could cure him of lust. Guest Master's conscience was like a barb in his skin.

When they had all recovered Sacristan placed the toe-nails on the altar. Then he read aloud the list of thirty-two authenticated miracles that was in the bottom of the wooden box. By the time he had finished even the retainers were on their knees. One of them, the Rising Sun who had wielded the poker, was so overcome by religious enthusiasm that he fetched Brother Joseph from the kitchen yard and told him all that had taken place.

Before he locked up the church that night Sacristan led in the two watchdogs and chained them to the altar. His dreams were happy.

In his locked room Novice Master sat with his hands on his knees and stared at his new-found belief. He was astonished that he had not seen it earlier. It was a beautiful belief, so logical, so understandable, so unmiraculous. The bread did not change into flesh. The wine did not change into blood. He was appalled that the whole Catholic Church should have lived under a delusion for so long. He felt it was his mission to tell them all—bishops, archbishops, abbots, cardinals, even the Pope himself—that they were mistaken. How distressed God must have been all these centuries to see man misunderstanding Him. Novice shifted on to his right buttock to ease his latest ulcer. His left leg was a mass of putrid bandages. 'I will tell the Bishop,' he thought, 'when he comes to see me. Perhaps I can make him see the truth.' Then he put his hands together and prayed that God would give him strength to remain loyal to his belief.

The village was shaken to its foundations by the revelation of heresy in the abbey. If heresy crept among the monks what hope was there for poor common peasants? And what price the monks' praying and chanting and being holy now that there was rampaging heresy in their midst? If one heretical monk why not another? It was likely that Novice Master had been talking them all round.

The peasants of Woodchester expressed themselves incoherently but their horror was real. When they toiled for their livings, when they braced themselves to bear the blows of nature, when they mourned the sudden deaths of loved ones, there was one unreasoning belief that gave them strength; and this was the Catholic faith that taught them that however dreary their lives on earth, in heaven they would enjoy eternal bliss. It buoyed them up to know that even sinners could get to heaven eventually, if they confessed their sins and received absolution. At least once a year they ate God's flesh and saw the priest drink His blood. In this way they felt themselves part of God and knew they would be saved by God's sacrifice. All they had to do to achieve eternal bliss was to be careful not to die in mortal sin. It was this knowledge that warmed them in winter, cooled them in summer, made their lives of toil tolerable. And now here was a monk, a holy man who existed solely to preserve a haven for the orthodox faith, lapsing into the most terrible heresy a Christian could think of.

Feeling ran high. There was much hot talk in the churchyard when the men gathered there in the twilight; and no talk was hotter than John Leys'. Resentments that hitherto had been only warm—the monks' aloofness, the land they would not let him buy, the threat to Rector's church—had been so fanned by fear of famine, so heated by the burning sun, that they had kindled flames of hatred that were rapidly not only consuming John Leys but also setting light to his friends and neighbours. There had been the reports that the abbey intended to buy up all the leases and evict the tenants at will, and now there were revelations of theft and heresy behind those grey walls; and finally, to crown it all, his daughter had brought shame down on his head. 'I 'ool winkle un out so be un be above t'ground,' he roared. 'And if un be above t'ground u'll soon be under un.' His temper had conquered his shame. Besides, if he did not spread the word how could he discover the man? 'When I uncovers un u'll wish un ne'er bin borned,' he ranted, tugging his red hair. 'Look out for un, chaps. Married man un be, and coupling with she in Rector's barn.' He peered from face to face, seeking the guilty glance, the look of fear. 'I 'ool whiffle un!' he said softly. 'I 'ool burn un to ashes, I 'ool break un to bits.' He beat a tombstone with his stick until the stick flew in three pieces. 'Ferret out t'married man as laid my girl in Rector's hay and I 'ool settle his'n hash.'

Their tempers flared to match his. There was no rain to douche them. Their arable was cracked into fissures three inches deep. Their corn was as sparse as hairs on a hog's back. Their pastures were sepia-coloured, the grass dying in the roots. Avon brook was run dry. There were only two feet of water left in the well. Already they were lugging water from Selsely springs. Cows and ewes had dried up. Four babies had died. Their pigs were skin and bone, their lambs dying in dozens. They looked down their days and saw nothing but suffering and death along the way. They were ripe for violence. They itched to vent their wrath on something or someone, some scapegoat.

'There bain't nought gone right for we,' growled Leys' friend Heaven, 'not since t'old Abbot shuffled off.'

'We 'ool be servants soon,' burst in Goodman. 'Working for thakky monks. Them's got no right to nab ourn land.'

'Them doan't work for thairn living,' shouted John Leys.

'Doan't be expecting thakky!' said Heaven. 'Them's thieves up along there, them's stealing rings and things. . . .'

'There be worser nor thakky,' Leys reminded them, rubbing the cracked skin round his mouth. 'Them's not proper monks, them's heretics, them's a-doing Satan's jobs. . . .'

'I reckon a mort of they soldiers be married chaps, John.'

'I 'ool thrash un out of she,' bellowed John Leys. 'If un be one of they Bears or Suns I 'ool hae un out of they gates if I mun drag un by t'heels.'

They lashed themselves into a fury of hatred and fear.

'Us bain't going to see they toe-nails,' shouted Leys. ' 'Ool us, chaps? They monks can whistle but us bain't a-going.'

And so strong was his hatred and his hold over them that they nodded their heads and said they were not going to jig to the monks' tune. Nor could Rector make them see reason. He concentrated on John Leys because he saw that where Leys led the others would follow. 'You are a churchwarden, John. You must set the village a good example. Why should they not have their chance for a cure for their ills?'

But all Leys said was, 'Keep t'eyes peeled for thikky married chap as laid my girl in yourn hay.'

Rector fingered the minute-glass in his pocket but he did not produce it because he knew John Leys' fiery temper and he was afraid he might murder Alice's lover in hot blood if he discovered who he was.

It was the day after Whitsunday, the day the Bishop was expected for the interrogation of Novice Master. There was no change in the weather. The water in the abbey well had dropped two more feet. If the underground springs dried up they would have to fetch water from the Selsely springs. If those failed they would be reduced to lugging water from the Frome a mile and a half away.

Lord Wenlock had returned from Monmouth but he had gleaned nothing more useful than that Ambrose had a purple birthmark between his shoulder-blades. Thomas Woodville had ridden twice to Silver Street. Nigel Woodville had still not reappeared. Henry Osborne, egged on by Abbot's Chaplain, had let it be known that he considered Nigel capable of stealing the Abbot's ring. Guest Master's ear was healed. Sacristan let Brother Joseph touch the toe-nails and was bitterly disappointed when there was no improvement in his sight. Secretly, when the dogs were being exercised, Brother Peter also touched the toe-nails but was not cured of his guilty passion. Brother Mark dogged Ambrose. Weary of his responsibilities, Prior longed for the Bishop's visit, surely the first prior ever to do so. Among the servants, betting on Ambrose stood at two to one. Not a penny was wagered on Nigel Woodville.

At midday the Bishop arrived with twenty servants in striped livery who immediately pitched tents in the Abbot's garden. Half the building fund was used in their entertainment. The Bishop dined in the Abbot's lodgings with Prior, Ambrose, Abbot's Chaplain, Henry Osborne, Lord Wenlock and Thomas Woodville. During dinner he informed Prior that unless Novice Master recanted his views at his first interrogation and did public penance he would not only be ineligible to vote in the abbatical elections but would in fact be removed to Worcester for formal trial before the Bishop's court.

After dinner they proceeded in procession to the Chapter House, for in the Bishop's honour Chapter had been postponed. Awed by his crozier the retainers were on their best behaviour. Fastidiously the Bishop picked his way through them. 'The sooner the King allows you to elect, the better,' was all he said. The customary business was got through; prayers, Martyrology, Epistle, offences and penances. Before the Bishop rose to speak the door creaked open and Thomas Woodville thrust in his yellow ringlets.

'My lord Bishop,' he said loudly, 'I ask leave to speak.' He slipped inside and shut the door behind him. His right hand was behind his back.

The Bishop considered. 'Speak,' he said. Thomas Woodville jumped on to the novices' bench, obliterating the end novice with the tail of his sleeve. He paused long enough to whet their curiosity, then with a flourish he whipped up his right hand and held aloft, between his finger and thumb, the Abbot's ruby ring. Guest Master's face turned purple, then crimson. Abbot's Chaplain was pale as a ghost. Henry Osborne stopped breathing.

'Abbot's Chaplain said Nigel Woodville had stolen it,' shouted Thomas, relishing his little triumph. 'Henry Osborne said Nigel was a thief. But it was not Nigel who stole it. I set my spies to looking and they found it in Reuben Abraham's pawnshop in Silver Street. Reuben Abraham is at the gate now waiting to give evidence. He has brought documents to prove who it was pawned the Abbot's ring.'

Abbot's Chaplain leapt up. 'My lord Bishop, will you accept the testimony of an infidel?'

Thomas Woodville crowed: 'He has brought the Talmud to

171

swear on. He has signatures. He can point out the man who pawned the ring; and the man who pawned it stole it.'

Guest Master sat still as a stone. Forty hearts hammered in the silence. Servants were sent and soon Reuben Abraham appeared, an ancient Jew with gold rings in his ears, his holy book under one arm and a sheaf of documents under the other. Mercifully he was brief. He described how a monk in black had come to his shop and pawned the ruby ring, saying that he was doing so on his prior's authority. He had made this monk a large payment of coin and he showed the Bishop the signatures. He described how Thomas Woodville had come to him and redeemed the ring with King's money, paying back the original sum plus additional interest. He put his olive hand on his Talmud and swore by the holy prophets that here was the man who had pawned the ring. And he pointed his finger at Guest Master.

From that moment Guest Master closed up tight as a clam. From that moment he never spoke a single word, except once to Nigel Woodville and once in the confession-box to gain absolution for his sin. It was the only way to support his degradation. The Jew was hustled away. The Bishop rose. There and then Guest Master was stripped to the waist and laid face down on the floor. One by one Prior and the other monks whipped his back with withies, three strokes each. Then he was hauled up and, supported by two monks, heard Bishop declare him deposed from his office and relegated to the ranks of the newly professed. Henceforth he was to eat at the lowest table, sleep in the dormitory, be without any privilege, never administer Mass. Every Friday for one year he was to be beaten on the chancel steps. Then he was dragged away and thrown on a bed in the dormitory.

Before the Bishop left the Chapter House, Abbot's Chaplain plucked his sleeve and asked in agitation, 'My lord, will Guest Master be eligible to vote in the abbatical elections?'

Coldly the Bishop detached himself. 'I advise you to be more careful in future how you speak,' he answered. 'You will do your candidate no good by these slanders. Yes, he is eligible to vote since he is not under any canonical cloud and has been chosen by the monks.'

Abbot's Chaplain's chagrin was a little comforted. At least one thing was certain: Guest Master would never vote for a Woodville.

That evening after Compline, when Guest Master was stonily preparing for his first night in the common dormitory for twenty years, Nigel Woodville returned to Woodchester Abbey. He eased his battered body off the herring-cart that had brought him from Stroud, gave the driver his blessing and crawled painfully up the slope to the north gate. He knocked and the porter let him in. The instant he set foot in the Abbot's garden all his dejected hopes revived. For there, wrapped in canvas, was the precious statue the King had promised him. And safe in his pocket was Brother Joseph's cure. Despite his hurts he had borrowed a horse immediately after his escape that morning and had ridden alone to Gloucester to fetch it. If Nigel Woodville failed to become Abbot of Woodchester it would not be for want of trying.

13

B Y MORNING the abbey was buzzing with activity. There
was the Bishop interrogating Novice Master. There was
Sacristan gloating over a golden money bowl and a jewelled
case for the casket of toe-nails and a marble statue of St Peter
that was now standing, still heavily shrouded in canvas, in the
north transept. There was Nigel Woodville, reeking of foxglove
ointment, bandages round both wrists and ankles, his face
purple with bruises, telling whoever would listen that he and
his party of three had been set on three days before on their
way back from Gloucester by a party of Lord Wenlock's men.
His servants had never been seen since. Nigel had been taken
to a shepherd's hut beyond Edge and there beaten and tied up
and left to starve. On the second day he had finally loosened his
bonds and broken down the door and staggered to a peasant's
house where he had been fed. The next day he had sufficiently
recovered to make his way to Stroud, ride to Gloucester for
Brother Joseph's cure—but Nigel did not mention his ride to
Gloucester—and return to the abbey.

Lord Wenlock rose bravely to his own defence. He defied
Nigel to prove that it was White Bears who had attacked him.
He accused Nigel of scourging himself in order to besmirch
Warwick's name. 'I do not believe you were captured at all!'
he roared. And in reply poor Nigel Woodville could only
point to his lacerated flesh.

Brother Peter was deep in the woods with his love. His plan
was made. He was not going to wait for the abbatical election
because he saw little chance of Nigel being elected. He would

wait only for his quarter's pocket-money and then he would run away. He would make his way to Rome and cast himself on the mercy of the Pope and beg for dispensation from his monastic vows. He would be able to offer little in the way of money but if he offered to join the Pope's crusade to win back the Holy City from the infidel perhaps His Holiness would look kindly on him. He might be away a year, two years, but Alice was to trust him and do as he said. 'As soon as you hear that I am gone,' he told her, 'you must go to the nuns at Brimpsfield. They will look after you and the baby until I return.'

Alice turned on him her innocent blue eyes. 'Cass-n't 'ee marry I now?' she asked. 'Now councillor's son bain't wedding I, why cass-n't 'ee run away and take I to wife and hae done with un all? 'Ee can wear a hat until t'hair be growed. Us can run afar off. 'Ee can take clerk's job. I do be wanting 'ee desperd bad for husband, Peter. I doan't care that 'ee be monk.'

He was speechless. How could he teach her to fear damnation if Rector had been unable to do it in sixteen years? How could he harrow her with pictures of everlasting torment? She was protected by her dreadful innocence. How could he tear her defences away? 'You do not understand,' he said at last. 'I cannot marry you while I am married to the Church. It would not be right. I will go to the Pope and he will undo my marriage to the Church. Nigel Woodville said so. Then I will return and marry you.'

Her lips trembled and her blue eyes filled with tears. She was young, she was an unmarried girl with child, her father beat her every night and bullied her to make her tell whom she had lain with in Rector's hay. She looked at the years ahead and saw nothing but beatings and an unwanted baby and perhaps, who knows, no husband at the end of it. She began to cry. She buried her face in his armpit and he stroked her shoulder where it was not bruised and murmured that he loved her, that he would come back and marry her, that the nuns would look after her and not let her father drag her home. Presently he stretched out a hand and picked up his crucifix on its plaited linen thread. He laid it between her breasts, then pressed himself against her so that it was held there by his own flesh. 'Swear,' he told her.

'Swear on God's holy Cross that you will go to the nuns at Brimpsfield and will wait there for me two years. If I have not returned or sent word by then you will be free to marry.'

She hesitated. The points of the Cross gouged her breasts. Brother Peter's chest heaved against her. His legs shifted, his mouth came down on hers, his hands touched her, making her shudder and cry out. 'I swear un,' she said. 'I swear un.' Their passion burst into flame. Brother Peter tossed the Cross aside and began to kiss her where it had lain.

'But you cannot believe such a terrible heresy,' said the Bishop, patiently. 'It must be devils prompting you to say these dreadful things. The Church has taught the miracle of the Mass for centuries upon centuries——'

'For five centuries, my lord Bishop,' interrupted Novice Master. 'If I may remind you it was not until the tenth century that the doctrine of the Mass was finally decided.'

'But it *was* decided,' said the Bishop irritably. 'It is holy doctrine. It is heresy to question it, and you know what happens to heretics.' He wiped the sweat off his face and sighed. The little room was already stifling, although the sun would not reach it for eight or nine hours. He retched from the stench of Novice Master's ulcers. He was distracted by the retainers' din. Prior irritated him by his gloomy aspect. His officer's pen squeaked. Yet he was very patient. He did not want this deluded man to damn himself. He did not want to send him to the fire. He wished, as they all wished, that Novice Master would see his errors and recant his startling views, do penance and receive absolution and be welcomed back into the bosom of the Church like a prodigal son.

'Let us go over it again,' said the Bishop.

Nigel Woodville, having done Wenlock and Henry Osborne as much damage as he could, limped off to the scriptorium to try to bribe Brother Joseph into supporting him. In his pocket was the cure for Brother Joseph's eyes. When he entered, Brother Joseph peered at him suspiciously. 'You need not think you can bring any printing-presses in here,' he grunted, blinking his scarlet eyes.

Without a word Nigel released the parchment from its press and held it up to the bright light. 'Your lines are crooked,' he said severely, 'and some of the letters run into one another. I wonder you waste your time on these manuscripts when you cannot do them better than this.' He flicked the page with his forefinger and added, 'Abbot Dominic would never have praised such work.'

Brother Joseph's anger was drowned in tears. He bent his head and let the tears run down the front of his cassock. When at last they stopped he said: 'Ever since I was a boy I have made manuscripts. It was psalms I copied, even when I was still an apprentice in my uncle's script shop, and litanies and parts of the Scriptures. I always wanted to live in a monastery and be a monk. I always wanted to make manuscripts and make them beautiful in God's sight. Do you know'—here he lifted his wet eyes to Nigel's and for the first time Nigel realized what a very old man he was—'for every line of my writing I say a Pater Noster. How many Pater Nosters do you suppose I have said in my life? For every illuminated capital I say a psalm and for every full stop I say an Ave Maria. Who is going to say prayers over printed pages?'

Nigel Woodville did not answer. There was no answer that would reconcile Brother Joseph to the simultaneous stamping of twenty lines of words on a piece of parchment. To him words were a labour of love; each was infinitesimally different from its like; each had devotion breathed into it at its birth. 'How will you employ yourself, Brother Joseph, when you go blind?' asked Nigel brutally. 'For you will go blind if you strain your eyes like this.'

'I shall wish to die,' replied Brother Joseph. 'It will be a terrible sin but I shall pray to die.'

With tantalizing slowness Nigel manœuvred an object out

of his pocket and placed it on the table in front of Brother Joseph. Brother Joseph stared at it. It was a hoop of thin iron. On to one side of this hoop two more smaller hoops were riveted. These were not iron but wood and they were riveted so that they hung down clear of the iron hoop. They were close together, barely an inch apart at their widest point. This contraption lay lopsidedly, propped up on one side by the wooden circles. Brother Joseph poked his finger through one of the wooden hoops but to his astonishment it would not go through. His finger met not air but a solid. He tried the other hoop, with the same result. He looked at Nigel.

'Close your eyes,' said Nigel Woodville.

Brother Joseph closed them. Nigel picked up the iron hoop and fitted it over Brother Joseph's head so that the two wooden circles ringed his eyes. 'Do not open your eyes yet.' He selected a parchment from a pile of Brother Joseph's earlier work. He unrolled it and pinned it top and bottom with paint-pots. He tilted Brother Joseph's head downwards. He crossed himself, uttered a silent prayer, then said loudly, 'Open your eyes.'

Brother Joseph's eyes flew open. Through the twin circles he stared at the writing. His face, half obliterated as it was by the grotesque contraption, was illuminated by a radiance so brilliant, so celestial, that he might have been gazing at paradise.

'Can you read it?' asked Nigel eagerly.

Brother Joseph did not hear him. As a man groping in a fog suddenly sees the mists blown away and familiar shapes spring up around him, so Brother Joseph found himself reunited with beloved objects he thought he had lost for ever. There they were, the square 'o's and 'a's, the aitches with their thin tails, the tall 's's so cunningly united to their 't's. Here were the hooks over the 'i's that Abbot Dominic had admired. Here were the forked prongs of the 'p's—how many months was it since he had been able to distinguish them? And the capitals! What intricacy! What minutae! He had forgotten how skilled his hands and eyes had once been. A tiny irregularity leapt into his view. In the third line the stroke over the 'u' was a fraction short. His hand darted to a pen but before he could grasp it Nigel Woodville's hand closed over his wrist.

'Read this,' said Nigel. And he unrolled in front of Brother Joseph a parchment page on which he had written a sentence of his own. Brother Joseph read:

This cure for your eyes shall be yours for ever if you will say that you wish me to be abbot and will vote for me in the abbatical elections.

It was signed *Nigel Woodville* with a flourish of swans' necks. The parchment floated to the floor. Brother Joseph's hands hovered about his head. His fingers curled into his palms, reluctant to touch his wonderful cure. It was a marvellous cure, but the price—the price was extortionate. He could obtain this miraculous device that made the letters leap out towards him but in return for it he must countenance whole pages stamped by a turn of a screw, unholy pages unblessed and unprayed over, pages so smooth one could not feel the depth of the ink with one's finger-tips. He must tolerate capital letters gouged out of wooden blocks and pressed inaccurately into spaces left for them. He must sanction books without any colour except the colour of the ink, books so drab and messy and indistinct they could bring no satisfaction either to their makers or to God.

'You must choose,' said Nigel Woodville. 'I will not give you this cure unless you support me and vote for me.'

Brother Joseph's hands wavered. He was a simple soul. He envisaged no way of obtaining this cure except through the man who was now offering it to him. He was also a devout soul. If he promised to support Nigel Woodville it would be with a sacred promise that he would never break. For him it was a question of choice quite cruel in its clarity.

Brother Joseph's hands opened and closed, tentative as sea-anemones. At last they made a decision, gripped the iron hoop and lifted it off his head. Across his brows the iron had made a red groove like a cauterizing scar. Brother Joseph laid the hoop down on the table and without a word Nigel Woodville picked it up and put it in his capacious pocket. In silence he walked to the door. Brother Joseph watched him until he disappeared into mist.

'No, no,' cried the Bishop. 'You must not say that, Novice Master. I cannot think where you have got these terrible notions. Can you not see that you are digging a pit in front of yourself and you are going to fall into it? Listen to the voice of the Church, I beg you. Be guided by me. Admit that the wine miraculously changes into Christ's blood and the bread into Christ's flesh. He told us so in the Scriptures. He said, "*Est enim corpus meum*," did he not? Why should He say that if He did not mean us to believe it?'

Novice Master replied, infuriatingly didactic: 'How can it have been His flesh, Bishop? Do you think He sliced pieces off Himself? Or cut a vein and held it over the wine mug? What He said was, "Do this in memory of Me." The texts have got muddled. They have deluded scholars.'

A dark flush spread up the Bishop's neck. 'Do you presume to tell me that for hundreds and hundreds of years the Church has been under a delusion? Do you presume to set yourself up in judgement on the Fathers of the Church and the Pope himself?'

'Yes,' said Novice Master.

The Bishop's jaw dropped. Here was a hardy heretic. Not content with questioning the miracle of the Mass he was now denying the infallability of the Pope! And with maddening certainty, as if he alone was favoured with God's intentions. Bishop laced his fingers and leaned forward. 'Novice Master, have you heard of James Wyllys?'

'Yes.'

'Who was he?'

'He was a weaver of Bristol.'

'What happened to him?'

'He was burned alive by the Sheriff of London.'

'Why was he burned?'

'Because he had been found guilty by the consistory court of the Bishop of London.'

180

'Of what was he found guilty?'

'Of heresy.'

'On what grounds?'

'Because he said the wine did not change into blood and the bread did not change into flesh.'

The Bishop leaned farther forward and tapped Novice Master on the knee. 'Have you ever seen a man burned alive in a fire?'

Novice Master shook his head, much as he might have done if someone had asked him did he want a second helping of pudding.

'Then I will tell you what it is like. He is put to stand in a barrel. Chains fasten his arms and legs to the sides. Faggots are piled round the barrel. A light is applied. Sometimes the faggots burn quickly, sometimes not. Sometimes a soporific sponge is allowed, sometimes not. When the body of the heretic is burned to ashes, the ashes are thrown in the river. The soul of the heretic, unless some miraculous repentance has taken place in the flames, is carried away by Satan and cast into hell where it is tortured throughout eternity, "cut off from God's sight".'

But Novice Master was not intimidated. He raised his calm eyes and answered: 'I shall never be cut off from God. It is God's truth that I believe. I shall join James Wyllys in paradise. You can burn my body, Bishop, but you cannot make me admit to a lie.'

The Bishop threw up his hands in despair. He took Prior and his officer with him out of the room, leaving Novice Master with his own thoughts. 'Has he been much to Bristol?' he asked, trying to find the least shocking reason why heresy had crept into Woodchester Abbey. 'There are many of these Lollards in Bristol. Perhaps Novice Master has been infected by their talk.'

But no, Novice Master had never been farther afield than Stroud, being totally occupied with the instruction of the novices.

'It is very bad,' said the Bishop. 'It sets such a bad example; heresy among monks.'

'You will take him to Worcester, my lord?'

'Oh yes. He will have to stand trial in Worcester. But you might try your monks on him, Prior. Send them in one by one. God sometimes chooses humble instruments.'

So all through the rest of that burning day the monks filed

one by one through Novice Master's stinking, suffocating room. They knew they ought to loathe him and his suppurating leg but they found they could only pity him, sitting there so calmly, impervious to their pleas. Guest Master was the only monk who did not speak to him; he simply stared stonily and marched out again. Brother Peter pleaded as persuasively as any, sad to see a man doomed to that very hell he feared so much himself. Abbot's Chaplain prayed over him very beautifully. Nigel could not help wondering whether another monk would be chosen to take Novice Master's place in the election. Henry Osborne rolled his thumbs. Ambrose exhorted him most fervently, but even his burning zeal could not shrivel up Novice Master's delusions. Prior, holding his sleeve over his nose to keep out the stench, urged Novice Master to consider the reputation of his abbey even if he would not consider his own salvation. Brother Joseph warned him to beware of the devil's tempting. But nothing would move the heretic. As he saw it, he was doing God's will.

Last but one came Brother Mark. He tripped over the threshold and caught his skirt in the door and had to open the door again to get free. He begged to be excused, pleading that nothing he could say would make any difference because he had been a great trial to Novice Master, he knew he was stupid, he would only vex . . . but Prior pushed him in all the same. He very soon lumbered out again, scarlet in the face, hurt by Novice Master's sharp tongue. Then Sacristan went in carrying St Peter's toe-nails in an attempt to infect Novice Master with their sanctity.

Sacristan heard the door close behind him. He waddled to the table and put the casket down. He sniffed. He looked at the tiny window through which the westerly sun was streaming, turning the room into an oven. Outside the window the hill reared up as steep as a spire, so close that he could have touched the withered bushes. There was not a whisper of wind. Sacristan sniffed again. He looked for flowers, then remembered that all the flowers were dead. 'You smell a lot better than when I last saw you,' he said cheerfully. 'Has Infirmarian done your ulcers some good at last?' He took Novice Master's hand and laid it on the box of toe-nails. He prayed earnestly that the toe-nails might cure Novice Master of his delusions.

But Novice Master shook his head. 'Nothing can change me,' he said. 'God has shown me the truth and I am prepared to die for it.' Sadly Sacristan picked up the toe-nails and rolled on his fat feet to the door. 'You are the last?' asked Novice Master courteously.

'I am.'

'Allow me to open the door.'

He rose, and Sacristan watched him advance and open the door. Sacristan stepped through it and heard it close gently behind him. He stood stock still. He shook his enormous head in vexation, like a bull worried by a fly. He turned to go back, then remembered Vespers and hurried away to the church. But his mind was disturbed. For days he was haunted by an unease he could not account for. It was not until Novice Master was safely locked up in the Bishop's prison in Worcester and had had his second hearing that Sacristan realized what was worrying him.

They left early next morning; the Bishop, his chaplain, his servants, his tents and horses and dogs—and Novice Master on a grey pony whose third rein was tied to a groom's horse. Before he left, the Bishop gave permission for the statue to be ceremonially unveiled and the relics revealed to the public on the Feast of the Commemoration of the Martyrs Peter and Paul in six days' time. He also, after profound thought, decided that no additional delegate should be chosen to replace Novice Master. To do so would be to invite the retainers to put other delegates out of action in the hope that monks more favourable to their candidate might be chosen. The Bishop had a keen nose and he had smelt violence in the abbey even though he had not seen it. Before dark they reached the Bishop's palace in Worcester and Novice Master was locked up in the Bishop's prison. The Bishop sat for an hour in warm water to ease his behind but he did not waste his time. He dictated a letter to the King at Northampton and despatched it at dawn by his fastest courier, beseeching the King to grant permission for the abbatical election at Woodchester to take place soon. He felt very anxious. He was convinced that Woodchester Abbey should get an abbot, any abbot, as soon as possible. He did not like what he had seen at Woodchester. He did not like it at all.

The instant the Bishop's back was turned violence broke out afresh. Cellarer sent a party of servants up with buckets to the Selsely springs but they found every spring but one guarded by villagers and villagers' dogs. 'One spring be enough for thakky monks,' John Leys told them. When they protested that there were nearly seventy retainers to be supplied they got the reply: 'Tell Prior to send they fromward then. Us doan't want t'Bears and Suns in ourn village.'

The servants were reduced to filling their buckets at the one remaining spring, which was such a miserable trickle it took them three hours to fill five buckets. 'Go up after dark,' said Cellarer. 'They will not be watching then.' But they were. The servants found a bonfire alight at each spring and villagers with cudgels and knives camped round them. ' 'Ee bain't stealing ourn water,' was the message they took back to Cellarer.

By this time the water in the abbey well had sunk two more feet and for the first time in living memory the monks knew what it was to fear nature's displeasure. Cellarer began to ration the water, a mugful for each man each day and so much for the kitchens. Washing stopped altogether. There was no shaving. A donkey-train began lugging water from the Frome guarded by White Bears with knives drawn. The day after the Bishop's departure a party of twenty White Bears toiled on their jaded horses up to the south gate, on either side of a queue of twelve donkeys, each one bearing river water in two wooden panniers. Suddenly, from behind the quickthorn hedge, there burst out a fantastic hullabaloo; a terrifying discordance of shouts, screams, barks, howls, whistles and rattles. The donkeys rolled their eyes and bunched up, jostling their panniers so that the precious water tipped down the sides. The din increased. Logs hurtled over the hedge in front of the leading White Bears, forcing them back. The donkeys tried to turn, jamming the outriders against the banks. In the panniers the water began to rock, swaying the donkeys by its weight. In a squealing, tumbling mass the donkeys began to slither down the slope, frontways, sideways, any way. Water slopped over and rolled down to the village. As the donkeys plunged downwards flaming torches flew through the air behind their rumps, cutting them off from the White Bears by a screen of smoke and sparks that the frantic horses would not pass.

The din subsided. By the time the smoke had cleared the donkeys had disappeared in a dozen different directions. When they were rounded up later their water panniers were empty. From that day onwards no retainer would escort the donkey train. The only way Cellarer could hope to get the water through was to send a monk with a Cross on the leading donkey. Even so, Cross or no Cross, every third lot of water was stolen by the villagers, always on the days that John Leys did not go out to his fields.

It was time for High Mass, a time that the monks had begun to long for as men in a desert long for an oasis. The procession round the cloisters had been shortened until now the monks hurried straight into the church individually as soon as the service bell rang. There was nowhere now that they felt safe except in their choir, only a few paces from the altar and the relics and the Holy Sacraments. This was their place. If they could find peace anywhere on earth it was here within these quiet walls, separated from the bustle of the lay world by the chancel screen. Here they had their job to do, their reason for existence. Here they laboured day after day, year after year, as monks had laboured for centuries past and would labour for centuries to come, to raise a wall of prayer strong enough to hold back the powers of darkness.

By this time there was no doubt at all who among them was the master-mason, the prince of wall-building. It was Ambrose.

Even Thomas Woodville, even Lord Wenlock, could not deny his holiness. They only had to look at him to be reminded of the saints. He was set aside by his gauntness, his self-denial, his silence, his brooding eyes. Morally and religiously he towered above them all.

Thomas Woodville had worked hard to convince the monks that Ambrose was too saintly to make a comfortable abbot but time and time again he had been confounded by a rush of religious enthusiasm—most marked since the exposure of the heretic—that with all his cunning he could not reason away. On this day he was all the more frantic to make Nigel Woodville abbot because he had that morning received a letter from his step-father the King informing him that if he got Nigel elected abbot he was to have an earldom. He hooked his fingers in the chancel screen and peered through its iron intricacies at the altar. He must succeed! He must! If only it was Henry Osborne alone he had to fight. It was not impossible to make headway against the Henry Osbornes of this world. But Ambrose . . .

Ambrose was taking Mass. He stood at the foot of the altar in his blood-red vestments. Over his shaved head hung the red altar-light. Behind him six white candles burned without a flicker, three each side of the silver crucifix, lighting up the bronze tabernacle, the casket of toe-nails, the cruets and bowls, the altar bell, the chalice and pyx and all the proscribed appurtenances of this the paramount ceremony of the Catholic Church. On his right stood the Abbot's empty chair and the Abbot's footstool of purple velvet edged with gold braid. In the shadowy nave, a dozen paces from where Thomas Woodville crouched, loomed St Peter's statue, enveloped in a canvas shroud threaded through at the bottom with a cord that was tied tightly and sealed at the knot with Sacristan's seal.

At the signal from Cantor the monks began the psalm, asking God why He had cast them off and made them sad. The psalm over, they all clasped their hands and confessed their sins aloud together, saying that they had all sinned exceedingly in thought, word and deed. Never had they confessed more fervently. What else but grievous sin could have brought

God's anger down on them so heavily? Ambrose made the sign of the Cross, joined his hands and gave them hope by saying, 'May the Almighty and merciful Lord grant us pardon, absolution and remission of our sins.'

'Amen, Amen,' they cried.

To give them even more hope Ambrose turned to face the altar, kissed the toe-nails of St Peter and cried, 'We beseech Thee, O Lord, by the merits of Thy saint whose relics are here that Thou wouldst forgive us all our sins.' His deacons swung the censers, and clouds of incense floated up towards the stone ribs of the roof and down into the monks' lungs. '*Kyrie eleison*, Lord have mercy!' they sang. Ambrose recited the Collect and together they sang the Gloria and listened to Ambrose chanting the Epistle and Gospel for the day. All rose for the Creed. They turned to face the east window whose mustard and blue and bloody segments glowed hotly in the morning sunlight. Together they recited the belief that held together the whole of Christendom, the whole of the Western world, a belief that was their passport to paradise. When they came to the words 'and was incarnate by the Holy Ghost of the Virgin Mary and was made man' they prostrated themselves as best they could in their narrow stalls, rising again with lightened hearts to declare their belief in the resurrection of the dead and in the life of the world to come. Their hearts beat faster. Now they were approaching the mysteries, the miraculous moment when God, working through his humble instrument, Ambrose, would change the wafers of bread into His Son's flesh and the jug of wine into His Son's blood.

Ambrose lifted the pyx in both hands and besought God to accept the unspotted Host that was offered for all faithful Christians, living and dead. Fortunate Christians, to have these earnest monks praying for their salvation day in and day out! With agitated pulses they watched Ambrose pour wine and water from the cruets into the silver chalice and offer it likewise to God for the salvation of mankind. They watched him wash his hands in the bronze bowl and wipe them on a white linen square. Again he kissed the altar and the relics and together they cried, '*Sanctus, sanctus, sanctus, Dominus Deus Sabaoth.*' Again Ambrose prayed God to remember all his faithful servants.

The deacon rang the altar bell. The monks strained their necks and their eyes, filled with the familiar excitement that never failed them. With his left hand Ambrose grasped the round stem of the chalice. On to his right hand the deacon lowered the pyx. Ambrose said clearly, 'Take and eat ye all of this.' He raised the Sacraments, one in each hand, and cried in triumph: '*Hoc est enim corpus meum. Hic est enim calix sanguinis mei.* As often as ye do these things ye shall do them in remembrance of Me.'

The bell rang three times. A sigh rose from the monks and mingled with the incense. The miracle had taken place. Ambrose now held in his hands the blood and the body of Christ. Ambrose laid down the Sacraments. He clasped his hands and prayed for the dead and living benefactors of the abbey. They joined him in the Pater Noster. Ambrose prayed that always they might be free from sin and secure from all disturbance. Then he opened the pyx, took out a fragment of the Host and dropped it into the chalice, thus mingling the Sacraments. The monks sang, 'Lamb of God, have mercy upon us.' Again Ambrose kissed the altar. Out of the pyx he took a piece of the Host, broke it in two pieces and said, 'I will take the Bread of Heaven.' He put the two pieces in his mouth, chewed a moment and then swallowed them. The bell rang three times. Ambrose struck his breast and made the sign of the Cross, then cried in a loud voice, 'I will take the chalice of salvation.' He took the chalice in his right hand and said, 'The blood of our Lord Jesus Christ preserve my soul into life everlasting, Amen.' He lifted the chalice to his lips and drank.

In the choir stalls the officials rose and came forward to the altar rail. They knelt. They bowed their heads, murmuring private prayers. 'O God, let Ambrose be made abbot,' prayed Prior. He opened his eyes and stared. A stream of blood, of wine, of something, was trickling down the altar steps. He looked up. Ambrose was on his knees, bowed over the chalice which was tipping its precious contents down his crimson robe and over the pavement. He sank lower and lower. He gasped and writhed. With a clatter of metal the chalice dropped and rolled down the steps, spattering the Sacrament over the communicants.

Prior leapt up and rushed forward in time to receive Ambrose in his arms. The officials hurried up the steps. The panic-stricken monks tumbled out of their stalls and crowded round the altar, the more agile among them leaping the altar rails. Laymen burst in from the nave. But not Thomas Woodville. Thomas Woodville had slunk away.

Under the altar light, surrounded by the brothers, his head in Prior's lap, Ambrose struggled with death. 'God save him,' they prayed, even Abbot's Chaplain, even Nigel Woodville and Henry Osborne. It was all they could manage. Horror had robbed them of all words but these. Violence had penetrated even this sanctuary, the ultimate refuge of the altar, their only haven from intimidation. Alas, what hope was there left for them if evil lurked even in the Holy Sacraments?

They did what they could for him. Infirmarian opened a vein. Sacristan endeavoured to hold St Peter's toe-nails on Ambrose's heaving chest. In vain. At the moment when he should have been reciting St John's Gospel Ambrose gave up the ghost. '*Requiescat in pace*,' whispered Prior, his world in ruins at his feet.

It was the third death.

Letters began to fly along the highways in all directions. Like a man in a nightmare Prior wrote to the Bishop, then in the thick of Novice Master's trial, telling him that Ambrose had been murdered. He also sent the terrible news to the King at Northampton, begging him to allow the election before anyone else lost his life. Nigel Woodville or Henry Osborne, it would have to be one of those two now. For an hour wild notions of another third candidate raged inside Prior's head but he knew he was beaten. He had screwed himself up to his gesture. He had induced a man to present himself whom he had considered—and still did consider—to be Woodchester's only hope of regaining something of its lost soul. But God had allowed that man to be snatched away. There was no time, even if it was God's will, for a candidate of Ambrose's calibre to be found and persuaded and presented. The King was bound to order the election at once. Even he, with his obsession to defeat Warwick's candidate, would not dare delay it much longer.

Thomas Woodville wrote to tell the King that he had great hopes of earning his earldom and that the Woodchester iron was now hot.

From Worcester the Bishop wrote to the King urging him again to allow the election. He also sent Prior instructions that Ambrose's body was to be placed in a tomb but not buried underground; that Prior was to start enquiries into the poisoning; and that the Bishop would come to carry on the investigation as soon as Novice Master's trial—and its outcome—was over.

Nigel Woodville wrote to the King that no candidate's life was safe and that his own chance of success was as great now as it had ever been. The bait was dangling in front of Brother Joseph. Sacristan was enchanted with the statue and the jewelled casket and the golden offertory bowl. Now that Ambrose was dead there was every chance that Prior and Brother Mark would vote for Nigel; he would make every effort to induce them. Brother Peter's vote he was already sure of. Novice Master was deprived of his vote. Guest Master was an enigma but it was possible he might be carried along with the others. Thus wrote the ebullient Nigel, ever hopeful, rejoicing, now that it was over and done with, that his most powerful opponent had been removed. Whoever had slipped the poison into the sacramental wine had certainly done Nigel Woodville a good turn.

Letters were also rushed to Warwick where he sat brooding in his castle at Raby. Both Lord Wenlock and Henry Osborne wrote optimistically, relieved that their great stumbling-block had been so unexpectedly removed. They were confident of victory. Brother Peter was hostile, but Henry Osborne knew a thing or two about Brother Peter that had persuaded him to change his tune. Now that Ambrose was dead Brother Mark could be cajoled or threatened. Prior could undoubtedly be persuaded, now his saintly third candidate had been removed, that it was his duty to support the more experienced and conservative of the two candidates that remained.

Abbot's Chaplain despatched a letter saying similar things in more elegant language.

Letters were sent in all directions but not one of the correspondents hazarded a guess—on parchment—at the identity of Ambrose's murderer. Only Prior had expressed regret for his death.

The King's letters reached him at Northampton. He read them carefully. He made his decision. If both Thomas Woodville and Nigel Woodville said the iron was hot then the time had come to strike. He would spike the guns of those who were spreading it abroad that he did not dare allow the election because he was afraid Warwick would win it. Besides, he did not want his own candidate murdered. That same day his chancellor drafted a licence for the abbatical election at Woodchester to take place on the Feast of St Barnabas in twelve days' time. The King signed it. Chancellor despatched it in the company of twenty soldiers who arrived at Woodchester two days later. They delivered the licence to Prior.

They also arrested Lord Wenlock on a charge of treason.

On that same day a messenger galloped his sweating horse into the courtyard at Raby. To his brother George's relief the news of Ambrose's death jerked Warwick out of his gloomy preoccupation. 'Thank God that Ambrose is out of the way,' he declared. 'I can beat that stripling of the King's with my hands behind my back.' But when three days later he learned that his hands were indeed tied; that his right-hand man, his dear friend and confidant Wenlock, had been declared a traitor and shut up in the Tower in London to await trial; then a devil entered Warwick, a ranting, raging devil that shook the walls of Raby to their foundations. The ice was melted, the dam broken, the walls breached. 'I will show him who is master at

Woodchester,' he shouted, he who had never shouted, except in battle, in his whole life.

Next day he despatched his cousin Mountjoy to Woodchester to take Lord Wenlock's place. He stood in blazing sunshine with his hand on Mountjoy's knee and said to him: 'Only God knows the importance of this election. It is my religious duty to put Henry Osborne in that abbot's chair. It is for the good of England.' Mountjoy looked at him curiously, then shook his reins and began his long and sweltering journey to Woodchester Abbey.

As he jogged southwards, far away in Northumberland a yeoman calling himself Robin of Redesdale was inciting his friends and neighbours to petition the King to govern properly, to dismiss all his favourites and listen instead to 'trusted and great lords of noble blood'. When the news reached the court the King laughed.

'A pack of yokels! What can they do with only a one-armed man to lead them?'

On the eve of the Feast of St Peter and St Paul, when Sacristan was bustling about the church preparing for the unveiling of the statue of St Peter, in the Tower of London Henry of Lancaster—only a stone's throw from Lord Wenlock and two flights of stairs away from where in the dungeons they were applying hot irons to the feet of Warwick's captured messenger —opened his eyes and said: 'I am hungry. Is Queen Margaret coming in soon to her dinner?' It was the first sensible thing he had said for five years.

But it was not any inkling of this marvel that halted Sacristan in the middle of his preparations. He suddenly realized what had puzzled him about Novice Master when he had taken leave of him in his room. When Novice Master had walked forward to open the door he had not dragged his leg.

14

AT THE fifth hour the sun burst over Woodchester as if impatient to sear the few blades that remained upright and suck up the last drops of water in the wells and streams. It set fire to the bronze Cross. It poked its burning fingers into the Chapter House and Prior's room and the monks' dormitory and the infirmary and the Guest House. It cast black shadows over the sepia grass in the cloister yard and over the kitchen cobbles and the retainers who sprawled there on their straw mattresses. It sucked a wisp of vapour out of the fishpond. It lay down in blue and red and yellow patterns on the choir pavement. Even at this hour it was cruelly hot.

John Leys, gazing out of his dormer window at the lapis-lazuli sky, knew that today would bring no relief. He peered up at the abbey wall that was one of his earliest memories. He remembered pissing against it as a lad. He remembered his ma throwing a silver penny over the locked gates when there was pestilence in the village and calling out to the monks to pray for his da'. His da' had died just the same and he had been forced to shoulder a man's responsibilities at fourteen years of age. Twenty-five years of toil and sweat, of coin accumulated and a good standing built, and still he had to go cap in hand to the monks to renew his lease and pay his rents. He had planted willows and hedges. He had dug a sheep-dip. He had built a lambing-pen. He had gouged out two ditches to carry away the water. Water! He spat drily and squashed a maybug with his thumb. What compensation had he received? None. And now those abbey-lubbers were going to take back the leases, and him with his lease due for renewal next Lady Day so they'd not need to pay him a penny for stealing his land.

In Amberley village a cock crowed, and John Leys jumped as if it had sounded in his ear. He scratched his belly, shouted at his wife and strode into the next attic to beat his daughter. The sun was rapidly inflaming his vices and shrivelling up his virtues. His view of life was being distorted by the same waves of heat that made the woods bulge and the fields ripple. He was blazing with hatred of nature, of the monks, of the retainers, of his daughter's seducer. More consuming even than his hatred was his fear, the fear of drought and famine and lingering death. But he had found that by giving free rein to his hatred, by ranting and throwing things, by threatening and running amok, he could, if not silence his fear, at least subdue it. So he went in to beat his daughter, convincing himself that it was his duty to take the skin off her buttocks and to go on doing so until she told him her lover's name. In the same way he was making a whipping-boy of the abbey. What did it matter if some of the things he ranted about were no concern of his? It was enough that some of his grievances were real.

John Leys wrenched up his daughter's shift. What did Rector mean, no concern of his? It concerned them all, what the monks did. They were supposed to be holier than ordinary folk. It was because they were holier and better at praying that they had been given all that land and wealth. If they stopped being holy and gave themselves up to theft and embezzling and kidnapping and heresy and murder . . . He swung his belt and Alice screamed mechanically. Both of them knew that she would never say her lover's name. Yet he beat her all the same.

In the abbey the monks one by one opened their eyes on another scorching day. In the dormitory Guest Master gloomed at the ceiling and stirred his dry tongue, tasting the bitterness of his son's disappointment. Brother Peter plucked another straw from the crack behind his bed. Only eight straws left. Eight days until he received his quarter's pocket-money and ran away to find the Pope. In the fourth bed Brother Joseph unstuck his eyelids and cocked up his toes to see if he could see them. He could not. He sighed and began his private prayers, well aware of the little devil who perched on his straw pillow and whispered wicked suggestions in his ear. In the bed next to the door Brother Mark nodded good morning to his lord Jesus Christ who was standing at the foot of the bed with the sun in His face. Brother Mark was aware, had been aware ever since Ambrose's murder, that his Lord wished to tell him who to vote for in the election. To Brother Mark life was very simple. He did what his Lord told him. That was why he was happy to be obscure and browbeaten. As long as he was unimportant, as long as people expected only foolishness from him, it was not difficult to do whatever Jesus Christ told him. Brother Mark had hopes that this morning his Lord would indicate whether he was to vote for Nigel or Henry. But no, He simply bowed and smiled and, when the bell rang for Prime, faded away.

Prior's eyes flew open at the first touch of the sun. For the first time in his life he committed a bad sin. Caught unawares, dazzled by light, he wished he had died in his sleep. The grooves between his eyebrows were like wounds. Sweat oozed out of his naked head. In two days his face had caved in between the cheekbones and the jaw. His eyes had retreated to the back of their sockets as if reluctant to look at the appalling question of choice that confronted them. Prior's thoughts flew to Ambrose, lying in his stone tomb in a side chapel waiting for the Bishop. All his hopes lay buried with him. Nigel or Henry? One was second best and one was third best, but which was which? Prior groaned and sat up, holding his aching head in his hands. Shouts from the kitchen yard told him that the retainers were already quarrelling over their water ration. He sighed, crossed himself and got out of bed.

Sacristan was up long before dawn. He waddled about his room, his flesh quivering, his red hair glowing, his piggy eyes gleaming with excitement. Novice Master had not dragged his leg! If he had not dragged his leg then his ulcers must be cured. Ulcers cured by the toe-nails of St Peter! Just wait until Winchcombe heard about this. Only let him get proof of the miracle and the pilgrims would come flocking. And Nigel Woodville had talked of faking a cure! That showed he was not fit to be abbot. Sacristan schemed busily. He must take testimonies from every monk who had visited Novice Master before him, to confirm that when they left the room the stink of pus was still there and that, if Novice Master walked at all, he was still dragging his leg. Not even the memory of Ambrose writhing on the altar steps, not even the fact that all the religious houses had refused his invitation to the unveiling, could undermine Sacristan's rapture. The ulcers cured and today the shrine to be unveiled! It was a pity the miracle could not be announced at the unveiling, but Sacristan was both honest and punctilious and he did not intend to divulge the miracle until he had proof of it. When at length the sun crept up to Sacristan's window it found him absorbed in a tactful letter to the Bishop.

Far away in Worcester Novice Master awoke placidly in the prison. He was smiling. No devils squatted on his pillow. To all their questionings and pleas he had one answer. 'God has showed me the truth. The wine does not change. The bread does not change. The Church is suffering from a delusion.' Out of all the community of Woodchester, he who had the hardest couch enjoyed the sweetest slumbers.

In Chapter that morning they said prayers of thanksgiving for the King's licence to elect. Prior preached them a sermon on the delegates' duties to cast out all considerations of their own advantage and to vote only for him whom they thought would make the better abbot. Chapter over, they marshalled themselves into two lines for the unveiling ceremony. The White Bears were oddly docile. Meekly they fell into line behind the monks. The King's men, curious and uncertain, bunched up behind them and made no disturbance while the inferior relic, the despised girdle of the blessed Honoria, was hoisted aloft and the tapers

lit and the Cross raised. Scarlet with excitement Sacristan
tweaked Prior's vestments and gave Cantor the signal and the
monks burst into their joyful psalm, 'O sing unto the Lord a
new song for He hath done marvellous things,' while Sacristan
hugged his marvellous secret like a warm brick. They went
once into and round the cloisters, then through the narrow
archway to the west door of the church. They passed the west
door and proceeded, singing lustily, through the Abbot's garden
to the north gate where the villagers had been told to wait to
join the procession.

There was no one there.

Not a man. Not a woman. Not a child. Not a single soul
had climbed the hill to see the new shrine, to admire the statue,
to touch the toe-nails of St Peter and be cured of whatever ailed
them. No one. Tears of disappointment rolled out of Sacristan's
tiny eyes. The religious houses were jealous—that he could
understand—but why should the villagers not come? They had
been told a dozen times the day and the hour. He peered out of
the gate down the dusty track. No one. He shrugged his gigantic
shoulders. It was their loss.

The procession moved on. They entered the church, journeyed twice round the nave, then came to a halt in front of the
shrouded shrine. This stood, a seven-foot canvas mound resting
on a stone base thirty feet round, on the east side of the north
transept. After prayers and psalms Sacristan fetched the casket
of toe-nails from the altar and, too agitated to do more than
glance at the sleepy watchdogs, put the sacred relics in Prior's
hands in readiness for the divine moment when the canvas
should be whipped off, the statue revealed and the toe-nails
reverently place in the niche prepared for them. In a short speech
Prior told them that the King had presented them with this
statue and the other appurtenances of the shrine. He explained
how pilgrims would be admitted. Then Sacristan cut the cord
and half a dozen servants dragged off the canvas and the shrine
was revealed.

They gasped. Those behind strained and jumped. Their
mouths fell open. There was the stone base and in the middle of

it a block of white stone with a rectangular niche cut out of the front. In the niche stood the jewelled box that sparkled under the candles with all the colours of the rainbow. There was a red cushion for pilgrims to kneel on and, to the left of it, a golden bowl for their offerings. And there was the statue of St Peter himself, the Great Fisherman, the Rock of the Church, six feet of Purbeck marble, dark as well-water with the same marvellous smoothness and translucence. This was St Peter. He stood, stocky and sinewy, on his block of stone, on legs like tree trunks and feet like roots. He flexed the muscles of his arms. He held out his hands to them. His beard rippled and his chest heaved. This was St Peter himself, naked, without so much as a leaf to cover him.

Their eyes bulged. Naked? No. Not naked. Round his organ someone had tied a silver ribbon.

Unadorned, it would not have offended. St Peter was a man and he possessed a man's appendage but he did not flaunt it like Worcester's bronze cherub. He was not proud of it as he was proud of his strong legs. He was not pagan. He said to them: 'This is how a man looks in the sight of God. This is the naked man beneath the silk vestment, the woollen cassock. Be humble but do not be ashamed.' This is what Sacristan had thought. This is what they all would have thought if one of Warwick's men had not drugged the dogs, cut the cord and tied round St Peter's manhood a silver ribbon stolen from Stroud market. The cord had been spliced. Abbot's Chaplain had returned the church key in the same way he had stolen it. A yard of tinsel had ruined everything, as Abbot's Chaplain had intended. It had transformed an object of reverence into an offence.

The retainers began to snigger and point. They made obscene gestures. The monks blushed crimson and looked at their feet. Sacristan lumbered forward and snatched off the ribbon. Spoilt! All spoilt! Without a word Prior laid the toe-nails inside the jewelled casket and closed the lid. Ignoring the nudges and whispers he walked to the altar and returned with the white linen towel. He stepped up over the red cushion and tied the towel round St Peter's loins. It was a rebuke.

In the background Thomas Woodville screwed his curls. Abbot's Chaplain smirked. The White Bears giggled. Even the Rising Suns grinned. Henry Osborne stroked his forearms with his thumbs, well pleased. Attack, that was what Abbot's Chaplain had told him, and here he was attacking and actually enjoying it. And Nigel? Already Nigel's agile brain was at work, making the best of a bad job, working out a way of dipping muslin in plaster of Paris and draping it round the offending member and, after it had hardened, painting it to match the marble. Although what all the fuss was about . . .

The fiasco ended at last. One by one they kissed the jewelled casket. No one was cured. Not a single retainer was cured of his pox or his piles or his corns or whatever ailed him. Monks and servants went out the same as they went in, except that Prior's spine sagged a little more. Sacristan tied the dogs to the rings in the side of the shrine, then he locked the church and went straight to his room. He finished his letter to the Bishop. In it he asked the Bishop to report the state of Novice Master's health, whether there was any remedy Novice Master required, for instance for his leg which had troubled him lately. Sacristan also enclosed a letter for Novice Master, which he begged the Bishop to pass on. In this letter he simply asked Novice Master to tell him what had cured him of his ulcers. He did not hate Novice Master. He knew he was a truthful man who sincerely believed his terrible delusion. He knew that Novice Master would tell him the truth about his cure. He sealed the letters separately and sent them off to Worcester together with two carrier pigeons in a basket. Sacristan wanted his answers in a hurry so that he could obliterate the memory of that tinsel ribbon. Then, being only human, he began to abuse Nigel Woodville because the King had sent a naked statue.

John Leys and Clive Heaven stayed at their stations, one at the foot of the north track and one at the foot of the south track, until the retainers began trickling into the village, guffawing and making ruderies with their fingers. 'There, I reckoned us bain't better go anigh thakky toe-nails and I be right. Un bain't proper, filthy statues and the like. U'll be naked wummen next, all tits and arse.' John Leys' fire was beginning to crackle and flare. Every new titbit of scandal from the abbey he welcomed as fresh fuel to his flames. He began cross-questioning every retainer he could catch hold of, waylaying them in the tracks and fields, singling out the married men and badgering them about what they had been up to before Rector's barn was locked and what girls they had tumbled. He cunningly shared bawdiness with them, egging them on to confidences and indiscretions.

He was not the only one making enquiries. Rector, too, was making his investigations, but discreetly. He did not question the retainers, partly because he did not want John Leys to know what he was doing, partly because the retainers were not his spiritual responsibility. It was for spiritual reasons, and not to pander to Leys' mania, that Rector wanted to discover Alice's lover. The man was married. The man must be about the village, because Alice had admitted that they had coupled many times, and since Christmas there had been no strangers except retainers in the village for more than a single night. Hence it followed that, if he was not a retainer, the man must be a parishioner. Being married and not having come to Rector for absolution, he was living in mortal sin. Therefore it was Rector's religious duty to discover the man and, if he was a parishioner, bring him to repentance.

Alice was as close as a mussel but Rector had one clue, the minute-glass that he had found in his barn. He took it out of his pocket and studied it. The longer he looked at it the more it puzzled him. What business had an ordinary man to be measuring minutes? Man worked from sunrise to sunset. He ate when he was hungry, drank when he was thirsty or when he could bear his thirst no longer. He went to bed when it was dark. The church bell told him when to douse his fire, when to come to church, when to say his Angelus. If he had a cow she told him when she wanted to be milked.

Rector turned over the minute-glass and studied it minutely. There was no name, no initials. It consisted of a glass tube squeezed in the middle so that the sand took about sixty seconds to run through. The tube was attached top and bottom to a wooden frame two inches long, that was itself bedded in a wooden block an inch thick. On this block there was a carving of a man crucified upside down. Evidently the owner of the glass had been born on one of St Peter's feast days. Perhaps he was even called Peter. Rector reviewed his parish. There were only three married Peters in his cure of souls and of these Peter Croke was seventy-one years old, Peter Clutterbuck had been laid up with a broken leg since the beginning of Lent and Peter Didlick was a henpecked husband with eight children. None of the three had two pennies to rub together. They could never afford a valuable thing like this minute-glass, even if they had a use for it.

So Rector worried and probed, groping his way blindly towards an appalling conclusion.

Inside the abbey interrogations and oaths were the order of the day. In an atmosphere as tight-packed with hysteria as a gunpowder-barrel, Prior set about his investigations into Ambrose's murder. During two gruelling days he sat on a stool beside the shrine, his head on a level with St Peter's loincloth, while a hundred and forty-eight men—monks, servants and retainers—filed past him. Each one placed his right hand on St Peter's toe-nails, his left hand on the girdle of the blessed Honoria, and his right foot on a copy of the Holy Scriptures. Each one was told that if he did not answer truly he would be damned. Each one was asked by Prior, 'Do you swear on these holy relics that you did not murder Brother Ambrose?' And each one answered, 'I swear on these holy relics, as I wish to be saved, that I did not murder Brother Ambrose.' Even Thomas Woodville swore. After all, he was damned already. If Archbishop Bourchier would absolve him of murder he would absolve him of perjury too.

This was all Prior could think to do, except lock up each jug of sacramental wine in his own room and hang the key on his girdle. This was bishop's business.

Sacristan, too, was busy. Under the pretext of investigating Novice Master's lapse from grace, he interviewed the monks one by one in the privacy of Novice Master's room. He made them vow on the Cross that they would tell him the truth. Alas, what hope was there for a monastery whose monks had to swear to speak the truth on a holy Cross, for fear that otherwise they might tell lies? Into his spate of questions Sacristan skilfully manœuvred the following: Had they smelt pus? Did Novice Master walk? How did he walk? How did he seem? What did he say?

By the end of the day he had questioned Prior and twenty-seven monks and had established that after Prior and the Bishop and the Bishop's officer had left the heretic's room they had all seen Novice Master. None of them had seen him move out of his chair. All of them bore witness to the appalling stink of putrid matter, a stink that Sacristan knew had vanished the instant he carried the toe-nails in through the door.

The twenty-eighth monk was Brother Mark, gaping foolishly as usual and wiping his ham-fists on his skirts. Brother Mark was so stupid that Sacristan did not attempt to disguise his vital questions. 'Swear to tell the truth,' ordered Sacristan briskly. He handed Brother Mark the crucifix. 'Come along, surely you have a tongue in your head.'

Brother Mark grinned, showing an expanse of scarred gum. 'Aye,' he said at last. 'I 'ool nobbut tell t'truth.'

Sacristan's eyes gleamed. He sniffed like a hound. 'When you last saw Novice Master in this room,' he said, loudly and slowly so that Brother Mark could understand, 'did he get up? Did he walk about?' Two questions at once were too much for Brother Mark. He stared stupidly. 'Did he get up?' asked Sacristan with monumental patience. Brother Mark considered, which in one of his limited intelligence meant scratching his pate and rubbing one foot over the other.

A bee flew in at the open window. Sacristan flapped at it.

'Noa,' said Brother Mark suddenly. 'Un didna budge.'

'What did he do?'

'Un sat on his'n bum and did thikky,' and Brother Mark turned his clumsy head to the right and to the left and back again.

'He shook his head?' asked Sacristan, but did not wait for an answer. 'What did you smell?' he went on. Brother Mark's eyelids lifted clear of the irises.

'Smell?'

'Yes, what did you smell?'

Brother Mark looked round helplessly. There were so many smells, how could he remember one among hundreds?

'What did you smell?' asked Sacristan for the third time. His heart pounded.

Brother Mark shrugged his shoulders. 'I doan't take count of smells,' he said.

Sacristan smiled. 'You may go,' he said.

Brother Mark did not move. He was staring at the window, at the stool Novice Master had sat on.

'Un were there,' he said, pointing with a finger as thick as a leek.

'Yes, yes,' said Sacristan kindly. 'He was there. Now you may go.'

Brother Mark stared, bowed and left the room, leaving Sacristan to gloat over the evidence. It was the toe-nails! Only let him get his replies from the Bishop of Worcester and he would be able to blazon the miracle. He would make the village sorry they had not come to the unveiling. He would make Winchcombe squirm. He went down on his knees, clasped one fat hand over the other and thanked God for this sign of His favour. God knows, Woodchester could do with it.

A conference of a different kind was at this moment proceeding behind a locked door in Abbot's lodgings. A conspiracy, Nigel Woodville would have called it. Henry Osborne and Abbot's Chaplain faced each other across the table. This was a new Henry Osborne. It was as if the old Henry Osborne had been softened in front of a fire and then fashioned into something different, something harder, uglier, sharper.

'I tell you you must fight for it,' cried Abbot's Chaplain, striking the table with his elegant fist. 'There are still seven days before the election. When the time comes the delegates will be locked away. Intimidation is not enough. Custom is not enough. You must make it impossible for the delegates to vote for anyone but you.' He wiped his anxious face. 'You owe it to our patron. It would never do to anger Warwick. He runs deep. There is no knowing what he would do.'

Henry Osborne straightened his shoulders. He no longer twiddled his thumbs. 'I have everything in my favour,' he said firmly. 'I am certain of Guest Master and Brother Joseph and Sacristan. Brother Mark will count for nothing, he will swim with the tide. Brother Peter's reputation hangs on my favour, he will not risk my exposing his guilty passion. But I must win Prior over to my side. How can I further discredit Nigel Woodville in Prior's eyes?'

Abbot's Chaplain leaned forward and whispered in his ear. Henry's eyebrows leaped. 'How do you know?' he breathed.

'Lord Wenlock's spies discovered it. Lord Wenlock confided in me the night before he was arrested.'

'Why did he do that? How can he have known the King was going to arrest him?'

They looked at each other and wondered.

Nigel Woodville reached Prior first. He started by asking his permission to experiment with muslin and plaster of Paris, bought that morning in Stroud, and to use Brother Joseph's paints to colour them. Prior bowed. It was a small price to pay for privacy. But Nigel had not finished with him. 'I think Sacristan will not be displeased with the statue when it is suitably draped.' Prior bowed again. 'I most deeply regret that the statue caused you offence. If I had known that Henry Osborne would play such a trick . . . ' He did not elaborate. He could not find words to say what he meant. He wanted to tell Prior not to turn his face away from new things just because they were not the old things. He wanted to urge him to make his mind elastic like knitting instead of hard like iron; to warn him that it was possible to dig so deep a groove that it became a grave; to show him that man's mind, even a religious man's mind, was for use and invention and creation. He wanted to cry out: 'Is the world to be like this for ever and ever? Is the abbey never to change, to grow, to progress?' But he said none of these things. Instead, being both sensible and clever, he noted the account books and rent-rolls scattered on Prior's table and hitched his stool nearer.

'The retainers are expensive,' he said quietly.

Prior sighed. He yielded to the temptation to share some of his anxieties. 'I have had to borrow,' he muttered, with as much shame as if he was confessing a mortal sin. 'Since the drought the rents have fallen off. The people have not the coin to pay. The price of food has trebled in Stroud market.'

'If the abbey had its own farms,' said Nigel, persistent as the proverbial water that by its dripping wears the stone away, 'then there would be no need to buy food. Drought or no drought, enough would be produced to feed thirty monks and sixty servants.'

'And seventy retainers,' said Prior gloomily.

'Ah, but the retainers will not be here for ever,' cried Nigel, falling smack into the trap.

'Then what will be the need of so much food when they are gone?'

There was silence, then Nigel began again. 'Ambrose was in favour of monks farming their own land. He was always talking of the dignity of labour.' Prior glanced first at his own soft hands, then at Nigel's. He said nothing. Nigel coughed. 'It has always worried you that the books would not balance. As soon as these bad times are over we can alter the finances so that there is no wastage. You will be amazed, Prior, at what efficient administration can do.'

Prior lifted his head. 'We are monks,' he said, 'not clerks of the Exchequer.'

Nigel flinched, then his youthful face resumed its customary eagerness. 'But you wish Woodchester Abbey to become famous, Prior? You wish it to be great, to have young men flocking to become novices.'

Prior raised his eyes. They were faded but not indifferent. There was a hint of wildness in their washed-out grey. 'Winchcombe is famous,' he answered. 'Evesham is famous. Tewkesbury is famous. Romsey Abbey possesses splinters of the true Cross. Tintern possesses the nipples of St Elisabeth of Hungary. Canterbury receives two thousand pounds a year from pilgrims visiting the shrine of St Thomas Becket. Do you know how many monks there were in these abbeys a hundred years ago?'

No, Nigel did not know.

'There were sixty at Evesham, fifty at Winchcombe, one hundred and forty at Canterbury, one hundred at Romsey.' A lump jerked in Prior's throat. 'And do you know how many monks there are there now?'

No, Nigel did not know.

'There are thirty at Evesham, twenty-six at Winchcombe, fifty-three at Canterbury, thirty-four at Romsey. Half or even one-third of what there were. Yet these abbeys are not in debt. Evesham and Winchcombe both have central bursaries such as you advocate. Canterbury is the richest abbey in England and has a shrine famous throughout the Christian world. Tewkesbury has a library. Llanthony breeds sheep and sells the wool in Calais. St Bartholomew's in London has a hospital, yet there are not half the novices there that there were in the Plantagenets' time.' Prior leaned forward on his sharp elbows. 'I tell you these are not the things to attract men into monasteries. They can breed sheep and add up figures and make money and read Greek texts out in the world, on farms and in universities and the King's service. They do not have to be monks to pray at shrines and get medical attention. These things are not what novices are looking for.'

Nigel jumped to his feet. He flung out his hands. 'What are they looking for?' he cried.

Prior closed his eyes. 'You are a monk,' he said wearily, 'and you can ask me that.'

Nigel hung his head. 'They want to get near God,' he muttered.

Prior opened his eyes. 'To get near God. To pray for themselves and for the benefactors of the abbey and for the sins of the world. To live good and holy lives. To shorten their own path to heaven. To sing the Holy Hours and obey the Rule of St Benedict. These are things they cannot do in the world. Such a life requires seclusion and dedication and time. That is why it is undesirable for monks to become obsessed with administration and accounts——'

'Then you must have a lay bursar!' burst in Nigel, the incorrigible. 'Let a layman shoulder your financial burdens and leave you free for religious duties.'

'But these farms——'

'You can have lay managers,' declared Nigel, forgetting all about the dignity of labour. 'Just as now you have lay stewards.'

'But this library, the printing——'

'It need not eat up your time. Employ clerks and scholars to conduct them for you.'

Prior rose. He was as pale as his parchments. 'It appears that you wish laymen to oust the monks altogether,' he said icily. 'Next you will be suggesting that laymen can take over the praying and the worship. Soon you will be saying that laymen can come as near to God as monks. You favour progress, Nigel Woodville. You wish to rush onwards and take the abbey with you. Beware you do not rush in the wrong direction.'

Blood surged in Nigel's ears. How Prior disliked him! He bowed his head and gradually his sanguine nature reasserted itself. There was still a week. Much could happen in a week. It was not as if Ambrose was alive. Henry Osborne was not much, surely he could defeat a man as ordinary as Henry

Osborne. But deep in his heart Nigel's resolution trembled. He knew that, now that Ambrose was dead, what he was fighting was not Henry Osborne but what he stood for, not a man but a tradition.

For as long as they could remember these monks had ambled along their calm, orthodox, cosy, traditional way. Their training had so conditioned them to the past that they saw the future only as a continuation of that past. Custom, tradition, established usage—these were as hallowed to them as they were to Warwick. They had no conception of a world in which things might alter, be discovered, be cast aside. They would no more, of their own free will, let Nigel Woodville interfere with life in Woodchester Abbey than they would let him interfere with the funeral service or than Warwick would let the King interfere with the traditional form of government. Nigel had become to the monks of Woodchester what the King had become to Warwick—a flaunter of tradition, an uprooter and destroyer. The fact that both of them, King and King's candidate, thought that their policies were for the best did not make them any more popular with those whose lives they were disrupting.

Prior pointed to the door. With a bow Nigel left the room, downcast but not so downcast that he could not climb out of his gloom and march straight off to ask Brother Mark to vote for him.

He found Brother Mark defending the well against a couple of King's men who were trying to sneak an illicit drink. He ordered them away but they were fractious with boredom and heat-rash and thirst and, as he had expected, they disobeyed him. So Nigel summoned some of Warwick's men and left the two sides to fight it out while he led Brother Mark past the dormitory into the lavatories. He leaned against a basin and poked his finger up the pipe. The conduits had run dry long ago. Brother Mark stood in front of him, spread-eagling his grimy toes. Six times Nigel said to him, 'Vote for me and you will be doing God's will,' weighting his words so as to penetrate Brother Mark's stupidity. He did not so much as dint it.

But Henry Osborne, when he discovered Brother Mark

feeding the doves after dinner, was lucky enough to find a chink to slip his chisel into. The new, resolute, unscrupulous Henry Osborne said to Brother Mark, 'Have you heard of my lord Earl of Warwick?'

Yes, Brother Mark had heard of Warwick who had sent all these soldiers into the abbey and was, some said, richer and more powerful than the King himself.

'You know that my lord Warwick wishes me to be elected Abbot of Woodchester?'

Yes, even Brother Mark knew that. Thirty-five White Bears had been dinning it into him for months.

'If you vote for me,' said Henry Osborne, 'you shall stay safely here in this abbey for ever. But if you vote for Nigel Woodville the great Lord Warwick will come and snatch you away and you will never be a monk again, never, never, never.' He left quickly before Brother Mark could ask any questions. Had he stayed to see Brother Mark's jaw tremble and his foolish eyes fill with tears, he might have concluded that perhaps after all even the saintly have their price.

On his way to Prior's room Henry Osborne reaped further satisfaction. He passed the novices giggling unsupervised on their stone bench; picked his way over the legs of a dozen retainers sprawled in the shade of the south transept; edged with conciliatory gestures behind a game of dice and prepared to mount the stone steps to Prior's room. A voice arrested him; a voice he had not heard, that no one had heard, for days. 'If I had an enemy,' said the voice, and it was like matter being squeezed out by subcutaneous pressure, 'and I wished to do that enemy the worst injury I could think of, I would make you his master and let you do what you liked with him.' It was Guest Master and he was speaking to Nigel Woodville.

When Henry Osborne tapped and entered, Prior groaned. Was he never to have any peace? He was a man on a rack. His arms and legs were being pulled in opposite directions. He was crying out in agony for the screws to be loosened and his torture eased. He wiped his sweating head and waved Henry Osborne to a seat. 'Yes?' he sighed.

Henry Osborne wasted no time. Nigel Woodville was not fit to be abbot. He had only been a monk a few weeks, he was too young by twenty years. He had no respect for the great tradition of the abbey. Who knew what he would get up to once he was abbot? And Prior must remember that he would command unquestioning obedience. There would be no appeal against him, as long as he lived a moral life. He would frighten novices away, not attract them. Under his leadership Wood-chester Abbey would become worldly and avaricious; it would lose all religious purpose. This was indeed a transformed Henry Osborne. No mention now of increased pocket-money or warm socks in January. 'It is the services that matter,' he cried, tearing page after page out of Ambrose's book. 'Nothing must come between the monks and their devotions.'

Prior thought of the officials biting their nails over their accounts. Henry Osborne noted his frown and coughed Abbot Dominic's cough. 'It is our sacred duty to preserve the fabric of the Church,' he continued. 'Do not be afraid that one day there may be no novices left. There will always be men wanting to escape from life and find peace inside these walls.'

Prior thought of his own noviciate, his blinding relief that now he could throw down his lance and retire from the lists for ever. Henry Osborne pressed on. 'How do you know Nigel Woodville will not tamper with the services?' he asked, for-getting how not a month ago he had been advocating cutting down the number of psalms.

Prior was no fool. He recognized the change of tune but he also recognized that although, in order to get elected, Henry Osborne might advocate such minor alterations as longer holidays, in fact he would alter nothing. He was not, as Nigel Woodville was, a man of his word; but then Prior did not want him to be. If he voted for Henry Osborne it would be for a man who would rule the abbey precisely as Abbot Dominic had ruled it and Abbot Jerome before him. There would be no innovations. How much better to have time to praise and worship and labour on the barricade of prayer that kept Satan at bay; even if it meant inefficiency and wastage in the administration.

'You cannot have it both ways!' burst out Prior in his agony, and Henry Osborne nodded wisely.

'Ah, but you can,' whispered Ambrose's ghost. 'Three hundred years ago, when these walls shone white with newness, the monks here laboured in their fields eight hours out of the twenty-four. Eight hours for sleeping and eating, eight hours for worship in the church, eight hours for labour in the fields. They worked hard, doing laymen's work, but they did it for God's glory and praise. They did not find it a hindrance or an interference. They did not find that it detracted from their spirituality. Think of the monks of those days! Where are they now? It is not the times that have changed, it is the monks. The spirit is missing.'

'But Ambrose is dead!' cried Prior aloud. 'How can the monks change, now Ambrose is dead?'

'Quite right,' agreed Henry Osborne. 'We do not want all this change. Change is an evil thing, you never know where it will get you.'

The sun burned relentlessly. Slowly, slowly, the millstones of everyday life ground to a stop. The well water sank to a single foot so that Cellarer had to use a smaller bucket. Six of the donkeys died. In four days only one donkey-van arrived at the abbey gates with full panniers. Two of the Selsely springs dried up. Driven nearly mad by itch the retainers quarrelled with monks, servants and one another. The monks were troubled with visions of fountains and lakes. Dirt collected under their nails, in their ears, between their teeth, in their groins and navels and armpits. They were sticky and filthy and ashamed of their filth. They began to count the hours to the election. Perhaps when they had elected their abbot God would relent and send the rain. The grain sacks dwindled. In Stroud corn prices soared. There was no milk, no eggs. In the village cattle and sheep and pigs were slaughtered and salted, while they still had any flesh on them. The villagers began searching the woods for bracken fresh enough to make bracken bread. More than one household was eating boiled rats. In the hedges berries shrivelled up and died before they were even born. The nuts did not swell. Cats and dogs vanished. Rabbits went deep underground and died there. Three more babies were buried. Fear retreated and panic took its place. Rector was busy night and day saying Masses for rain and trying to restrain his flock who, goaded on by John Leys, were snapping and snarling and not caring who they bit.

Two hundred miles west in Calais a sweating and disgruntled garrison despatched a message to their captain Warwick confirming their loyalty to the Nevilles 'whatever might betide'. Two hundred miles south in Harfleur the Bitch of Anjou began to amass forces, French forces paid in French coin. She pitched her tent and there she sat, hopefully gazing northwards.

The same sun that skinned her soldiers' backs penetrated even the six-foot walls of the Tower, making Henry of Lancaster scratch and ask for water. When the water was brought he astounded his gaoler by saying: 'Why do you not bring the silver bowl with roses engraved on it? It was a christening present from my uncle Bedford. I hope it is not lost. I should like my dear son Edward to have it after I am gone.'

It was the same sun that made Lord Wenlock sweat in his stifling cell with its iron bars in the window, but even its heat could not penetrate to the dungeon, twenty feet under the ground, where Warwick's luckless messenger was being put to the torture for the third time. He did not need the sun; there was a glowing brazier and red-hot irons instead.

The same sun set fire to the golden spire of Westminster and made a dazzling square of the parchment between the King's hands. It was a holiday sight: the young King crowned with golden curls, his blue eyes sparkling, his legs sprawling, munching marzipan and jingling the silver bells on his marigold sleeves. He tossed the parchment into his chancellor's black lap. 'Tell them to continue with the irons,' he said, his mouth full of sweetmeats, 'but to give the man rests so that he does not collapse altogether. I must have names, Chancellor, more than one name. I want the names of all the men in England who have so much as breathed treason in their sleep.'

Chancellor shifted uneasily. 'My lord will remember that under torture a man will say anything, any name, that he thinks may ease his agony? Is it wise to continue with the irons? There may be no traitors for the man to name.'

The King leapt up and strode to the window. 'He gave us Wenlock's name, did he not?'

Chancellor shrugged. 'Yes, my lord. After Wenlock's arrest. After Wenlock was lodged in the Tower. Do you think the messenger would have said his name if he had not heard from the gaoler that Wenlock was already in custody?'

The King gazed at the sparkling river. 'I cannot trust them,' he muttered. 'I cannot afford to trust them. Their allegiance is not to me but to England. Soon they will be saying that to serve England and to serve me is not the same thing.'

Greatly daring, Chancellor ventured: 'It is not you the Nevilles object to, my lord. It is your counsellors.'

The King flung himself round. Dazzled by the sunlight he saw only a black figure seated on the couch. 'I loved him once,' he cried, exasperated that life would not do just what he wanted, that he could not keep Warwick's affection without doing his will. He began to argue with the black figure. 'I have a right to appoint my own counsellors. I want to build up my own party, faithful only to me, owing everything to my favour. How can I do what I think right with a cartload of barons breathing down my neck, telling me I cannot do this, I cannot do that, that is not the custom, I am breaking sacred traditions?' He thrust out his hands to the black figure. 'Can you not see? You are living in the past. I am thinking of the future. I want to do great things for England. I want to increase her trade; lead her into glorious victories; build palaces for her filled with beautiful books and statues and pictures. I want to make her rich and famous so that travellers flock to her as they now flock to Italy. How can I do these things if I bind myself hand and foot to a council of barons who squash progress as if it was a snake? I want to trade

213

in my own ships: oh no, that is a vulgar occupation, not fit for a king. I want to make war on Louis of France: oh no, England cannot afford to go to war, let us stay at home and let him scheme against us. I want to employ Italian painters and sculptors to make beautiful things for my palaces: oh no, they will depict nakedness and nakedness is evil. I want to set up a printing-press in Westminster: oh no, printing is an invention of the devil.'

He let his hands drop. The black figure rose and became Chancellor. He began to speak of tact, of disquieting news from the north, of rumours from Harfleur. 'Can you not give a little, my lord?' he pleaded. 'It is not wise to shut them out entirely. Extend a hand. Invite Warwick and Northumberland and Oxford to this parliament. Perhaps'—he glanced at the King's downcast eyes—'it might be advantageous at this moment to send one or two of the Queen's relations on diplomatic journeys. John Woodville, perhaps; he makes mischief easily. Lord Scales is complaining of ennui. Or Earl Rivers, a pilgrimage to Rome. . . .'

The King raised his eyes. They were the blue of steel. 'And you, Chancellor,' he said coldly. 'Where will you care to go?'

Chancellor jumped and protested: 'But I am not a Wood-ville! I am a bishop. Warwick cannot object to a bishop being your counsellor. Bishops always have seats in the Great Council. What the Nevilles object to is your taking counsel of men who are distinguished not by birth or honour but simply by being your wife's relations.'

'No.' The icy syllable chilled even that broiling air. 'No.' The King came close to Chancellor, who trembled. With a tinkle of bells the King raised his right hand and laid it on the crucifix that hung round his neck. He said: 'It is not the Wood-villes that Warwick objects to. It is not the men I choose that he minds. It is the fact that I choose at all and that I have chosen to exclude him.'

There seemed nothing more to say. This was a different king, more mature, more independent; following a policy rather than a whim, clutching Woodvilles round him not simply to pander to his queen but because they enclosed and protected him and did what he told them without criticism. Nothing more was said about despatching Woodvilles abroad.

'News from the north, my lord,' said Chancellor, consulting another parchment. 'Five hundred yeomen have attached themselves to Robin of Redesdale and are moving south towards Durham. Their demands are the same, that you should dismiss your present counsellors and readmit the ancient barons of the realm.'

The King brooded. Five hundred. What could five hundred do? Nevertheless it might be judicial to write to his brother-in-law Charles of Burgundy requesting troops and ships to be made available. At this point the Queen entered. The King jerked his head at the door and Chancellor scuttled away. Even in pregnancy she had lost none of her allure. Every pore of her white skin breathed out animal lust. Her yellow hair was plaited and coiled and drenched in perfume. Her lashes were tipped with charcoal, her lips reddened with cochineal. Her crimson dress was gathered into folds under her breasts and armpits. Her muslin bodice did little to conceal the attractions underneath. The King was pulled towards her as if by strings. He put one hand on her neck and pushed the other inside her dress. Her hands gripped his curls. He began to tremble and sweat. He pulled her to the cushions and began to fumble with her laces. 'My lord, remember what the Bishop of London said. Not until——'

'God damn the Bishop of London!'

He burst the laces and flung himself over her.

Later, thinking to please her, he murmured in her ear, 'Your cousin Nigel will soon be abbot.'

She stretched like a cat and pulled his head down to her breast. 'Abbot? Abbot?'

She had forgotten all about Nigel.

15

O N THE fifth day before the date of the election
Lord Mountjoy reached Worcester. Choked by dust,
blinded by sun, reeking with sweat, he and his party
had ridden thirty miles a day in order to please their lord Warwick. Mountjoy claimed the Bishop's hospitality and was
admitted to the Bishop's palace. When he asked the cause of the
hustle and bustle he was informed that a monk from Woodchester Abbey in Gloucestershire was being tried for heresy.
He was at this moment having his last hearing. If Lord Mountjoy
cared . . . Lord Mountjoy did care. He was given a seat at the
back of the court. He watched and listened.

The heretic stood behind wooden railings on the left of the
dais. He was dressed in white, with a hemp girdle round his
waist. His feet were bare. His face was covered with stubble.
His flesh had shrunk so that Mountjoy could see the bones that
supported it. His eyes were as calm as two pools of water.
Bishop was frantic. He eased the sweltering robes round his
neck. He mopped his scarlet face. He turned with helpless
gestures to his two archdeacons, to his chaplain, to the dean and
the priests and officers. He sighed. 'If you are determined to go
to hell there is nothing I can do to stop you.'

'I shall not go to hell,' replied Novice Master, placing his
dry hands on the wooden railings. 'God has told me what is the
truth about the Mass. I am prepared to die to uphold God's
truth.'

Bishop threw up his hands in despair. For eight days he
and his clergy had worked on this hardy heretic. They had
prayed, cajoled, threatened, besought, persuaded, intimidated,
pleaded. They had recited recantations to him and begged for a

sign, a lift of the finger, a nod of the head, to show that he repented of his error. They did not want to burn him. They longed to save his soul. In vain. Novice Master clung to his delusion and stiffened himself to suffer the flames.

With sorrow the Bishop rose and read the condemnation of the court. He told them that a disease such as this heresy could not be cured by gentle remedies but must have harder plasters. In doing this the Church was hurting the heretic medicinally for his own good as well as for the good of Christians everywhere. He told the court that it was his religious duty to pluck up by the roots and burn all heresies that might undermine the true faith. Novice Master bowed. Rapidly and distastefully the Bishop ordered his officers to hand over the heretic to the Sheriff of Worcester, to be burned publicly in the market place in two days' time. But, he added, priests and monks were to sit with him and pray for him continually; if they felt so much as a breath of repentance they were to run for the Bishop at once.

Novice Master bowed again and was led away. He looked the happiest man in the room. He walked out of the room, neither limping nor dragging his leg.

Lord Mountjoy dined with the Bishop and heard tales of Woodchester that made him wish Lord Warwick had chosen someone else for this mission. At dawn he was saddled and away. As he left, the Bishop gave him a letter for Sacristan. 'It will save my messenger a journey,' he told him. But before Mountjoy had gone five miles he was overtaken by a Bishop's servant demanding the letter back. For the Bishop had suddenly remembered Sacristan's pigeons. He was ashamed he had not replied earlier and he did not want to appear discourteous, so he ordered his clerk to copy his own reply in brief in mapping hand on a scrap of waxed paper. This he fastened to one of the pigeons. On another scrap of paper his clerk copied the two words that Novice Master had written in reply to Sacristan's appeal. This scrap he fastened to the second pigeon. His servant carried the birds up to the top of the cathedral tower and there released them. After circling twice they flew steadily southwards towards their home. The Bishop was pleased he had remembered the pigeons but he never learned what a colossal weight hung on that thread of memory.

The pigeons passed high over Mountjoy's head at Severn Stoke but he did not notice them because one of his horses had developed a swollen fetlock. He decided to rest the horse for a day and take advantage of the delay by having all his horses reshoed. What difference could one day make? The election at Woodchester was not for four days. There was plenty of time.

At the ninth hour William Leys, John Leys' eldest son, spotted the first pigeon over Lightpill where he was gathering fungus for his mother's stew-pot. It arrived over the abbey a few minutes later and, scared by the whirling fists and boots below, began circling round and round the spire. In vain Sacristan spread precious corn on the belfry sill. In vain he heaved himself up a ladder to the roof of the pigeon house, cooing and clucking like a demented hen. The pigeon was wary. Soon she was joined by the second pigeon. They wheeled in the still air, afraid of the noisy men in stockings and breeches. At last they ventured down on to the dormitory roof and began walking up and down the roof-ridge. Sacristan called for a ladder but by the time the servants had lugged it from the pigeon house the retainers had fished out their slings and were taking pot-shots at the pigeons with stones.

'No, no,' roared Sacristan. 'These are carrier pigeons.'

He waddled towards the men, shouting and waving his fists, but they had come a long way since the day they had quailed before Sacristan's fury at the altar rails. They saw waddling towards them not a monk, not a priest, but a mountain of fat; a wobbling sweating hulk of a man as filthy as themselves, his face disfigured by red stubble, his eyes inflamed, rivers of dirt striping the insides of his colossal forearms. A pebble kicked up dust at his feet. Another pinged on the stone behind him. He turned and ran for safety. He toiled up the steps and pushed open the dormitory door. Sobbing with heat and haste he hurried past the beds and climbed the wooden ladder. He pushed open the trapdoor and poked out his head. A stone clipped his right ear. Below, the yard was cobbled with onion heads, each turned up towards him and painted with a gaping mouth and two eyes. He sank back until only his blistered pate showed above the trapdoor. He turned his head. There were the pigeons, each with her tiny cylinder strapped to her left leg, marching up and down the ridge a pace from his forehead. 'Coop!' he said. 'Coop, coop, coop!' The men mocked. Sacristan straightened his knees and engineered a handful of corn out of the trap. Ping! A stone split his thumb-nail. The men roared. This was a good game. Sacristan's hand came to life again. His knuckles crawled up the tiles.

The first pigeon eyed the corn and ventured off the ridge. Ping! Ping! Stones hit the roof on either side of her but she was hungry and the corn gleamed. On she came. She knew this hand. It had never hurt her. She pecked. She stepped into Sacristan's palm and his sausage fingers closed over her. One. Under cover of the trap he slipped the cylinder off her leg and popped it into his pocket. He dropped her into the dormitory and scattered corn for her. The instant his red pate poked up again the onion heads screamed with excitement. Stones began to fly like hail. He was struck on the temple and the cheek. Threads of blood got entangled in his stubble. Ping, ping, sang the stones but to Sacristan they were no more than flies. All he was aware of was the second pigeon, a gunmetal shape against dun woods and brown pastures. He offered his corn. The pigeon waddled towards it. Softly his finger and his bleeding thumb closed over her leg. Gently he pulled her towards the trap. The onion heads howled and jeered. A flint flew through the air and ploughed a furrow across Sacristan's scalp but he never released his hold of the bird and a second later the cylinder was in his hand.

He backed down the ladder. Oblivious of the blood that was pouring down his back and between his buttocks on to the floor he opened the cylinder and prised out the Bishop's letter.

Heretic burns, he read. *Health exc. Legs perf. Bishop comes.*

So he was right. Novice Master's ulcers were cured. He kissed the letter, rolled it carefully, pushed it into its cylinder and secreted it in his inside pocket. He took out the second cylinder and extracted Novice Master's answer. He began to tremble. The scrap of paper jerked and he had to steady it with his other hand before he could read the two words written there.

Two words? What two words? Toe-nails? St Peter? The relics? What two words had Novice Master used to describe the miracle that had cured him? The words danced, grew tired, lay still. Sacristan's eyes read them. His eyes told his brain what the words were.

Brother Mark. Brother Mark. Brother Mark.

Sacristan's fingers rolled up the words and secreted them in his inside pocket. He closed his eyes. All of a sudden life became too burdensome and he pitched forward on to his face.

At noon William Leys reached home with the fungus which was soon bubbling in the pot along with bracken and roots and rooks' bones. They ate together, John Leys and his sons William and Thomas and Arthur and young Geoffrey and Mistress Leys. The disgraced Alice could wait for her grub. She had been sent with the last of the pigs deep into the woods in search of last year's acorns, and if she found solace there in her lover's arms surely God could not blame her.

After dinner John Leys sent William and Geoffrey up to guard the springs and Thomas and Arthur to the salting and he himself, after warning his wife on no account to leave the last of the grain unguarded, walked down the slope to speak to Rector about his daughter Alice. In spite of the heat Rector's door was shut. John Leys should have knocked but he was tormented by heat-rash and he had sore places in both armpits so he kicked the door irritably and burst in in time to see Rector scrabble for something on his table. Before he could carry it to his pocket John Leys' fingers closed over his wrist. The red hairs on Leys' head bristled with suspicion. His grimy fingers tightened. With a little gasp Rector opened his hand and the minute-glass fell on to the table. Leys snatched it up.

'What be 'ee hiding thikky for?' he growled. A knowing look crept into his eyes. ' 'Ee bin stealing, Rector?'

'No, no.' Rector made a snatch for the glass but John Leys held it high above his head.

' 'Ee be mighty pertickler along of thikky glass,' he said softly. 'Not yourn, be un?' Rector shook his head and bit his lower lip. 'Where be from then?'

Rector screwed himself up to lie but could not squeeze out a drop of deceit. He blushed scarlet and muttered, 'I found it.'

'Found un? Whereby found un?'

With a sigh Rector shifted his responsibilities. He was only human. He had done his best. He was certain it did not belong to any married Peter in the village, nor for that matter to any married man in the parish. Perhaps it belonged to one of the retainers. There must be many married men among them, many Peters. Perhaps it even belonged—but Rector's imagination would not jump the last ditch. He looked at the minute-glass in John Leys' hairy hand. 'I found it in my barn,' he said.

Slowly the wheels of John Leys' brain began to turn. With a grind and a thud the first cog engaged, then the second, then another and then another until the whole machinery was whirring and shuddering. Leys' blue eyes bulged. His hair crackled. His mouth opened and shut. With a scream of rage he crashed his free hand on the table. A mug jumped on to the floor. ' 'Tis his'n!' he roared, spitting all over his chin. ' 'Tis his'n what laid my wench and disgraced I.' He was like a man possessed by devils. He beat his fist on the table until the skin split. 'I 'ool mammock un! I 'ool jigger un! I 'ool hackle un . . .' He gasped for breath.

'It is no man in the village,' said Rector quietly. 'I have made investigations and I swear it.'

The machinery gathered speed. Leys' forehead puckered with the effort going on behind it. 'I 'ool show un to she,' he said softly, patting the buckle of his belt. 'Her 'ool tell I whose it be and then there 'ool be a wapping and a larroping.' His eyes gleamed at the thought of finding a legitimate target for his wrath. He gloated over a picture of himself beating into his daughter's lover all the fears and frustrations and furies of his own life. Whack, whack, whack, whack! If only he could serve those abbey-lubbers the same way.

In the Abbot's garden, happily free from Cellarer's scolding, Brother Mark sat crumbling bread saved from his dinner for the Abbot's doves. There was a blissful lull, an oasis of quiet. Worn out by the excitement of the pigeons, weighed down by a dinner of porridge, the retainers dozed in the kitchen yard. In the infirmary Sacristan opened his eyes and felt for the two cylinders in his secret pocket. He groaned, not because his head hurt him but because he saw a road before him, a road that split into two roads; only one of these was the right road and he had to choose between them. He knew which one he wanted to take, the one carpeted with palm-leaves and hung with bunting and flooded with sunlight; the one where birds sang and pilgrims lined the way. The other road was obscure, quiet and apparently deserted; a humdrum, dusty road that did not look as if it led anywhere important. Sacristan did not like the look of it. He closed his eyes to shut it out. 'Just a little bleeding,' he heard Infirmarian say. 'And a foxglove poultice for your head.'

Brother Mark smiled. Now there were four doves, six pigeons, two sparrows, a thrush and a mouse feeding off the crumbs. If he stretched out a hand he could touch the thrush. He touched her. The thrush hopped on to his knee and pecked his thumb. Brother Mark stroked her feathers, starting with her soft forehead and ending with her tail. The doves fussed. The sparrows swallowed crumbs too big for them. The mouse curled up on Brother Mark's big-toe joint. The thrush shut her eyes in bliss as the clumsy finger swept down her back again and again and again.

'Idling as usual, brother!' Abbot's Chaplain's scorn shattered the peace of the Abbot's garden. The birds flew off. The mouse ran up Brother Mark's leg. 'You are wanted at once in the cloisters so you can leave your daydreaming and do God's work for a change.'

With a sigh Brother Mark got up and brushed his skirt. He was too stupid to resent the interruption. Or perhaps in an obscure way he realized that while he was thus browbeaten he was safe, because as long as his superiors bullied his body they would never think of bothering with his soul. He dawdled. He said good-bye to the birds and wandered along the passageway between the west wall of the abbey and the west door of the church. Through the archway ahead floated noises of altercation. He was not in a hurry to get closer to them. Level with the west door he stopped. He turned to look at the doorway that he had passed through hundreds of times in procession. Behind the closed door he pictured the shadows of the nave, the pillars soaring up into the roof like beech trees in winter, the rectangular brasses, the statue of St Peter made decent by a concoction of Nigel Woodville's that in the gloom could scarcely be distinguished from marble. He imagined the wrought iron of the screen, the side chapel where Ambrose lay, the choir stalls, the Abbot's empty chair, the brass rail, the altar steps and the altar that was the centre of their lives. Such a beautiful church deserved a beautiful entrance. Brother Mark's eyes travelled up to the Norman arch, five perfect semicircles sprouting from ten clustered pillars. Each semicircle was set back from the one above it so that the receding arches seemed to beckon. Brother Mark stepped forward. Between each semicircle there was a band of decoration, four bands altogether, two of rose pattern and two of dog's-tooth. He looked at the dog's-tooth. Up, down, up, down, up down, up down, it went. Its symmetry pleased him. He moved nearer. And there, not at all to his surprise, was his lord Jesus Christ. Jesus did not smile. He watched Brother Mark intently, seriously and for a long time, long enough for even Brother Mark to realize that this was a meeting of special importance. Yes, Brother Mark understood. His lord Jesus Christ was telling him something. Perhaps it was the name of the new abbot? Would Jesus speak? Would He make a sign? Brother Mark nodded violently. Yes, he was ready to listen, to watch.

223

Jesus raised His right hand and pointed upwards—at what? The archway? The semicircles? The decoration? The west window? The roof? The sky? Brother Mark investigated all of them in turn. What did Jesus mean? Steadily Jesus pointed upwards, His compassionate eyes fixed lovingly on this sweating, lubberly, stupid young monk. Then Brother Mark saw what He meant. Up down, up down, up down, up. Brother Mark sighed with relief. There was no need to bother his head any more. Jesus Christ had shown him how to vote.

When Brother Mark eventually arrived in the cloister yard he found all the monks assembled. It was Henry Osborne who had summoned them, in order to effect his *coup de main*. Sacristan, his head a mass of bandages, was placed solicitously on a bench, Brother Joseph beside him. The novices squatted round the dry pond. Guest Master stood apart, fingering his disfigured ear. Brother Peter leaned against a pillar. Brother Mark stroked the mouse that had taken up lodgings in his pocket and wondered why Sacristan was staring at him so. Scenting drama, servants and retainers crammed the cloisters and wangled themselves into inaccessible places.

The stage was set. Abbot's Chaplain fetched Prior from the church and as the clock struck the hour Henry Osborne appeared leading a puzzled Nigel Woodville by the sleeve and engaging him in pleasant conversation. They reached the centre of the cloister yard. Instantly Henry Osborne dropped Nigel's sleeve as if it were verminous. He contorted his stubbly features in disgust and shouted at the top of his voice: 'This man is not fit to be abbot. I can prove it.' He forgot his dignity and began jumping up and down screaming, 'I can prove it, I can prove it.'

The retainers roared. It was better than a show. Thirty or so monks all looking like something the dog brought in: filthy, bedraggled, blotched, scratched, bandaged, sweating, intimidated. There they were, bellyaching about whom they should choose for abbot, slinging mud at one another and rolling in muck; and the two they had to choose between no better than the rest, a tubby clown who did what the one with the bashed-in nose told him, and a black-eyed pirate with curls over his ears who never knew when he was beaten.

Henry Osborne flung up his arms. 'Nigel Woodville cannot be abbot,' he shouted. 'He is not a true priest. He is illegitimate!'

There was silence. The seriousness of the charge robbed it of all comedy. They had all seen Nigel administer Mass.

'Blasphemy!' shrieked Abbot's Chaplain. 'Nigel Woodville has perjured himself at the altar.'

Sacristan laid his aching head in his hands. No more dear God, no more. Prior closed his eyes. With no prompting from Thomas Woodville, Nigel leaped to his own defence. 'I am a true priest,' he cried. 'I had a dispensation from the Bishop of Lincoln. The Bishop is still alive. You can write and ask him.'

'No man born out of wedlock can be a priest,' intoned Abbot's Chaplain, getting his own back for not being a whole man.

'Do not be ridiculous,' snapped Thomas Woodville. 'Everyone knows a bishop can dispense with bastardy. Is that not so, Prior?'

Prior inclined his unhappy head. Under his sunburn Henry Osborne turned pale. Wenlock had unearthed nothing about a dispensation.

'He lies!' he roared, astonished at his own vehemence. 'He has never had a dispensation.'

Mud flew.

'He is too young, he has scarcely been a monk five minutes.'

'What does that matter? St Thomas Becket was not made a priest until the day before he became archbishop.'

'If you make Henry Osborne abbot it will be Abbot's Chaplain who rules you. Who wants an impotent ruling Woodchester Abbey?'

'If Nigel Woodville is abbot you will not be able to call your souls your own. Under Henry Osborne the abbey will be safe. Nigel Woodville will ruin it with his new fangles.'

'Make Henry abbot and the abbey will be bankrupt in five years.'

'Henry Osborne concealed heresy.'

'Nigel Woodville pretended he was kidnapped. . . .'

Thus Nigel and Thomas Woodville threw mud at Henry and Abbot's Chaplain, who caught it and threw it back again. The monks watched, turning their eyes from one assailant to another as if they were watching a tennis game. The retainers jeered and egged on their favourites. But deep down they all knew that it was not battles like these that would decide the victory.

'I have the King's favour and the King's wish is paramount.'

'A king is not a true king whose wishes are dictated by his wife's relations.'

'Henry Osborne has the favour of the great Warwick.'

'Warwick is a traitor!' burst out Thomas Woodville.

A dozen White Bears snatched their knives. Thomas Woodville was promptly enclosed, and Prior with him, by a circle of Rising Suns.

'Henry Osborne is the image of Abbot Dominic.'

'Tell him to unbend his finger!'

'Nigel Woodville will fill the abbey with naked statues.'

'Listen to him! He has good cause to be ashamed of nakedness.'

In twos and threes retainers began to creep down from their perches and crowd in behind their friends. Instinctively the monks started edging into the east cloisters. Sacristan heaved himself up and barged unsteadily, Brother Joseph in tow, towards the south transept. Brother Mark prised Guest Master out from between two Rising Suns and piloted him past the Chapter House towards the south door of the church. Brother Peter slid like an eel in the same direction. Individual fights broke out. Adeptly the servants made themselves scarce. From the safety of his Rising Suns Thomas Woodville suddenly yelled: 'It is Henry Osborne who is not fit to be abbot. He has a whore, a concubine, a kept woman.'

There was uproar, a babel of shouts and yells clearly heard in the village. Abbot's Chaplain denied the charge at the top of his voice. Those with sharp ears caught snatches of Henry Osborne's protests. 'Fifteen years ago . . . renounced her on . . .

Bishop's pardon . . . penance. . . .' It did not really matter what he said. It was not past scandals but future intentions that sat in the scales.

By this time the monks were hemmed in in the east cloister and Prior had fought his way through the Rising Suns at the door of the tower. He had made a decision, not *the* decision, not the almighty and everlasting decision, but one big enough to show him that his will, although ailing, was certainly not on its deathbed. He took a key from his girdle and unlocked the tower door, the same door from which Abbot Dominic's seizure had been announced aeons before. He spoke to Sacristan, to Brother Joseph, to Guest Master and Brother Peter and Brother Mark. 'Get inside,' he told them. 'You will be safe in the tower and servants will bring you food and drink and mattresses.' Obediently they filed past him into the tower, although Brother Peter's feet dragged. Prior slammed and locked the door after them.

'Are you not going to lock yourself in too, Prior?' asked Cantor fearfully. 'What if the retainers . . .'

But Prior shook his head. It was not physical violence he feared. Besides, some semblance of authority, however faint, must remain in the open. What would the Bishop say if he arrived to find Prior not in the cloisters to greet him?

Immediately Cantor rang the service bell and the depleted monks hurried into the church for Nones. Prior followed them in and locked the door. It was the first time in the history of the abbey, the first time in three hundred years, that the church door had been locked during a service. The door secured, Prior called the five delegates to come down from the tower room by the inside staircase. Whatever disaster happened, the services must go on. There had never been a service missed, not even when the kitchens caught fire, not even when half the community died of the plague. They sang their service.

The delegates climbed the stairs to the tower room. Servants brought bread and wine and a brown jug of water. They lugged up five straw mattresses and arranged them in a row against the north wall. They made arrangements for night-soil. They fetched missals and bibles. They brought up inks and paints and parchments for Brother Joseph and ointments and bandages so that Brother Peter could dress Sacristan's wound. This small square room, twelve feet by twelve feet, was to be their home for four days. Until they had elected their new abbot they were to look out of no windows but these.

Brother Joseph lay down and fell asleep. Guest Master sat down at the table, piled one tiny hand on top of the other, crossed his ankles and stared at the blank north wall. He never spoke a word. Brother Peter leaned against the east window and gazed at the village. He imagined Alice tying up her bundle and hiding it in her bed in readiness for flight to the nuns. He wondered if after all he would have to run away without his pocket-money. He wondered how he was going to get out of the tower. Brother Mark sat down on a stool by the door and fished his mouse out of his pocket. It ran up his sleeve and popped out under his chin. Brother Mark put it back on his hand and it ran up his sleeve again. He tried it with the other sleeve. He balanced it on his instep and let it scramble up his calf and over his knee. He closed his thighs so that it could hop on to his other leg. He wedged a grain of corn between each of his toes and grinned his gap-toothed grin when the mouse accepted his invitation to dinner.

From under his turban of bandages Sacristan watched him. So this was the miracle-worker. Not the precious relics that had cost fifty pounds and travelled all the way from Rome but a simple-minded youth who played childish games and made mistakes even in the *Te Deum*. A miracle-worker. There had not been a living miracle-worker in any English abbey since the thirteenth century. In those days there had been the anchorite walled up in Pontefract, he was said to have worked miracles. There had been Philip of Evesham, Gilbert of Sempringham, St Hugh of Lincoln; all these had been monks and had worked miracles while they were still alive. But their kind had died out two hundred years ago. Now it was always the dead, and their

precious relics, who worked miracles. But Brother Mark—
Sacristan eyed him where he sat playing with his mouse. There
was a red-hot iron searing his scalp but in his excitement he
scarcely felt it.

The sun was very bright on the road ahead of him. The
air was filled with Hosannas and Alleluias. The way was thronged
with pilgrims: on crutches, on litters, crawling, hopping,
dragging themselves on wooden contraptions. Here were the
blind, the deaf, the barren, the impotent, the imbecilic, the
possessed, hundreds and hundreds of them making their way to
Woodchester Abbey so that Brother Mark might heal them.
He would dress Brother Mark in white and seat him on a marble
chair beside the shrine of St Peter. The pilgrims could be admitted
between Nones and Vespers every day. There must be a book
to record the cures. Brother Joseph could decorate—here
Sacristan's wound pierced him. Brother Mark must have
touched Brother Joseph dozens of times yet the old man's
failing sight had not been restored. Ah, but even Jesus Christ
had not cured everybody. They would still come, even if
Brother Mark cured only one in a hundred of them, because
the afflicted never give up hope.

Brother Mark laughed and clapped his beefy hand over his
mouth. Sacristan gazed at him. The light from the east window
shed over him a radiance Sacristan had never seen before. It was
the radiance of happiness. Sacristan's fingers closed over the
letters in his secret pocket. He had only to produce them and
Brother Mark's life would be transformed. Instead of being the
butt of the convent he would be revered by them all, even by
Abbot's Chaplain. He would have a place of honour. Each time
he lifted his hand everyone would wonder if a miracle was
about to take place. Pilgrims would crawl to his feet. Even
Winchcombe would send its sick monks. Young men would
beg to enter a monastery that had a living miracle-worker.
After his death Brother Mark might even be proclaimed a
saint. Woodchester would be the first English abbey for centuries
to have one of its brothers canonized. What a splendid, shining
road for a man to choose. Sacristan drew the letters from his

pocket. He held the tiny cylinders closely in his sweating hand. He opened his mouth to say, 'I can show you a wonderful thing.' But he found he could not move his tongue. 'I . . .' he began. 'I . . .' Brother Peter turned to look at him. 'It is nothing,' muttered Sacristan, astonished at what his tongue was doing. He laid his bandaged head on his arms. Later. He would tell them later.

The sun set. In the village Alice drove the pigs up over the dry brook. Faint with heat and hunger, she toiled after them up the slope and herded them into their pen. She pressed a hand to her stomach, her breast, her burning eyes. She tasted Brother Peter's kisses on her parched mouth where his spit had dried. When she reached her own threshold she was panting for water. She dragged herself over the sill and fell on her knees beside the crock. She seized the iron spoon and had gulped one mouthful when a sound made her look up. There was the table shining in the setting sun. There was her father, legs straddled, belt in hand. And there was her lover's minute-glass, lost months ago and never recovered. She screamed. She screamed and screamed so loudly that all the neighbours came running and her father was ashamed to beat her. Besides, he had his answer. Find the owner of the glass and he had found his daughter's seducer. While the wives were still slapping Alice's face and loosening her dress he was on his way up to the abbey to question the retainers. But he was too late. Curfew rang while he was a hundred paces from the gate. The gates were closed, bolted and chained, and no amount of ringing or shouting could persuade the porters to open.

Night came. The five delegates slept on their mattresses in the tower room. Nigel and Henry tossed on their feather beds in the Abbot's lodgings. Prior paced his hot room, flogging his will to a decision. In the village Alice lay on her side, awake and afraid. How could she warn Brother Peter that her father had his minute-glass? It could not be long before he discovered who owned it. She must send him a message; no, feeling ran so high in the village she would never persuade even a child to take it. She must go herself as soon as the gates were open. She must warn Brother Peter not to wait for his pocket-money but to run away at once. She turned over and rubbed her swollen stomach.

Among his sons and neighbours John Leys dozed at the Selsely springs. The minute-glass was snug in his pocket. He too was waiting for the opening of the gates. In Severn Stoke Lord Mountjoy slept lightly, ears cocked for the birds' dawn song. In the blacksmith's stable his horses stamped their new shoes. At Westminster the King lay with his queen. In Raby Castle Warwick sat beside a single candle, making patterns with the corpses of insects perished in the flame. In his prison Novice Master slept like a baby, oblivious of the faggots piled in the market square, of the barrel and the chains.

At the fourth hour Novice Master was roused. He was stripped naked except for a cloth round his loins and a rope round his neck. His left leg was whole and unmarked. The Bishop came in his nightcap and begged him in vain to recant. The prior of the cathedral carried in the Holy Sacraments and begged him to admit the miraculous change. Novice Master shook his head. In spite of Brother Mark's cure—or perhaps it was because of it—he had not changed his mind. With tears running down his face the Bishop ordered the execution to proceed. As the sun came up the procession was formed of monks and clergy, with the heretic in their midst. The way was lined with people kept silent by sadness and horror and relief that they themselves were not similarly deluded. In the market place they were met by the Sheriff. Prayers were said and the second and thirty-seventh psalms sung, proclaiming that God would bruise the ungodly and break them in pieces, burn them and wither them and root them out. The silent crowd gathered round. The Bishop prayed aloud that even in the flames this hardy heretic might repent of his ways and be saved from hell. Two men lifted Novice Master into the barrel and fastened the chains round his waist. He asked for a Cross and the Bishop gave him his own, made of ivory with a silver figure on it. The faggots were piled round the barrel. A dripping sponge was put in Novice Master's hand but he dropped it. It was then fastened on to the end of a pole and pushed against his face but he said: 'I do not want it. I want to suffer so that you will see the truth.'

The Sheriff clicked his fingers and six men came running with flaming torches. They thrust the torches into the faggots and the pile blazed like a bracken fire. Flames leapt ten feet into the air, singeing the Sheriff's eyebrows. Novice Master never made a sound. His hair, beard, flesh, sinews, nails and bones were burned to ashes. When the fire died down there was nothing left but the chains, the iron hoops of the barrel, ashes, and something black that had been the Bishop's crucifix.

It was over. The Bishop watched the remains being shovelled into a weighted sack and thrown in the river, then he returned to his palace to prepare for his journey to Woodchester for the investigation into Ambrose's murder and for the abbatical election.

An hour before dawn Lord Mountjoy saddled his horses and set off for Woodchester Abbey.

When the first cock crowed Alice put on her dress and crept up to the north gate of the abbey, ready to ask the porter, when he opened the gate, to fetch Brother Peter to speak to her.

At daybreak John Leys roused himself. He lugged water down to the village, snatched a crust for his breakfast and sat down with his friends to wait for the opening of the abbey gates.

The monks rose for Matins at midnight and then returned to their beds. At five o'clock the retainers began to stir. At half past five the two porters emerged sleepy-eyed from their shelters and took a look at the clock in the cloister yard. Half an hour before the bell rang for Prime and they could open the gates.

But the gates never opened.

At ten minutes to six a woman screamed in the village. A terrible wailing broke out. Women and children rushed up the street, screeching and crying. Some hammered on Rector's door. Some toiled up the slope shrieking to their men to come down. Up at the springs the men jumped up. Their hands flew to their knives. Was it an attack? Had the retainers run amok? They plunged down the track. On the other side of the gate the porter shot back the Judas-grille and peered through. Six paces from his nose the villagers met. The women wept hysterically. Many fell on their knees. Children were trampled. The men appealed for information. How could they put the trouble right when they did not know what it was? At last a woman put a name to the disaster. A name. A single word.

The porter's face blanched. He snapped the grille shut. The retainers pressed round him. What was it? Why did he not open up? What was wrong with the women? The porter opened his eyes.

' 'Tis t'plague,' he said.

In the terror-stricken silence that followed, one voice was heard. It was the voice of John Leys. He shook his fist at the abbey gate and shouted, 'Thairn prayers bain't no good!'

16

'THAIRN prayers bain't no good!' What a depth of disillusion was there in John Leys' bitter words! They were terrible words, words that tunnelled like sappers under the monastic ideal, undermining its defences. 'Thairn prayers bain't no good.' They no longer had the power to keep evil at bay, that was the dreadful thing John Leys was saying.

A woman scrabbled at her bosom, flung back her arm and hurled a penny over the abbey gate. 'Pray for my lad,' she screamed. 'Pray for Walter Heaven.' Her husband knocked her down. Not John Leys. Her husband. He gripped her wrist. 'Thakky monks bain't praying for no lad of mine,' he growled. 'Let Rector do t'praying. Them be bad men in there.' He spat in the dust. Where he had spat John Leys spat, and his sons and his friends Loveday and Goodman and Luker. One by one the villagers spat on the threshold of the abbey and cursed the monks whose sins had brought down on them this most terrible of all God's afflictions.

Their hearts nearly died of despair. Drought they could fight, even if it meant trekking to the Severn and camping there until the rain came. Famine they could fight, even if they lost the battle, even if they were reduced to boiling earth and beechhusks. But plague! For plague there was no remedy. Plague chopped people down as a sickle chops barley-stalks. One day they were erect and healthy, the day after—or if they were unlucky the day after that—they were dead. They became disfigured with black boils the size of walnuts. Before they were even buried their families might be dying on the same beds. Before now whole villages had been wiped out by plague. A hundred years ago a third of the people of England had died of it, so it was said. Like a poisonous snake it lurked in the undergrowth and was lured out by heat and dryness to feast on innocent victims.

'Us bain't done nought,' shouted William Leys. ' 'Tis they abbey-lubbers did ought to get t'pestilence, not we.'

'Hush up, boy,' muttered his father. 'Them do be going to get t'pestilence sure enough.'

They trailed back to the village and immediately Rector was besieged by men and women clamouring for Mass and prayers and confession. They feared the plague but what they feared more was dying of it so abruptly that they had no time to be absolved of their sins. Prayers said, John Leys hurried with his friends to see what could be done for Heaven's boy. They found him unconscious and bathed in sweat. There was a black swelling behind each ear, three on his chest, one in his groin and six on his legs. While they watched him two more began to push at the skin on his forehead.

'What can us do for un?' asked John Leys, and when Rector answered that the only thing they could do for him was bleed him Leys immediately took charge of the operation.

They did what he told them without a murmur. They never questioned his leadership any more than sheep question the ram with the bell round his neck. Leys took out his knife and wiped it on the blanket. He stretched out the boy's arm and selected a vein. Rector brought up the basin. In went the knife and the boy's blood welled out into the basin. Leys counted slowly. When he reached a hundred he stamped his thumb on the cut and then tied a cheese-muslin round it. Mother and children sobbed. Rector arranged on the floor by the mattress the appurtenances of the last rites: the holy oil, the lambswool, the crucifix, the holy water, the wine and bread. He put his stole round his neck. '*Kyrie eleison, Christe eleison,*' he began. John Leys got up and went out into the brilliant sun. Ahead of him he saw endless endurance but his body yearned for action, for something to thrash and break. He picked up a stick and slashed at some sheepgrass that was the only faintly green thing within reach. At the third slash his hand hit his pocket. He dropped the stick and pulled out the minute-glass. Well, at least it would be useful for the bleeding. For an hour he had actually forgotten it.

Before her father reached his house Alice had crept down

from the north gate and was away with the pigs, finding a crumb of comfort in the thought that at least her father could not get at Brother Peter now.

Fifteen miles away to the north Lord Mountjoy reached Tewkesbury. He stopped for ale at an inn and there heard from a pedlar that plague had broken out in Stroud and in some of the surrounding villages. The pedlar had seen four doors north of Stroud marked with a white cross and he was running away as fast as he could go. Lord Mountjoy turned northwards and began the long journey back to Raby. He did not possess Lord Wenlock's devotion. On his way through Worcester he told the Bishop of what he had heard and immediately the Bishop ordered his bags to be unpacked. 'Thank God I remembered the pigeons,' he said. 'The monks of Woodchester will have to elect their abbot without me.'

For an hour or two a dozen retainers and a couple of servants who had been shut out the night before hammered for admittance on the abbey gates. When the gates did not open they sought lodgings in the village. No one would take the retainers, who eventually trudged into Stroud and lost themselves there. The two servants found a lodging with Robert Cordwell, who was grateful to Sacristan for selling him land.

At noon a man called Thacker fell down in Woodchester churchyard and was carried home raving to his terrified wife. He had three black boils on his neck. John Leys opened a vein and let out twenty ounces of blood. Instead of counting to three hundred he took out the minute-glass. He upturned it and watched the brick-coloured sand run five times through the squeeze in the glass. He enjoyed slipping his knife into the vein. It was a hurtful action. It released a fraction of his pent-up fury.

When he was summoned to the third victim, the pregnant wife of Philip Luker, he jabbed so hard he cut two veins and blood splashed his face. 'I wish we had Infirmarian to help us,' said Rector with an end of bandage between his teeth.

John Leys wiped his knife on his sleeve. 'Catch thakky monks risking thairn necks!' he replied. 'Village can perish but them 'oon't budge t'finger.'

236

'I do not know that this bleeding brings much benefit,' said Rector sadly.

Leys stuck his knife in his belt. 'Un be doing good to I,' he said. He prowled round the room like a lion seeking a way out of a cage. His red hair flamed. He flung up his arms and stamped his feet. To lash the air and the earth was better than doing nothing. Rector watched him anxiously. This man was ripe for violence. Pray God he found nothing to justify it!

If the village was in terrible straits the abbey was not to be envied. It was in a state of siege. Plague beat on its doors and tried to insinuate itself through chinks and cracks. Inside these walls were cooped up seventy retainers, over sixty servants and thirty-one religious, none of whom dared put a foot outside. There were ten inches of water in the well. The only drink they had in abundance was the sacramental wine. What was to happen when the well dried up? There was grain for perhaps a week. There were four dozen hams, a cellar full of onions, a hundredweight of last year's black puddings, a quarter of oatmeal. What was that among a hundred and sixty men? The plague might last for weeks, even months if there was no change in the weather. It seemed to Prior, whom this latest disaster had turned into an old man in a day, that sooner or later they would have to choose between starvation and plague. And what of the retainers? Here were dozens of undisciplined men packed like herrings inside the baking walls. There was no one who could control them. They were owed a month's wages. They were terrified of death. They were crazy with itch and sweat-rash. The ale was finished. Their diet was porridge and salt ham that made them mad for water.

In the tower room Brother Joseph had arranged his writing materials at one end of the table. In a semicircle in front of him were his ink, his charcoal, his ruler, his eraser, his quills, his paint-pots, his brushes. On his left hand was a psalmody. In the centre was a sheet of clean parchment clamped on to a wooden frame. He began measuring the sides into half-inches, preparatory to drawing lines. After an hour of smudging and peering Brother Joseph began to cry. Brother Mark came and sat beside him and patted his hand. Despite his aching head Sacristan turned the parchment over and ruled heavy lines for him. Brother Peter selected the best quill and put it in his hand. 'Do not worry if you cannot copy as you used to,' he told him. 'There are hundreds of your manuscripts in the book cupboards. You are leaving a wonderful legacy to the monks of the future.'

Brother Joseph wiped his nose and made the downstroke of a very shaky 'P'. Guest Master sat like a statue, feeding on his hatred. They spoke little. Prior had forbidden them to discuss the candidates. If they did not mention the plague it was easier to forget it. After Mass Brother Peter intercepted Prior and asked him about his pocket-money. Prior was astonished. He asked sternly, 'How can you think about pocket-money at such a time?'

Brother Peter blushed and stammered: 'On the tenth. The quarter is up on the tenth.'

Prior answered: 'There is time enough for pocket-money when the plague has gone. How can you speak of it when you cannot leave the abbey?'

Brother Peter bowed. So he would have to go without his pocket-money. He could not wait. The election was in three days' time. He could not break his solemn oath to the two White Bears nor risk Henry Osborne exposing him. He was sorry for Nigel Woodville. He would like him to be abbot. But he did not imagine his own disappearance would make Nigel's chances any smaller than they were already. He returned to the tower room to change Sacristan's bandages.

Sacristan grunted as Brother Peter eased off the bloody wool. He was perplexed but not by the question of abbot. He wanted Henry Osborne to be abbot, not because there was anything remarkable about Henry Osborne but because Sacristan did not want as abbot a man who did not believe in miracles. No, Sacristan was perplexed because he could not bring himself to tell Prior about Brother Mark's powers of healing. Every time it came to the moment he could not utter the words. He was not seeing the right pictures. He tried to imagine Brother Mark seated on a marble chair in a white robe and all he could see was Brother Mark playing ridiculous games with his mouse. As Brother Peter tied the last knot Sacristan looked at Brother Mark. For the first time it occurred to him to wonder how Brother Mark was going to vote.

Down in the church Prior and Cellarer were busy hearing the retainers' confessions. It had taken the plague to drive these unruly men into the confession-box. All through that broiling day Prior and Cellarer sweated inside their boxes listening to sins so hair-raising they did not have a name for them.

The day crawled on. The gentry of Woodchester, Thrupp, Ebley, Pitchcombe and Slad debated how best to warn strangers that they were entering a plague area. No right-thinking man wanted the plague to spread and none of the plague-infested population wanted foreign mouths to feed. Notices were posted on the highways. White crosses were chalked on trees. Sir Thomas Arundel devised a startling plan for warning any travellers using woods or sheepwalks or travelling by night. He began arrangements for sounding regular warnings from the Amberley slopes that overhung the valley opposite Woodchester Abbey.

In the night Heaven's boy died and plague seized another victim, a little girl of three, Rector's brother's child.

Brother Peter did not run away that night because Sacristan was feverish and needed constant attention.

On the day before the day before the election the sun came up quickly and beamed at the havoc it had made. Prime. Chapter Mass. Sext. High Mass. In the village Rector came out of his confession-box to read the burial service over Walter Heaven. The ground was so hard they were forced to use picks. There was no doubt the mood of the village was changing. It was not browbeaten but belligerent. John Leys' fire was rapidly bringing them to the boil. Old resentments bubbled. Even the women began to shake their fists at the walls. There were no more pennies thrown over the gate. It infuriated them to think of men protected by those high walls from a danger that they themselves could not avoid. They were terrified by every twinge. Covertly they inspected their friends faces for signs. They felt they were doomed men, destined to die of starvation if not of pestilence, and like most doomed men they wanted to take others with them, preferably those they blamed for their misfortunes.

After the burial Leys tapped off four ounces of blood from Rector's little niece, measuring the sixty seconds by the minute-glass. The more he handled it the more significant the glass became and the bigger his loathing for its owner grew. Rector watched little devils twitching Leys' arms and legs and pulling his mouth about. To the villagers he insisted that the heat had turned John Leys' brain, but they did not believe him. John Leys' obsessions had become their obsessions.

All except Robert Cordwell, who had bought land from Sacristan. But he broke out in black swellings after dinner and would not be long in this world to protest.

In the abbey the monks cleaned their faces with their own spit. At every available moment Henry Osborne and Nigel

Woodville badgered Prior to vote for them; told him he must use his influence with the delegates. After Vespers Prior put his hands over his ears, hurried to his room and locked himself in. Only thirty hours to go until he could order the election. The Bishop had named the date and Prior had no power to advance it. Besides, St Barnabas' Day was an auspicious day.

The day blazed to its end behind Selsely Hill. In the tower room Brother Joseph took his tears to bed. Guest Master unpiled his little hands and lay down on his mattress. Brother Mark fed his mouse with crumbs and started to snore. Sacristan drank his medicine and declared he felt better. He soon fell asleep. Brother Peter lay wide-eyed, his heart hammering. At midnight Cantor's bell roused them for Matins. In pitch darkness they felt their way down the stairs to sing the hours of Nocturn and Lauds. In the choir the candlelight was merciful to their filthy hands and faces, their inflamed eyes and bedraggled habits, their dirty teeth, their black nails, their rashes and sores and stubbles of beard.

Brother Peter managed to sit in the end stall nearest the south side of the altar. When they had sung the last *Gloria Patria* he darted out of his stall into the shadows. Crouched over, he tiptoed along the empty back stalls until he reached the chancel screen. Sacristan, Brother Joseph, Guest Master and Brother Mark detached themselves and disappeared up the tower stairs. They would never miss him in the dark. Prior doused the candles and led the file of monks out through the nave into the south cloister. In the darkness no one noticed the extra hooded figure on the end of the crocodile's tail. Brother Peter followed the queue of monks along the east cloister. When he reached the door of the scriptorium he slipped into the archway. Prior locked the church door and then passed him, taper in hand, and disappeared. There was a padding of felt boots on the dormitory stairs. Doors thudded. Brother Peter waited until he could distinguish the roofs from the sky, then he moved cautiously towards the dormitory. Yes, it was still there, the ladder that Sacristan had intended to climb to lure in his pigeons. He did not climb it at once. He stole round the corner of the refectory and inched along the wall, a pace away from three snoring retainers, until he came to the kitchen. Outside the kitchen was a closet and from this he stole the clothes of the dead kitchen boy. He tied the clothes round his neck and hitched his cassock over his girdle. He climbed up the ladder and stepped into the lead gutter, then edged along it, leaning his weight on the tiles. In this way he traversed the roofs of the dormitory, the infirmary, the Guest House and the disused almonry. A solitary light burned in front of the porter's shelter. The yard was littered with grotesque bodies, arms and legs abandoned in sleep. A century before, alms had been dispensed to the poor from a window in this almonry but when the monks stopped dispensing charity it had been bricked up. Brother Peter hung from the wall by his hands and found the lintel with his toes. His fingers found two cracks previously selected. He groped with his left foot and found the window-sill. He clung to the lintel. He muttered a prayer and leapt backwards into space. He landed on all fours, unhurt, on the track. He changed into the kitchen boy's clothes and hid his cassock in the willow copse. He crept down through the village to the highway and began running south towards Bristol.

Dawn. The day before the election. Luker's wife, and the child inside her, had died in the night. Thacker was unconscious, no more than a penny's width between his boils. Rector's niece whimpered and tossed. Robert Cordwell had had to be strapped to his bed. At midday his wife begged John Leys to bleed him if only to weaken him into lying still. Leys snatched out his knife and ran to Cordwell's house. He had a grudge against Cordwell and enjoyed slashing him. He jabbed with his knife and out welled the blood, dark blood that gave Leys a sensuous pleasure. He stood the minute-glass on a stool and watched alternately the trickling of the ruddy sand and of the crimson blood. He crouched between his knees; his pale eyes darted to and fro. The whispering in his head changed to a mutter, then a shout, then a roar. Mechanically he turned the minute-glass once, twice. Heat weighed him down, crushing his head between his shoulders. His muscles shuddered. Monstrous thoughts filled his brain. He turned the glass again and then again, so that St Peter stood on his head, but he did not clamp his thumb on the vein. Fascinated, he watched the blood flow. With every ounce of Cordwell's blood a little more of Leys' sense drained away, until at last he was not a man but a puppet dancing on devils' strings.

There was a sound of footsteps and a man came in. It was one of the two abbey servants who had been locked out two nights before. 'I see 'ee got Brother Peter's minute-glass,' he said. 'Infirmarian were mighty mad with un for losing un.'

The floor rocked under Leys' haunches. Brother Peter! They all knew Brother Peter, the young one with black eyes always mooning about the woods looking for herbs. Brother Peter! Leys' brain clicked frantically. Miraculously the bits dropped into their proper places. His daughter's seducer was married—to the Church. His daughter had been ravished by an adulterous monk. His daughter's lover was a monk from Woodchester Abbey, the hated abbey that was going to gobble up all their land, the loathed abbey that harboured brawlers, thieves, murderers, heretics, plague-mongers—and now adulterers. The last thread of John Leys' control snapped. He seized the minute-glass and rammed it in his pocket. He jumped up and rushed from the house. His bellows of rage brought the village running. ' 'Tis a monk bedded she,' he screamed at them. ' 'Tis thakky Brother Peter. Un bain't fit to live, coupling with my lass, snaking into she. . . .' Foam spattered his lips. He was mad, and like all madmen he won their allegiance by leading them into acts they would not dare on their own.

'He is mad,' they said to themselves. 'We will do what he says and the blame will be his because he has bewitched us.'

'Us be going to winkle un out,' Leys shouted. 'Us 'ool bust into t'abbey. Us 'ool larrop thakky Peter for what un done to my girl. Us 'ool give it to they monks.' Then he threw up his arms and roared, 'Us 'ool give t'monks t'plague!'

His madness infected them. A knot of men gathered round

him: his sons, his friends Luker, Heaven, Goodman and Loveday with their sons and nephews. The women snatched up their children and hurried home. Leys surveyed his forces, fifty able-bodied men thirsting for action, any action so long as it hurt those they hated. Leys shouted his orders and the men scattered to find ladders, flails, pitchforks, cudgels and knives. They never asked themselves what exactly they were going to do once they had scaled those walls. They were going to punish Brother Peter and they were going to give the monks the plague. That was all they knew.

In vain Rector pleaded for restraint. John Leys' answer was to lock him in his own belfry. The two abbey servants were caught and trussed before they could give the alarm. In his house Robert Cordwell bled to death.

They made their preparations stealthily. Ten ladders were laid on the north track in readiness. Each man sharpened his knife. Seven carried flails, twelve carried pitchforks, ten carried rabbit-bows and the rest carried cudgels. Leys armed himself with a chain off his waggon-wheel. But their most deadly weapon was invisible, the infection they carried on their skin. Each drank and swallowed a crust of bread. Each kissed the crucifix that hung round his neck, for already they had become God's avengers. They squatted silently in the dust, waiting for the Nones bell, for they wanted to catch the monks in church before Brother Peter could be hidden. If any of them thought of first asking for Brother Peter to be handed out of the gate to them he did not suggest it.

It was hotter than ever. The baked landscape wavered in the heat. Sweat rolled down their faces, making rivers in the grime. Then the abbey clock struck two and Cantor's bell rang out, so loud in the scorching air that Sir Thomas Arundel's men heard it in Amberley. Leys jerked his head. Twenty men hoisted the ladders and in a shuffle of dust the villagers moved up the slope to the north gate. The bronze Cross flashed in their eyes. No one spotted them. They propped five of the ladders against the north wall. Two men mounted each ladder carrying another ladder between them. When the leading men reached the top of the wall they laid the ends of their ladders flat on the stones and pushed them out over the Abbot's garden. It was not until the bottoms of these dropped with five thuds on to the Abbot's grass that the drowsy porter came out to see what was up. He yelled and rushed to the church and began hammering on the north door but by the time Prior had unlocked the door a score of villagers were already in the garden and a dozen more were on the inside ladders, their weapons over their shoulders.

'Them's village!' sobbed the porter. 'Them's plaguey.'

Prior ventured a few steps into the open. 'What do you want?' he asked. 'Leys, Heaven, Luker, why have you climbed the wall?'

Leys stepped forward. The last of the villagers reached the grass. Monks' faces peered out of the north door. Leys fished the minute-glass out of his pocket and held it up in the sunlight. 'Who be t'owner of thikky?' he demanded.

Prior peered. 'Infirmarian!' he called. There was agitation in the church and Infirmarian shuffled forward. 'Is that one of our minute-glasses?'

Infirmarian gazed in Leys' direction. 'I cannot see,' he complained.

Leys marched forward. With a gasp of terror Infirmarian stumbled back. Contemptuously Leys stood the glass upright on the ground and retreated four paces. Infirmarian advanced and looked at it. 'It is Brother Peter's,' he said.

With a shout of triumph Leys kicked the glass and smashed it against the church wall. In the nave the dogs growled. 'Fetch un out!' he bellowed. ' 'Tis Brother Peter tumbled my wench in Rector's hay. I want un.'

A spasm contorted Prior's face. 'But he is gone,' he stammered. 'He ran away in the night.'

Heaven laughed. 'Expect we to credit thakky, monk? 'Ee got un hid safe away.'

'No, no. He ran away in the night. I swear it. He was found to be missing at Prime.'

Leys lurched forward. ' 'Tis lies. 'Ee got un hid.'

Prior clasped his hands. 'I implore you to believe me. Whatever his sins, Brother Peter is not here to answer for them.'

By this time the west end of the garden was packed with retainers who dared come no nearer for fear of catching the plague. They bunched up like cattle showing the dirty whites of their eyes. Behind them the servants crouched. The villagers flourished their weapons but the retainers had no intention of fighting the abbey's battles. Let the monks settle their own quarrels. The retainers' only concern was to keep well away from infection. Nor did the servants, not even Prior's steward, intend to fight. They feared the plague and none of them liked the monks well enough to fight for them. Let them get on with it. The monks were forbidden by their Rule to fight. Whatever Leys wanted of them he could take without violence.

Prior retreated a step. 'Brother Peter is not here,' he insisted. 'I swear it on this holy Cross.' He snatched his crucifix and held it up. 'Go back to the village, Leys. You can do no good here.'

'Then I 'ool do 'ee harm,' shouted Leys. He darted forward whirling his chain. Prior stumbled backwards and fell. Mad with frustration Leys swung back his chain and heard . . .

The end of the world.

A noise like a million drums burst over them. It rocketed into the air, bounded from hill to hill, rolled up and down the valley. Out of the cloudless sky it fell on to their heads, splitting their eardrums and sending them frantic with terror. It was the Day of Doom, like Rector had told them. Leys dropped his chain. He fell on his face and waited for the earth to open under him. Behind him his men fell. The retainers scrabbled in a heap. Speechless with dread they lay like dead men, hands clutching the backs of their necks, waiting for judgement. But nothing happened. The waves of din retreated. They felt the sun burning their calves. There was grit under their tongues. They heard the doves flap one by one back to their house. A thrush sang.

On Amberley Hill Sir Thomas Arundel's men surveyed their ten smoking muskets. 'Thikky 'ool warn travellers,' said their sergeant. 'Nobody bain't coming nigh when un hears thikky rumpus.'

Inch by inch Leys jerked up his head. Prior was gone. All

the monks were gone and the north door was tight shut. It was a trick. He sprang up. 'There bain't nought to fear,' he shouted. ' 'Tis only t'thunder.' He rushed up to the door and rattled the handle. Locked. He hurled himself against it and the oak tossed him back like a pebble. 'Bust un open!' he yelled. The sound of chanting reached him. He shook his fist. 'Babble on, monks. 'Ee 'oon't do Brother Peter no good, not once I do catch un.' But he was not completely lost, not yet. There was still a jot of reason free of the devil that possessed him. 'We 'ool search t'abbey first. If we doan't winkle un out we 'ool bust t'church door in shatters.'

He gave his orders for a search and they obeyed them without a murmur, as men will always obey the reckless and the obsessed. He posted four men at the north door, in case Brother Peter should be inside and make a dash for freedom, then he gathered his little army about him and made for the passage that led into the cloisters, carving a way through the mass of retainers and servants as easily as a leper. Men retreated ahead or dodged back into the Abbot's garden. Others flattened themselves against the west door, under the dog's-tooth decoration, and when Leys walked towards them to try the lock they melted away like butter under a hot knife and crammed themselves into niches or crouched on the ground thinking themselves invisible. When the villagers trampled over them they lay there quaking, feeling little plague-worms crawling down their backs. His men at his heels, John Leys tramped on into the west cloisters. His power was going to his head. Like Moses, he had only to raise his hand and the waters divided in front of him. He amused himself by darting at tardy retainers, making them scream and shrink. Soon his lieutenants Loveday and Heaven and Goodman and Luker began to copy him. Another four men were posted at the west door and another four at the south door and two at the tower entrance.

'Us 'ool turn t'abbey topside down, chaps,' said Leys, winding his chain round his fist. 'Everywheres, mind.'

He ordered Luker to take ten men into the kitchen yard and to watch the south gate. Loveday was to take ten men and investigate all the east buildings. Goodman was to search the refectory and the cellars. Heaven must do all the officials' rooms. Leys himself would search the Abbot's lodgings.

They scattered and set to work, driving retainers in front of them like sheep, crowding them in confined spaces, repaying them for their thieving and bullying and wenching. At first it was almost a game. The villagers ran in and out of forbidden places, excited as children. All their lives, and their da's' lives and their granda's' lives, as far back as anyone could imagine, this abbey had been sacrosanct. For centuries it had cast its shadow over the village. They nearly all owed it rent. Yet here they were, made free of all its secrets, given *carte blanche* by their leader to poke and pry; and no one to stop them because no one was willing to touch them.

They began harmlessly enough. In the kitchen yard Luker's men ransacked the stables, the smithy, the bake-house, the masons' lodge, the empty chicken-houses, the shambles and the brew-house, which they were disappointed to find full of nothing but empty barrels. They hurled stones down the well and listened for groans. They rampaged through the kitchens. When they found no sign of Brother Peter they began ripping open closets, shifting sacks, peering in ovens and salt-barrels. They searched the pigeon-house. They slashed open the retainers' mattresses and tossed the straw about with their pitchforks, as if Alice's lover might be lurking inside.

On the east side Loveday and his men searched the old almonry, the dormitory, the Guest House, the infirmary, the warming house, the scriptorium and the Chapter House and Prior's room above it. They raged through the buildings like an earthquake but they found nothing—except Thomas Woodville skulking under his feather bed in the Guest House. They pawed him until he babbled in terror, then chopped off his ringlets and his twenty-six-inch sleeves and pushed him out into the yard with his mouth stuffed full of feathers. But it was still fun, nothing more. For a while they amused themselves by daubing one another with Brother Joseph's paints. Those that could write scribbled obscenities on the walls with his charcoal. They poured

Infirmarian's medicines into the bathtub and smeared foxglove poultice all over the mattress on which Abbot Dominic had died. They played games on the benches of the Chapter House. They tore up Prior's account books and hacked open his oak chests. But they found no money inside, not a single penny. Neither did they find Brother Peter.

Meanwhile Goodman's party was making hay in the refectory, dancing on the tables, kicking up the rushes, lugging up from the cellars what was left of the grain and the hams and the onions. And still they meant no harm, no serious harm, except of course to Brother Peter.

In the officials' rooms Heaven and his men made a systematic search, prising open cupboards and chests. They found nothing; no monks, no money. In disgust they scotched their initials on the doors and then withdrew to compare notes with their leader.

John Leys had drawn a blank in the Abbot's lodgings. He had turned it upside down from attics to cellars and found no trace of his daughter's seducer. He too had broken open the money-chests and found them empty, for all the Abbot's accumulated coin had either been spent or been taken away by the King's official. There had been no rents to reimburse it. But what he had found was the abbey's stock of sacramental wine, ten butts of the finest Bordeaux, enough to give fifty men the courage to commit sacrilege. 'Whet t'whistles, lads,' Leys told them; and they came running with mugs, horns, ladles, jugs, whatever they could lay their hands on, and drank and drank this delicious red liquid that they had never tasted in their lives. They found it did marvellous things to them. It made them brave and strong and righteous so that when Leys shouted to them to lash the ten ladders together to make a battering-ram they rushed to obey him, never doubting that it was proper to batter down a church door in order to chastise one wayward monk.

Inside the church the monks crouched with hammering hearts at the altar, the officials and the old men clinging to the altar stone and the younger monks on the next step stretching over their shoulders to touch the altar hangings and the novices on the lowest step each hanging on to a monk's skirt. Abbot's Chaplain had insinuated himself near the centre. His beautiful lips moved in prayer but his less beautiful mind was wishing that the villagers would burst in and mistake Nigel Woodville for Brother Peter and give him a jab too many. Sacristan squeezed St Peter's toe-nails between his massive knees. Brother Joseph rested his cheek against the blessed Honoria's girdle and sang softly the age-old supplication for help. As the most lowly of them all, Guest Master knelt the farthest from the altar Cross and reflected grimly that this was what the abbey deserved for serving him so badly. Brother Mark thought nothing at all. He opened and shut his mouth and listened to the yells from the Abbot's garden and the growling of the dogs tethered to the shrine.

'Under the shadow of Thy wings shall be my refuge,' they sang, Nigel and Henry as loudly as any. Prior huddled in the midst of them, his forehead pressed to the door of the tabernacle. 'Until this tyranny be over past I will call unto the most High God,' he sang. Tears trickled down his face. He had sunk into a despair so profound that he could not imagine ever struggling out of it. How he had failed his monks. How the villagers must hate them. How angry God must be with Woodchester Abbey to allow this terrible thing.

Crash!

Something hit the north door like a cannon-ball. The dogs leaped and snarled on their chains. The chant wavered and stopped. The monks huddled closer to the altar. The smallest novice put his arms round Brother Mark's waist. Closer and closer they pressed, trying to creep into God's bosom. Again the north door jumped on its hinges. They heard John Leys shouting. The dogs rattled their chains and snapped at the panting, heaving men on the other side of the oak.

Crash!

The monks burst into their favourite prayers and clutched their Crosses with their free hands. Abbot's Chaplain had a sudden vision of himself as a fifteenth-century Thomas Becket, martyred on his own altar and performing miracles before his brains had dried on the pavement. Sacristan took a fresh grip on the toe-nails and hoped the dogs' chains were long enough to allow the dogs to bar the north entrance. Both Henry and Nigel prayed to be spared so that they might do good to Woodchester Abbey. Brother Joseph reflected that soon death might relieve him of his agonies of indecision over the spectacles. Brother Mark patted the little novice's hand. Guest Master thought of his son Francis and all he had hoped to do for him. And Prior wondered if there was going to be an election at all or if with their murders the abbey would die too.

Crash! The lock held but the door was giving at the hinges. Whatever they were using, Leys and his men were swinging their ram as freely as a tent-pole. Crash! Oak splintered. 'Un be going!' yelled Leys. The monks pushed closer, like children seeking a way back to the womb. Panic seized them. They stopped thinking, they stopped praying, almost they stopped breathing. They fastened their lips on their crucifixes and listened to iron wedges being hammered between wood and stone. They heard a rending and a scraping as crowbars were pushed home, then a sickening splitting as the door was prised away from its hinges. A shuffling and a muttering. Snarls from the dogs. A last deafening crash as the ram hit the door and the lock burst open and the door fell thunderously on to the pavement. With the last of his strength Prior ordered his monks to be still. 'Do not move from the altar. When they come in, turn your face to show that you are not Brother Peter. But do not move. You will be safe if you do not move.'

Behind their backs they heard the dogs choking against their collars and the arguments of men afraid to pass them. The voices retreated. Still the dogs plunged and yelped. A novice jerked up his head. He had heard a sound he knew, the soft twang of a rabbit-bow. The crunch and the scream came together, then the dragging of the chain, the scrape of claws on stone and the gasp of a dying dog. The bow twanged again and the second dog dropped with a rattle and a thud.

The village came rushing in over the corpses. Headed by John Leys they burst into the choir. 'Where be thakky Brother Peter?' he screamed, dancing like a devil, all red hair and red eyes. They swarmed in after him, drunk on sacramental wine, their feet red with the dogs' blood. Slowly the heads at the altar turned. The heads became faces. Leys looked at them and they were all faces of Brother Peter. He bounded forward brandishing his chain. 'I 'ool lam un,' he roared. 'I 'ool wap un for laying my wench.'

Suddenly Brother Mark heaved himself up and, with the little novice still clinging to his girdle, bounded down the altar steps. ' 'Ee bain't a-coming up to t'altar,' he shouted. 'Ee got no call to come over t'rail.' The voice jabbed a nerve in Leys' arm. His hand flew open and his chain shot across the choir and crashed into the tower door. He looked again and faces were no longer Brother Peter's but Prior's and Sacristan's and Cantor's and Infirmarian's. He knew then that Prior spoke the truth, that Brother Peter had slipped through his fingers. But he searched first before doing the terrible thing.

He and his men searched the tower room, the belfry, the bells, the staircases. He searched the Sacristy, the choir stalls, the nave and the side chapels. He levered the slabs off Ambrose's tomb and Abbot Dominic's tomb to make sure there was only Ambrose and Abbot Dominic inside. When he had searched everywhere he led his men back into the choir. He stood quietly at the gap in the altar rail until the villagers were ranged four by four behind him. The monks stared like paralytics. The clock in the cloisters struck five. John Leys walked quietly between the rails and stepped up to the first novice. He laid his filthy hand on his shoulder and said, 'In God's name I do curse 'ee and give 'ee t'plague.' Then he moved on to the next novice and the next, cursing each one in the same words. Then without haste he touched and cursed every one of the officials and monks, saying, 'In God's name I do curse 'ee and give 'ee t'plague.'

After him the villagers lurched, pawing every monk and novice and uttering their slurred curses. In this manner each member of Woodchester community had the plague wished on him fifty times.

When the last villager had uttered his curse John Leys led them out through the south door. The door was shut. At the altar not a soul moved. They were petrified by so much hatred. They crouched with their faces hidden, as immobile as St Peter, almost as dead as the dogs. The clock struck six. There was another burst of muskets from Amberley. Noises reached them from the cloisters: shouts, catcalls, the crashing of latrine seats and then, soon after seven o'clock, certain thumps in the vicinity of the novices' benches. Brother Joseph's head jerked up like a fox that hears the chase. 'You hear it?' It was the first word spoken for two hours. More thumps. A call for straw.

Brother Joseph struggled to his feet. 'It is the book cupboards!' he cried in anguish. 'They have broken open the book cupboards.' He tried to clamber down the steps but Sacristan hooked him round the waist and held him. 'But they will damage the books,' sobbed Brother Joseph. When the smell of fire reached them from under the south door he shrieked like a mother who smells her children burning. To muffle the dreadful sounds they sang all the penitential psalms. It was not until the third psalm that Prior realized they had missed Vespers. It hit him between his eyebrows like a stone from a catapult. They had missed a service and not even realized it. The routine of centuries had been broken. They had made a chink in the wall of prayers that could never be stopped up.

When the psalms were sung he said that they would now sing Vespers, although he knew that the little devils had already slipped through. So they sang Vespers, squatting on their numb haunches, trying to drown the hubbub outside. Smoke began to drift in the north door.

At last the shouting stopped. There was silence. Flies buzzed over the dead dogs. The sun streamed in the west window, setting fire to the brasses in the nave. Brother Mark fell asleep with his mouth open and Sacristan watched the dribble run out of the corner of his mouth. Brother Joseph sobbed for his burned manuscripts. Guest Master unbent one short leg and found a grim pleasure in the agony of pins and needles.

Eight o'clock. Shadows doused the brasses. Their sweat

cooled a little and they began to grunt and shift. Abbot's Chaplain detached a novice's hand from his skirt. Nigel sniffed the bonfire and smelled hope in it.

At last Prior rose. 'Let us sing Compline,' he said. They staggered into their stalls and struggled through the last service of the day. Everything was quiet. 'Come.' They tucked their hands into their sleeves and tottered in procession through the chancel gate. Prior unlocked the south door. They turned their backs on the dead dogs and the smashed north door and walked out through the south door into the cloisters.

'Let me see!' cried Brother Joseph.

Nigel jumped forward and led the old man up to the smoking pile that had once been Brother Joseph's reason for existence. Brother Joseph sank on his knees and dabbled his hands in the hot ash. 'They are all gone,' said Nigel brutally. 'There is not a book left in the cupboards. They have burned all your manuscripts, all the books the abbey possessed.' Brother Joseph covered his face with his hands and bent his aged back so low Nigel could count the knobbles of his spine. It was ominously quiet. There was not a shuffle, not a whisper.

They left Brother Joseph and crept past the ruined scriptorium and the shattered glass and the scrawled obscenities into the kitchen yard. There was nobody. No villagers, no servants, no retainers; only a sea of straw, a scattering of onions and, in the open gateway, a burst sack of flour. Cellarer hurried down the cellar steps and a minute later returned with terrible news. 'They have taken everything. All our stores, the grain, the flour, onions, puddings, hams, everything. They have left us nothing.'

Like men in a nightmare they drifted to the well and Sacristan, still clutching St Peter's toe-nails under one arm, wound up the bucket. It came up one-third full of muddy water. They drank. For the third time Sir Thomas Arundel's muskets blasted them but they were too dejected to be afraid. They shovelled the dirty flour into a sack, working speechlessly in the last of the light. Then they lit torches from the embers over which Brother Joseph was still grieving and made a melancholy inspection of the havoc. They trailed through their little world, mourning the smashed chests, the slashed mattresses and broken beds and ripped hangings, the strangled pigeons and scotched panelling and ruined medicines. They found the bell-ropes severed, the vestments cut into ribbons, their horses gone and most of the pewter stolen from the refectory. Four cats were strung up in Prior's room. Someone had poured wine into the salt-barrels. Only their beautiful church was untouched, except for the dogs' corpses and the smashed door and the two desecrated tombs. Wearily they covered Ambrose and Abbot Dominic up again and fetched picks to dig a grave for the dogs, who were already smelling.

Sacristan put St Peter's toe-nails on the altar. Refectorian lit the kitchen fire and began baking grimy dough. Two of the novices ran away home to Stroud. Prior shut and bolted the south gate. The rats had deserted. Even his own steward had run away. They had braved the plague rather than stop in an abbey with a curse on it. Now the monks were alone for the first time in months; alone to draw the tatters of their lives round them and elect their new abbot. Before he shot the bolts, Prior peered out of the gate and spotted a man lying on the track. He ventured out and found Thomas Woodville face down in the dirt with a broken-off pitchfork buried in his back. Hastily Prior crossed himself and muttered an absolution just in case there was a spark of life or repentance in the man. But he was too late. Thomas Woodville was dead and his soul was already suffering in the hell of unrepentant murderers. Now he would never enjoy the earldom for which he committed such a terrible crime.

In the kitchen Brother Mark blundered into a table and upset a precious half-pint of oil. In the east cloister Brother Joseph searched the book cupboards in vain for an overlooked volume. In the light of a candle Sacristan pushed his sweaty needle in and out of a ripped surplice so that Prior might have something to wear for Mass. He smiled to himself. He had solved his dilemma. He had forsworn the cures and the fame, the rejoicing pilgrims and Winchcombe's jealousy—unless, of course, St Peter's toe-nails should furnish him with these things. At some time during these last days he had come, quite quietly,

with no revelation, to the conclusion that—God forgive him—
he could not do it. He could not tell the monks about Novice
Master's ulcers and Brother Mark's powers of healing. He could
not turn the limelight on Brother Mark and take away his
happiness, not even for the sake of the blind and the crippled,
not even for the glory of the abbey. Sacristan threaded another
needle. He would make up for it. Brother Mark must be very
near to God. Only a few hours and Sacristan would make
amends. He made a knot at the end of his thread and plunged
the needle into the surplice.

Henry Osborne and Nigel Woodville were wielding picks in
the Abbot's garden, each trying to swing higher and dig deeper
than his rival. Between swings Nigel held forth to Henry about
how, now that they were likely to catch plague anyway, they
could go up to Selsely for water. Since there would be only
thirty of them, they could make shift on very little food. If
they pawned some of the church plate they could raise enough
to live through the lean months. Surely between them they
could restuff the mattresses. . . . Henry spat on his blistered hands
and sighed.

Smoke still hung about the cloisters. The clock struck
ten. Only two hours and it would be St Barnabas' Day, election
day. Only two hours and the delegates could retire with Prior
to the tower room and elect the new abbot. In the relief of
knowing that soon the ship would have a captain Prior almost
forgot that he still had to decide which captain was most likely
to bring the ship into harbour.

At half past ten Prior finished scraping foxglove poultice
off Abbot Dominic's mattress and came out into the kitchen
yard. He looked northwards and saw that a cloud had come
between him and the stars. A cloud? Could rain be coming?
Then he saw that it was not a raincloud but a cloud of smoke
rising like incense from the roof of the church.

17

PRIOR sank beneath his burdens. He slid down on the
cobbles and laid his head in the dirt. The church was on
fire. Their beautiful church, focus of their lives, walled
and pillared and vaulted in Cotswold stone, roofed with square-
cut oak shingles pegged with sheep's bones and topped by a
two-hundred-foot spire; their lovely church was burning. There
was nothing they could do. They had no water and, even if
they had, no way of throwing it. Those oak shingles, scorched
and dried by months of burning sunshine, would flare like
straw. Then the rafters would catch, the tower would fall. . . .

Someone lumbered past him and he heard Sacristan shouting:
'The relics! Get out the relics and the valuables.' When eventually
he struggled into the Abbot's garden he found rescue operations
under way. The cloud of smoke had become a column. Both
nave and choir were full of smoke but Sacristan knew the
whereabouts blindfold of every article of value, even to the silk
bookmarkers; and he drove the monks like a slave-master, even
Nigel and Henry, even Abbot's Chaplain. Coughing, half-blind,
their faces swathed in wet cheese-muslins, they groped their
way in and out of their church, laden with relics, tapestries,
jewels, caskets, hangings, chalices, cruets, candlesticks, images,
lamps, carpet, vestments, cushions, pyxes, handbells, altar-
cloths, crucifixes, service books, bowls, patens and the great
Bible; while overhead the rafters cracked and spurts of flame
shot out like tongues from the cornices. For an hour they toiled,
their skirts tucked up round their thighs, lugging out their
treasures and piling them round Prior and Brother Joseph
where they sat speechless with their backs to the north
wall.

'St Peter's statue!' cried Nigel. 'Can we not save it, Sacristan? If we tied ropes round it and pulled from the north door . . .'

Henry Osborne heard him and rushed for ropes, ever mindful of the election that must take place, fire or no fire, the next day. Sacristan had just fastened the ropes round St Peter's neck and waist and Brother Mark and four other large monks had just mounted the base of the shrine to topple St Peter over, when a central beam crashed down into the nave.

'Out! Out!' screamed Prior.

They ran for safety. As they reached the north wall a flame twenty feet high fountained into the sky and within minutes the whole roof was ablaze, nave and transepts burning so fiercely they lit up the slopes of Amberley and almost drowned Sir Thomas Arundel's fourth salvo of muskets. They watched it burn. For hours they watched it burn, the roof that had sheltered three centuries of Woodchester monks, and the tears poured down their filthy cheeks.

Eleven o'clock. Twelve o'clock. St Barnabas' Day and the day of the election. In the glare of the fire they bent their heads and muttered Nocturns and Lauds, giving thanks to God that He had spared their lives and their treasures; although once the plague-worms hatched on their skin . . .

At one o'clock the roof of the church caved in, falling down between the pillars with a roar that could be heard in Nailsworth, carrying with it tons of vaulting and tracery, the rood, the corbels and the tops of the pillars. But the tower stood firm, together with the blackened pillars and the sturdy outer walls. At dawn the last of the flames died down and they were able to peer in through the north door at the charred and smoking ruins. The Stations of the Cross were obliterated. St Peter's statue was smashed into splinters by a lump of masonry. The chancel screen was buckled. But when later they inched open the hot west door they saw that the altar was untouched and that the east window was casting its rainbow colours over the havoc as beautifully as ever.

They sang Prime on the altar steps, having reached the altar from the tower staircase. Through their sandals they could feel the heat of the stones. Prior added a prayer that he and the delegates might be guided by God in electing their new abbot, then he collected together Brother Joseph, Guest Master, Brother Mark and Sacristan and led them up the stairs to the tower room.

Nigel and Henry sank on their knees in the choir and launched into continuous, audible and conflicting prayers. Abbot's Chaplain buried his broken nose in his hands and peeped through his fingers. The other monks knelt or squatted on the warm stones, coughing and fingering their beads and watching the smoke fuming over the ruins.

In the tower room Prior placed before each delegate a pot of ink, a quill and a scrap of parchment. 'Pray,' he told them. 'Ask God to show you which man He wishes to be our abbot. Then write that man's name on the parchment and give it to me.'

They bent their heads in prayer. They were sitting round the table, Sacristan and Brother Joseph on one side, Guest Master and Brother Mark on the other, Prior at the head with his back to the sun. Under his sooty bandages Sacristan's wound throbbed like something alive. He shaded his smarting eyes and peeped at Brother Mark from under his hand. He was going to make amends. He was going to follow the course of Brother Mark's pen and write down the same name as he did. Sacristan tucked his fat little finger out of the way so as to get a better view.

At Brother Mark's right hand Guest Master did not need to ponder. He knew, had known ever since Thomas Woodville exposed him, who he was going to vote for. He hated the Woodvilles but he hated Woodchester Abbey more. The abbey that he had milked for so many years had become his enemy the day that it had disgraced him, stripped him and beaten him in Chapter, and sent him to sleep with the junior monks. The abbey had humiliated him and, far worse, had stolen Francis' shop away from him so that now Francis hated his father and had not sent a word of greeting for weeks. The abbey was his enemy and, as he had once told Nigel Woodville, he knew what was the most terrible injury he could do to that enemy. That he

259

himself, being chained to the abbey, would suffer with it, gave him a masochistic pleasure.

He unrolled his parchment and wrote on it Nigel Woodville's name.

Opposite him Brother Joseph was in difficulty. He could see the pen and he could see the ink-pot but he could not dip the pen in the pot without feeling for the opening with his left hand. But if he used his left hand to feel for the pot he could not use it to keep his parchment flat. And he could not, when his quill was inked and therefore not to be laid down, unroll his parchment with his left hand alone. At last he solved the problem by pulling the ink-pot under his nose, unrolling and pinning the parchment with both hands, and then dipping the quill at close range. Unfortunately, he knocked over the ink-pot and black ink poured over his fingers and the parchment and into his lap. Prior found him a larger piece of parchment and a fresh pot of ink, wiped his hands on the bottom of his skirt and shifted him to a clean place at the bottom of the table. He pinned the parchment flat for him with two empty mugs, dipped the quill for him and put it in his hand. Brother Joseph bent his rheumatic spine and made his first downstroke. He did not pray God for forgiveness because he knew he had no choice. The villagers had burned all his precious manuscripts, his fifteen psalters, his missals and breviaries and works of St Augustine. They had burned all the works of former monks. The abbey did not have a single book left except the service books and the great Bible chained to the lectern in the choir. There was no time to be lost. There would be no spare money to buy books from the Gloucester scribes, indeed it was unthinkable that Woodchester should have to put up with their inferior workmanship. Brother Joseph must set to work at once. He could not work without seeing; he could not see unless he had the spectacles; and he could not get the spectacles unless he voted for Nigel Woodville. Even the thought of a printing-press did not deter him. The beautiful manuscripts that he would now make would survive long after printing-presses were broken up for firewood and printed pages nothing but a distasteful memory.

Brother Joseph completed Nigel Woodville's name and blew on the ink to dry it.

At the other end of the table Brother Mark had conveyed black ink to his fingers, his nose and his eyebrows. He turned out his elbows and bent down until his left ear was six inches from the table. He squinted sideways and poked his tongue through the gap in his teeth. Sacristan watched him from under his colossal hand. Brother Mark jabbed his quill in the ink and, holding it west and east with his right elbow cocked up, brought the end to rest on the parchment. Sacristan pressed his belly against the table. Brother Mark breathed noisily. Up, down, up, down, up, down, up, went the pen. That was all. It was Nigel Woodville's initials. Jesus Christ had pointed them out to Brother Mark over the west door where, many times repeated, they formed the dog's-tooth decoration. Brother Mark threw down his pen, blotted his dog's-tooth with the ball of his thumb and extracted his mouse from his pocket.

Sacristan dropped his hand. So be it. That was Brother Mark's choice and who was he to question the choice of a miracle-worker? Although how God could choose so unsuitable a man; too young, too sceptical, too worldly wise—Sacristan heaved a sigh and wrote Nigel Woodville's name on his bit of parchment.

For Prior, sitting with his back to the sun, with blistered hands and feet, a fortnight's growth of beard, dirt that could be scraped off him, two sores in his groin, parched, hungry, despondent—for him it was no longer a question of choice. The nave was in ruins. It was going to cost hundreds of pounds to rebuild it. The abbey would need to make a great deal of money and there was only one man capable of making it. If Ambrose had lived—but Ambrose had been murdered and there were few Ambroses in this world. Prior's lofty principles must bow to necessity. There could not be an abbey without a church. Better a worldly abbey than no abbey at all. And perhaps after all it was too late to return to the glorious past, to monasteries both spiritual and loved, to monks who were indeed lodged in God's bosom. Perhaps Ambrose's austerity would have become unpopular, perhaps the monks would have revolted against manual labour. Thus Prior laboured to justify with reason a decision from which his instinct recoiled. He would not be happy with Nigel Woodville. If there had been no fire, no attack, he believed he would have chosen Henry Osborne; so restful, so conservative, so like Abbot Dominic. But John Leys had wrested choice away from him. Henry Osborne did not have Nigel's administrative and financial ability and without it Woodchester Abbey could never rebuild her church.

Prior sighed. He pulled the ink-pot towards him, dipped his pen, and wrote Nigel Woodville's name.

Thus it came about that Woodchester Abbey elected an abbot it did not really want, to whom all its instincts were opposed.

It was one week after the election.

There had been no more cases of plague in the village. None of the monks had succumbed.

The monks, all but Abbot's Chaplain, had received the news calmly. They had kissed Nigel Woodville's hand and reflected that nothing that Nigel could do to them could be worse than the months they had just endured. And, who knows, he might not be so progressive as they feared. There was always hope.

Henry Osborne bowed to the decision and trudged into Stroud to buy a horse for his solitary trek back to Salisbury. Now that he had lost, he did not envy Nigel his task. Perhaps, after all, provided the great Warwick did not take the news badly, his stall in Salisbury Cathedral might be more comfortable than that blackened abbot's chair.

Abbot's Chaplain was Abbot's Chaplain no longer. Diplomatically Nigel had put him in charge of the six remaining novices and, now that Brother Peter was not available, had taken as his chaplain a young monk called David who had proved himself intelligent and resourceful during the fire. The new Novice Master overcame his chagrin amazingly quickly. Despite the broken nose the novices proved dutiful and admiring; and he did not want to make an enemy of the new abbot. After all, Brother David might die of plague or be squashed by a bit of masonry. As long as his patron Warwick did not come thundering down on him . . .

'Obedience!' he exclaimed in his thrilling voice. 'Obedience is your first duty. Obedience to me. . . .'

In the restored scriptorium Brother Joseph sat down in front of his page. He fitted the spectacles over his head and adjusted them so that his eyes looked through the glass circles. Ah, there they were, his 'a's and 'o's and aitches, as neat as ever. And there was the capital 'O' awaiting the fig tree that he intended to twine round it. He smiled with pleasure. He dipped his brush accurately in the green pot and began to paint fig-leaves. Happy Brother Joseph!

Guest Master toiled with the junior monks at clearing the floor of the nave. With wet muslin draped over his head, he spent the hours between services lugging stones from the church to the north wall and scraping up the dogs and burying them. He skinned his hands and broke his nails. His half-mugs of water were quickly sweated out of him. In his brief intervals of rest he sat with his tiny hands folded and waited for Woodchester Abbey to go to the devil.

Sacristan was doing two men's work. He had rolled his sleeves to the armpits and pinned his skirts knee-high so that he seemed all red: red beard, red hairs on his arms and legs, red eyes, face roasted red by the sun. In between lugging water from Selsely and pushing a needle through the vestments, he laid out on what had once been the Abbot's grass all the splinters of St Peter that he could find. Alas, they were beyond putting together. He took his problem to Abbot Nigel; in future they would take all their problems to Abbot Nigel.

'Abbot, I want to make another shrine for St Peter's toe-nails. If you will allow me to make two entrances into the Sacristy I will put the toe-nails in there and pilgrims can approach from the north gate.'

For a moment Abbot Nigel stopped stuffing straw into mattresses. He wiped the sweat out of his eyes. 'Certainly,

Sacristan,' he said. 'You may use some of the undamaged tapestries. I will spread the word around the village that they may come and visit the shrine despite what has happened. God said forgive our enemies and do good to them that hurt us.'

There was no doubt that, now the cloak of authority had descended on him, Nigel Woodville was fast growing to fit it.

Sacristan waddled away, his turban of bandages slipping over one ear. He made straight for the Sacristy. Yes, the door-ways could go there and the toe-nails there, on the stone block with tapestries hung on three sides of them. The cushion there and the offertory bowl there.... Sacristan cocked his head on one side and the turban slid straight. He grunted with pleasure. He could see them all, the blind and crippled and deaf, the idiots and the possessed, creeping in through one door and bounding out through the other, laughing, singing and praising God. He fished a measure out of his pocket and set to work.

Near the top of Selsely Hill Brother Mark squatted beside the abbey's spring and waited for the trickle to fill his bucket. A hundred paces away William Leys and young Goodman shuffled their feet and studied the cloudless sky. Were they not so sunburned they might have been blushing. Brother Mark took no notice of them because his lord Jesus Christ was walking down the hill towards him, smiling, the sun full on His face. He sat down on a stone and placed His hands on His knees. Brother Mark could see the marks of the nails. Jesus Christ smiled. ' 'Ee done right well, lad,' He said.

In the village John Leys sat, cap in hand, at Rector's table. ' 'Ee mun find my girl a husband,' he pleaded.

'She has taken an oath to wait two years,' said Rector.

'But thakky be nobbut nonsense. Her cass-n't marry thakky · Peter. Un be monk.'

'Alice tells me Brother Peter hopes the Pope will absolve him.'

'Pope bain't such a fool. 'Ee doan't reckon t'Pope 'ool oblige, do 'ee, Rector?'

Rector shook his head.

'There 'ee be, then. 'Ee just free my girl of thakky vow and find she a husband and I 'ool give 'ee twenty shillings.'

Rector thought for a long time. 'The Bishop is the one who should absolve her.'

'Bishop bain't a-coming into plague-spot.'

'You must wait, then.'

'Her cass-n't wait. Her be months gone. Do 'ee want she to bear t'baba unwed?'

Rector pondered. 'I will absolve her on one condition. That you swear to leave those monks alone.'

Leys laughed bitterly. 'I 'oon't touch they with t'barge pole.'

Next day Rector received Alice in the church and absolved her vow. What else could the girl do? She was no heroine but a betrayed country girl who needed a father for her baby. Her lover was gone, perhaps he would never come back nor be able to marry her. What else could she do but obey when her father, her mother, her four brothers, her cousins and aunts and uncles and neighbours and Rector all told her that she must marry?

Within a week Rector had found a husband for her in Stonehouse, which had four cases of plague. He told her she was lucky because he was neither old nor ugly and was prepared to wait for her dowry until times were better. She married him a week later. After her baby was born she was not unhappy.

And Brother Peter? God was merciful to Brother Peter. God may not have been able to save him from hell—although there is always hope that some secret act of contrition may, even without absolution, save even a mortal sinner from the final penalty—but He saved him from discovering his loved one's treachery. On the day that Rector talked with John Leys Brother Peter was drowned. The boat in which he had sailed from Bristol sprang a leak off Hartland Point and sank within sight of the coast in a millpond sea. Brother Peter could not swim and he drowned quickly. No one in Woodchester ever knew what became of him.

The day Brother Peter drowned, a Stroud man reached the King at Huntingdon. The messenger had carried his own food and drink and had slept on the road. He had white crosses sewn on his jacket. Half a mile from the castle he had skirted an army of fifteen hundred men led by Robin of Redesdale, who had pitched camp outside the town and was waiting patiently for the King to reply to his sixth petition. The letter announcing Nigel Woodville's election was tossed on to the drawbridge and carried to the Chancellor in a pair of tongs. Chancellor unrolled it with scissors, read it and promptly burned it. He then carried the good news of Nigel's election to the King.

'That is one in the eye for Warwick,' shouted the King inelegantly. 'That will teach him who is master.' He kissed his Queen's neck and squeezed her left breast. 'That will put those Nevilles in their place,' he said. 'They cannot give me orders.'

Chancellor looked the other way and coughed. The King rose. He flung his emerald arm round Chancellor's shoulders and propelled him out of the room. 'Now to business,' he cried, in high humour. 'I have a message for my brother Burgundy. My wool ship can take it when she sails to Calais. And I want enquiries made about William Caxton. I hear he has set up a printing-press in Bruges. I have a mind to lure him to England to build a printing-press in Westminster. We must move with the times, Chancellor. . . .'

They went out.

The second messenger, similarly equipped, did not reach Middleham until two days later. He offered the letter he carried on the end of a pole. It was taken and the contents conveyed to Warwick where he sat brooding on the ramparts gazing southwards towards France. Mountjoy told him of his defeat. 'They have elected Woodville,' he said fearfully. 'The villagers burned the church down and the monks chose Nigel Woodville.'

Warwick did not reply. Soon Mountjoy left him. When he was alone Warwick closed his eyes. So it had come. The King had ignored him, flouted him, insulted him, deprived him, treated him like a traitor, and now defeated him in an abbatical election. Very well. Now he knew what he must do. He rose and went down the stone steps to his bedchamber. He called for ink and parchment; without hesitation, without searching for a word, he wrote a letter and sent Mountjoy with it to Scarborough with orders to commission a boat and carry the letter to the Bitch at Harfleur.

He wrote quickly so that he might not have time to contemplate the rivers of blood that flowed between himself and this woman. He refused to remember her offering Calais to the French or butchering five thousand innocent people on the Great North Road. He did not dwell on his father murdered by her orders, or on himself declared outlaw by her ten years before; on her son whom he had labelled a bastard; or on her friends Somerset and Wiltshire whom his soldiers had slaughtered in cold blood in the civil wars. He turned his back on the past and wrote:

To Queen Margaret of Anjou, at Harfleur. Madam, we send you greetings. After heavy thoughts and devout prayers we have seen it as our duty to restore to our country a king who will respect its ancient institutions and take counsel of its hereditary nobility. Deploring a ruler who flouts convention and takes heed only of puffed-up favourites and who seeks to make war on your kinsman, France, we now send our cousin Mountjoy to you with plans for restoring your husband Henry of Lancaster to his rightful place. . . .

And Nigel Woodville?

Abbot Nigel, with Prior in tow, was making a tour of his domain. He squatted down beside a pile of valuables. 'These are what we must pawn,' he explained. 'We shall be forced to buy food at high prices but we must be able to redeem our treasures when times are better. We will pawn this and this and this. . . .'

Prior scratched frantically on his slate. They moved on to the stables.

'Buy one horse,' said Abbot Nigel. 'I must ride round the estates and see which we can farm for ourselves next year. Thatcher had no sons. We can take in his lease. There are four leases due to fall in in the spring. We will renew Leys' lease because we must keep him in a good temper but we will not renew the other three.'

Prior made a note. They entered the Abbot's lodgings and found Brother David poring over accounts.

'I have sent for Walter Penny,' said Abbot Nigel. 'He is in Lord Hastings' employment but he will be glad to leave him when the plague has gone from here. He will take charge of our finances. He is an advocate of central bursaries. The abbey will employ him to keep our accounts in proper order. Being a layman he will have more time than a monk for seeing to our financial reorganization.'

Prior bowed. They came to the ruined nave.

'We must create a special fund for the rebuilding,' said Abbot Nigel. 'We must salvage the good stone and take our quarries into our own hands as soon as possible. The present lessees can be kept on to manage them. As soon as the plague has gone I will engage masons. They will accept low wages if I promise them plenary indulgences.'

They moved on. 'About the new Chapter House . . .'

Prior sighed and poked his scratcher into the grooves between his eyebrows. 'Yes,' he said. 'Yes, yes.' He foresaw countless days like this, endless endeavour. He did not doubt that Abbot Nigel could do all that he planned. But Prior was not happy. He seemed to see Ambrose listening, gently shaking his gaunt head as if to say, 'This is not how I would go about it.' Yet he might be mistaken. His head ached and he slept badly. Perhaps this was the way; to build up the body of the abbey and hope that the spirit would come to inhabit it. Perhaps he was just tired. Perhaps there were better times coming. They had been presented with a clean slate. Perhaps Abbot Nigel Woodville would after all draw something beautiful on it. Perhaps . . .

Prior scratched his head and hurried to catch up with his abbot.

EPILOGUE

In the summer of 1538, seventy years after Nigel Woodville's election, King Henry VIII's greedy eyes alighted on Woodchester Abbey and on her fabulous riches. He declared the abbey and all its possessions forfeit to the Crown.

Before the monks could hide any of their valuables the King's commissioners arrived. Into oak chests they packed all the convent plate, the golden chalices, the silver pyxes and stoups and patens, the bronze Cross, the embroidered vestments, the crucifixes, the Flemish hangings, the pearl box that had sheltered the girdle of the blessed Honoria, the jewelled casket made for the toe-nails of St Peter, the pewter tableware, the brass lamps, the silver candlesticks, the Abbot's ruby ring. They lugged the abbey bells to the foundry at Gloucester and there had them melted down. They sold the clock to the new Bishop of Oxford. Every jewel, every precious thing, every scrap of metal or material that could be turned into money, was seized in the King's name and for the King's enrichment.

They prised the brasses out of the pavements. They broke open the abbots' tombs in search of valuables. They chopped up the choir stalls, the rood screen, the wainscoting, the lecterns, even the floorboards, to make bonfires on which to melt the lead from the roofs into convenient bars. They smashed the plaster statues of Christ and the Virgin Mary and the saints. They broke up St Peter's shrine. They threw St Peter's toe-nails and the girdle of the blessed Honoria into the River Frome. They ripped down the altar hangings. A solitary uncompleted psalter found in a cupboard was tossed on the fire. The famous collection of printed books and Greek and Latin manuscripts assembled by Abbot Nigel they sent to London in twelve ox-carts together with all the stained glass and some of the finer carving and the three chests of silver coins accumulated during the previous seventy years. The abbey's thirty horses they sold in Stroud market, all but the white stallion which they sent to Thomas Cromwell at his own request.

The abbot's London house was sold at a favourable price to a wool merchant. The twenty tons of best Cotswold wool waiting baled in the Gloucester warehouses for shipment they sold in Calais on the King's behalf. Woodchester's livery stables in Gloucester and Cirencester, patronized by eighty thousand pilgrims, they sold to local hostlers. Of Woodchester's twenty thousand acres, the two thousand acres which was farmed directly by the abbey's servants the commissioners gave or sold to supporters of the King, the lion's share going to the abbey's lay bursar who had greatly assisted them by his unrivalled knowledge of the abbey's resources. The leases and tenancies of the remaining eighteen thousand acres they left undisturbed, the rents and payments henceforth being rendered to the Exchequer. The grain, wine, beer, farm machinery, animals, furniture and medicines they sold in Stroud market.

Of the inmates of the abbey itself, Abbot John was given a pension of ten pounds a year, his prior a pension of six pounds a year, the six officials pensions of two pounds a year each. All went to live with relations in the shire. The eight remaining monks were turned out to make a living as best they could. The single novice returned to his father's farm which he lived to inherit. There was nowhere else he could learn to be a monk, because the King was destroying not only Woodchester Abbey but also all the other abbeys of England. The fifty servants drifted into other employment.

Such was the death of Woodchester Abbey. Not a hand—save one—was lifted to prevent it.

One week after the last monk had left, one day after the departure of the last King's commissioner, the villagers moved in. Whatever the commissioners had not taken they took. They stripped the roofs, giving to the most important families the new stone tiles that Abbot Nigel had used to re-roof the church after the fire. The last of these tiles was carted away by George Leys, John Leys' great-great-grandson, to roof the new house he was building in Laggar Lane. They sawed off the rafters. They lugged away the stones of the inside walls. They dragged out the stone fireplaces and window-frames. They took the fish from the ponds and the ropes from the belfry. They searched the yards for old nails and drippings of lead. By Hallowe'en Woodchester Abbey had been stripped of every single thing of any use.

The years passed. Sun, rain, frost and wind wrought havoc on the shell of the abbey. The staircases fell in. Timber rotted away in the long grass. Thistles and docks flourished where the cloisters had been. Bit by bit the remaining walls crumbled and rolled away down the hill. Couch grass crept over the tombstones and the broken pavements. One stormy night in the year 1570 the tower collapsed. At first light the villagers swarmed over it like ants. In two days there was nothing of its blocks and traceries to be seen. The stone built three new houses in the village. The bronze Cross from the top of the spire, for which the King's commissioners had not risked their necks, was stuck on top of the parish church.

Within sixty years the ruins in summertime were scarcely visible over the tops of the wild foxgloves. In a hundred years there was nothing to be seen at all except a few grassy mounds and a little rubble, and these were soon swept away by a small landslide. Soon men forgot Woodchester Abbey altogether. They did not mourn it. Why should they, when in the time of their ancestors not a hand had been raised to save it?

Save one.

When the King's commissioners had come trampling up the nave on that blazing July day in 1538, an ancient monk had been the only one to bar their way. He was ninety years of age and had lived as a monk in the abbey since his nineteenth birthday. He was a big man still and he stood under the rood screen and lifted his trembling hands to stop the commissioners' advance. They pushed him aside, not unkindly, and went about their business. When the monks left he wept and clung to the only statue they had not yet destroyed, but they thrust him out of the south gateway—the great oak gates had been sold to Sir Charles Arundel long before—and he wandered away and was forgotten. But when a week later, soon after dawn, the first of a queue of ox-carts reached the south gateway, the villagers found him dead on the threshold, his ancient forehead couched in the hollow worn by four centuries of monks' feet.

It was Brother Mark.